Praise for Forgetting Me

"It's a testament to Tirado-Ryen's talent that readers will sympathize with Anne and her plight ... the naturalistic dialogue and brisk pace will keep readers engaged, as will the unpredictable plot. A breezy romantic thriller with enough intriguing twists to satisfy fans of the genre."

— *KIRKUS REVIEWS*

"Tirado-Ryen (*Two Weeks of Summer*) delves deep into the psyche of a woman set adrift after an accident robs her of her memory and identity ... Tirado-Ryen beautifully illuminates human resilience and the journey of self-discovery. [An] enthralling story of memory, identity, and redemption."

— *BOOKLIFE* (EDITOR'S PICK)

D1242625

"Katherine Tirado-Ryen has crafted a deeply engaging and emotive novel that delves into the complexities of memory, love, and the human spirit ... *Forgetting Me* is a compelling and emotionally resonant story that will leave readers reflecting on their own definitions of self, and I could not recommend it highly enough for fans of emotive female-centric fiction."

— *READERS' FAVORITE* (STARRED REVIEW)

"In a trope rife with possibility, this gripping amnesia romance makes excellent use of internal conflicts, dark twists, and likable characters ... the story arc is so engrossing that readers might overlook how smooth the author's storytelling actually is. A riveting novel about a woman forced to own up to lies she can't remember and live with pain she can't forget, *Forgetting Me* is a tender tale that will steal your heart."

— *INDIES TODAY* (STARRED REVIEW)

"Tirado-Ryen's ability to evoke emotion through her words is truly exceptional, adding depth and resonance to an already enchanting story ... Readers will be captivated by the finely drawn characters, the suspense, and Anne's journey to redefine who she is. A page-turning narrative with abrupt and unexpected twists and a denouement that will leave readers spellbound."

"A fascinating look at identity, memory, and the relationship between them—as well as a rather sweet and tender love story."

Forgetting Me

Also by Katherine Tirado-Ryen

NOVELS

Forgetting Me

The Secrets Inside

Two Weeks of Summer

BLOOD OF THE WARRIOR QUEEN

The Traitor's Prophecy (Coming Soon)

Forgetting Me

A NOVEL

KATHERINE TIRADO-RYEN

MEADOW LAKE PRESS

Printed in the United States of America.

A Meadow Lake Press Book.

Tirado-Ryen, Katherine.

Forgetting Me / Katherine Tirado-Ryen

ISBN: 979-8-9896849-1-5

Published in 2014 by Meadow Lake Press.

To my husband, Chris,
and our sons: Nolan, Aidan, and Jackson

Thank you for being with me through every word
You are the great loves of my life

Part One

IN THE DARK

Chapter One

A SMOKY FOG pressed on her brain. How long had she been there? She stirred, weighted in the darkness, trying to free herself from unseen shackles.

A sound in the distance. Repeated at intervals. The chiming of a bell?

Was she dreaming?

Her thoughts fractured. Then—reverse diving, swimming up in her mind. Breaking through a shell, rocketing over the bend...

She opened her eyes.

A bright white ceiling. All lights snapped on to full wattage. The smell of bleach emanating from the firm pillow under her head.

She tried to swallow, but the saliva burned her throat. She shifted her head.

She was in bed. But not her own bed. At least, she didn't think it was her bed.

Starched white sheets. Scratchy. Her hands felt heavy when she lifted them.

She tilted her head again.

Something pinched her arms. Tubes: thin and clear. The end of one punched between two knuckles of her hand. Everything tethered to various machines that beeped and whirred about her.

Past the thick bandages squeezing her arms, squares of white acrylic tipped her fingernails—all save her thumbs, broken to the quick.

She considered these details for half a minute, looking about in a daze.

I'm in—this is... She strained for the word, then latched on: a hospital. Yes. She was in a hospital.

Why am I in a hospital?

A tickle ignited in her throat, and she coughed. Hard. She moved her hand to cover her mouth when something released, and the machine next to her exploded in a series of alarms.

The sliding of doors, a gasp of wind. A large nurse in green scrubs lowered a plastic rail beside the bed and bent to inspect her. She clicked buttons on the machine, touched the tube in her hand. Then the nurse leaned close, so close that two silver studs winked at her from the woman's earlobes.

"Hi there. My name is Theresa," the woman said

in a slow, loud voice. "I'm your nurse. Can you understand me?"

She nodded.

"Can you speak?"

She coughed again, dislodging stale air. "Yes."

"How do you feel?"

She searched her body for clues. She felt heavy as a stone. A whirlwind threatened to suck her in. "Dizzy," she managed.

"Okay. Try to take a few breaths."

She did. The room slowed, and then stalled. Her stomach picked up. She drew a settling breath.

"Better?"

"Yes."

"Would you like some water?"

She nodded and closed her eyes. When she opened them, the nurse held a clear plastic glass in one hand and pressed a nearby button with the other, lifting the bed in a series of rattling clicks. She shakily accepted the water and Theresa tilted the rim to her lips. The water had cooled to room temperature, sliding down her throat and into her stomach.

She thought she had drained it all, but when she released the glass, it remained half full.

"Better?" Theresa asked.

She nodded.

"Do you know where you are?"

She nodded again. "Hah—hospital."

"Good. Do you know your name?"

She stared at the woman, and the moment stretched between them. It was there, just beyond her mental reach. The answer. *Her* answer.

"Do you know your name?" the nurse asked again, more intently.

Oh God. What's happening? She felt hot, winded. Afraid. *What nightmare is this? What's wrong with me? Why can't I remember?*

Panic squeezed her throat.

"Shhh, you're okay." Theresa reached down and clasped her shoulder through the web of wires and tubes. "The important thing is that you're awake. The rest should come back. Just try to relax and I'll call the doctor, okay?"

She fell back into a wave as darkness slammed over her as solidly as a coffin.

Someone peeled open her eyelid. White light shot into the back of her skull. Darkness again, and then light exploding in her other eye.

Warm breath plumed over her face before everything snapped into focus. It was a man, one eye obscured by the light, the other peering at her intently. "Hello, I'm Dr. Porter," he said with grave authority. He was in a long white lab coat, gray shirt, and striped tie. "You were in a car accident and sent here to New York Presbyterian Hospital. Do you understand me?"

She nodded.

"Good. Your nurse tells me you were feeling dizzy earlier. How do you feel now?"

She considered. "Not dizzy?"

"Okay. Does your head hurt at all?"

She tried to lift her hand to show him the point of pressure, but her limb fell like a paperweight. "On my eye."

"Left? Right?"

"Right."

"Okay." He studied her. "Can you tell me your name?"

My name. My name. Panic stirred. She thought hard and caught the first letter: V. It began with a V. "Begins..." she began, but her voice slurred. *Is this how I sound?*

"Good," he said encouragingly. "Try again."

"Begins with..." She drew in a breath and forced the rest out, "...with V."

"Your first name begins with a V?"

She nodded.

His smile didn't reach his eyes. "Well, it's a start. I guess 'Jane Doe' won't cut it anymore. Maybe Veronica Doe?"

There. She caught it. "Vickie!" She drew a breath and blew it out. "My name is *Vickie.*"

"Okay, Vickie. Do you know today's date?"

Her confidence melted. No. She didn't know the date.

"That's okay. What about the month?"

She glanced at the window. Snow blew past the frost-bitten glass. "December?"

The doctor followed her gaze. "Clever. Yes. How about the year?"

Worn gears clicked in Vickie's mind. She studied the doctor as she answered. "2010?"

He blinked, but his expression gave nothing away. "No, Vickie. It's 2013."

Her heart fell. Something was very, *very* wrong.

The doctor held up one long finger inches from her eyes. "It's all right. You're doing fine. Just try to follow my finger, okay?"

It moved to the right, then left. Up and down.

"Good, good. Can you puff out your cheeks?"

She looked back at him. *What?*

"Like this." He pinched his lips and blew. His cheeks inflated like two balloons. She followed him. "Good. Now stick out your tongue."

She closed her eyes and opened her mouth, and he examined her for several seconds. "Can you smile at me?"

She did.

"Bigger. Like this." He grinned like a circus clown.

Vickie smiled so enormously she suspected he could see her molars.

"Great. Can you frown?"

She tried to pinch her eyes together, but had trouble.

"Try again," he said.

She did.

"Hmm." He picked up a chart, jotted a few notes.

"What?" she asked him.

"Could be several things. Perhaps some neuropathy, but maybe…" He leaned closer to inspect sections of her face. Her forehead. The sides of her eyes. Around her lips. "Have you had any Botox recently?"

She stared at him blankly.

"Injectable fillers? Wrinkle minimizers?"

There was a long pause. Theresa called from a machine. "You know. Botox? Restylane? Juvéderm?"

"I don't know…" *What are they asking me? What do they mean?*

"Here, in the nasolabial folds…" He touched the skin between her nose and mouth. "There's slight bruising inconsistent with your other injuries. And you're having difficulty moving some sections of your face. But your epidural hematoma wouldn't account for this type of maxillofacial nerve paralysis…" He scrutinized her again. "It's a bilateral pattern more suggestive of a recent series of facial injections."

His words bled together. *Injections. Facial fillers. Is he asking if I purposefully injected something into my face? Why would I do that?*

He must have seen her frustration, because he said, "It's okay. We'll worry about that later. Vickie, I need you to think back—"

A sudden movement silenced him. Doors slid

open, and an unfamiliar voice crackled. "Is she awake?"
A man's face punched into her vision. Two-day stubble. Rimless glasses. Brown, flat hair. He was waving a
form. "Great! I need her to sign this confidentiality
agreement..."

But the nurse intercepted him. "Sir, I've already
told you—"

"Yeah, yeah. If she could just sign this..." He
clicked a pen. "It'll only take a second..."

Dr. Porter snapped the form from the man and
pointed to the door. "Either you leave or I call
security."

He shot the doctor a look of warning. "Do you
even know who I represent?"

"I know exactly who you represent, and I don't
care. You have two seconds to leave the ward or we'll
kick you out. Understand?"

The man sighed. He snapped his pen and glumly
abandoned the paper. "Fine. Have her read it over.
And you can tell Mr. Post yourself—"

"Out!" said Theresa, pointing a threatening finger.
After the man slunk out the doors, Theresa returned
to the bed and whispered to the doctor, "I wish it were
Jack Post coming here instead of that lawyer. God,
don't you just *love* his movies?"

Dr. Porter studied the various screens that glowed
with fluctuating numbers and percentages. "Sure.
That's probably why he makes more money than the
rest of us put together."

Vickie watched them with some detachment, when something knocked behind her lids. "Ooh." She groaned, closed her eyes. "My head..."

Dr. Porter redirected his attention to her. "Are you having a headache? How would you rate your pain? On a scale of one to ten?"

She opened her eyes and saw him pointing to a laminated poster of cartoon faces, each etched with mounting levels of pain. She considered, then pointed to the little red face with lips caught somewhere between a straight line and a downturn. "Maybe five?"

"Moderate to severe pain?"

She nodded and then peered closer at the images. Two words labeled her chosen face. *Dolor fuerte.*

She knew these words. They meant "strong pain." But how did she know that?

Her mind gripped in a vise of pain. The doctor spoke to her again, explained future tests, procedures, and steps to be taken. Everything blurred. The nurse gave her two small pills and the rest of the water. After downing the pills, Theresa arranged her pillows—stiff from the plastic beneath the case—and helped her settle in.

When the nurse left, Vickie realized she still didn't know how she got there. She only knew her first name.

Chapter Two

A GLOW BEHIND HER EYELIDS. Warmth.

Was she dreaming?

Vickie opened her eyes to a drawn window with glints of sunlight peeking beneath the blind. She was still in a hospital bed, but a different one, in an unfamiliar room. The lights were almost dim. A machine beeped beside her. Only a few tubes connected to her now. A small gray clip pinched her opposite index finger.

When she gazed at her left hand, it gave an involuntary tremor. A few reddish scrapes were visible past the tape of the bandages, as were some dark discolorations. But the pain in her head was gone.

Vickie thought back. *How did I get here?*

Words exploded in her mind, echoing through her mental universe. *Parasailing*, said one. *Sashimi*, said another. *Matinees.* Braveheart. *Catholicism. Impressionist paintings. Graham Greene martinis...*

Stop, she thought, but the words peeled past her like race cars.

Rock climbing. Crate & Barrel. Warren, Michigan. Private planes. Horseback riding. Skydiving. Frette linens. Organic produce. Purple. Tantric yoga. Magnum condoms...

Magnum condoms? What the hell is going on?

Vickie closed her eyes, tried to pinch them, to block out the white noise. She wondered where all this was coming from. It was like a fracture in a dam she desperately wanted to mend.

What do these words mean? Are they connected to me? Do I like to parasail? Do I eat organic? And what about those magnums...

The door to her room opened and a nurse with bright red hair came in. "Ah! You're awake."

"Yes," Vickie said, sitting up a little.

"Do you remember me?"

She nodded. This nurse had looked after her yesterday, had even asked if she wanted her fake nails removed. She remembered the woman trimming the tips of her nails before soaking her hands in a pungent fluid, and then patiently scoring everything down with a file. She remembered the kindness. "You're Maureen. My nurse."

"Oh, great. That's terrific." She puttered around the room, looked at the machines, and then passed

Vickie a glass of apple juice. "Can you remember anything else?"

Vickie took the cup, sipped gingerly. "Some things." She hesitated. "I think I might like skydiving."

"Skydiving! Really?" Maureen's eyes pitched to the ceiling. "Not in a million years for me. No, ma'am. I'd sooner eat maggots than jump out of an airplane."

Vickie envisioned hurtling through clouds, the earth yawning open before her, unable to stop herself from certain death. "Maybe not," she said doubtfully. "But it was one of the first things that popped into my head."

"You're speaking so much better," Maureen said with a cheerful smile. "What else do you remember? How about your last name? Or where you're from?"

"I know my name is Vickie. I think I'm from..." She thought back. "Michigan?"

"Michigan," Maureen echoed. "Good. Good. Keep going."

Like a flashlight shining on a stone, she saw it before her. "Vickie Winslow," she said, flushing with triumph. *I'm remembering!* "My name is Victoria Winslow."

Maureen nodded in approval. "Very nice. It's a thousand times more exotic than Maureen Davis, if you ask me. So where in Michigan are you from?"

Vickie searched for a few moments, but came up empty. "I don't know."

"It's okay. I'm sure that'll come, eventually. What else can you remember?"

She related her strange collection of unconnected words.

Maureen laughed and arched an eyebrow. "Magnum condoms, huh?"

She reddened. "It's probably nothing."

"Or maybe that's one memory you want to get back ASAP." Maureen flashed a conspiratorial grin before her expression turned solemn. She approached the bed, resting her hip against the rail. "Listen, Vickie. What can you remember about the accident?"

"Accident?"

"The report said that a car struck you. And so close to Thanksgiving!" Maureen gave a sympathetic tut-tut. "Do you remember anything about it?"

Vickie searched the empty tunnel of her mind, but all she held in her mental hands was vapor. "No. Nothing." She smoothed the hair from her face. "Was I hit by a car?"

But before Maureen could answer, the door to the room opened. Vickie turned to lock eyes with a man, and something in her began taking shorthand. Dark hair flecked with gray. Olive skin. Striking blue eyes. Late forties. Fitted cable-knit sweater and khaki pants.

Undeniably handsome.

Even in her current state, Vickie knew his beauty was unmatched. When he entered the room, his presence filled the space. Did he know her somehow?

"Oh my god." Maureen came forward, almost slack-jawed. "Jack—I mean, Mr. Post. It's a real honor, sir. I'm Maureen Davis, the registered nurse on duty."

He took the woman's proffered hand. "Pleasure, Maureen. How's our patient?" When he turned to Vickie, she saw him hesitate, and a strange expression crossed his face. But this momentary lapse passed so quickly that Vickie wondered if she had imagined it.

Then his face brightened with a ready smile, but she saw the smile did not reach his eyes. There was something in them she could not place. *Anxiety? Fear?*

"She's doing amazingly well," Maureen informed him. "They transferred her from the ICU yesterday. Now we're just monitoring her. Really, she's a miracle case." She gave Vickie a winning smile, as if she was the prize horse at the Kentucky Derby: a specimen to be shown off, glorified, and studied.

Vickie flashed to her lead physician calling others into her room. Unknown men and women who had scrutinized her charts, examined her face, and tested her reflexes. Her near-full motor function astounded them. They spoke of patients with similar brain injuries who had never walked again, much less fed themselves, or breathed independently of a machine. And yet here she was, suffering only the occasional hand tremor, with bandaged wounds that would heal. She could breathe. She could speak and understand. She could even make fresh memories. But for the near loss of her life, she was physically whole, and lucky to be alive.

"Has she regained her memory?" Jack asked the nurse.

"Bits and pieces. It's a slow process, especially considering the severity of her accident."

"Right." He swallowed as he drew near her bed.

"Hello," Vickie said.

His eyes filled with relief. "Oh, thank God. You're speaking. How do you feel?"

"Okay. Who are you?"

He blinked. Something passed over his face.

Surprise? she wondered. *But why is he surprised I don't know him?*

He coughed into his fist. "You don't know who I am?"

"No," she said. *I barely know who I am.*

He cleared his throat. "My name is Jack Post."

She said nothing.

He frowned. "*Jack* Post."

She nodded.

"You still don't know who I am?"

"Am I supposed to?"

His chiseled face broke into a wide grin. "No, I guess you're not *supposed* to."

Vickie shifted in the bed, trying to draw all this together. "Are we related?"

"No, no." He shook his head, some of his earlier humor gone. "Not that I know of, anyway. But then there's always some random person claiming to be my fifth cousin or something." He laughed awkwardly. Maureen laughed with him.

"Listen," Jack said, his gaze sweeping the room. His eyes locked on a chair, which he dragged beside the bed so that he could sit across from her. He lowered his voice. "Before any of this gets out, I just want to say that I'm sorry. I really didn't see you, and I feel terrible. And I was stupid to be—" He paused, then seemed to reconsider. "Well, not in the best frame of mind."

"Okay," Vickie said, not understanding any of this.

"So..." His expression turned troubled. "Do you...I mean, can you remember anything?"

"About what?"

"About what happened. What put you here?"

She shook her head. "No. I barely remember who I am."

He blinked. "Seriously? Not a thing?"

"Well, I know my name. Victoria Winslow."

"Victoria Winslow," he said. "Beautiful name."

She smiled.

"Anything else you remember?"

"I'm not sure." She thought over her unconnected mental explosions. "Different things. Like my favorite color."

"Which is?"

"Purple," she told him, though with little conviction.

"Great choice," he said. "That's mine too."

"Really?"

He nodded. "Are you from New York?"

"No. At least, I don't think so." Again, she ran over her fractured list. "Maybe Michigan?"

"Really?" His face changed again, but she could not read his expression. "I'm from Michigan. Where'd you grow up?"

Vickie sped through the list, clinging to it like a lifeline. "Warren?"

A smile tugged on his lips. "What a world. *I'm* from Warren."

"Really?" said Maureen. "I thought you were from Detroit."

"It's a suburb of Detroit," he explained, looking at Vickie with renewed interest. "Well. Maybe we're related?"

She smiled. She was finding it easy to smile around him.

The door opened again, and a small, hurried man stepped into the room. "Great! You're both here. Okay, Jack, I've already handled the rest of the staff. So let's get her to sign this before any of the rags get a hold of this." He pulled a packet of paper and a pen from his jacket. It all seemed very familiar.

Maureen stepped forward. "Sir, we've already been through this. If you want me to call security—"

"I'll handle this, Maureen," Jack said smoothly. He turned to the man. "Sam, for God's sake. We can't do this now. She just woke up."

"Now's the best time. Does she even remember what happened?"

"You're the man who came in here before," Vickie said, loud enough that all eyes immediately turned to her.

"Oh, Christ. She's remembering." Sam stepped forward and thrust the papers onto her lap. "Okay. So this is just a standard NDA..."

She blinked up at him. "NDA?"

He glowered, as if she was wasting his time. "Means non-disclosure agreement." He spewed a litany of words that Vickie barely understood. Proprietary information. Restriction of third parties. No monetary gain.

But before he could finish, Jack Post stripped the packet from her lap and glared at the man angrily. "I said this could wait. My God, where the hell are your manners? Did you even introduce yourself to her?"

"Now hold on. I just—"

"Vickie," Jack said pointedly, "this is my lawyer, Sam Winters. He's usually a lot more polite." He turned back to the man before adding, "At least he better be."

"Jack, I—"

"Sam. That's enough. Go home."

Sam stood there, flummoxed. "If the tabloids get a hold of this story..."

"Then we'll let the PRs handle it." His jaw set. "She's not signing some goddamn agreement."

With an exaggerated sigh, Sam reluctantly folded the packet in half and tucked it into his inner jacket pocket. "You know I'm just looking out for your best interest."

"I know, Sam. And that's why you're still here. But I don't need you right now. Go home and I'll call you later, okay?"

Sam gave Vickie a long, piercing glare, as if she were about to claw to death the man he so obviously worshiped.

Who are these people? Vickie wondered.

"I'm sorry, Mr. Post," Maureen said eventually, "but visiting hours are over. I'm afraid you both are going to have to go."

"But we'll be back," Sam announced ominously.

Jack gently squeezed the three free fingers of her left hand. "You take care, Vickie from Michigan. I'll be back to visit as soon as I can. Okay?"

She blinked up at him. "Okay."

One more squeeze of her hand, and he was gone through the sliding glass doors. He turned left down the hall and disappeared behind her head.

"Whoa," Maureen said with a slow shake of her head. "I just can't believe it."

"Believe what?"

"Jack Post. In this room. I actually shook his hand!" She grinned excitedly. "Did you see me?"

Vickie nodded. "So who is he?"

Maureen strode to her with a grin that threatened

to topple her over. "Jack Post? Oh, he's only the big-gest movie star on the planet." She resumed the seat Jack had left behind and then animated a list of specifics. "Two Oscars. Twenty-mil a picture. He used to be married to a gorgeous Victoria Secret model. Or maybe two of them? Anyway, now he's mostly retired, only coming out once a year for the summer or winter blockbuster." She sighed. "Other than that, he's just like you and me."

"Oh," was all Vickie could think to say. Jack Post. Illustrious movie star. The man who apologized for putting her in the hospital.

After Maureen left, Vickie remained still for a very long time, playing over recent events, trying to make sense of everything, but it was all such a mess. *What's happened to me? Why does this man—this Jack Post—care anything about me?*

And why can't I remember?

Chapter Three

"THERE," said Sandra, the new nurse, as she eased the catheter from between Vickie's legs. There was a long pinch, and a small rush, like Vickie had just wet herself. "It'll take some time to adjust, but you'll do fine." Sandra pulled down the dressing gown and gave Vickie's leg a reassuring pat. "How's that?"

"Weird," she said. "So, can I use the bathroom by myself now?"

"Sure. Do you have to go?"

"No. Just curious."

"How are you feeling otherwise?"

"Okay. A little dizzy now and again, but Dr. Porter said that's normal."

"I'm sure it is." Sandra fluttered about, putting notes into a chart. Then she turned to Vickie, and her smile twitched. "Vickie?"

"Mmm?"

"Can I ask you something?"

"I guess."

"Great." Sandra drew a breath. "What's he like?"

Vickie blinked at her. "Who?"

"Jack Post. What's he like? And how do you know him?"

"I don't know him."

"I mean, before your accident. You must have known him before, since he's visiting you all the time."

"He is?"

Sandra fingered the bedrail. "Well, I've not seen him here myself, but Maureen said that he visited you most days in the ICU."

"He did?"

"You don't remember?"

"I just remember the one time a couple of days ago."

"Maybe it was mostly while you were in recovery, before you completely came to. Anyway, all his effort says something."

"It does?"

"Sure, hon." Sandra paused. "Do you think you guys dated?"

"Dated? Jack Post?"

"Yeah."

Vickie considered the possibility. "No. He would've said something. I don't think I even know him."

"You'd think he'd be a memory you couldn't erase," Sandra said wistfully. "But the mind..." Her voice trailed as she took in Vickie's open face. "Sorry."

Vickie shrugged. "It's okay."

Sandra's lips tightened as she smoothed the sheets draped over Vickie's legs. "Maureen said you're remembering bits and pieces?"

Vickie shrugged again. "It's still really a blur. There're some things. Stuff I like to do, I guess. That's it."

"You've got to start somewhere." Sandra smiled down at her. "You think you've got any family?"

"I don't know. Is that something people can just sense? Because I don't really sense anything."

"The mind is a powerful thing. I've seen people lose decades through Alzheimer's, to where they don't know or even recognize their own children." She paused, seeming to consider her next words. "But you're the reverse. You're aware that there's memory loss, and you're trying to regain it."

"You think I will?"

"Don't know. That's a question for Dr. Porter."

She turned to leave, but Vickie stopped her. "Sandra?"

"What, hon?"

"Can you give me a mirror?"

"A mirror?"

"Yeah. I'd like to see what I look like."

"Really? With your dressing and injuries?" Sandra

looked doubtful. "Okay, well, you should first know that your hair *will* grow back. I promise. They just had to shave a small section when they worked on your intracranial bleed."

Vickie touched the dressing on her head, just above her right ear. She was bald under the gauze? She sighed. "Please. I just want to see myself."

Sandra disappeared into the bathroom and returned with a small plastic hand-held. "Here, hon."

Vickie took it from her, her grip still unsteady, and turned it to her face. A large white dressing squeezed around her head, with a scattering of cuts, bruises, and stitches marring her exposed skin. But she could see herself. While not for the first time, it certainly felt like a novel experience.

Vickie gaped at her gray-green eyes and singed eyebrows. Her overly plump, pale lips, and the limp blonde hair hanging past her shoulders. She touched the gauze above her ear, scraping her scalp through the bandage. No hair crumbled beneath. They'd shaved it smooth, just as Sandra said.

Vickie dropped her hand and studied herself, taking in every bruised and scarred part of her face.

I am... she thought, then immediately corrected herself. *No, I was pretty.* She could see past the bandages and injuries and imagine an untarnished face, with unburned brows and hair freshly washed. Indeed, she had been pretty. But what else was there? Vickie narrowed her eyes at the woman in the mirror.

Who are you?

She tried to frown, but something stopped her, an unseen presence pulling up at her forehead, the sides of her eyes. All Vickie could manage was to squint, and even that didn't look right.

Perhaps this was what Dr. Porter had tried explaining earlier. What had he said? That she'd had facial injections? Paralyzed her own face? For what purpose? To look young? Younger? How old was she?

"How old do I look to you?" Vickie asked the nurse, who had been watching her struggle to control her face.

Sandra considered her question for a few moments before finally shaking her head. "This would be easier if you'd come in with some sort of ID." She paused. "I don't know. Thirty?"

"You think?" Vickie picked up her chin, analyzed every curve and feature. It was difficult to tell. *Am I twenty-nine?* she wondered. *Thirty? Thirty-five?*

"A *young* thirty," Sandra qualified at length.

Vickie glanced at her. "I don't care how old I am. I just want to know."

"Great attitude," Sandra said, then narrowed her eyes. "If that's the case, I'd put you at a solid thirty-two."

"I'll go with that," Vickie said, grinning at this bizarre conversation. "Now, if you can tell me if I have any living parents, or brothers or sisters, that'd be very helpful."

Sandra opened her hand for the mirror and Vickie handed it back. "Sorry, hon. That's beyond my expertise."

"Yeah. I guess so." She dropped her hands against the sheets. "Can I use the bathroom?"

"You ready to get up?"

She nodded.

"All right." Sandra lowered the bar on the bed and helped slide out Vickie's legs. When Vickie winced, Sandra asked, "You okay?"

"I'm really sore," said Vickie, her eyes watering at the sparking pain in her shoulders and back of her arms. She grasped the nurse's hand, wishing they hadn't lowered her medication.

"Yeah, you will be for a few more weeks. Try to be easy on yourself." Sandra helped her take a few shaky steps from the bed. "You want me to walk you to the bathroom?"

Dull pain snaked up Vickie's thighs and into her lower back. She winced, but the pain was manageable. "No. I think I've got it."

"Okay." Sandra reluctantly released her arm, and Vickie managed a few cautious steps on her own. "I'll be out here if you need me."

Vickie left the door slightly ajar as she palmed the cold steel of the sink. An unframed mirror hung directly before her, and she caught sight of her reflection again. A stranger stared back at her. A stranger in a head bandage. She wondered how long it would be before she recognized herself.

After maneuvering herself onto the toilet, Vickie urinated, then rose to wash her hands. She was especially gentle with her nails, which were still tender from removing the broken acrylics.

It was as she dried her hands that Vickie had a moment to take in the rest of her body. And the first thing she saw—and could not believe she missed—were her breasts.

They stood before her like two prized melons. No soft curvature downward, but a severe upward thrust. Vickie touched them through the fabric of the hospital gown, surprised by the hardness. She opened her shift to stare down at them. They were appendages that stood apart from her, as unnatural as synthetic limbs. *Are these really my breasts? What's wrong with them?*

"You okay in there?" Sandra called from outside.

"No. Can you come in?"

Sandra opened the door fully and took in the sight of Vickie staring down at herself. "What is it, hon?"

"There's something wrong with my breasts."

"Something wrong?"

"They don't feel right."

Sandra's face dimmed with concern. "Did you find a lump?"

"A lump? No. They just, they feel..." Vickie shook her head, took in a breath, and opened her gown.

Sandra glanced at her bare chest. "They look okay to me."

"But they don't feel right."

"Aren't they implants?"

"Implants...?" Vickie's mind reeled back and then clicked. Yes, she knew this term. "No. Yes. I don't know."

Sandra extended a hand. "May I?"

Vickie nodded.

The nurse reached out and took one breast in her hand, squeezed lightly at first, then more firmly. With her opposite hand, she palpated around her breast. "It feels like an implant," she said, "but I don't see any sign of a scar." She trailed her fingers under Vickie's breasts before moving to her armpits. With a scowl, she touched Vickie's bellybutton, pausing on the rim's small cleft. "Wow. I've never seen one before."

"Seen what?"

"A TUBA augmentation."

Vickie blinked at her. "A what?"

Sandra shook her head, "Sorry, hon. I used to work primarily in plastic surgery. They usually do the implant under the breasts, or through the nipples, or under the arms. But this time they went through your bellybutton, here, to put them in."

"So they *are* implants?"

Sandra nodded. "Very expensive implants."

This news centered somewhere in Vickie's brain, laid among the other facts she safeguarded. She had fake breasts. She paid someone to stuff her chest. Someone to inject her face.

She closed her gown.

"You okay?"

"No," said Vickie, neither liking how this puzzle was fitting together, nor the person she was turning out to be.

"Knock, knock," came a voice from the door.

Vickie shifted her gaze from the window overlooking the small, frosty courtyard to meet eyes with Jack Post. He stood just inside the room, cradling a crystal vase with a dozen lavender roses.

She smiled at him from the bed. "Hello."

"Hello, Vickie." As he shuffled in with the flowers, a wedge of light crossed his face. Vickie lost her breath, stunned by the brightness of his blue eyes and his effortless beauty. How many men were this flawless? This symmetrically perfect? "These are for you," he said, his voice uncertain. "You said you like purple."

"I remember."

His brows shot up. "You do?"

She nodded.

"That's great." He gently set the arrangement on a shelf near her bed.

"They're really nice," she said. "Thank you."

He shrugged. "It was nothing. I'm glad you like them."

She hesitated before asking, "Can I see them?"

"See...?" He followed her gaze. "Oh! Sure." He snapped up the vase and brought it to her.

The roses, cut short to fit the heavy square vase, beckoned from her lap. She closed her eyes and inhaled their soft, calming fragrance. She envisioned these petals floating on the surface of a bath, brushing her skin with each ripple of water.

She smiled up at Jack. "Thank you."

His gaze was warm and unrestrained. "Sure, Vickie." He pulled a chair next to her bed. She returned the vase to him, but he had to help her lift it, as her grip was still unsteady. He replaced the nodding flowers on the shelf and said, "So, how are you feeling?"

"Better. I'm still really sore, but the dizziness is almost gone." She tucked a stray hair behind her ear. "Jack?"

"Hmm?"

"Why are you here?"

He blinked, clearly surprised. "What do you mean?"

"You're pretty famous, right?"

He nodded.

"And I'm literally a nobody. So why do you care? How did we even meet?" She wondered at his face and its handsome, secure confidence. *Have we dated?* she wondered, and not for the first time. *Been intimate?*

Sandra was right. How could she have forgotten such a thing?

"Technically, we've never formally met."

"*What?*"

Jack reached out to touch her hand. "Listen, Vickie. You know you were in an accident, right?"

"Yes." She hesitated. "Were you the reason for it?"

He nodded slowly. "Yes. I was driving the car that hit you."

This didn't shock her. As good an actor as he might be, he couldn't hide his guilt. Vickie pressed him for details, hoping that one word might break the spell trapping her mind. "Then you need to tell me what I was I doing that I got hit by a car."

"You weren't doing anything," Jack blurted. "It was all my fault, and I'm so sorry."

"What happened?"

He sighed and briefly passed a hand over his face. "I was driving in New York, heading home. You—well, I think you were crossing the street, but not at a crosswalk. I didn't see you at first, but when I did, I hit the brakes. Maybe it was the clutch? I'm not sure. I lost control. You got hit and went over the hood." He winced, as if mentally replaying the moment. "The ambulance brought you here."

A disconnected image coalesced in Vickie's mind. It was a far cry from a full, genuine memory. "But what was I doing? Why was I there?"

"I don't know. I just remember that you were

crossing the street and were too close for me to stop. You don't remember any of this?"

"No."

"Have you talked to your doctor?"

"I met with him this morning."

"Any good news?"

"Only that everything else with me seems to function, other than my mind." She gave a short laugh.

"It makes sense. You have retrograde amnesia."

She blinked at him. "You spoke with my doctor?"

"A couple of days ago."

Again, this didn't surprise her. A man like Jack Post could buy such information.

"Do they know when you'll regain your memory?" he asked.

"I may never."

"Really?"

"Really."

His face darkened. "Anything else?"

"They said they'll discharge me soon."

"When?"

She sensed he already knew, but answered him anyway. "Within a day or so. Dr. Porter said he would do my follow-ups over the next few months, should I stay in New York. So that's good." She sighed. "I just don't know where to go from here. I don't so much as have a driver's license, so it's going to be pretty tricky to find out where I live. They've recommended a rehab center—"

"Listen, Vickie," Jack interrupted, any trace of humor gone. He passed a hand over his face and sighed into his palm. "I want you to come stay with me. I have about a dozen guest rooms that are completely empty, and you're free to stay in any—or all—that you want. At least until you've figured out your next step."

She said nothing. When several moments passed, Jack grimaced and added, "I'm saying that you are welcome to stay at my house while you recover. It's not far away. I live in New Jersey, and we can take the car to the city for any follow-ups—"

Vickie shook her head emphatically. "You don't have to do this."

"Do what?"

"Be so nice."

He grinned. "Am I?"

"Yes. And I know what it is. Guilt." She looked at her hands, bruised purple and yellow from the various IVs. She contemplated what she must say next. "I was also told that someone paid for all my medical expenses, including flying down a pair of surgeons to repair my face. Was that person you?"

He didn't hesitate. "Yes."

"Well." She took in a breath, folded her hands over her lap. "I guess I owe you even more thanks. But I'd like to know why."

"Why...?"

"Why you're doing any of this? If it's how you said it was an accident. You don't owe me anything. You don't have to pay for my treatment, and you certainly don't have to put me up in your house. I'm a stranger to you. You don't have to do anything." She said these words, but a knot began forming in the back of her throat. She was terrified that he was going to nod, agree, and walk out of her life forever. And that part—growing greater by the second—saw Jack as her only contact in a world that had become a wall of strangers. Though an interloper in his otherwise charmed life, his familiar face remained her only anchor.

"Maybe you're right," he said finally.

She waited for him to continue. Her pulse beat in her ears.

"You're right. Guilt plays a part of this. But there is another part that says I can't leave a woman who can't remember anything alone in a strange city. Why do I have all these resources if I can't help someone in need?"

"And you believe that?"

He smiled as he took her hand. "Set aside my motivations. Your only other option is a rehab center, and I can assure you my abode is much, much nicer. If you like, I can commission a fleet of nurses and therapists to be at your bedside. You wouldn't have to worry."

"I just don't know."

His expression turned dubious. "If you prefer, I can arrange a hotel. Would that make you more comfortable?" When she said nothing, he continued, "What I'm trying to say is that no matter what happens now, my actions caused you to be here. But the decision is up to you." He paused, his face open and pleading. "So, Vickie. Tell me what I can do for you."

She had few choices. Jack was her only link to the outside world, and she was desperate for answers. She looked at the roses, nodding at her from the shelf. They were nice. *He* was nice. "Okay," she said. "I'll stay with you. At least until I figure out what to do next."

"Good." Jack stood, and the sunlight that dappled his face earlier faded behind a cloud. "There's only one more thing."

"What?"

He unbuttoned his blazer, reached inside, and removed a folded packet of papers. "Before you leave, I need to ask a small favor."

"Anything."

He gave her the same disarming grin that must've earned him his superstar moniker. "I need you to sign this non-disclosure agreement."

She peered at the packet in his hands. "Is that what the lawyer tried to have me sign?"

"Yes."

"Do I have to sign it?"

"No, you don't. But it'll protect both of us if you do. They would dig up every bit of shady history that you have and put it on a world display. I know you're unaware of the degree of my fame, but for years, I was the target of the paparazzi, and they chomp at the bit for news like this."

"Movie stars sending unknown women into hospitals?" Vickie asked, smiling.

He returned with a winning grin. "Or something like that. It just says you won't run to *People* with an exclusive. That sort of thing."

"And that's it?"

"The short of it, yes." He opened the packet and pulled a pen from his inner jacket pocket.

Her eyes swam with the legal jargon, the page after page of text and bullet points. Her name appeared several times, with places for her to sign and initial. Vickie met Jack's encouraging smile. She sensed she could trust him—that she *had* to trust him. She took the pen and signed the papers, initialed where instructed, and returned the packet.

"Great." He folded the papers and tucked them away. "Now. Let's work on getting you out of here."

Chapter Four

"AND THIS IS YOUR BATHROOM." Jack touched a wall and instantly soft, golden light spilled from a crystal chandelier into an immaculate bathroom. Vickie marveled at the marble floors and veined granite countertops. The plush designer robes, towels, and throw rugs. The enormous Jacuzzi, gilded shower, and glistening trashcan. And it was only the guest bathroom. One of *three*.

"This is a neat feature." Jack snatched a remote from inside a brown leather case and pressed a button. Light flickered from behind the mirror, suspended over the double sink. The light coalesced into CNN. "You can set it to any channel," he explained, cycling the numbers up into the triple digits. "And of course you've got the movie stations. HBO. Showtime. You know, whatever you want."

"People watch TV in the bathroom?" Vickie asked him in awe.

"Mostly when they're in the tub. But you saw the TV in the bedroom, so you can watch whatever you want there too. And it has Blu-ray and surround sound, and the acoustics are great." He shrugged. "I mean, I've not slept there. But I hear it's great." He shifted on his heels, and Vickie realized he was nervous, although she didn't know why.

"Thanks," she said.

"Sure. Do you need anything?" His hand went to his head. "Oh! I completely forgot. You don't have any clothes."

"I have clothes. The hospital gave me some." This was true. The nurses had folded two pairs of jeans, three sweaters, a handful of socks, and a set of scuffed black boots into a faded Macy's bag. The donated collection slumped beside Jack's enormous front doors.

Jack made a disgusted face. "Those don't really count. No, we should send for some. I'll take care of it, so don't worry. I'd say you're a—" He gave her body a fleeting glance. "A size two?"

She spread her hands. "Your guess is as good as mine."

"Should work. We'll get you some basics. I have some oversize T-shirts you can sleep in tonight, if you'd like."

"Okay. Thanks."

"Sure." He swayed back on his heels again. "So. Are you hungry?"

She considered. "Maybe some soup?"

"We can get you some soup. No problem." He paused. "Do you want to settle in first?"

Vickie glanced around the suite. "Not really."

"Right." He shrugged. "Think you can handle the rest of the tour?"

"Sure."

"Let me know if you get tired and want to rest, okay?"

She nodded and followed him out, catching sight of her reflection as they entered the hall. No dressing on her head. No more stitches. But her scars—a long pitchfork and two smaller lighting bolts—remained bright red and marred her face. Not to mention the shaved part of her head.

Vickie glanced away.

She followed Jack into the dining room. Platinum-trimmed plates and sterling silver flatware studded a polished mahogany table. Before she could admire the crystal wine glasses sparkling from their geometric cuts, they passed into a living room punctuated with broad leather divans, ornate tables, and ambient light. Finally, they arrived in a pristine kitchen arrayed with stainless steel appliances and three ovens. Two people scurried to the sharp orders of one: a shockingly small man with sinewy arms who beat the rim of a large Dutch oven with a spatula. Vickie expected to be introduced, but Jack passed through the kitchen without a backwards glance. Vickie hurried after him.

They moved on to what Vickie surmised was the trophy room. A filigreed stand showcased an impressive array. Two Oscars. Seven Golden Globes. Four Screen Actor's Guild Awards. Three Emmys. And a slew of other statues, plaques, and recognitions that Vickie had no time to count.

"Impressive," she said, wondering how she recognized them.

"Do you want to see them?" Jack asked.

"See them?"

Jack grinned broadly as he produced a key and unlocked the trophy case's double doors, then spread them open like a pair of wings. Seeing her hesitation, he said, "You're more than welcome to touch them. Pick them up, even."

Do people want to touch them? Vickie wondered, momentarily picturing an alien from a distant world flummoxed when a human offered his hand in greeting.

She moved to stand beside Jack and peered at each level of the case. Centered just above her nose was a bright gold man, his body ramrod straight, with arms crossed at his breast and his elbows resting atop what appeared to be a podium.

Vickie glanced at Jack, who nodded his approval, and she reached up and lifted the Oscar. The weight of it surprised her. She ran her fingers over Jack's name, etched into the metal.

"This is beautiful," she said.

He nodded, seeming to admire it as much as she did. "You know how they say it's an honor just to be nominated?" He didn't wait for her response. "Every schmuck knows that's a big fat lie. *Winning* is the real honor. No one ever remembers the nominees."

"Wow." She turned the figure over in her hand, and the gilded man with the hollow eyes stared back at her, unsmiling. "It must be some honor."

"These are some of the best nights of my life." His gaze fixed on the glowing case. "There's all the fanfare behind it, of course. The pre-parties and post-parties, press junkets and interviews. Lots of shaking hands and sit-downs. You feel you're in a whirlwind half the time, especially if you're on a production simultaneously."

"So you've been to a lot of these?"

"Indeed." He grazed his index finger against the second tier of glass. The various medals winked back at him. "These are just the awards I've won. They've nominated me dozens of times over."

She considered his words, and questions bubbled to her lips. "So, is it like that all the time? All that...fanfare? Don't you ever tire of it?"

"Not really." He opened his hand for the trophy and returned it to its rightful place on the glass shelf. "No, that life is mostly behind me. I only do about one or two films every couple of years. Hardly any interviews lately. I'm getting too old for it, honestly."

"You're not too old," she said.

His eyes softened. "You're sweet. But for this world, I'm practically a dinosaur. I'm what you would call 'overexposed.'"

"Overexposed?"

"They've seen too much of me. There's a word for it...existential, maybe? Anyway, you go rent a movie—that is, when people actually *drove* to rent movies—and see yourself on a cardboard cutout, or framed in a poster, and on display in every single genre in the store. You know that you've made it, but it does something to your head. You get kind of crazy with it. You lose perspective."

He stopped, and they stared at each other. Vickie absorbed his words, imagining life as he described it, and it sounded to her like something out of a dream: unreal, fantastic, and detached.

"So have you?" she asked him finally.

Now it was his turn to look confused. "Have I what?"

"Regained it?" she said. "Your perspective?"

"Ah. Let's just say it's a gradual process." He glanced over her shoulder. "You ready for dinner?"

"Sure."

"Then I'll have it served. You can rest in here if you like."

"Okay."

He left, but Vickie was too alert, too awake, to rest. Her shattered world had finally stopped spinning. Perhaps if she examined each detail, she could piece it back together again.

She set out to explore the rest of the room, beginning with a nearby table fanned with almost a dozen frames. Despite her memory loss, she recognized many people with Jack: Presidents Bush, Clinton, Bush Junior, Obama.

Vickie's nerves frayed. *How can I know the faces of presidents but not my own?*

She moved on to Jack, sitting cross-legged beside a bemused Dalai Lama. Jack on an elephant with a cluster of bushmen. Jack holding onto an airplane's safety bar seconds before plummeting through the stratosphere.

Skydiving. Had she done this? A part of her said yes. She *had* flung herself from an airplane. Another part screamed such a feat was too terrifying to contemplate.

Her inner compass spun in a blur.

Flustered, Vickie left to explore the room adjacent: Jack's library. Bright oriental carpets, their fringes neatly combed, muted her footfalls. A fire crackled in a stone hearth on the left, filling the space with ancient smells. Custom bookcases extended on three walls into the second story of the house. Rows of dusted hardbacks embossed with delicate gold calligraphy. An entire shelf dedicated to the *Encyclopedia Britannica* series. Another to biographies. Still another reserved for nautical travelogues.

Vickie spun around, taking in the space's beauty. She wandered about and paused before a section entitled "19th-Century Fiction" with a gold plaque. Scanning the titles, she selected a copy of *Jane Eyre*. The book was small, hardbound, with raised bands, red and green spine labels, and pages edged with coppery stains. She sensed this was an original edition, and very expensive.

She carefully turned to the first chapter. The novel called to her, its words an almost familiar hum, and she wondered if she had read these pages before, where she was when she read them, and why. Glancing up, Vickie realized the book split into three volumes. She turned to the second book, skimming over Jane's blossoming love for the wealthy and elusive Mr. Rochester. Pressing to the last volume, Vickie smiled as the characters reunited. How Jane loved Rochester despite his maiming and blindness. Jane gleefully accepting his proposal. Rochester recovering his sight just in time to see her cradling their newborn son—

"So you're a Brontë fan," said a voice to her left, and a yelp caught in Vickie's throat.

She closed the book with a *thump* and smiled nervously at Jack, who stood with glasses of red wine in each hand. "Sorry..." She hastily returned the volume to the shelf. "I didn't mean to snoop. It was just...I think I've read this book before, and I—" She paused, wondering what she was trying to say. "I guess I just wanted something familiar."

"No, I get it." He passed her a glass. "It's strange that you chose that one, though."

"Why?"

"It's my favorite book."

"Really?"

"Yes. My very favorite out of the entire collection."

"Why?"

He regarded the binding thoughtfully. "My mother read it to my sisters and me every other winter, right until she died. Hers wasn't a first edition, of course, just a paperback she bought at a local bookstore. I hated the thought of listening to the plight of some British girl, but it grew on me. I actually started looking forward to the next time she'd pull down that book and call us all to the fireplace."

"You should play Mr. Rochester," Vickie suggested, her tone playful.

A frown wrinkled his forehead. "I actually did, Vickie. That's the role that won me my first Oscar. That award you picked out of my trophy case."

"Oh." Vickie crossed her arms, trying to hide her embarrassment. Perhaps this knowledge was akin to knowing the names of all fifty states, or who won the Civil War. Something that everyone knew, or should know, and she did not.

"It's not a big deal," Jack said, seeming to discern her feelings. "And it'd be ridiculous to expect you to remember that. Anyway, it happened almost twenty years ago." He chuckled. "It's not every day that I have to explain my work history."

"I'm sorry—"

Jack raised a hand. "No, don't be. You don't know how refreshing this all is." He gazed at the book, secured now on its shelf, and then reached out to touch the binding. "The second I saw this, I knew I had to have it. It's a first edition. Very rare. Printed in a full tree calf with morocco labels."

"Wow," she said, though not in understanding. "Must be worth a lot."

"About forty thousand."

"Dollars?" she exclaimed.

He nodded.

She gazed about the enormous library, wondering how many other treasures hid amongst the shelves. "And when you see this book now, you think of your mother?"

He gave a solemn nod. "Every time. From the second I open its pages."

"That's nice." She wondered when another moment might slingshot her through her fractured memory. Could she regain an image or a genuine feeling for her own mother?

"So," Vickie managed, "do you come from a large family?"

Jack shrugged. "Depends on what you consider big. I had two older sisters."

"And you never wanted children of your own?"

"I have children. Three, actually."

"Oh." She frowned, and her eyes cut glances around the room. "I just thought, since I didn't see any photos—"

"You're probably right in that I should put some up for public view," he said, his formally jaunty voice now thick with a detectible heaviness. "I tried keeping them out of the limelight, but perhaps I took it too far since you can't even tell I have children after touring my home. It's complicated with their mothers. I only see them a few months a year, when their mothers are off traipsing in Boca or St. Barts—enjoying *my* money."

"I'm sorry," Vickie said, shifting awkwardly. "I didn't know."

"How could you?" Jack sighed and shook his head as if to clear it. "It's fine. I love my kids, but I didn't alter my life for them. I can't blame the business, because plenty of actors at my level have children and dedicate every spare minute to them. There are days when I wish I could go back and reset the clock, but what are we if not the sum of our experiences?"

His words pressed Vickie like weights. As a silence stretched between them, new questions spun like a maelstrom within her. Hadn't she had her own clock reset? Not by choice, but by circumstance? Could Jack be right that, deep down, she was simply a collection of her own life experiences?

A bleakness gripped her heart. *What if I never remember my life? Who am I, in the end?*

Her mind tunneled, then stirred. Were people more than the sum of their experiences? Or did memories carve people like water through stone?

Not ready to face the implication of these questions, Vickie took a quick sip of wine, surprised at its sweetness.

"You like it?" Jack asked, returning his attention to her.

"Mmm. What kind of wine is it?"

"It's actually sparkling grape juice. You're not supposed to mix alcohol with your medication."

She smiled gratefully. "Thanks. I forgot."

"Sure." He took a sip and made a face. "Nope. Way too sweet."

She was about to ask why his wasn't wine when an accented voice called from the doorway, "Mr. Post?" A small woman in her late fifties smiled cordially at them. "Dinner is ready, sir."

Her accent stirred something familiar. Vickie strode to the woman and asked, "*¿Habla español?*"

The woman glanced at her in surprise. "*Sí, señorita.*"

"*¿Y de dónde eres?*"

The woman hesitated, her eyes flicking to Jack. "Argentina, *señorita.*"

"*¡Genial!*" Vickie exclaimed, grinning. "*Cuando yo era una niña, tenía...*" A wall in her mind stopped her voice. The easy flow of words, their familiar cadence, became unknown.

A pressure built behind Vickie's eyes.

"*¿Señorita?*" said the woman, peering at her with concern.

"I'm sorry," said Vickie. "I need to go."

"Vickie—" said Jack, but she was already past him.

She flew down the hall, choking back tears. What must Jack think of her now? Or that nice woman? She was being ridiculous. Completely unhinged.

She stopped in her tracks and wiped her eyes. The world cleared through her haze of tears. A gilded frame glinted at her from the wall. An oil painting of a haystack, muted in the fading sun. She stared at the colors and furiously worked at pushing back more tears.

Why am I crying? What's wrong with me? Vickie shook her head, angry with herself. *Why can't I remember?*

"Vickie," said Jack, nearing her. "Hey, Vickie. Are you all right?"

She wiped her eyes, already damp. "No. I don't know. I thought I had it for a moment. A real memory."

His hand went to her elbow. "It'll come to you. I'm certain of it. But it has to happen organically, like it did in that room. You can't force it."

"Easy for you to say." She shook her head.

"Everyone in the world knows who you are. If you forget, all they have to do is hand you a book."

He laughed. Vickie glanced at him, shocked at the smile tugging at her lips.

"Okay, here's what we know," Jack began. "We know you're a Brontë aficionado, and that you speak Spanish."

"Not much to base an identity on," she said dismally.

"But it's a start. Do you know what you said to Maria?"

"Who?"

Jack made a swift motion with his hand. The woman Vickie had spoken to quickly strode to them. "Vickie, this is Maria. Do you remember what you said to her?"

"No." Vickie shook her head again. "I can't remember."

"That's okay." He turned to Maria. "Can you tell us what she asked you?"

"*Claro*," Maria said. "The lady asked if I speak Spanish. I said I did."

"And after that?"

"She asked where I am from. I told her Argentina."

"Very good." Jack waited for her to continue. When she didn't, he pressed, "Was that it?"

"Well..." Maria hesitated. "She started to say something, about how when she was a little girl she had something, but she didn't finish."

"Ah!" said Jack. "That's good."

"How's that good?" Vickie demanded, her frustration boiling over.

"It shows that something she said triggered a memory from your past. It shows that it's there, just under the surface. You're a scratch and sniff ad, Vickie. Everything you have may be just one word away."

He turned animated at this prospect. She was, Vickie realized, some unearthed treasure that Jack had set about to piece together. But she wondered how long she would interest him, and if—like all treasures grown old—he'd cast her aside for something new and unbroken.

They were about to settle in the dining room for dinner, but by then the aches in Vickie's back and thighs were throbbing anew. After Jack gave orders, everything moved into her guest bedroom. Maria offered a tracksuit to sleep in, a glass of ice water, and a Percocet. Maria stirred the fire in the hearth and helped Vickie into bed, propping the pillows behind her back. A table slid across Vickie's lap with homemade chicken noodle soup steaming from a platinum-trimmed bowl. Jack dragged a table and chair next to the bed and dined on *coq au vin*, but they only talked for about fifteen minutes before the full weight of Vickie's medicine took hold.

"You rest now," said Jack, sweeping aside the bed table and taking up her empty bowl, spoon, and linen napkin.

When he touched her hand, Vickie smiled up at him. "Good night," she said.

"Good night, Vickie." He shut the door behind him, and the space sealed with the warmth of the fire embers and the flickering light.

Chapter Five

VICKIE SLEPT until noon and would have slept on had Maria not gently shaken her shoulder and asked about breakfast. She pushed herself from the enormous down pillow, rubbed the sleep from her eyes, and cramped with the first pang of hunger. Vickie told her so and Maria related that the head chef, Francis, wanted to meet her. "That's fine," said Vickie, and quickly smoothed her mussed hair, wondering why she was being given any attention by a chef.

Appearing minutes later, Vickie recognized him as the man giving orders to the kitchen staff the previous night. Today he wore a starched, clean apron and a bright, ready smile.

"I hear you like my soup," he said in a faint, unfamiliar accent.

Vickie sat up in bed and pulled the covers to her armpits. "From last night? Yes. It was great. Thanks."

He beamed. "Well. Mr. Post has asked me to look after your culinary needs. I can make anything you want. Give me a challenge! *Crêpes Suzette*? A smoked salmon frittata?"

Vickie had not expected this. Challenge him? Would she insult him over a craving for Frosted Flakes?

"Can you make anything..." She tried to find the right word, and settled on, "...simpler?"

"Simpler." He said the word as if it was his first time speaking it. "Simpler. Like a yogurt parfait?"

"Yes!" Vickie exclaimed, seizing upon his suggestion. "Yes. That sounds perfect."

He nodded animatedly. "Very well. I'll have it to you in a mere moment."

She smiled after him long after he was gone and then cast her eyes to the floor-to-ceiling windows. Pale sunlight spilled in dusty pillars. Beyond the glass was an expansive snow-covered garden with manicured hedges covered in ice. How often did Jack stroll his property? Or did he only enjoy it through occasional glances?

Maria returned with a young man—tall, thin, whose brown eyes appeared enormous behind a pair of rimless glasses—who carried a garment bag over his arm.

"Hello, Ms. Winslow," he said pleasantly. "I'm Justin, one of Mr. Post's personal assistants. I've brought some clothes I'd like you to try on." He unzipped the bag and lay the contents on the divan. A lavender cashmere sweater with matching pants. A pair of socks and fluffy black slippers. He'd somehow concealed another bag, this one with pale pink panties and a matching bra.

"This is all for me?" Vickie asked him dubiously.

"Yes, ma'am. I thought this fabric would feel good, yet still be loose on your wounds."

Vickie nodded. "But how do you know what fits me?"

He grinned. "That's part of my job, ma'am."

He seemed nice enough, but Vickie was still uneasy. "How will I pay for these? Where are they from?"

"Mr. Post has made all the arrangements," Justin said briskly. "You're not to worry, ma'am."

"I see." She stared at the arrangement of fabric. "Thanks."

"No problem. Maria will help you dress, and I'm here if you need me to find some alternatives."

When he left, Vickie moved to stand from the bed when sudden pain sparked from almost all of her joints. Maria saw her face and helped ease her to the floor, then opened a Terrycloth robe to drape over her shoulders. Vickie noticed her pain pills on the nightstand, along with a sweating glass of ice water.

Maria followed her gaze. "It is time, if you want them now."

"Yes. Please." Vickie took the Percocet and water, swallowing both quickly.

Maria placed two ibuprofen pills on the night-stand. "Remember to wait two hours. After breakfast, so you have something in your stomach."

"Okay." Vickie shuffled to the bathroom, then paused. "Is Jack here today?"

"Yes," Maria said, already smoothing the bed sheets and folding the comforter back onto itself. "But he's meeting with his assistant."

His assistant, Vickie thought. *What a world he lives in. The cooks, the housekeepers, the personal shoppers. His lawyers, managers. PR specialists. Whirlwinds of people all serving one common purpose: him. And what am I to him?*

What am I to myself?

Maria offered to help her shower, but Vickie said she would try it herself. Vickie shut the bathroom door, peeled off the tracksuit, turned on the shower, and stood outside the double blasts of water. She waited a few seconds before easing beneath the faucets, angling her still-tender face from the jets. The pressure wasn't too much.

Vickie exhaled her held breath and let her mind drift into the vanilla-scented steam. As she massaged a sudsy loofah along her arms and stomach, she found she couldn't fully bend for the pain in her sides. Setting her foot against a shelf to sweep the loofah across her legs, she noticed four small cuts on each of her inner thighs. They were nearly identical in length, the scars white and paper-edge thin.

She traced her fingers across the cuts. When had sustained them? Why were they so symmetrical?

Vickie gave a resigned shake of her head. Maybe she would never know.

She found an unused razor and managed—with some effort—to shave most of her legs and underarms to the smoothness of a newborn. She liked the slick sheen on her skin that emerged after toweling herself dry.

Eventually Vickie settled at a gold-plated vanity and gazed once again at her reflection. No bandages hid the pale patch of scalp above her right ear, or the scars that traversed her face. Vickie must have glimpsed herself a thousand times before the accident. Yet this face she'd known since childhood felt as unfamiliar as the robe knotted about her waist.

On the warm marble vanity, Vickie discovered a blow dryer, a vented styling brush, and an inexplicable tray of Estée Lauder makeup. For her? Or leftovers from a girlfriend?

But everything was unopened, everything store-bought new, and so Vickie decided on the former.

Drying her hair was a cumbersome effort as her grip was still uneasy, her scalp ached in places, and her hands trembled occasionally. But by the time she finished, the medicine had taken effect, and she even laughed at the sight of her hair, which had fizzed into a bright blonde poof about her head.

Vickie considered the untouched makeup, picked up a circular case, and set it down. She touched her face experimentally—still sore, but not at all the fiery pain she remembered in her murky glimpses of memory.

As she inspected a pot of cream near a stand of brushes, something tickled the back of her mind. Her left hand opened the cap while the right smoothed blue cream on her face and neck. After a quick massage of her eyebrows, Vickie reached for a set of tweezers. With a dozen deft plucks, the uneven feathering of her brows thinned. With a careful application of powder and liner, she fashioned from her mangled brows two reasonable arches.

She moved to a small tube and a tapered brush. With practiced strokes, she applied concealer beneath her lashes, over her eyelids, and across her scars.

Vickie watched all this from a distance, an audience member witnessing an orchestrated ballet. Her hands knew the steps, and she let them carry on. The ivory foundation and symphony of brushes. The rouge and eyeshadows and liners. Curling the lashes and setting mascara. A swipe of lipstick, another of gloss. She pursed her lips before the mirror and cleared a smear of liquid liner beneath an eyelid.

With the rhythm finished, Vickie stepped back.

I am...

But her thought trailed. What was she? Was this the face she was supposed to know? Lacquered and plucked to perfection?

She didn't recognize herself—at least not the self from the hospital. Her scars had reduced to half a dozen faintly raised lines, easily concealed beneath a clever hairstyle and strategic hand placement. If one were to focus only on her face—ignoring the patch of exposed scalp from her surgery—Vickie appeared, for once, normal. Almost pretty.

She had an almost primal need to wash everything away, but suppressed the urge. She decided that if this was truly who and what she was, she must become reacquainted.

After combing her hair over her jarring bald spot, Vickie returned to the bedroom to find a parfait glass chilling in a champagne bucket. She freed the glass and wiped down its sides, admiring the stacks of yogurt, strawberries, blueberries, and a singular dollop of whipped cream. She sat on a corner of the freshly made bed, snatched the spoon, and devoured the parfait, delighting in its flavorful combinations and textures. *Francis,* she thought, *you're a genius.*

It was only when she returned the glass that she noticed a small envelope tucked beside her prescription bottle. Someone had etched her name across the envelope. With mounting curiosity, Vickie peeled it open and removed a stiff piece of monogrammed stationery.

Dear Vickie,

I hope you slept well and enjoyed breakfast. I forgot to mention that my house has a spa. You're welcome to its services. Tell Maria if you wish to connect before dinner at 7 pm. Otherwise, relax and enjoy yourself.

Regards,

Jack

She smiled as she reread his note twice more. How unbelievably kind. And a spa service? What it must be like to live in such luxury!

Jack had everything—or at least everything he could buy. Reflecting over the pictures strewn about the home, Vickie couldn't recall glimpsing any family. Was he lacking in all but this? Did he consider his life fulfilled?

Vickie wondered at the details of her own life, the one beyond these walls. Did she have a family? Children? A boyfriend? Perhaps a husband? Why couldn't she sense the answers to these questions? Perhaps the reason was because none existed, and that she was—in fact—utterly alone in the world.

She sat in silence as December frost splintered across the windowpane. She had wanted answers from the moment she had awoken at New York Presbyterian Hospital, yet now the prospect of the truth frightened her. What if she didn't like what she found? What then?

There came a knock on the door. "*Señorita* Vickie?" called a muffled voice. "Are you dressed?"

Vickie started from the bed, disrobed, and shimmied into her proffered clothing. "Almost! Wait just a sec!"

With the cashmere sweater straightened and her stocking feet snug within the fluffy slippers, Vickie opened the door and smiled at Maria. "Sorry," she said, a little winded.

"You didn't have to rush. I was just checking on you." She paused as she took in Vickie's face. "*Dios*, you look good! So healthy!"

"Thanks," she said. "The makeup certainly helped. Not to mention the shower."

"*Bien*. And you like the clothes?"

"Oh yes. They're great. Thank you."

"And how was breakfast? Did you enjoy?"

Vickie nodded. "Very much. Tell Francis it was another hit."

"I will."

A moment passed when neither one of them knew quite what to say next. "So..." Vickie began at last. "Is Jack still with his assistant?"

"Assistant?" echoed Maria. "No. I believe he is in his study. Would you like to see him?"

"Not if he's busy."

"No, no. I'll tell him. Would you like to wait here?"

She considered. "Would he mind if I went to the library?"

"Not at all." She turned to leave. "I'll tell him."

Vickie was about to close the door when she remembered her medicine. Though the shower had taken the edge off her achy limbs, she certainly didn't want a repeat of last night. She pocketed the two remaining pills and in seconds was down the hall.

She reached the library without trouble. Strategically placed windows brightened the room, though a slight draft had Vickie crossing her arms for warmth. Clumps of snow slid from the roof and flecked the room in gray an instant before their muffled landing in the garden below. She wandered about the space, noting the swept fireplace. Everything looked pristine as a museum exhibit.

Vickie wondered at living in a home with no fingerprints. Did Jack find it stifling? Certainly, she was wary of disturbing anything.

For now, she ignored the stacked bookcases and searched instead for more photographs, anything that might tell her an immediate story. But all she discovered was a series of still lifes. She had almost given up when she discovered a small frame tucked inside the 19th-century literature section. She stepped closer to gaze upon the faded photo.

It was three small children—a boy and two girls, perhaps aged three to ten—and an older woman. They were sitting around a small fireplace and the woman was reading from a book opened across her lap. They appeared unaware of being photographed, and the image had a familiar authenticity.

Jack said his mother loved *Jane Eyre*. Were these his sisters?

Sisters. *Sister.*

A memory stirred at the back of Vickie's mind. Just as it coalesced, footsteps sounded outside the door.

"Good morning," said Jack as he strode into the library.

She turned and smiled up at him brightly.

"My God!" he exclaimed as he took in her face. "You're like a completely different person!"

"The magic of makeup, I guess," she said with forced nonchalance. "Sorry if that makeup was meant for someone else, but I thought—"

She stopped when he stepped to examine her as one would an oil painting. He was so close that Vickie felt the heat of his arms through the fabric of his shirt. He shook his head and said, "But your scars..."

Vickie brought a hand to her roughened face. "I know. It's—"

"It's like they healed overnight!" he said, misinterpreting her next words. "How did you do that?"

She shrugged and dropped her hand. "I don't know. It was..." How could she put this? That the process was almost instinctual? She shrugged instead. "Maybe I'm a makeup artist in real life."

"Maybe." He nodded approvingly. "Very good. Very..." His voice trailed, and he shrugged. "It's just great. Amazing."

Vickie warmed again. She pulled the picture from the shelf and held it to him. "Is this your mother?"

He looked as if he wanted to say something more, but obligingly took the frame. "Ah. Yes. I put this out last night, after we talked." He gazed down at it for a time. "It was in a box upstairs. Haven't taken it out in years."

"Do you have any other pictures of your family?"

He shook his head. "Yes, and no. I have pictures. But since we hadn't spoken in some time, it didn't feel right to put them out."

She wanted to ask why, but his expression was clouded and she didn't want to upset him. "Sorry," she said instead.

"It's not your fault." He said this crisply, without a trace of emotion, and replaced the frame on the shelf. "So. Any more memories?"

"Well, what have I told you so far?"

"That you're from Warren, which I am still excited about. And that you speak Spanish and love the color purple. And, apparently, you're a magician with makeup. What else do you know?"

His face was bright and open again, and Vickie seized on this moment of levity. The list was still fresh in her mind, as she ran over it constantly. "I think I like to rock climb. And go to matinees. I like skydiving—"

"You do?" he said, clearly intrigued.

"I think so. Why?"

"It's one of my personal pleasures."

Vickie nodded. "Yes, I saw the photo."

"How many jumps have you done?"

"I don't know..."

"Sorry," he blurted. "I didn't mean to interrupt. Keep going. This is great."

"Okay. I like paintings and Graham Greene martinis..."

He stopped her again. "Did you say Graham Greene martinis?"

"Yes."

"You're serious?"

"About what?"

His expression furrowed. "But you're so specific. It's just—it makes me wonder..."

"I'm sorry, Jack. What are you talking about?"

"It's my favorite drink. I've not met anyone who knew what they are, much less mentioned it in passing."

Doubt crept into Vickie's heart. "I think I like them. I mean, why else would I remember them?"

"I don't know." He shook his head. "Sorry again. What else?"

"I think I may be Catholic..." She mentally reviewed her list. "And that my favorite movie is *Braveheart.*"

"Mine too," he said eagerly. "God, I wish I could have been on that set. Continue."

She paused. "There was the color purple. Wait, I said that already. And parasailing. Something called sashimi—"

"It's a type of sushi."

"Okay, then. Sushi. And that I'm from Warren. And eat organic produce." *What else?* "Oh. The linens."

"What linens?"

"A brand called Frette linens."

"It's what you're sleeping on."

"Sorry?"

"The linens. From Frette. It's all I ever buy."

"No, I mean I *like* those linens."

"You mean you liked them before you came here?"

"Yes. Or at least it was on my mind in the hospital."

He stared at her in wonder. "Amazing."

Doubt crept in even as Jack beamed at her with pleasure. What were the odds that they liked the same things? Once more, she tumbled through her mental list. "And then there was something called tantric yoga—"

"Really?" His eyebrows shot up. "You're into that?"

"Maybe." She spread her hands. "Or at least it popped into my head. What is it?"

"It was a series of movements meant to free the mind of ignorance. In a sense, become *reborn*."

"Really?" She was on the brink of laughing, but he looked so enthusiastic she didn't have the heart to admit it sounded silly.

"Indeed." He leaned into her. "A friend turned me onto it a few years ago. Terrific stuff. Is that it?"

"What?"

"All you can remember?"

"I guess."

"Nothing else?"

She reviewed her list and realized only one thing remained. She blushed.

He saw her face. "What? What is it?"

The magnum condoms. But she couldn't tell him that. She thought quickly, "Oh, it's nothing. Just a type of shampoo I guess I used."

"Oh." His face lost some of the excitement. "Well. That's not much to go on, but it's something. Fantastic."

"Mr. Post?" called Maria from the door. "You have a call."

He waved at her dismissively. "Tell them I'll call back."

"But it's Mr. Zuckerman from Universal—"

"Doesn't matter who it is. It can wait."

A hesitating moment passed between them, and Vickie thought that this must be something Maria found very odd. The woman wavered for another instant before she nodded and quipped, "Yes, Mr. Post. I'll have him leave a message with your service."

"Very good."

Vickie tensed. Why was Jack being so kind to her? Was there guilt beneath that generosity?

No. That didn't make sense. Jack had no reason to feel guilty. *She* had been the one at fault, not him. Yet despite these facts, Jack paid for all of her treatment, opened up his home, and catered to her every whim. What had she done for him?

It was happening again. That strange tickling, falling sensation at the back of her mind. A warmth emanating from somewhere dark and deep. An image coalesced as if in a still pond. Vickie nearly had it when Jack exclaimed, "Holy shit!"

She jumped, and the image blurred. "What?"

His hand went to his face. "I can't believe I hadn't thought of it."

She waited, wishing desperately she could bring the moment back. She willed it to return, to no avail.

"Vickie," he said, "it's ingenious. I'll hire a PI."

She blinked. "A what?"

He practically glowed with triumph. "A private investigator. What do you think? We could pay someone to find out who you are. Just throw money at the problem."

"Really?"

He nodded. "God, why didn't I think of this before? With any luck, we could have this whole thing resolved in a matter of days."

"You know someone who can do that?"

He shook his head, undeterred. "Not personally, but I'm sure Sam has connections. We have your name and hometown. I think that's all they would need. Lord knows my Internet searches have been fruitless. Wait here, and I'll make the call." He took a few steps from her, stopped, and then turned around. "Is this okay with you, Vickie? Me hiring an investigator?"

"Why wouldn't it be?"

"Well, we would technically invade your privacy."

"But I don't even know what's private."

Jack shook his head and laughed. "True. So this is fine?"

"I guess."

"No skeletons in the closet?"

"Skeletons...?"

"Nothing you don't want found out?"

"Oh." She thought for a moment. "Well, if I did, how would I know?"

Jack laughed again, as if she were the world's greatest comedian, and not the center of some mysterious tragedy. "Okay. I'll make the call."

He left, and Vickie remained alone in the center of the room. Skeletons in her closet. Secrets to unearth. What would the investigator find? Who would she turn out to be?

She sighed into her hand, printing her lipstick onto her palm. *I just hope I like myself.*

A coldness gripped her insides. What if she didn't like what she found?

"You look so good that I feel like I should take you out for a night on the town," Jack said as they settled at his gleaming dining room table for dinner.

Vickie blushed, for the first time unable to meet Jack's penetrating gaze. She took a few sips of ice water, served in heavy Waterford crystal, and regarded the meal set before them. Francis—unconcerned with Vickie's limited digestive range—had prepared three lavish courses. A leek and potato soup with an antipasti salad. Beef tenderloin medallions and garlic mashed potatoes slathered in a portabella cream sauce. Finally, a dark chocolate cake layered with sambuca mousse.

Her stomach turning at the sight of the prosciutto and salami, Vickie asked Maria for any leftover chicken noodle soup. As Maria disappeared into the kitchen, Jack regaled Vickie with yet another story about life on a movie set, to which she only half-listened. Whenever an unfamiliar staff member appeared, she tensed, anticipating Jack's private investigator. That man held the details of her life. He knew if she was married, had children, held a job, was happy.

Vickie was almost sick with nerves and hardly tasted her spoonfuls of soup. She nodded and smiled during Jack's few pauses, all the while stealing glances at the door—ever hopeful and wary.

"...so what do you think?" asked Jack, finally taking a breath. "Can you believe he went with Cruise instead of me? After having the gall to demand an audition? That's why I refuse to work with him. Keep your loyalty to the ones who put you first, even if your latest work grosses less than studio estimates."

Vickie sipped her water. "Right. That makes sense."

Jack grinned as he leaned back in his chair. "God, Vickie. It's so great talking to you. It's fantastic that you know nothing about me. You know how far I'd have to travel to find that?" He leaned forward, intent once again. "Years ago I was in Salta and these children who literally had no shoes knew who I was. They even wanted my autograph."

"Why?"

He blinked, seeming not to understand. "Why what?"

"Why would they want your autograph?"

"I don't know. Probably to sell it. Anyway—"

"Did you give it to them?"

"What?"

"Your autograph."

"I don't remember. That part's irrelevant. Point is,

with you, I can completely open up. There's absolutely no judgment."

Finished, he sat back and regarded her. Vickie didn't know quite how to respond, so she didn't.

"What do you think?" Jack persisted.

"About...?"

"About what I just said."

She shifted in her chair, uncomfortable with this line of questioning. "I'm not sure what you're saying, Jack."

He opened his hands before her, as if in an offering. "I'm saying that you're a blank slate."

Vickie considered this. "And that's a good thing?"

"The best. I think that's why my relationships have all disintegrated. They were damned from the beginning, because I could never be sure if they wanted to be with me for me, or for the fame." He spread his hands. "But you don't know this. You're just perfect."

Perfect. She reflected on this word, his particular choice of it. What did Jack consider perfect? An arrangement of qualities, of ideals? Was it her innocence to his worldliness, the vague glimpses of her past, her made-up face, her cashmered body? Certainly it couldn't be for the whole of her, since she barely even knew herself.

Meanwhile, Jack was magnificent. His face symmetrically flawless, with sunshine perfectly dappling his features. The world revolved around him, and even Vickie orbited around the gravity of his existence.

She chafed at an unseen shackle—the unspoken deference she must pay him. Yet for Jack, she was someone he sought. While others would pay dearly for such a compliment, she longed for the freedom of another life. *Her* life.

Vickie blinked. All this had occurred to her in a matter of seconds, and she found herself breathless.

A smile played on Jack's lips. He picked up his plate and moved down the table until he sat alongside. His gaze was heavy upon her, his hand only inches from her own. "What will you do, Vickie, when you discover who you are?"

"Do?" She tore her eyes from his to glance about the table, at the lavish meal going untouched.

"Yes," he said. "Will you leave?"

She didn't know what to say. She felt pressured to please him, but was uncertain of what answer to give.

"Say you have a family," he continued. "You'll want to return to them, yes?"

"I suppose I would."

"And how do you feel about that?"

"Feel?"

He chuckled as he traced his index finger along the middle of her right hand. She noticed how small she was next to him, how easily he could take both of her hands into his one. "Why do you repeat everything I say, as if it were the most amazing thing you've ever heard?"

"I'm sorry," she said, wondering at the heat of his

touch, his magnetic pull. She realized he was working some sort of magic, trying to draw her in like the moon to the tides. A part of her wanted to give in to these strange new feelings, but another, greater part, resisted.

She withdrew her hand.

Surprise scrawled across his face. "You think you're married?"

Another beat of silence. "I don't know."

"You don't even have an inkling?"

"No, I don't. I don't know anything, Jack." She picked up her spoon, stared down into the cooling bowl of soup, and dropped the cutlery with a clatter. "I'm sorry. I'm not feeling very well."

She stood, and Jack mirrored her movement. "You okay, Vickie? Is it something I said?"

"No—yes. I don't know." She shook her head. "I don't know. I just want this to be over. To know whether I'm married. Whether I have children. Or parents. Or sisters. Brothers. Friends. Do I even have a job? Am I even being missed?" She sighed, her head swimming with unanswered questions. "This just all feels...wrong. So wrong. I just want this to be over."

"I'm sorry."

She shook her head again. "I just want to know who I am. But I'm also scared to know."

"Why?"

She hesitated. "What if I don't like what I find?"

"Why wouldn't you?"

But how could she tell him? How could she explain the little clues she found etched across her body, the fragments of her mind? "I don't know. Maybe it's all fine. But I just want to *know*." She laughed mirthlessly. "*You* may like a blank slate, Jack. But I'm finding it a horrible state to live in."

"You're right, Vickie. I'm not saying any of this right at all." With a grimace, he reached to cup her shoulders. "I'm just saying it's nice to have you here, to have you around. Sad, isn't it?"

"What's sad?"

"I hardly know anything about you, yet I feel I've more in common with you than my own family. The things you like—from your favorite color to your hometown—I couldn't have created a more synchronous woman. Understand?"

"A little," she said. Then, as his eyes filled with an unknown meaning, she added with a nervous laugh, "Okay. Maybe I don't."

Jack grinned. "Why don't we call it an early night? Maria can get you whatever you want, and we'll start over again in the morning. We can even see if you're ready for a day out. What do you think? Maybe a stroll in my garden?"

"Okay," she said, then glanced out the far window. "But what if it's too cold?"

"Then you have the library. I'll clear up some conference calls tonight, and then I'm all yours in the morning." He called for Maria to turn down her bed and glanced at Vickie one last time. "I am glad that you're here. Strange as all of this is, this place is better with you in it."

She thanked him and slipped from the dining room before he could say anything further. During her long walk down the corridor, her scattered thoughts whipped into a maelstrom. She still suspected the sincerity of Jack's kind words. She sensed he liked her, and also that a part of her wanted that. Yet the rest of her remained at war. Were she capable of sprouting wings, she'd fly through the vaulted ceiling, back through time, and into her old life—whatever life that turned out to be.

Chapter Six

THE SNOW-FILLED trees snapped through the tinted windows of the town car. Vickie's face was near enough to the glass to feel the cold seeping through the pane, but she didn't care. She gazed at the vista with the reverence of a child. Jack sat beside her, thumbing through his iPhone, as Vivaldi's "The Four Seasons" played over the stereo. The driver sat mutely at the wheel, tapping his thumbs on the pulled black leather.

"So how close are we?" she asked Jack.

Without averting his gaze, he called to the driver, "How far, Timothy?"

"We're almost at Bridgeport now, sir. About fifteen minutes if traffic stays light."

"Very good." Jack pressed a button and the phone's screen darkened. He pocketed it inside his jacket and turned to her. "How are you feeling? You still up for this?"

"I'm okay." She sat back in her seat and smiled at him. "Still sore, but the medication really helps."

"You're remembering to alternate your meds every few hours?"

"With Maria's help," she admitted. "But today's the best I've felt so far. I even went an extra two hours before the second dose."

"Wow. That's real progress."

"Thanks," she said, thrilled to escape the boundary of Jack's estate. She'd enjoyed their walk outside where Jack showed her where the hyacinth and forsythia would blossom come spring. They stayed out until the cold forced them in, warming themselves by the library's crackling hearth—one of the few places Jack truly relaxed. As he read aloud a favorite literary passage, the perpetual tension in his face momentarily released, and Vickie was relieved to see it.

Still, Vickie craved more, and had lain awake all night wondering if the day might trigger a memory from her past. Running her hands along her puffy black parka, she gazed into the snow-filled world.

Over a week had passed with no word from the investigator. The waiting consumed her thoughts. When she'd expressed a desire to leave the house at dinner, Jack offered to take her anywhere. It'd been her idea to visit a market. She knew Francis bought produce at an organic food store in Bridgeport. Jack had never been, and Vickie figured it was as fine a place as any to test her stamina.

When she stepped from his mansion into the icy chill of winter, she lost her breath. Wind flayed her cheeks red. A brutal cold gripped her bones.

"You okay?" Jack asked, studying her face.

"Fine," she said. Better than fine. It all felt *real*.

She shuffled along the gravel driveway into the awaiting car purring beside a granite fountain. She would remember every one of these details—and she relished it.

She stared out into the world until the edges blurred. She didn't know she dozed until Jack tapped her shoulder. "Vickie. We're here."

She sat up, rubbed the frozen spot on her forehead, and opened her eyes. They'd parked outside the store whose electric doors slid open and closed. Jack tucked his scarf into his coat, slipped on a pair of sunglasses, then stepped from the car. Her door immediately opened and Timothy helped her out and into the parka. Taking her arm firmly, he guided her across the icy asphalt, then past the sliding doors into the indoor market.

As Timothy discussed the parking logistics with Jack, Vickie slipped off her coat and folded it over the handlebar of a shopping cart. A chilly breeze snapped through the store as the door behind them slid open. She crossed her arms, thankful to be warmed by her thick turtleneck and wool skirt.

When the driver left, Jack stepped to her and said, "So. What do you want to do first?"

Vickie gazed at the aisles of wares. The small kiosks offering free samples. The curved glass counter stacked with exotic cheeses and pastries. Customers milled about with their small shopping carts filled to the brim. How easily they selected a russet potato or a can of cherry pie filling. They turned it over in their hands and either placed it back or tossed it into their carts. They had purses and billfolds, all with crisp identifications. Some had friends or family chatting beside them, others with children bounding about. Vickie throbbed with envy for this mass of strangers. She wished she could so easily shop for the day ahead, knowing she had something to return to. She longed for a life in a home she couldn't remember.

Maybe this was a mistake, she thought, and chastised herself. She shouldn't feel so perpetually sorry for herself. From what she gathered at the hospital, she should be grateful she could clasp a glass of water, that she was ambulatory, that she could think. Her memories were gone, but she was creating new ones. Maybe even *better* ones.

She glanced at Jack, still awaiting her decision. The oddity of this moment, of this man, struck her like a whip. His was a magnetic presence, his handsomeness known the world over, with wealth beyond her imagining. And what was she? A woman with only a name, her history stripped in a single afternoon. Yet there they were, in a market, with only the space of several steps between them. She wondered what her other self —the self that existed in her forgotten life—would think of such a circumstance? Vickie smiled at him and said finally, "Can we just look around?"

He nodded. "Of course."

She started for the cheese section, taking in the enormous wheels of gouda, cheddar, and smoked provolone. While she longed to try the pegged squares upon a proffered dish, her medication roiled her stomach. Instead, she sated her visual appetite. Jack dutifully followed as she meandered down the casements, bent with her as she examined the glassy eyes of sea bass and flounder arranged on beds of ice.

"Look at that." She pointed to the bright pink salmon fillets, then the vegetable and beef cutlet kabobs.

"Do you like those?"

"They look good. But my stomach's still not great."

"So we'll cook something light for dinner," he suggested. "Why don't we—"

"Excuse me," interrupted a voice from above them.

Jack stiffened. Vickie glanced up and said to the man leaning over the counter, "Yes?"

"Can I get you anything?"

"Oh. No, we're just looking."

When the man smiled and moved on to another

customer, Jack tapped her side. "Why don't we keep walking?"

"Oh. Okay," she said, not understanding his urgency. They continued a punctuated walk down the line as Vickie glanced at the many tantalizing arrangements. Glistening pearls of mozzarella. Bruschetta topped with crimson tomato wedges. Buckets of Spanish and Greek olives. The order of the food stirred a memory. She closed her eyes, trying to catch it.

"Excuse me, sir?"

Vickie straightened, assuming it was another grocery worker, when she stared into a mobile phone. A click sounded, and the woman behind the phone said, "I knew it! You're Jack Post. Honey! Look who it is!" She waved a man over, and—noticing the excitement —another couple followed.

"Mr. Post," said the man, a grin threatening to take over his face. "I can't—I just...it's a real honor, sir. *Payton's Landing* is my favorite film, ever."

Jack put on his most winning smile. "Glad to hear that."

"Can I have your autograph?"

"Of course."

The man searched his coat pockets before glancing imploringly at the woman beside him. She immediately began ransacking her purse, removing a checkbook, a packet of gum, and finally, a paperback novel.

"That'll work!" the man exclaimed. He snatched

the book, folded it open to the first page, and thrust it at Jack.

"Do you have something to write with?" Jack asked in a patient voice.

"Oh! Yes. Sorry." He threw a frantic look at the woman, as if Jack was about to vanish. She again dug through her purse, tucking her billfold and a pair of gloves under her chin, and produced a pen. She shoved the cap off with her thumb and thrust the pen at Jack.

Jack smiled and said, "Who should I make it—"

"Doug and Debbie," the man put in. "Winston. Doug and Debbie Winston."

"To Doug and Debbie..." said Jack, writing quickly. He tapped twice after his signature and re-turned the book and pen. "Thanks for your support."

"So, are you filming anything now?" Debbie asked him. "Is it another drama? Oooh! Is it a sequel to *Lydell*? I love that movie!"

"Nothing at the moment," said Jack. "Thank you for your support. But we really have to—"

"Oh my god!" said a man directly in front of them. "It is! Oh my god. Jack, can I have your autograph?"

"Me too!" cried another. "I have something right here..."

Someone grabbed Vickie's shoulder and asked, "When's *Plymouth* coming out on DVD?"

Fans surrounded them. They yanked receipts from their coat pockets, clicked open pens, asked for autographs, for pictures, details of Jack's latest film. And who was she, they wanted to know? Was she a relative? A friend? A *girlfriend?*

Jack was cordial throughout the bombardment. He shook hands, scrawled a few signatures, smiled for pictures. But as the crowd thickened and more questions poured in, with some shouting over each other, Jack put up his hands and said they were late for a meeting. But they had a difficult time turning through the crowd that didn't readily part for them. They hustled through the store with phones and cameras clicking away, ducked into the town car, and sped onto the road.

Vickie glanced through the back window. People massed at the store's entrance. "What was that?" she asked, flabbergasted.

"That," said Jack, scowling as he furiously texted a message into his phone, "is the *real* world."

When they returned home, Jack shut himself away in the study. Vickie lingered in the hallway, uncertain. His voice fell through the broad oak doors, demanding to know the start date of principal photography.

Sensing this would take some time, Vickie returned to her room and sat on the bed. Her weight wrinkled the pressed linens, scented vaguely with lavender. She wriggled out of her boots, dropped them on the floor, and noticed her pain pills on the nightstand next to a glass of water. Smiling at Maria's thoughtfulness, Vickie downed the pills and arranged herself more comfortably. She gazed out into the white expanse of Jack's backyard, at the icicles threading down the window casement. Then she eased into the pillows and closed her eyes, telling herself it would be for just a moment.

When she awoke, the room and windows were dark. Unfamiliar smells scented the air and a band of light peeked from beneath the bedroom door. Intrigued, Vickie slid off the bed, opened the door, and turned down the hall. She half-expected to bump into Maria or a member of Jack's staff, but the house was quiet.

As she walked, she differentiated the various scents: cooking meat, a beefy broth, peppers. Her mouth watered as she stepped into the kitchen.

"You're finally up," Jack called from the massive eight-burner stove. "You must feel better."

"I do, thanks." She glanced about. "Where is everyone?"

"I gave them the night off."

"They're gone?"

"They are."

So we're alone. She sensed a yawning expanse behind her, the dearth of people in the house. She missed Maria's familiar face.

Jack didn't appear to notice her unease—or even her. His singular focus was his cooking and the orchestrated stages of dinner. He removed a tray of toasted almonds, shook over a handful of sea salt, and returned it to the oven. Checking the contents of his skillet, he sashayed the pan across the burner with a flourish.

This piqued her curiosity, and Vickie moved to stand by his shoulder. In the skillet were several cups of fluffy rice, bubbling in a brown liquid. A pot of broth steamed on the adjacent burner. "What are you cooking?"

"Almond risotto with stuffed bell peppers," Jack said, gesturing towards a whirling machine perched on the granite countertop. "That bad boy is making us some homemade ice cream. I culled the Madagascan vanilla beans myself." He grinned at her. "Impressed?"

She laughed, remembering their earlier exchange. "This is what you consider a light dinner?"

"I think it should be fine. But if it's too much, we can always reheat the broth."

Vickie hoped it wouldn't be too much, as it smelled incredibly delicious. "It really looks fantastic, Jack." *Fantastic,* she thought, *and somehow familiar.* She anticipated his next draw of broth, the wake he pushed into the rice. She somehow knew he was testing to ensure each sliver maintained the right texture, that it was a delicate process that required a steady vigil.

I know this, she thought. *But how?* She chased her

thoughts down the dark alley of her mind, but just as she was about to grasp the memory, it dissipated into vapor.

"A penny for your thoughts," said Jack, breaking her reverie.

She shook her head. "I thought I had something."

"What?"

"A memory. This all seems so familiar."

"What does? The food?"

"Yes. The risotto, specifically." She paused. "I think I've cooked it before."

Jack halted his deft movements and said, "Perhaps if you take over?" He stepped aside and passed her the ladle.

The weight felt right in her hand, much like the makeup brushes earlier. Encouraged, Vickie stepped to the stove, took up a spatula, and folded the rice over itself. She surveyed the bubbling broth, checking for burns. When the rice was ready, she scooped broth into the ladle and eased it into the mixture.

"You know what you're doing," Jack said.

She shook her head again. "I don't know why."

A companionable silence fell. While Jack stuffed bell peppers with prosciutto and mozzarella, Vickie stirred broth and toasted almonds in the pan. Careful not to burn herself, she dipped a spoon in the mixture and plucked a few shards of rice. They were crunchy and soft on her tongue, and the flavors swam through her. The flash of a memory glimmered in her mind, a dizzying sense of *déjà vu*. Once she had stood at a similar—though much less illustrious—range before, tasting risotto, with someone familiar at her side.

Vickie glanced over and was a little surprised to see Jack standing next to her. But then, who else would it be?

Jack's eyes met hers, and he smiled. "I'm almost ready to plate. Do you need anything?"

She blinked. "Actually...yes. Do you have any raisins?"

Jack searched his pantry and passed her a box, and she tapped a handful into her palm to scatter across the risotto. Jack knew better than to question her tactic and perhaps break her rhythm. They agreed to dine in the family room, and assembled casually on adjacent couches, their dinners set on two leather ottomans with glasses of ice water.

Jack took in a forkful of risotto. He closed his eyes.

"What do you think?" Vickie asked, as she too took a small bite.

"Delicious. I'd never thought to add raisins to this." He smacked his lips. "It adds a certain *je ne sais quoi*."

"A what?"

He smiled at her. "A certain something. A sweet punch. It's excellent, Vickie."

Grinning, she tasted the stuffed peppers, but decided these might test her sensitive stomach and so pushed them aside.

"Too much?" he asked.

"Sorry."

"Not a problem." He sat beside her. "Come on. Pass it over." She did, and he scooped up the pepper, downing it easily. "Yum," he said, as if making a point.

She offered him her second one, which he ate with an exaggerated relish. She laughed, but halted when she noticed his smile had changed, become more serious.

Her stomach knotted. Searching for something to say, her eyes fell on their respective glasses. She said, "Why do you always drink water? It can't just be out of sympathy for me."

He followed her gaze. Several beats of silence passed, and Vickie wondered if she had said something wrong.

"You really want to know?" he said.

She hesitated. When he didn't fill the silence, she said, "I don't—"

"I'm an alcoholic," he said, the words hanging between them, heavy as rocks. "Well, I used to be. I'm much better now." He sighed. "No, that's not right either. I'm still an alcoholic. Always will be."

She grimaced. "I'm sorry. I shouldn't have said anything."

"Don't be. It's under control. I had an unpleasant episode recently, but I'm back on the wagon."

"That's good," she said, hoping the wagon was a good place to be.

"There's something I've been wanting to tell you, Vickie." His tone had changed again, becoming almost grave. "The afternoon I hit you with my car..." He drew a breath, as if his next words would pain him. "I was drunk."

The words settled on her, but didn't surprise her. She waited for him to continue.

"I'd just gotten a call that my youngest sister had died—"

"Oh, Jack," she said, her mind filling with the photograph of his family, seated around their mother, listening to *Jane Eyre*.

He shook his head. "I'm okay now. I just hadn't seen her in three years. Couldn't even remember the last time we spoke. That, and some other things, put me in a bar, with drinks in my hand, and—" His voice trailed. "I don't really remember how the chain of events unfolded after that. I remember getting into my car against common sense. I remember driving." He gave her a furtive glance. "And I remember you— splayed across my windshield."

These details summoned no memory, but Vickie stiffened anyway.

"I'm sorry," Jack said, reddening. "I meant to tell you the truth. It was my drinking that led to the accident and—well. Everything that followed." He shook his head bitterly. "I'm a terrible friend, a terrible son. I neglect my family. I only think about my career. I'm lonely, even though I'm never alone. What I mean to say is that I'm sorry. I'm really, truly sorry that I did this to you."

Vickie touched his hand. For once, she knew exactly what to say, and she believed the words as she said them: "I forgive you, Jack." And she did. It helped that she never harbored anger towards him, for she didn't know what she was missing, not really. But she saw him now, this man sitting beside her, and the well of pain in his eyes seemed genuine, even though she knew he was an actor and paid well to summon such emotions. But she sensed his sincerity. The truth in his words.

He abruptly stood, announced he needed to check on the ice cream, and was gone.

She sat alone in the family room, staring at the risotto on her plate, a meal that she helped cook, if not from memory, then surely by instinct. Once again, her mind crammed with questions. Who was she in her other life? Would she ever know? What had she lost?

Jack returned with two chilled bowls and spoons. He passed her one of each as he sat next to her. Vanilla scented the air. Vickie gazed at the two creamy mounds, peppered with small black flakes, and took a spoonful. And then another. And another. "Delicious," she said, smiling at Jack.

She finished the bowl in triumph. She had finished her first meal outside of the hospital. And the pain that had lanced her body weeks ago was now a distant hum

—present, yes, but no longer in control of her. She sensed herself recovering.

"I'm glad you liked it," Jack said, setting his bowl aside. He cleared his throat. "I want to thank you, Vickie. Thank you for understanding. I know this can't be easy."

"Of course," she said. She felt herself accepting this new life, having been born fully grown, with her future open before her. Perhaps fate had guided her here. Perhaps this was a second chance. Perhaps...

Her mind stalled as Jack eased the spoon and bowl away. With one hand, he cupped the side of her face, his knuckles grazing her cheek. His face closed in, and then his lips were on hers in a slow, gentle kiss.

He shut his eyes, but Vickie kept hers open, rapt by the new sensations. The taste of peppers on his tongue. The silky-smooth texture of his shaven face. The musky amber of his cologne and aftershave. As the kiss deepened, she wanted to both draw him closer and push him away, and it was as if two minds were at war, wrenching her in opposite directions. There was the ghost of her, cheering to open herself to him. That she desired his touch. His closeness. His attention. But there was also her present self, inexplicably confused and repelled. In a flash, she saw another man before her: a man with castigating eyes the color of threaded blue ice. A man who smelled like mint and amber musk. A man who felt like home. It was that image that filled her body, the one that guided her hand to gently—defiantly—break the kiss.

Jack sat back, breathless. "What's wrong?"

"I'm not sure." She shook her head, weary of her conflicting mind. "I just know I can't. I'm sorry."

She needed to escape. She stumbled when she tried to stand. Jack helped her up, and a moment passed where they leaned awkwardly against each other.

Vickie spoke first. "If it's okay with you, I think I'll head to bed."

"Listen, I'm sorry. I don't know what I was thinking." He shook his head, not meeting her eyes. "You're only just recovering, and I'm sorry if I took advantage of you. Again, I don't know what I was thinking—"

She put up her hands, surprised to find herself on the verge of tears. "Please don't apologize. I'm fine, okay?"

He nodded in understanding, though confusion etched across his face. She wondered if any woman had ever denied him. Perhaps this was a first for both.

Unable to summon anything further, Vickie turned to leave, when she glimpsed a figure leaning against the doorframe. She leapt back, startled.

The man stepped forward, and Vickie instantly recognized him as Jack's lawyer, the man who had accosted her at the hospital. His eyes pinned hers as he said, "Getting comfortable, are we?"

Jack blew an exasperated sigh. "What are you doing here, Sam?"

"I might ask that of her." In an instant, Sam produced a thick manila folder, which he jabbed in Vickie's direction. "I just got this from the investigator we hired. I think you'll find its contents very interesting."

"You know who I am?" Vickie asked, hearing the desperation in her voice. She was about to say more when Sam glared at her, his eyes cutting. The lift in her heart fell instantly, replaced now with an unknown fear. In the space of a moment, she realized that Sam, and the pages in his hand, were maligned against her, and that her life was about to change all over again.

Chapter Seven

"WELL, GET ON WITH IT, MAN," Jack said, clearly irritated at the interruption.

Sam's beady eyes narrowed at Vickie. "I'd say introductions are in order. Shall we start with your name?"

Jack shook his head. "Sam, I don't know what you're playing at, but this—"

"What *I'm* playing at? Don't you wonder why it took my guy over a week to track her down? Of course, it would've helped to have the right name and hometown. Don't you see? This whole thing was a massive charade." Sam's eyes turned to her again. "Isn't it, *Anne*?"

Vickie shrunk from him. "I don't know what you're talking about."

Sam opened the folder as if to accost her. "Aren't you Anne Strafford, née Turner, of Tulsa, Oklahoma?

Born to Valentina and Jacob Turner? Sister to Elena Lewiston? Married to Frederick Strafford? Living in Ohio?"

The information struck her like an avalanche. She had parents? A sister? A husband? *Wait,* she thought. *My name...*

A line creased between Jack's brows. "You're married?"

"And living in Ohio," Sam added with great contempt. "She's nothing she said she was, Jack. She's an imposter. A charlatan."

"Wait," she said as the world shifted under her. "You said my name before."

"Stop playing games with us!" Sam strode to her and thrust the document before her eyes. "It's all here, in black and white. You know exactly who you are."

She took it shakily into her hands. On the first page was a photocopy of her driver's license. The picture was the same face she saw in the mirror, sans scars. But the rest of it—her name, her hometown—everything else was different.

She blinked against a wave of dizziness. No, that couldn't be right. How could everything be different? What about her memories? What about everything she'd told herself? Was none of it real?

She read the name, Anne Strafford, like an incantation that could summon her lost memory. But nothing came. She tried her maiden name, said the word out loud, carefully pronounced "Turner". But it weighed on her tongue, its cadence unfamiliar. Surely she had said this name a thousand times before?

"It's all legitimate?" Jack asked, coming to stand by her shoulder. "It checks out?"

"One hundred percent." Sam folded his arms over his chest, regarding them both. "It wouldn't surprise me if she planned everything. Made this whole amnesia thing up as a ploy to stay at your house. It wouldn't be the first time a pretty girl got through the gate, now would it? Perhaps she's here to take a few incriminating photos. Sell it to the highest bidder."

"Wait..." She tore her eyes from her history with great effort, sensing that Sam was weaving a web that she could not get caught in. "Wait. What are you saying? I didn't make anything up!"

"Your name," Sam spit out, "where you're from. It's all here. It even says you have a chronic fear of heights, that you had to go to some sort of treatment center!"

"I don't see how—"

"But you said you like to skydive," Jack interrupted. "And parasail."

That stopped her cold. She remembered saying these words to him, how this shared liking had linked them in the beginning. But she feared heights? Why would she have remembered otherwise?

"Listen, Jack," Sam said, his tone softening. "She tricked you, and that must hurt. But don't blame yourself. She was incredibly thorough."

"What are you talking about?" Jack said wearily.

Sam waved his hand at her, as if she was nothing more than a trail of smoke, a bothersome insect. "She did her homework. She knew what you liked, what you wanted. She knew what to say. None of this is your fault."

"You think she planned this? Truly?"

Sam nodded. "I do. I really do."

"But it doesn't make sense!" she cried, unable to stop the pressure from building behind her eyes. Hot tears tracked down her face, beading off her jaw. "I didn't plan any of this! I don't know what's going on!"

Jack held her gaze. The three of them were still for a long time, when Sam broke the silence, "Jack, listen—"

"No." Jack turned on him. "*You* listen. I've worked with the best actresses in the world, Sam. And she's not one of them. I believe her."

Sam tensed. "But the investigator—"

Jack put up his hand. "I understand what you're saying. And if you say her history checks out, then I believe you. But it doesn't mean that her brain didn't get scrambled when—I mean, Jesus, Sam. I hit her with my *car*. I saw her break the windshield. I watched her bleed on the side of the road. I was there after her surgeries. I was there when she woke up. And she didn't know me. She didn't *know* me." Jack rubbed his temples. "The rest of it? Who the hell knows? So she got her name wrong, where she was born, who she is. You weren't there with her doctors, Sam. You didn't see the CAT scans. She was lucky she could feed herself, let alone speak English. You think with what mental acuity she had left, she's going to fabricate an entire history just so that she could gain access to my house?"

Sam spread his hands. "Wait. Just listen. What I'm saying is—"

"No," Jack returned, his voice taking on a hard edge. "That's it. Thank you for what you've done. I know you're only looking out for my best interest. But you're done. I can take it from here."

Sam glanced between them and gave a slow nod. "I'm here if you need me, Jack. And if—" He cast Anne a suspicious glance. "—*if* you still want to help her, then I can make some arrangements."

"Thank you."

"Of course." He lingered a moment longer, then reluctantly departed. But he'd left the world shifted.

Anne—for that was her name, her *real* name—looked at Jack with a renewed sense of wonder. He believed her. She didn't think he would, not with Sam's evidence. But even though Jack knew her motives were pure, she herself had doubts. It had all seemed so real, the history her mind created. There had been so many details, as if handed to her on a card. Why were they there in the first place?

Jack smiled as if to put her at ease. "Listen, Vic—I

mean, Anne. I'll give you time to read over the report. I know you must want answers."

She nodded, once again struck by the deepness of his understanding, and his kindness. "I am."

"Okay. I'll leave you to it." He squeezed her shoulder encouragingly, his eyes dropping to the papers in her hands, and then left too.

Anne returned her attention to the folder, its various photocopies calling out to her. She sat upon a divan and flipped through the pages. She found a marriage license with her husband's name: Frederick Strafford.

Frederick Strafford. Her *husband*.

She waited for happiness to rise like a bubble. Instead, a slick of guilt twisted her insides.

She set aside the copy of his driver's license and lifted an enlarged picture of Frederick. He'd dressed in a nondescript black suit, his body lean but not overtly muscular. He had an angular, unsmiling face beneath a tuft of brown hair peppered with gray. Not as handsome as Jack, of course, but a decent-looking man.

Anne studied Frederick's eyes—a light, powdery blue—and slowly, like dawn creeping in, her cheeks warmed. Was that affection? Was that love?

Anne feared chasing the feeling, lest it slip through her fingers like water. Did she love him?

She examined her husband's face. He must be older. But by how much? She checked his driver's license and gasped at their age difference: fifteen years.

She snatched the copy of the marriage license. They'd been married six years. *Six years!* Surely she knew the man. They'd shared a home and a bed. She must harbor details privy only to a wife. She combed her mind for a single, powerful feeling, but nothing emerged. She gripped his picture like a talisman. *Come on! Why don't I remember anything about you?*

Discouraged, she turned her attention to her family history, hoping that would shed light on who and what she was. Her father was an adjunct professor of 19-century literature from Cleveland. Her mother an Argentinean tango instructor from Buenos Aires.

At least that's one mystery solved, Anne thought with great relief. *That must be the reason I know some Spanish.*

She read about how she had started college in Cincinnati with a major in British literature. She'd dropped out after three years, one month after her parent's death by the hands of a drunk driver.

Anne sat back. *They're dead. My parents are dead.*

This realization sunk into her core, leaving her breathless and heartsick. Was this grief over their deaths? Or fear that she'd never remember them?

Her eyes pounded. More tears fell. She craved her memory, even if it would bring her pain.

She turned the page, and there: a black-and-white photograph of her parents. Her father, fair-skinned and bright eyed, tall and slim, next to her mother, curvaceous and dark. An obituary adhered to the back, describing them as a loving couple, taken too soon.

Anne traced her fingers over their faces, and as she did so, an image ripened in her mind. A book spread before her. A gentle hand at her back. A large finger tracing the words as a voice intoned them. Her small hands touching the printed words. Turning back to ask a question. Seeing the familiar snaggletooth smile. The red fluffy beard. Eyes glinting in kindness—and love.

Anne lost her breath. It was her father, surely. She saw herself on his lap, reading literature instead of the singsong Doctor Seuss books popularized by her peers. The joy of being close to her father, of riveting his attention, making him proud of her efforts.

When the feeling dissipated, Anne searched unsuccessfully for a memory of her mother. *But it's there*, she thought, smiling with relief. *I just have to find it.*

She read now about her sister, Elena, who was married and living in Cincinnati. Anne wondered if they were close, even best friends. Perhaps Elena was searching for her even now, wondering if she was all right?

Anne looked at Elena's picture, her oval face framed by long, almost black hair, with wide brown eyes and ivory skin. *We look so different,* Anne thought, then wondered at their age difference.

She turned to the biographical details of her family

and stopped. She read her sister's birthdate and read it a second time.

Could that be right?

She flipped back to her driver's license, and it was there. They were both thirty-two years old, born on March 11.

They were *twins?*

Anne could not breathe for a moment, and then a rushing spasm of excitement poured through her. *I'm a twin! I have a twin sister!*

Not only did they share a family bond, but they had once shared the same *womb*. True, she and Elena could not look more different. But there had to be a connection that nothing—not distance, time, or even lost memories—could extinguish.

On impulse, Anne picked up the phone on the end table. She scanned for her sister's phone number, found it, and dialed the ten digits. As she waited, she thought about what she would say, how she would say it...

"You've reached the Lewiston's residence," announced a deep male voice. "I'm sorry we're not in right now. Please leave a message after the beep..."

The beep sounded. Anne stalled for a few beats and blurted, "Hello, yes! Sorry. Uh, Elena, this is Anne. Your sister. Your twin sister." She stopped, giddy with her own words, and forced herself to continue. "I'm calling because I'm in New Jersey. There's been an accident. I was in an accident. The doctors say that I've lost my memory, and when I—well, my friend, the one I'm staying with—searched for my history, your name and number came up, so I'm calling you." She paused. "I'm sorry. This must be such a strange message. I'm just searching for anyone that knows me. Can you please call me back?" She scrambled for Jack's number and found it written on the underside of the phone. "So if you can please call that number—and if Jack answers, tell him who you are and he'll get me. Oh! And his name's Jack Post. He's works in the movies, so you may actually know him. I know this all seems very strange, but if I can just explain—"

A loud beep. An automated voice prompted her to either accept the message or re-record it. Wary of attempting the exercise again, Anne simply hung up and hoped she'd done it right.

She sat there in silence, expecting the phone to erupt at any moment. But as the seconds slowly ticked away, Anne realized she couldn't wait, that she had to make contact. Particularly if she had a sister—a *twin*—out there: the woman would be doubtlessly worried about her.

Anne found the details of her husband and dialed the first number provided. There came a single ring and an unfamiliar voice, "Daily & Johnston, Wanda speaking. How may I direct your call?"

Anne hadn't expected this. She squinted at the list, at the five phone numbers printed in bold beside her husband's name. Why had she called his work first? "Frederick Strafford, please?"

"Sorry, I didn't hear you. Can you please say the name again?"

Anne cleared her throat. "Frederick Strafford?"

"Oh, hello Mrs. Strafford. I'm sorry; I didn't recognize you. Please hold."

Another stretch of silence. Anne's stomach churned with excitement. *Mrs. Strafford*, the woman had said. Someone knew her!

A crackle sounded in Anne's ear. "Mergers and acquisitions," called a tired voice. "Frederick Strafford's desk. This is Carol. How may I help you?"

"May I speak to Frederick Strafford, please?" Anne said, a bit more strongly.

"Of course, Mrs. Strafford. Please hold a moment."

After a click, the line quieted. In the interim, Anne tapped her fingers beside the phone and played over how she would explain everything to her husband. *Her husband.* How surreal to be legally bound to someone she couldn't remember. What was the man like? Was he kindhearted? Funny? Passionate? Were they happy together?

She imagined his voice on the line. His relief at hearing from her. It had been over a month since they'd seen one another. She envisioned her speech, beginning with, "I'm so sorry, Frederick. But I've been in an awful accident..." She would tell him everything, holding nothing back. He would be heartbroken but understanding, desperate to help her remember him.

Before Anne slipped away into thought, Carol returned. "I'm sorry, Mrs. Strafford. Your husband is in a meeting."

Anne hadn't expected this. "Can you tell him it's an emergency? A medical emergency?"

"Are you all right?"

"I am now," she said. "But I was in a severe car accident. I—" She wanted to tell Carol everything— from meeting Jack Post to the private investigator— but stopped herself. It was too much at once. Better to take it slow. "Just tell him it's an emergency. I've been in the hospital."

"I certainly will. Please hold."

Anne waited. A full minute tic ked by before Carol said, "I'm so sorry, Mrs. Strafford. But your husband requests I take a message."

"A *message*?" Anne sat back, flummoxed. "But did you tell him—"

"I did, ma'am," Carol interjected. "I'm very sorry, but he can't step out at the moment. Why don't you leave me a message and I'll have him call you the second he's available?"

"Oh. Okay." Anne recited Jack's number and endured a few more apologies before the line went dead.

It had to be a very important meeting. He knew she'd been in a serious accident. Why not speak to her?

Was it because she was well enough to call that he didn't need immediate contact?

No. That didn't sound right at all. She'd been gone for weeks. Hadn't he been worried? Hadn't he thought of her at all?

Anne decided she was overthinking this. His actions must be reasonable somehow. The instant his meeting was over, her husband would rush to the phone, desperate to hear her voice.

Anne stared at the phone, willing it to ring. She was an orphan, with only her husband and twin sister for family. What would Elena sound like? Did their voices match in tone and inflection? Would her sister scream with joy? Or weep over Anne's injuries? And what about Frederick? He'd cry buckets when he learned of Anne's shattered memory. He would crush her to his chest, never letting go.

Maybe it won't be that dramatic, Anne thought with a smile. At least she could count on them hopping on the first plane. How could they not want to see her?

Anne envisioned dozens of scenarios, all of them ending in a warm embrace and her family taking her home.

Chapter Eight

ANNE WAITED for the phone to ring for the rest of the day. Each time it did, her heart lifted, only to fall once she realized the call wasn't for her. She bided her time by studying the investigation report, wanting to become an expert on herself and her own history. She reviewed the major events in her life and recalled them as she would for a final exam. She recited her birthday, birthplace, her parents' occupations, her husband's major corporate deals and philanthropic contributions.

Anne methodically arranged every picture. This was her family. Her whole family.

She snapped her head up when Jack reentered the study. "Any calls?"

"No, sorry." He sat on the couch across from her. "Anne, I need to talk to you."

She saw the seriousness in his face, and immediately set aside her materials.

He sighed. "Sam's putting a great deal of pressure on me, and it doesn't help that I have a shoot coming up in a few days..."

Jack let the sentence draw out and Anne nodded in understanding. "You want me gone."

"It's not like that. I just think you should be with your family. You being here had always been under the pretense that it was an end-stop until you found your family, and you have."

She nodded, unsurprised. "I know."

"You do?"

"Sure. I knew I couldn't stay forever. It's okay."

He breathed a sigh of relief. "Oh good. Because, to my own ears, it sort of sounds like I'm throwing you out."

"I'd never think that. You didn't have to do any of this, but you did. I really appreciate everything you've done for me." She quirked a smile. "Of all the people in the world who could've run me over, I'm glad it was you."

He gave a startled laugh. "That's a glass-half-full mentality. I'm sorry I'll miss you for Christmas. We could have had a lot of fun together."

She envisioned a tree heavy with twinkling ornaments, a crackling fire in the stone hearth. Familiarity. "I'm sorry too," she said.

"I'll miss you, Vickie—" He caught himself and shook his head. "Sorry. *Anne*."

"I think I'll always be Vickie to you."

"I think you will."

Without letting herself think too much about it, Anne stood and clumsily reached to embrace him. "Thank you, Jack. I don't know what I would've done without you."

"You would have found a way."

"I'm not so sure."

He pulled back and hesitantly stroked her face. His fingertips traced her scars, more exposed since she'd traded her lacquered mask for a more natural appearance. A little blush, two coats of mascara, and a swipe of beige lipstick. Nothing more.

Her scars were mending well. That was because of the plastic surgeons Jack flew from New York to treat her face. Still, Anne found her appearance jarring. A salmon-colored pitchfork ran from her right temple to jawline. Two small lightning bolts marred her left eye and collarbone.

"I wish I could take these away," Jack said, dropping his hand. "God, I'm so sorry I did this to you."

She shook her head. "At least I'm alive. What are a few scars compared to that?"

"I know women who would choose death over a single visible scar, especially on the face."

Anne blinked at him. "Really?"

"Yes."

"What sort of person could do that?"

He considered. "Let's just say in my line of work, that's not a unique characteristic."

Anne couldn't understand this. "How can you be happy if you're always terrified of something happening to your face? What happens when you get older?"

"Money solves a lot of those problems," Jack said flippantly, then sighed. "I am going to miss you, Anne. You're a breath of fresh air in my upside-down life."

"I'm going to miss you, too." She managed a small smile. "After all, you're the only person I know."

Humor lit his face and his laugh that time was true. "I don't know if that's a good or bad thing," he said.

"It's a good thing," she assured him. "I think I was lucky, in a way."

"You think fate brought us together?" he said, then cocked an eyebrow. Even this simple movement was practiced, and undeniably handsome. Anne wondered if he rehearsed this look for his films. Did a legion of fans swoon over his penetrating gaze?

Jack moved to pull a stray hair from her eyes. A certain playfulness had returned to him. Anne's body turned warm and languid, as if filled with hot caramel.

"You sure you're married?" he murmured.

She dropped her eyes to the report, spread on the far table. "Well, according to that..."

He waved a hand. "Could've been a typo."

"And if it was?" said Anne, her tone equally playful. "Would that make a difference?"

"It'd make it easier for me to kiss you."

She touched her lips to his cheek. "Better?"

"Infinitely," he returned with an easy laugh.

Anne laughed with him, comfortable in his proximity, the familiar touch and smell of him.

Her buoyancy vanished when she realized she'd soon lose Jack. How would she manage? At the moment, he was her entire world.

Jack saw her face. His grin faded into a frown. "What's wrong?"

Anne's throat closed before she could respond. She tried to convince herself that the fear was ridiculous, that she would be fine. But the unknown that faced her was more terrifying than thrilling. She wished she could take Jack with her, pocket him in her suitcase, and if things turned sour, she could take him out for his companionship and comfort.

"It just hit me I'm really going," she said instead.

"But you're going home to your family."

"I know I am, but..." She gazed down at her stack of papers, at the image of her husband, her life's history, sprawled on the topmost stack. "I know it says I'm married, that I have a family, but..."

"You're still afraid."

She blinked at him, wondering how he could know. "Yes. What if I remember nothing about them?"

"Dr. Porter said there's still a chance for a recovery..."

"But he also said it's just as likely the damage is permanent." Anne instantly regretted the forcefulness of her remark, for he winced as if she'd slapped him. But what she said was true. Just as she may never know what she had lost, Jack may never forgive himself for what he had done.

"There's a chance I'll remember," she amended, for his sake, "but if I don't, what will these people think of me? Will they still want to be with me? And why haven't they returned my calls?" Her eyes stung as she forced back an onslaught of tears. She knew she was leaving, and soon, but to what? This was the only life she knew. She had awoken five weeks ago, born into an adult body with only three known abilities: her freedom of movement, fluency of language, and ability to form new memories. Whatever skills and attributes she possessed in her previous life were unknown to her. She had to have a cheat sheet to even remember the names of those purportedly closest to her. What was she going to do with her life?

"Anne," said Jack, gently bringing her back to the present. He hesitated, then placed his hand into his jacket pocket and removed a leather billfold. "I want you to have this. For your travel expenses, and whatever else you need." He peeled open the wallet, removed the contents, and passed a neat stack of bills to her.

She counted the crisp money in confusion. "Ten thousand dollars? Why are you giving me this?"

He covered her hand, the one with his money, with his own. "There's more if you need it. Much more. I know Sam and my accountant would disagree, but I want you to have anything you need. I can't have you wandering the world lost and alone. The money should help, at least a little."

"I can't take this."

"You can and you will."

She sighed, knowing better than to fight him. Anne knew Jack was wealthy, but he had no requirement to pass any of his fortune to her. She rationalized that, perhaps, this amount would be like ten dollars for the average person.

Anne searched her mind for words to convey her gratitude. Unable to find the right ones, she settled simply for, "Thank you, Jack."

Something in his gaze foreshadowed the end of their journey together. He said, "I'm having my staff find you the nicest flight to Ohio. And please stop thanking me."

She smiled. "Force of habit."

He raised his hand, hesitated, and then settled on patting her shoulder. "I'll have Maria arrange your things."

"What things?"

He gave her a playful wink. "I'm not letting you go home without some souvenirs."

She was about to thank him again when the phone rang, its echo carrying down the hall. There came a rush of footsteps and Maria's voice. "Mr. Post? The studio is on line one."

Anne's heart fell.

"Right." Jack turned to her. "Better go. Let me know if you need anything, okay?"

Anne managed a smile. "I will. Thank you."

Jack left without further ceremony. Anne sat alone in the study, wondering why her husband and sister still hadn't called, and who—or what—would be waiting for her when she returned home.

Chapter Nine

"PLEASE WAIT until we have taxied to the gate. Be careful, as some of your items may have shifted during flight," intoned a voice over the loudspeaker.

Anne came awake with a lurch. Her neighboring first-class passengers had pulled their purses and briefcases into their laps. Others reached for their parcels stowed overhead.

Anne shifted in the seat and rubbed her eyes, then jumped when she realized she might have smeared her makeup. She reached into her purse and extracted a small round compact, scrutinizing her reflection in the powdery mirror. No, she was fine. She ensured her eyebrow liner was intact and feathered her hair over the scars hooking her cheeks and forehead. She didn't want to startle anyone with her singed brows and mangled skin. Better to wear a mask until she could explain.

Anne settled back into her seat with a rattled pulse. When had she fallen asleep? It must have been shortly after takeoff. In the space of two hours, she had left her dreamlike existence in New Jersey with Jack to awaken in her alleged home in Ohio.

"I'm excited for you," Maria had said, as she and Justin helped pack her new suitcases the evening before her flight. Jack commissioned half a wardrobe as a parting gift. He'd laid everything—from cashmere sweaters and pressed pants to leather boots and matching gloves—in precise stacks on Anne's bed.

"I'm excited too," said Justin as he folded a viridian turtleneck under his chin. "You'll have to tell me what your family thinks of these combos. You still got my number?"

"I do," Anne said, grinning. Maria and Justin had been especially kind to her during those last few days, trying to ease her nerves. She'd spent hours staring at the DMV photos of her family, trying to dredge up memories. She'd formed only nonsensical fragments. A moment at dinner. A backwards glance in the car. A stolen kiss. She tried to attach feelings to these memories, but they remained as vague and disconnected as watching a film through the slits of her fingers.

Maria must have seen something in Anne's face, because she said, "*Todo está bien, nena. Está bien.*"

"*Yo sé,*" Anne said, even though everything was not

okay. But she smiled despite herself, because it gave her pleasure to hear the ease with which she sometimes spoke Spanish. She'd tried practicing with Maria. Some days she could remember, could communicate—albeit briefly. But then the linguistic door would slam shut, and she'd resume her native English.

"I'll miss you, *nena*," Maria said. She embraced her warmly, and Anne buried her face in her close-cropped hair, breathing in Maria's gardenia perfume.

"Me too," Anne said, blinking away tears.

"It's not like this is goodbye forever," Justin piped in, arranging a silver vanity case with the makeup Anne had barely touched. "I'm sure we'll see each other again."

Anne knew they probably would never see each other again—especially if Sam had anything to do with it. Her time there had been like a stolen dream, never to be resumed upon waking.

Jack had seen her off himself, donning his usual disguise of nondescript clothing and sunglasses. "Call me if you need anything," he had said, holding her to him with a gentle firmness when they reached airport security. Once again, he assured the doctors had cleared her for travel. He'd even provided a list of occupational therapists in Ohio, should she need further help.

"I hope they know how lucky they are," Jack said, trying to be reassuring. So far, the only person to return Anne's calls was a young housekeeper. Jack tried calling her husband and sister himself, to no avail. Had they deemed his messages a prank? It didn't matter. Anne insisted on going home. Despite his misgivings, Jack arranged a luxury flight and car service.

But what about after? Anne wondered. *What life am I stepping into?*

Anne clutched her sleek new purse and sunglasses as she walked down the terminal. Families and friends rushed to embrace each other at the gate. Some wept with joy. Others entwined in a passionate embrace.

Anne passed these people and thought of her next steps. She needed a new driver's license and a cell phone. Good. That she could control. That was manageable. Other fears loomed larger. What if she felt nothing when she saw her family? What then?

Anne mulled over these thoughts when she spotted a uniformed man boasting a sign printed with STRAFFORD. Jack told her to expect this, so she approached the man and introduced herself. He retrieved the rest of her luggage from baggage claim and Anne followed him to an awaiting limousine parked at the airport's curbside.

He opened the door, and she slipped into a dim room with Beethoven strumming from concealed speakers. A bottle of white wine and champagne chilled in silver buckets. She spotted a tray of crustless sandwiches and shelled pistachios.

Ignoring the provisions, Anne rummaged through her plaid rucksack and removed the investigation report. Memorizing her husband's details would make their reunion less awkward. It might even awaken her other memories.

Her husband—"Frederick," she said, again and again, "Frederick, my husband..."—had an impressive history. Born in Connecticut and raised by his father, a European dealer in antiquities, he went to Yale and then Harvard Law School, graduating second in his class. He was in one firm briefly before his twenty-year tenure with Daily & Johnston as their head of mergers and acquisitions. He joined its seventy-two-member partnership fourteen years ago. According to the report, he juggled 80-hour workweeks and an impressive dedication to fitness. He'd even placed ninth in his age group in an Ohio triathlon.

Anne read his report several times before ticking away his sundry accomplishments. Though it wasn't until now, sitting in the back of a cavernous limousine, that she began wondering how much time they had actually spent together. If he saw her at all, it would have to be after work and his Olympian workouts, which left them little time.

How did they make it work? Anne envisioned his loving calls throughout the day. Romantic dinners to fancy restaurants. Flying away to fabulous vacations. Cheering Frederick as he rounded the race track.

Had they ever thought about children? Given his age, it would appear that such an experience was not in the cards for them. She wondered if she was fine with that, or if this was a dream she secretly—or vocally—harbored.

Anne lifted her gaze from the report. The city had disappeared. Now they meandered down narrow, winding roads. "How long until we're there?" she called to the driver.

"About another forty minutes," returned his voice on an intercom.

As the minutes ticked away, Anne polished off all the nuts and three of the sandwiches. She helped herself to the icy bottle of chardonnay and was a little worried she was slightly drunk. But the alcohol and food eased her nerves. They trundled into the outskirts of the city, pulled down a private driveway, and stopped before a three-story Victorian.

The door opened, and the driver helped her out. Her boots clicked across the flagstone walkway and through drifts of snow as they traversed the broad white porch to the front door—her front door. The driver, holding her rucksack and two matching suitcases, waited for her.

Anne raised her fist to knock on the beveled glass and spotted a doorbell tucked near the frame. She pressed the button, and a ring tinkled down a deep corridor inside.

As they waited, Anne swept her gaze across the exterior. It was an old house, surely, but recently renovated. The creamy paint on the door, gray-blue paneling, covered porch, and archways were new, with no telltale signs of age or wear. Christmas wreaths speckled with light bulbs hugged the exterior windows. More lights strewn the rooftop's edge and along the steep gables.

Fresh snow covered the expansive lawn with two dozen mature trees. How long had she lived there? Were any of the design choices hers? Had she picked these colors, those hedges, or that curtain peaking behind a windowsill?

She ascended the porch, passing a wooden three-seater swing suspended from an archway. A window of stained glass twinkled in the winter sun.

Anne's shoulders relaxed. The home felt deeply personal. Perhaps she'd picked it herself.

The door opened inward and an unfamiliar face peeked outside.

"Hello," Anne said pleasantly.

"Mrs. Strafford." The woman—a stout, dishwater blonde in her fifties—regarded her cautiously. Her eyes widened as she took in Anne's appearance.

Anne touched the worst of her scars. "I know. I look different. But we know each other, right?"

The woman hesitated before giving a grim nod. "I'm sorry. It's just—well. Welcome home, Mrs. Strafford." She stepped back and opened the door fully.

Warm air enveloped her as Anne stepped inside. She caught the scent of pine and mint, and her heart surged. She was *home*.

The driver set her bags inside and tipped his cap at

her before departing. Anne turned to the woman who greeted her and said, "Are you Nicole? The one I talked to on the phone?"

"That's my daughter," the woman intoned. "I'm Miranda Burns."

An awkward silence fell as the two women regarded each other. Anne said, "So, do we know each other well?"

Miranda blinked and seemed to take her in fully for the first time. "It's really true, isn't it? That you lost your mind?"

"Well, I didn't lose my mind exactly..." Then, thinking it over, Anne amended, "Okay, maybe I lost it a little." She smiled at her attempt at a joke, but the woman didn't so much as crack her stony expression.

"You really don't remember me?" Miranda eyed her suspiciously.

"I'm sorry, no."

The woman shook her head. "Good God. I didn't believe Nicole when she told me, thought there had to be more to it. But you really don't remember me?"

The warm feeling Anne experienced coming through the door waned. "No, I don't. Have we known each other for a long time?"

"Long enough. Mr. Strafford has employed me for two decades. I met you six years ago."

"You've known my husband that long?"

Miranda nodded.

"And is he a nice man, my husband?"

"Mr. Strafford is the kindest employer I've ever had." Miranda's gaze was unwavering. "He certainly doesn't deserve to be put in this situation."

Anne nodded, in full agreement that no one deserved the hardship of a wife who no longer remembered her husband. "Would you say we get along well? My husband and I?"

Miranda Burns was about to answer, then stopped herself. She finished with a small grin, "Oh yes. You two get along *swimmingly*."

Anne flooded with relief. She had so many questions to ask, though wondered how much a housekeeper would really know about their relationship. "And do you know where my husband is?"

"Saudi Arabia."

"Saudi Arabia?" Anne echoed dumbly.

"Yes. It's a country in the Middle East." The corner of Miranda's mouth twitched. "He's there for a few more days."

"Oh." Anne's fantasy of her husband returning home and sweeping her into his arms broke into fragments. "Well...okay, then."

Wary to meet Miranda Burns' gaze, Anne cut glances around the foyer. She glimpsed a dining room table—set for dinner—through a set of double doors on her left, and what appeared to be a study on the right. A polished staircase rose to the second level, with a spacious catwalk fenced by a mahogany handrail.

Anne turned back to the woman and said, "Miranda..." Anne paused, trying to shake her discomfort. "I'm sorry, do I call you Miranda?"

"You call me Mrs. Burns."

"Right." Anne cleared her throat. "So, Mrs. Burns, what do we do now?"

"Well, when you come home, you usually dismiss me for the day." Mrs. Burns crossed her arms, her gaze a challenge.

Anne blinked at her. "Right. Okay. Then...well, where's Nicole?"

"She'll be back to decorate for the Christmas party."

"There's a Christmas party?"

"On the 23rd."

"Right." Anne swayed on her heels. "So, then I guess you're leaving?"

"I am." Mrs. Burns snatched up an enormous bag, oversize black coat, mittens, and a hat. "Good afternoon, Mrs. Strafford."

"You too."

The woman slipped behind her and slammed the door. A key scratched in the lock, setting a deadbolt into place.

Anne was alone for the very first time in her brand-new life.

Chapter Ten

EVEN AFTER AN HOUR, Anne still had not made it to the second story of her house. She wanted to drink in its contents the same way sommeliers imbibed their finest wines. Slowly, with an appreciation for its structure, taste, and overall balance.

Anne wandered the downstairs, running a hand along the ornate dining room table, lifting the heavy flatware and crystal wine glasses. She strolled through the kitchen and peered at its light granite countertops, twinkling pot rack, stainless steel cutlery. She entered the study and inspected two bookcases housing dozens of hardback books—all legal texts. None of the variety found in Jack's behemoth of a library. Anne opened every closet, discovering not only two pantries but a narrow stairwell to a cellar with two stainless steel wine refrigerators. She pulled at one door, swinging it open with a sigh and a cold gust of air. She studied the wine bottles, hoping to induce a memory. All it triggered was an alarm that the temperature had floated above 57ºF, and so she shut the door.

Anne returned to the main level and opened every available cabinet and drawer. Beyond piles of envelopes and monogrammed stationery, she found nothing personal or telling. Her favorite color might not be purple at all, but crimson. That shade lived in abundance on the walls and the satin roses and peonies accenting nearly every available table. At the end of a three-panel mahogany desk, she found a stack of mail neatly arranged in a basket.

Anne hesitated, feeling like an interloper, but resolved that it was her house and *her* mail, and that she had every right to inspect the envelopes, even open them. She fanned through the stack. Most were addressed to her husband, save for some lingerie and household catalogs with her name printed on the front: Anne Strafford.

That's me, she thought, tracing her name. *These are my magazines.*

Anne moved to an end table with an inexplicable series of silver-framed photographs stacked into a tower. She slowly fanned through them. All were of her and her husband on their wedding day. Her blonde hair fell past her shoulders in thick, bright waves. Her smile radiant as she leaned into her tuxedoed husband with a bouquet of pink and white orchids nestled at their side.

An enormous canvas propped against the fireplace. She pulled it back, revealing a captured moment after their vows. Anne wrapped in Frederick's tender embrace, her hand cupping the back of his head as she kissed him for the first time as his wife.

Anne's heart pinched. *That's true love.*

Why couldn't she remember it?

She examined the photos, feeling as if she gazed at a stranger with an uncanny resemblance to her.

Eventually, Anne ascended the stairs and peered past several doorways. An unused guestroom next to an office with an executive desk adorned with a vase of fresh flowers. A gym with a treadmill, recumbent bike, and a TV suspended from the ceiling. She examined a broad white bureau speckled with an odd arrangement of empty picture frames, all of which lay across from a pristine four-poster bed.

Not quite knowing what to make of this room, Anne moved on to the master bedroom at the end of the hall. She opened the door and took in the vaulted ceilings and crown molding. The clean sweep of ivory carpet and matching walls. The king-sized bed decorated in vibrant emerald and chocolate fabrics. She was about to pass into the en suite bathroom when she spotted a pile of canvases in a corner next to the walk-in closet.

Intrigued, Anne eased herself onto the carpet and

gently overturned them. The images were once again of her wedding day. Anne realized she hadn't seen one picture taken sooner than six years ago. Every image had been stripped, piled, or braced against a wall.

She flashed to Jack Post's mansion and its dearth of any personal photographs. Meanwhile, her home remained frozen in time.

Anne spread out the three canvases. Two of the prints were bridal portraits of herself and her husband. The third was their race to a black stretch limousine, holding fast to each other, laughing and clearly happy. A gilded mahogany frame and gold matting encased each canvas.

Nailed hooks studded the bare walls. Someone had forgotten to display the prints.

Anne hung them herself. The singular portraits on either side of the bed. The landscape opposite. She filled the bare walls within minutes.

Deciding the space could stand some light, Anne thrust open the grommet curtains, revealing two sets of bay windows. Cold, bright sunlight spilled into the room. She smiled in triumph.

Her ebullience dissipated once the silence of the house settled in, and Anne stood in a bedroom with no sense of what to do next. Her husband was out of the country, her sister had yet to return her calls, and she was no closer to regaining her memory than she was on the day she awoke in the hospital.

Her eyes dropped to the end tables beside the bed

and, before she considered what she was doing, Anne crossed the room and opened the bottommost drawer.

She blinked in surprise at a tangle of lingerie. Crimson lace bras and satin teddies. Thongs and bikini-cut panties in a rainbow of colors. She crunched the cool fabric in her hands, pushed them gently aside to see what was beneath. All she found was a medium-sized envelope with the words "Color Swatches for Bedroom" scrawled across the top. Curious, she picked up the envelope, surprised by the weight.

She peeled the lip apart and reached inside to remove a small black leather photo album.

Success! Anne thought ecstatically, placing the album on the bed as delicately as if it was an unearthed Babylonian treasure. Perhaps it contained photographs of her parents, of her and Elena in their youth, of her husband when they first met, or even a picture as recent as two months ago.

Strange, she thought, *that I would have put it in a mislabeled envelope.*

Anne peeled back the cover, grimacing at the empty photo sleeve. She had to flip several sheets before reaching the first photo.

Anne studied the picture. A frown crept into her face.

The shot was a close-up of two faces, hers and an unfamiliar man. Their teeth were a stark white against their matching tans. He was shirtless, with a gold cross twinkling in a nest of chest hair, and she had the white

V of a bikini top just visible between her shoulders. Her straw hat obscured most of the background, but she glimpsed an ocean behind them with a bright sandy beach. The man saluted the camera with an emerald drink. The way his cheek pressed hers, Anne sensed they knew each other well.

But she didn't know his face, and she hadn't come across a description of him in the investigation report. Was it a cousin? Or a co-worker?

She considered this photograph for a few seconds, but since no memory surged, she moved on. Several blank sleeves later, she came across another photograph of herself, with another man. But this one was different. Instead of a beach, they appeared to be in a bar. He was leaning into her and saying something that must have been hilarious, because the photo caught her mid-laugh. He was older than the previous man, perhaps in his forties, and clothed in a business suit— no jewelry.

Anne pursed her brows together in concentration. *Do I know him?*

Again, nothing.

She moved on. She found another photograph of herself and yet another man in a restaurant with twinkling chandeliers and a bustling bar. Then later, with a different man in a lobby of an unfamiliar hotel. She counted four pictures in the twenty-five-picture album.

Where was her husband? Who were these people?

She must know them, surely, because why would they be sitting so close, smiling those smiles, so easily embraced?

Anne replaced the album in the envelope, re-sealed it, and almost returned it when she spotted an exposed photograph snagged under a navy bra. She removed the photo, and the two women were herself and—

"*Elena!*" Anne exclaimed, relieved to recognize someone at last. She was standing next to her sister in a simple white sheath, her gown unadorned with beads or crystals. Caught with a full, radiant smile and wearing bold red lipstick—matching Anne's burgundy gown—Elena looked happy, fulfilled, and—

In love.

Anne had seen pictures of her brother-in-law, Andrew. An average-looking man, he was shorter than her sister, with a flop of blonde hair and wide hazel eyes. Her sister—tall, thin, and with a penchant for black-framed glasses—seemed destined for someone attractive, or at least physically memorable. Or perhaps that was only Anne's hope.

Anne sensed she must have looked at this photograph often. There was real love there. She *had* to try again.

She reached for the nearest phone and dialed the number she'd memorized. Two rings sent her to voice-mail and her brother-in-law's monotonous message. Anne waited for the beep, and said in a rush, "Elena!

I'm in town, at my house. Can you please call me? I need to talk to you. Please call me back." She was about to hang up when she snapped the phone back to her face. "Oh! Sorry. This is Anne. Please call me back."

She dropped the phone in the receiver and regarded the photograph again. She wondered why it wasn't on a shelf somewhere. Anne decided—instead of returning it to the drawer—to prop it against the lamp beside the bed so that it would be the first image she saw upon waking.

The phone erupted in a ring. Anne jumped, and the phone rang a second time, then a third.

She hesitatingly picked it up. "Hello?"

"Stop calling me!" cried a woman's voice down the line. "Stop filling my voicemail with your stupid messages! All right? Enough is enough! Stop calling me. Stop getting people to call me pretending to be movie stars. You think I'm an idiot? I've had it with all of your bullshit drama and I'm done. I'm through with it, okay? *Good*bye..."

"Wait!" Anne shouted. "Wait! Who is this? I'm sorry, I don't—"

"Oh, stop playing your little amnesia game with me!" The voice sounded on the verge of breaking, with pain and cruelty equally intermixed. "You didn't lose your memory, but you've certainly lost your mind if you think I'm going to believe anything you say to me—"

"Elena?" Anne cut in. "Is that you? Are you my sister?"

"Yes, it's Elena! What, now you're pretending not to recognize my voice? Oh, that's rich. Listen, save all this melodrama for someone who cares, because it's not—"

"I'm not making this up!" Anne cried, her voice rising sharply over her sister's. "I'm not! I had an accident in New York, and I don't remember anything, and I..."

"You missing any arms? Legs?"

"Uh, no," said Anne, surprised. "But I have a note from my doctors, and my scars—"

"You sound fine to me. Let me know when you're done with this act—actually, don't. Don't call me at all. We're through. Forget you even know me. And if you call me again, I'm having the number changed."

"Wait!" Anne cried, desperate for the barrage to stop. "Please! I don't know what's wrong here. Please talk to me. You're the only one I can talk to—"

"That's your own damn fault," Elena snapped. "You have no one to blame but yourself. You're a God-awful human being, and you deserve everything coming to you. Call Cindy if you want someone's ear. She's your match in every way."

"Who's Cindy?" Anne asked desperately. "Wait! Who's Cindy?"

An abrupt click. The line went dead.

The phone hung in Anne's hand, strange as an amputated limb.

She glanced at the photograph beside the bed. She and her sister. Smiling together. *Happy.*

Nausea churned Anne's stomach. *What the hell just happened?*

Chapter Eleven

EVERYTHING IN ANNE screamed to call her sister back, beg her to talk, apologize for whatever she had done. But Anne heard the echo of her sister's words, and the fear of what might happen paralyzed her. She sensed Elena was being truthful with the threat of changing her number should she attempt further contact. What if Elena followed through on her threat to cut Anne off? Anne fantasized about hunting her sister like a fugitive, cornering her with a weapon, and demanding an accord. But she shook her head, knowing that wouldn't solve anything.

Desperate for answers, Anne called the woman Elena mentioned: Cindy. She tried to be resourceful and find the number herself, but she could not so much as locate an address book on any of the desks throughout the house. She pulled the investigation report from her purse and studied it like a "Where's Waldo?" puzzle. Anne traced her finger over the text, searching for any mention of a Cindy.

But there was nothing.

Finally, after locating the investigator's number, she called his office. The secretary told Anne they couldn't help. Any request for information had to come from the one who commissioned the report.

Stymied, Anne had no one else to call but Jack. But what could she tell him? That her sister wasn't talking to her? That her husband was out of the country? That she was completely alone in her own house? She'd wanted to be a success. Prove she could take care of herself. That she didn't need Jack Post.

But Anne had no choice. She searched through her carry-on bag and smoothed out the crumbled spool of numbers Jack had written for her just before her flight. She elected not to call his cell phone, but try the main house first. She breathed a sigh of relief to hear Maria's clipped voice. "*¿Alo?* Who's calling?" Jack had instructed Maria to delay acknowledging who lived in the house, initially pretending she was the sole matriarch.

"Hi, Maria. It's Anne."

"Anne!" she cried, her formal voice melting into friendly recognition. "*¡Dios mío, nena!* We have all been thinking about you. *¿Estás bien?* Have you met your husband yet?"

"Not yet," Anne said, hoping Maria wouldn't ask

many questions. "He's out of town right now. I'm sort of settling in."

"Ah, well, that's good. Oh! I can't forget...Justin wants to know how your family has liked your new clothes. What did your sister think?"

Anne glanced at the beige sweater and gray sweatpants she had pulled on rather haphazardly that morning. *Justin would be mortified.* "Well, everyone's sort of busy right now, so I haven't had time to show anything off yet. But tell him I really love everything."

A long pause made Anne wonder if she'd lost the connection. Then Maria returned with a lowered voice. "What's wrong, *nena*? Why is everyone so busy?"

Those eight innocuous words cut Anne like a knife. She sucked a breath and tried to mask her desperation. "Oh, it's okay. I'm really just settling in. It'll smooth over once I'm able to meet everyone and they can see that what I'm going through is real." *Not even here twenty-four hours,* Anne thought, *and already I'm going to cry. God, I'm hopeless.* She cleared her throat and focused on the task ahead. She would not reveal her worry to Maria, at least not yet. They said knowledge was power, and Anne intended to gather all that she could. "Listen, Maria. I need you to get in contact with Jack."

"Of course," Maria said, suddenly all business. "What do you need?"

Anne told her quickly and with little details. When

she hung up, she realized she was playing yet another waiting game. Waiting for someone on the other side to provide her with information so that she could get on with her life.

Luckily, the wait wasn't interminable. In less than an hour, the phone rang, and Anne—hoping it wasn't her husband or sister, at least not until she puzzled things out—picked up the receiver. "Hello?"

A crackly voice introduced himself as the lead investigator, and that Jack Post himself had requested he call to provide anything she desired. Anne related what she needed, surprised to hear the man's tenor change into something close to amusement.

"This is most unusual," he said. "You want me to do what, exactly? A secondary investigation?"

"No, no," Anne said quickly. "I mean that, I just... well. Okay." She took a steadying breath. *How to explain this?* "I've been told that I know a woman named Cindy and that she's the only one I can call at the moment. And at the moment, I'm out of people to call, and I have to talk to someone. So I need to know if you came across anyone with that name in your investigation."

"Cindy. Cindy..." The line filled with the sound of cracking paper. Anne waited. The man's breathing turned ragged as he typed at a keyboard and flipped more pages.

"My sister said she's a friend of mine," said Anne, hoping this detail might prove useful.

Anne remembered the coldness in Elena's voice, the distant pain edging her every word. *What did I do to her?* Anne thought miserably. *How long have we been this way?*

"Aha!" said the investigator. "There's a Cynthia Harper who lives in Dayton. Do you need the address?"

"And the number, please." Anne wrote both on the investigation report, with "Cindy Harper" scrawled in the margin with capital letters. "Thank you. You don't know how much this'll help." *Hopefully,* she added inwardly.

"So it's really true?" asked the investigator. "This whole amnesia thing?"

"Unfortunately, yes."

"Amazing. Well, good luck to you, kiddo. If it's any consolation, at least you're rich. Or, more accurately, at least your *husband* is. So you better watch out, since you signed a prenup."

"Right," Anne said, though not in understanding. "Okay, well, thank you again."

"Sure." He clicked off.

Anne dialed the woman's number. Two rings before the line picked up with an ecstatic greeting, "Hey *you*! I have been waiting for you to call for weeks! What the hell *happened*? Tell me everything!"

"Cynthia Harper?" Anne glanced down at the number and address. "Or Cindy?"

"What?" A confused laugh. "What the hell are you talking about?"

"Are you Cindy Harper?"

"Of course I'm Cindy! What's going on? Did you just get home? You better've not been home long, you bitch!"

"Um..." Anne, caught a little off guard, was unsure how to proceed. "So we know each other?"

"What is going *on*, sweetie pie? What's with all these bizzaro questions? Oh—" Her voice dropped a few decibels. "Is your husband there? I thought he was going to be in Europe—"

"Saudi Arabia," Anne corrected.

"Then who's with you? Luke? Eddie? Do you need to call me back?"

"No one's here. It's just me." Anne paused. "Who's Luke?"

"Didn't he get back in touch with you? I thought —" Cindy abruptly stopped, then said, much more slowly, "Wait. Why are you calling me from this number?"

"What do you mean?"

"I mean, where's your cell phone? Did you lose it?"

"I guess," said Anne. "Why? Does it matter?"

"I thought Frederick didn't like you talking to me." Another pause, then a worried, "Won't he trace this call or something?"

Anne's head spun. "What are you talking about?"

"Isn't that why you got the secret line? So you could call me, or Luke?"

Anne shook her head. "I don't know what you mean. Listen, I just want to talk to you..."

"Do you need me to come over?"

This stopped Anne. Come over? Someone from her real life was offering to see her, speak to her face-to-face? "If you can..." Anne began, but Cindy cut her off.

"I'm *there*!" she said. "Give me twenty-minutes."

An hour and a half later, the doorbell rang. Anne, who had anxiously waited by the door for the first forty-five minutes, was by then in the kitchen pantry, rooting for something to eat. She emerged with an enormous bag of salt and vinegar potato chips, which she crumpled into the crook of an arm as she opened the door.

A woman with a mess of platinum blonde hair and teetering heels spilled into the house as she scooped Anne into a hug. "*Hon*-ney!" Cindy cried, giving her an extra squeeze. She dropped an enormous grocery bag on the floor and switched her purse to her opposite arm. "My God! Why didn't you *call* me? When did you get in? How long have you been here? I've been *dying* to see you!"

Anne, taken aback, tried to work the chips from her arm so that their contents wouldn't crush to dust.

She pushed herself free and offered a wan smile. "Hi. Cynthia?"

"Cindy, *Cindy*! What the hell's up with all these formalities? Why are you acting so strange?" Cindy finally glimpsed Anne's face and stepped back in shock. "Oh my god! What the hell *happened* to you?"

Anne instinctively reached to touch her scars, to cover them, but she stopped herself. "I was in a car accident."

"Jesus." Cindy's nose crinkled. "When was this? Are you okay?"

"Sort of..."

Anne was about to tell her about her memory loss when Cindy's face changed and she said, "Well, you know the right guy to fix you right up. Which reminds me...I've been meaning to tell you that you need to be careful."

Anne blinked in surprise. "What? Why?"

"I think Freddy hired an investigator. Someone called me last week asking questions. I'm not an idiot." She wagged a finger at Anne. "Watch yourself."

Anne opened her mouth to explain when Cindy waved a hand at her face. "Has Luke seen you like this? What does he think?"

"Who's Luke?" Anne asked.

"You're hilarious. Are you this good with Freddy? 'Cause you almost have me convinced." Then, as she regarded the potato chips in Anne's arm, she winked and added, "Hung over a bit, are we?"

"What?" Anne followed her gaze. "No, I'm just hungry."

"Yeah, right! I've never seen you eat chips unless you're recovering from something." Cindy clicked her way into the foyer. Anne took in the woman's long legs, swathed in black nylon beneath a short yellow minidress, just visible under a long white coat with a fur-trimmed collar. Cindy paused by the stairs, resignedly snapped open the gold buttons of her coat, and draped it over the banister. "So..." she drawled, giving Anne a conspiratorial wink before she peered cautiously up the stairway, "...seriously, where is he? I miss him!"

Anne stared at her blankly. "Who?"

"*Who*?" Cindy rolled her eyes dramatically. "Who do you think? I know you're hiding him somewhere, but you don't have to do that for me. I totally forgive you for what went down on your trip."

"Trip?"

Cindy barked a laugh. "Boy, you're hung over. Are you taking something because of your face? Is that what's making you like this?"

"Not now," Anne said with a frown.

Cindy cast a dubious glance around the house. "So he's really not here?"

"It's just us."

Cindy's smile faded. "Seriously?"

Anne nodded, not knowing what to make of the

woman. What was she talking about? And who was this Luke character?

"Ah shit." Cindy snapped her fingers and began rummaging through her red leather purse.

Anne watched her with curious interest. "What are you doing?"

"Finding..." Cindy fanned through various magazines before pulling one out, opening it to the middle, and brandishing it before her. "...this! You *bad* girl! You think you could keep this from me?"

Beneath a headline entitled "Celeb Sightings" was a pictorial of half a dozen people in dark sunglasses trying to dodge the camera. It took Anne a second to register what she was seeing, as almost all the faces were unfamiliar. But then one caught her eye.

Jack! His name erupted in Anne's mind like a cannon shot.

At the bottom left corner of the page was Jack Post, passing through a pair of supermarket doors. And behind him, holding his hand—

"Is that me?" Anne asked, confusion and nostalgia weighing her voice.

"You bet it is!" Cindy pointed to the picture. The fair hair framing Anne's face. The high black turtleneck. And the emblazoned words, "Jack Post's Mysterious New Lady."

"You might have thrown me a little with your weird conservative vibe," Cindy continued, "but I'd recognize that face anywhere! I just couldn't believe you didn't call me. You know I waited by the phone for like three days, wanting to hear how things were going!" She paused, and then said as slowly as if the realization had just dawned on her, "Oh my god. Do you think Luke knows?"

Anne took the magazine. "I don't know who you're talking about."

Cindy cackled. "You're a riot! But then I guess after Jack Post, I'd be saying the same thing."

Anne peered at the spread of pictures. She took in Jack's stony expression. Her own confused gaze staring out while all those shoppers snapped photographs. She remembered how tired Jack had been when they'd returned to the car. How he'd shut himself away in the study. What was supposed to have been a simple market outing had devolved into some sort of wild spectacle.

"I take it the plan worked," Cindy said, breaking Anne's thoughts. "But how the hell did you pull it off?"

Anne forced her eyes from the picture. ""Pull what off? What are you talking about?"

"What is *with* you?" Cindy's eyebrows twitched somewhere between bewilderment and surprise. "I haven't heard from you in like six weeks. *Six weeks!* I mean, you called me your first day there, and that was fine, but now it's been like a month and a half! You really had me worried."

Anne sensed an expected apology. "I'm sorry?"

Cindy gave a cavalier shrug. "Whatever. I just mean you put me in a bad position. I was really worried something had gone wrong, and I couldn't exactly call your husband to find out, now could I?"

"Why couldn't you?"

Cindy gaped at her. "God. Are you *mental*? Could you imagine me calling Freddy and saying, 'Hi there, Anne's husband! So I just wanted to check in to see if everything was still a go with Operation Seduce a Movie Star. Could you give me a status update?' God, that man would have killed me!"

The ground tipped under Anne as Cindy's words replayed in her mind. "Wait. What are you saying?"

"I'm saying tell me how you did it! I know we spent like weeks—months!—preparing. I don't even want to think about how many times we talked about it over cocktails before that, but to actually go out and do it! Holy crap! You're officially my guru!" Cindy strode forward and clutched Anne's shoulders. "I want details, girl. *Details!*"

Anne shrunk back. A part of her wanted to admit she had amnesia. That she had copies of her medical report as evidence. Instead, she tried to be evasive. "Sorry, but I still don't know what you're talking about."

Cindy dropped her hands and for a long moment seemed to study her, as if Anne had donned the flesh of her previous friend and replaced the core. "Something is wrong with you—" Cindy stopped. Her eyes rounded as she snapped a glance upstairs. Her voice returned in a whisper. "He's *here*, isn't he?"

"Who?" Anne whispered back.

"Freddy. Did he come home early?" When Anne didn't respond, Cindy nodded sagely before calling up the stairs, "Sorry, sweetie! I guess *I'm* the one who's hung over. I don't know what I'm talking about half the time. I'm so glad that you enjoyed your trip with the girls. Everyone said they had a blast with you. Sorry I had to leave New York early. Next time you go, though, I'm totally staying the whole time!"

Cindy nodded meaningfully to Anne. "I'll let you go. Call me when he's gone, okay?"

Anne, still rattled, didn't stop her. The woman clicked to the front door and removed a long black jacket from the grocery bag discarded by the entryway. With deft movements, Cindy slid her arms through the sleeves, shook her hair over the collar, pulled on a pair of matching gloves, and opened the door.

The December wind cut across Anne's skin, but she made no move to cover herself. Just before Cindy disappeared, Anne cried, "Wait!" She pointed to the fur-trimmed coat draped over the banister. "Aren't you forgetting this?"

Cindy gave her a strange look. "You sure that accident didn't knock your head around a bit? I thought you'd be salivating at that Gucci." She laughed mirthlessly. "I'm actually surprised you didn't do your usual victory dance."

"Victory dance?"

"Yeah. Thanks for showing some restraint. That's really not like you! But, seriously, call me ASAP. I've just got to hear the details about how you did it."

Anne blinked at her. "Did what?"

"Sleep with Jack Post, you idiot!" Then, with a glance up the stairs, she whispered, "I know we'd planned it for like forever, but when I saw the proof, I just couldn't believe you pulled it off. *Genius*!"

Cindy blew Anne a kiss, and in an instant, was gone.

Chapter Twelve

ANNE STAGGERED UPSTAIRS. For the next half hour, she was in a manic state. She tore open the bedroom drawers, the desk, and the armoires for any evidence of Cindy's claims. She fanned through paperwork, scrutinized an assortment of Post-It notes with, unfortunately, nothing more titillating than grocery lists and reminders to pay off credit cards. She even searched the medicine cabinet. Nothing.

What was she missing? There had to be something.

Anne crossed her arms. *If I were really part of the plan that Cindy says I am, wouldn't there be evidence of it somewhere? Anywhere?*

Anne trudged up the stairs, exhausted. She didn't know who or what to believe. Were she and Cindy really best friends before the accident? Whatever she thought of Cindy before, she found the woman appalling now.

The sunlight dimmed, darkening the bedroom. Anne stood at the threshold, listening to the sounds of the house settling, and finally slogged to bed.

A nap'll make me feel better, she thought, pulling back the duvet cover and creamy bedsheet.

Her hand froze.

Sitting on the bed was an enormous beige envelope. On the front, in thick black ink, were the words, "To: Anne. Love, Frederick."

"Oh my god," Anne whispered. *A letter from my husband!*

She sat on the bed and wondered why he hadn't left it somewhere visible, like on the foyer table or a kitchen counter. But she pushed away the thought as she excitedly peeled open the envelope and peered inside.

Anne frowned, instantly disappointed. She didn't know what she'd expected, but it had been something other than a formal stack of papers, with paperclips dividing it into two sections.

Anne pulled out the packets and spread them on the bed. Clipped together were two batches of e-mails, followed by a nondescript manila folder, which she set aside.

Must be something with work, she thought as she arranged herself more comfortably on the bed.

Lifting the first stack of e-mails, her eyes stalled on

a section highlighted at the top. She squinted to read the text—it appeared to be the e-mail's sender—which read "ASSexyDD". Next to this odd moniker was her name, inked into the margin.

That's supposed to be me? Anne wondered with a deepening frown. *ASSexyDD? What the hell does that stand for?*

Before the thought even finished, a voice rose within her to answer, "Anne Strafford, Sexy DD."

Anne glanced down at her chest and rolled her eyes. *Good grief. Why would I choose that as a name? Is it some sort of joke?*

She tucked her legs beneath the mountain of pillows behind her and began to read. The first page was an e-mail written by her to "SexKitten78", which, if the sidebar identification was accurate, was an alias of Cindy Harper.

> *Hey Chica! Can't wait 4 NYC in 2 days. So I'm staying at the Plaza—hell yeah!—and I've gone over the list a thousand times. I'm a total pro on this guy. This may be the ultimate dare, but who else do you think could pull this off? I hope you're ready to pony up that Gucci coat! Luv ya! ~ AS*

The Plaza? Anne thought. *But the investigator never mentioned a hotel.*

Anne turned the page, hoping the next correspondence would shed light on this cryptic message. The letter was dated a few days earlier, again to Cindy:

Hey Chica! So I'm calling around for the best places. Where do you think puts me in the best locale to run into him? I know he's doing a shoot in Central Park. Maybe somewhere on 5th? Luv ya! ~ AS

The next e-mail was from a day earlier, this one from Cindy:

Hey Mrs. DD! I'm so getting that Armani dress. Did ya hear Post loves to skydive? How're you going to manage that? Didn't you go to some fear of heights camp a few years back? I'm totally gonna win this! Add that to your list, bitch! ~ Cin

Anne's stomach twisted as her mind crowded with questions. *What the hell am I reading here?* she wondered. *What's this bet? That I'm somehow going to sleep with Jack Post? Why did I do this? And what is this list?*

Anne forced herself to read through the e-mails detailing her excitement for the trip, her travel arrangements, her plans for seduction. She'd make it through the flight—traveling an unholy thirty-five thousand feet in the air—by throwing back a Xanax and a couple of apple martinis on the plane. She had been uncertain how to trick Jack Post into believing she loved skydiving, but figured the right lingerie rendered such details moot.

She reached for the last e-mail in the stack. As Anne read her letter to Cindy, her skin prickled with goosebumps.

> *Okay, Cin. Here's what I've got so far. Para-sailing. Sashimi. Sunday matinees. Graham Greene martinis. Impressionist paintings. Rock climbing. Skydiving, Organic produce. Tantric yoga. Anything you want to add to the Jack Post Loves List? ~ AS*

The words blurred as Anne trembled. *That's part of my list!*

She flashed to her hospital bed, those exact words spilling through her mind. She'd taken them as her identity. Her passions. The very core of her. Sam doubted them. So had the investigator. Now she'd bashed those illusions to pieces.

None of it was real. It had all been a lie. A massive charade to seduce a man she'd never known beyond a movie screen, for the spoils of bragging rights and a designer coat.

Anne was dizzy with this unexpected knowledge. But she still could not quite accept it as her personal truth, because it was not really *her*. She felt disembodied, gazing down from the ceiling at herself, alone in her marital bed.

Anne lowered the first stack of e-mails to her lap. Then, hesitatingly, she picked up the second stack and peered at the top. Again, her provocative moniker, "ASSexyDD", was highlighted. But this time it was addressed to someone unfamiliar: Luke Harris.

Luke. Cindy had glanced up the stairway, asking for a man by that name. Was this the same one?

Anne scanned the page and noticed this correspondence was longer, more flowery. She slowly read the words, *her* words, and sensed the distance from herself closing.

> *Dearest Luke,*
> *Thank you again for everything you've done for me. You're truly an amazing man, someone I never thought I deserved. Everything you've done for me is so selfless, so wonderful. I feel honored to have you in my life. Your gift to me is truly irreplaceable, and I know you'll love seeing the girls in person! I look forward to seeing you soon, and holding you in my arms.*
> *Yours forever,*
> *Anne*

Her throat dried. She tried unsuccessfully to swallow. *Maybe this means nothing. Maybe he's just a close friend.*

Anne feared reading what was hiding underneath that sheet of paper. But her fingers moved on their own accord, and she saw herself turning over the page, and staring at the next e-mail:

> *Dear Anne,*
> *I know it's only been two days, but I couldn't stop thinking about you. I'm at work, but I'm having difficulty concentrating on the procedures. My mind keeps returning to those last incredible hours we had together. You're the only one I want to be with, the only one I think about. I think my wife's suspects, but frankly, I don't care. You're the only one I care about. Watching you leave the hotel was the hardest thing I've had to endure. I can't stop thinking about you. Your touch. What you do for me. I'm so glad that the surgery went well and you're happy with your breasts. If anyone ever deserved a pair of gold standard tits, it's you, baby. Let me know if you need any more money. Your bastard husband should keep you in gold and diamonds, but at least I can treat you the way you truly deserve.*
> *Yours forever,*
> *Luke*

Anne read his letter to her again, then a third time. *My breasts,* she thought with mounting despair and disbelief, *my breasts!* She gripped her front, where the hard mounds strained against her sweater. *I'm cheating on my husband. I'm cheating on him with a married man who paid to stuff my chest.*

Anne swallowed, closed her eyes. New realizations flamed through her mind, burning her with shame. *He cheated on his wife to be with me. Oh, God. His poor wife. My poor husband.*

An unknown hurt squeezed her like a vise. Her throat ached, her eyes pounded, and she realized that for these last few minutes she had been fighting back tears. Anne drew a few deep breaths. An almost physical weight pulled her down at the shoulders.

Her fingers trembled as she turned to the next e-mail, expecting it to be more love proclamations to Luke Harris. Instead, the highlighted sender was a man name Edward Tallow. His e-mail was shorter, but his message—dated only two days before her professed love for Luke—was unflinchingly clear:

> *Hey Double Delight,*
> *Last night was amazing. I swear I've never met a woman who could satisfy me in so many nasty ways. When're you free again? I know you said you wouldn't agree to anything less than a five-star hotel, but that really stretched my budget last time. Can we take it down a few notches, maybe an express inn or something? Let me know. I'm free day or night for your amazing ass.*
> *Later,*
> *Eddie*

Anne's stomach turned again, this time with a sickly flip. Her mouth watered, and she realized she was going to be sick. She rushed to the bathroom and knelt by the toilet, but no heaves came. Only a rocking nausea that leveled her. She sat with her forehead pressed to the cool porcelain, the smell of Clorox stinging her nostrils. She tried in vain not to think of Elena or Luke or Cindy or her husband. She wondered why had she divided herself among so many, why she had done any of this.

When she returned to the bedroom, the e-mails stared accusingly from the bed. Though sickened by herself and wanting to stop, Anne forced herself to push on. Even if she uncovered nothing remotely re-deemable, she had to know the truth of herself. She feared if she didn't, she'd catch in the fog of her own existence, never knowing what her life had once been.

As the e-mails continued and their contents be-came more explicit, Anne tried to align her previous vision of herself with her current reality. But the effort was too much, and she resolved simply to make it to the end.

When she finally reached the last of the e-mails, dated two months earlier, Anne dropped the packet on the bed as if she had been holding putrid waste. She wondered how many other men she had slept with. Had she ever feared for her safety or con-tracting a disease? Were all these men married and cheating on their spouses? That photo album hidden in the nightstand. Was that a collection of her conquests? Each captured image holding a special, secret meaning?

Anne couldn't imagine returning home after a night with one of those men. Sitting across from her husband at dinner. Pretending nothing had happened. What was it like to live such a life of duplicity? Lies predicated every decision. And all for what? A cry for attention? Feelings of insecurity? Loneliness? A need to escape?

Anne scrubbed her face with her hands. *Sam was right. I am a fake. Everything about me is wrong. Twisted. I can never fix this. Not in a hundred years.*

Another thought struck her like a mallet. Her heart hitched in her throat. *Frederick knows. He knows everything. He left this packet here for me, in this bed for me to discover. He's read everything in these e-mails.*

Anne pinched her eyes closed. *What had that been like for him? To read my words to these men? My plans for New York? No wonder he never took my calls or called me back.*

She saw her husband hunched over the e-mails. His shoulders sagging with each successive page. His face hardening to stone.

Anne opened her eyes and reached for the envelope that had contained everything spread out on the bed. She turned it over and her husband's words devolved into a hateful scrawl: "Love, Frederick."

Why did he write that, knowing what was inside?

Anne thought in confusion. *Does he still love me? Or is he trying to hurt me?*

Anne remembered the manila folder, the one she'd set aside seemingly a millennium ago. It'd been pushed under the comforter, one small corner exposed.

Anne took up the folder and opened it to the first page. At the top, in bold black ink, were the words:

OHIO DISSOLUTION OF MARRIAGE FOR PARTIES WITHOUT MINOR CHILDREN OF THE MARRIAGE

Tucked alongside were several Post-Its. She turned to the first tabbed page. At the bottom was a blank for her signature.

Below it was her husband's. Already signed.

Chapter Thirteen

ANNE SAT in the large soaker tub in the master bathroom. The cooled bathwater pooled into her armpits. She propped her feet on a ledge and fingered the near-empty water glass sweating on the tiled floor. Her skin shriveled and chilled, but Anne refused to get out. She turned the faucet to its highest setting, wincing as the stinging hotness turned her lobster pink. After finding a loofah, Anne had been intent on scrubbing away the memories, as if they existed on her topmost layer of skin. But no matter how hard she scrubbed, she couldn't get deep enough.

First, the shattering phone call with her sister. Then her baffling meeting with her alleged friend Cindy. Now the package left by her husband.

So far, this was the worst puzzle *ever*.

Anne took a long drink of water, forcing herself to

finish the glass. She wiped her mouth with the back of her wrinkled hand and set the glass down with a clatter.

And now that I'm home, I'm supposed to do...what? What the hell am I supposed to do now?

She didn't know how long she could stay in the house. Could she, with the divorce proceedings? Frederick would probably toss her on the streets by Christmas. And she couldn't really blame him.

Her mind turned to Luke Harris, author of several of the most descriptive and titillating e-mails.

Did I really love him? Anne wondered. *Was there something really there? Something meaningful? Or was I just using him?*

Or were we using each other?

Anne cupped her face in a hand. The wet, icy chill seeped into her skin. When she had first drawn the bath, she had resolved not to leave until deciding her next step, but she was no closer than before. All she could think about was making everything right again, somehow reclaiming some sense of who she really was, or who she wanted to be.

But how to begin?

Anne sighed, weary of the entire enterprise. *All the people I want to talk to aren't speaking to me. And the ones who are, I want out of my life.*

Another thought tumbled through her mind, at first frightening in its implications. But as it settled, it burrowed, and soon it was deep within her, consuming every fiber.

Anne stood up in the tub. The water tracked down her skin and splashed against her calves in a tumult. *That's where I'll start.* That's *how I'll make it right.*

She snatched two towels and twisted one around her hair and the other about her chest. She rushed into the bedroom, seized the packet of e-mails, and made her way down to the study. A renewed sense of purpose filled her, and it was exciting and terrifying in equal measure.

She turned on the computer and waited for the welcome screen with its bright wallpaper of rolling meadows. She double-clicked on the Internet browser, opened her e-mail, and saw blanks for her screen name and password.

Shit.

She remembered her screen name—ASSexyDD— but the password eluded her, and there had been no mention of it in the file her husband left.

"Think, Anne, *think*," she commanded, working her mind like a muscle. She tried various names: "Anne," "Freddy," "Frederick," "Elena," "Cindy," "Vickie," "Victoria," "Jack," "Jack Post." Then others: "Marriage," "Love," "Sex," "Sexy," "Men," "Affairs," "DD", before she sat back in frustration.

"What would I pick?" she thought aloud. Deciding

she needed a mental break, she padded into the kitchen towards the investigation report stacked on the center island. She flipped through a few pages and returned to the study, cradling its contents. With dwindling hope, Anne entered her niece's name, "Charlotte," her father, "Jacob," and then, resignedly, her mother, "Valentina."

Instantly, Anne was sent to her inbox.

Her fingers leapt from the keyboard. *What?*

Her brows pursed in confusion. There it was. Her e-mail. She'd entered the correct password.

Anne glanced at the report, at the last name on the page. Her mother's: Valentina.

Scared to lose her e-mail, Anne opened another browser and again logged into her e-mail account, typing the nine letters of her mother's name carefully. Once again, she was sent to her e-mail, with over three hundred unopened letters waiting in the inbox.

Her mother. *Valentina*.

No time to think about that now. She needed to embark on her cyberspace mission now, before she lost courage. In the search field, she entered "Luke" and pressed ENTER. Several hundred e-mails appeared, and she quickly discerned his screen name: LukeHarris86MD. She opened his most recent letter.

Anne —
Why haven't you returned my calls? Where are you? I came by your house yesterday, but your housekeeper wouldn't speak to me. How does she

know about us? I know your husband is out of the
country, so he can't be keeping you from me. Please
write when you can. I miss you every second we're
apart. Write soon.
 Yours Forever,
 Luke

Anne read his e-mail twice over, and one statement chilled her. Her housekeeper knew about Luke? How?

She flashed Mrs. Burns' icy greeting. The way she had told Anne that she and her husband were happy together.

Anne's throat tightened in shame. *God. Frederick knows. Now Mrs. Burns. Who else knows about him? Elena?*

Before the questions could spin her out of control, Anne hit REPLY and defiantly typed out a response:

 Luke —
 This is Anne. I just returned from New York
 and want to tell you that whatever relationship
 you think we have is over. Please don't contact me
 again. Do not call me or write to me or visit my
 house. Go home to your wife and try to find happi-
 ness there. Because you will not find it with me.
 Sincerely,
 Anne

She sent the message with a single click. But just

before Anne closed the search field, she noticed an e-mail near the top of the page, with the attached screen name AmandaHarris31.

Amanda Harris... Anne thought. *Harris. Is she related to Luke?*

Anne clicked the message, and a single paragraph appeared in a separate window.

> *I can't even make myself type your name, even though yours is the only one I think about lately. I've thought about what to say to you for what seems like forever, but the right words elude me, and there is no rulebook to follow. So I'm just going to write about what I feel. The anger and hurt and pain manifest themselves in new ways each day. Mostly I'm sick, but sometimes I feel like there is a cancer inside me, and that cancer is the knowledge I carry with me every second of the day. I cannot look at my husband without seeing traces of you. Our children sense something's wrong, broken between us, though I'm trying to repair it—repair us. I don't know who you are or why you chose my husband. You knew he was married, that he has children, but you didn't care, so that has to say something about you. I just want you to stop seeing him. If you have a shred of decency or kindness left in you, you will leave my husband and our family alone. Please get out of our marriage and out of our lives.*

~ Amanda Harris, Luke's Wife

Pinpricks pierced the back of Anne's eyes. *What have I done? That poor woman.*

Anne sat in the chair for a long time, reading over the woman's words. *If you have a shred of decency or kindness left in you...leave my husband and family alone...get out of our marriage and our lives.* Were these sentences really meant for her? Could someone she had never met truly hate her so much? Could her name alone really conjure feelings of sickness and disdain from another?

Anne covered her face with her hands. Perhaps if she blocked out the world, she could stop this avalanche that seemed destined to break her. *My God,* Anne thought. *What the hell did I do with my life?*

With trembling fingers, Anne hit "REPLY" and wrote a message to Luke's wife, reading her few words carefully before sending it:

> *Dear Amanda —*
> *I cannot express the shame I have for what I have done to you and your family. You don't have to worry any more. It's over between us. Again, I am deeply sorry for what I've done to your marriage and hope that you can work things out with your husband.*
> *Sincerely,*
> *Anne*

Her words were paltry, and she doubted they'd bring genuine comfort. Still, she hoped that Amanda Harris might eventually reclaim a margin of happiness. That her family would regain their husband and father.

"One more to go," Anne said, gritting her teeth. She typed "Edward Tallow" in the search field.

She was a little surprised to find no recent message from Eddie, only the e-mail that her husband had printed and left for her on the bed. Anne wrote a terse reply:

> *Eddie –*
> *Please do not contact me again. I am back*
> *with my husband and do not want to see you.*
> *Sincerely,*
> *Anne.*

One click, and it was done.

Anne sat back, bleary-eyed. The toxic men in her previous life were gone, wiped clean like a dirty dinner plate, and she had done it herself. Of course, she'd not counted on discovering an e-mail from a jilted wife, but she had needed to see it, needed to experience a fraction of the pain she had caused. She struggled to bear the guilt of actions that felt disconnected from her, as if committed by someone else. But the evidence was there, and the reality, Anne figured, was hers to do with what she could.

Perhaps her words could assuage the wife's hurt. Perhaps she could do the same for Frederick, should she ever see him again—or for the first time.

Frederick.

The name resonated in her mind, his name once more opening a well of warmth. Anne wondered if this was something close to love, a shadow of what she might once have felt.

Even if she missed the chance to fix her own marriage, she could at least tell her husband that it was over with these men. That she was trying to make amends with those she had hurt—though the list seemed to expand by the minute.

With a sigh, Anne shut down the computer and dragged her feet up the stairs. It was close to nine o'clock and her bedroom was dark as slate. She inched carefully to the bed and slipped beneath the covers, the towel at her waist bunching up against the mattress. She didn't bother to throw on a nightgown or even a pair of underwear. Instead, she pulled the comforter to her chin, burrowed her face and wet hair against a mass of pillows, and hoped to awaken in a different house. In a different body. And in a happier life.

Chapter Fourteen

AT FIRST, Anne didn't recognize the sound. In her dreams, she was falling in an elevator, with the screech of break cords tearing her eardrums. Then, as she groggily opened her eyes, she realized it was the telephone clamoring beneath her husband's divorce papers, next to the digital clock that read 3:32 a.m.

Anne reached for the phone, missed, and knocked against the folder. The papers dashed to the floor in a violent cascade. She hissed and pawed the nightstand until her fingers made successful contact. She dragged the receiver to her ear. "Yes? Hello?"

"What the hell do you mean that it's over?" snarled a deep and unfamiliar baritone.

"What?" Anne sat up in bed, tried to rub the sleep from her eyes. Was she still dreaming?

"What do you mean that it's over?" demanded the

voice. "How can you do this to me? After everything we've been through together?"

Anne pulled the phone back, examined the connection, and returned it to her ear. "Listen, I don't know who you are, but I—"

"Who I *am*?" The man sounded like he was choking something back—a laugh, perhaps? A scream? "Anne, I'm not up for one of your stranger games. Just tell me why you broke up with me via e-mail. Tell me *that*."

"Stranger games?" Anne echoed, having some difficulty following his thoughts. "Sorry, *who* is this?"

"Are you kidding? It's Luke, goddamn it! *Luke*."

"Luke!" A chill swept through her. "Why are you calling me? What about your wife? What about..." She searched her shoddy memory. "Amanda?"

"*Don't*," he warned. "We never speak their names. That's our deal. It's only ever *us*."

"What deal? You mean who we're married to?" She had the urge to drop the phone in its cradle, but morbid curiosity latched her ear to the receiver. A part of her had to know, had to understand.

"What's wrong with you?" he said to her now. "You're acting so strange. Did something happen in New York? Did you and Cindy have a falling out?"

"Cindy? She wasn't with me in New York."

"What are you talking about?" Confusion mixed into his tenor. "Weren't you up there for some girl's weekend or something?"

Anne hesitated. "Um...no."

Another pause. "Then why were you there?"

A fair question, but she didn't owe him an answer. "Listen, Luke. I'm sorry that you're hurt. But we can't see each other anymore. We're married. It's wrong."

"That never stopped us before."

Anne winced, recognizing the hurt in his voice. "Luke--"

"Don't forget," he snapped, his expression hardening. "*You* pursued *me*. Nothing was stopping you then."

"I don't remember," she said, hoping he'd understand. "Listen, I'm sorry for all of this. I really am. But we have to move on and forget this ever happened."

"Forget?" He was near shouting now, and Anne cringed. "Just like that? Forget each other? Like it was nothing? Like it was all some fantasy? Are you kidding? We *love* each other, Anne!"

"We don't love each other," she said, and then amended, "Or at least, I don't. Not any more."

His breath turned labored. "So you were using me. You used me to get your lousy tits done, is that it? Do you know what I went through to get Jason to do the surgery? I had to do three cleft palates!"

Her world spun as she aligned the details. "So, you're a doctor?" she said. "You had someone put these implants in me?"

"What's going on with you?" Luke roared. "What

the hell happened in New York? What aren't you telling me?"

Cringing at his savage tone, she blurted, "I've got to go," and dropped the phone in its cradle.

It rang a few seconds later. She lifted it up long enough to hear, "Don't you *dare* hang up on me..." before dropping it again. Another ring, another diatribe sounding in the earpiece, and she cut him off again. Two more rings, two more clicks, and then the house was quiet.

Anne slumped back into bed, more awake now than she ever remembered being. *So that was Luke,* she thought. *I wonder what I did to deserve him?*

Anne couldn't sleep. Luke's voice haunted her, triggering new—or old—memories that surged through her mind like a crashing surf. Anne saw herself in a series of thick leather armchairs. Sipping dry martinis in first-class cabins and pretending not to know the man beside her in the Prada business suit. They'd laugh and she would feign rejecting his advances until he seduced her with lavish compliments and clever rhetoric. Their games always ended the same: tumbling together across a wide clean bed, and afterwards ordering drinks and dessert from room service.

Did I love him? Anne wondered again, chasing the

memories down the dark alley of her mind. She scraped through threads of memory. Saw herself spread on smooth, starchy sheets. Luke's arm tucked under her face. Being satiated by the touch and taste of him. But the moment he left to shower or attend a medical conference, loneliness and regret swiftly consumed her.

Not love, Anne thought. *But something else...a need? Why did I need him? What was I missing in my life?*

But no answers came. As the hours ticked by and she tried in vain to sleep, all she could feel was relief at never seeing him again.

By morning, Anne had made another decision. Despite her sister's explicit order, she was going to see her. *Today.*

In the bathroom, she unscrewed the various containers of shimmering powder, rouge, and foundation Jack Post gifted her. But as she blended powders into her skin, her scars rang anew with pain. They fairly throbbed beneath the brush, so much so that Anne filled the basin and dabbed warm water to her face, then soaked her forehead and cheeks with a soft towel. The pain faded into a manageable ache.

She glimpsed her reflection with her blotchy skin, stringy hair, pink scars, and mangled eyebrows. She hoped her sister didn't run away screaming.

After dressing, she entered the study and reviewed her sister's home address in the investigator's report.

She found an online website for driving directions. After typing the streets and zip codes into the computer, she discovered Elena lived exactly 43.1 miles away.

Anne considered her options. She could try renting a car—she still had Jack's $10,000 folded in a large clump in her wallet—but she itched to try something from her old life.

"I'll drive my own car," she announced. "I'm sure I have one." She smiled, finding more and more comfort in hearing her own voice, even if hers were the only ears to hear it.

Anne opened the door to the two-car garage and found two hulking shapes sitting in the near-darkness. She trailed her left hand just inside the doorframe and flicked a switch. Bright incandescent light filled the darkness, spotlighting a black Mercedes sedan and a silver Lexus SUV. Anne tried to discern which was hers and which was her husband's. The Lexus was probably hers, since the sedan was better suited for Frederick's business. But the Mercedes—with its glossy exterior and tinted windows—called out to be driven.

But where do I find the keys?

Like an after-burn image, a flash flared to life in Anne's mind. She returned to the kitchen and yanked open the drawer to the center island. Between a box of plastic sandwich bags and aluminum foil were two sets of keys, each discernible by their car model decal.

"Oh my god! I did it!" Anne cried, the echo of her

words filling the house. She snatched up the keys and held them in her hand, staring down at the winking metal. *I remembered something. I actually remembered something!*

An enormous smile spread across her face. Her first time smiling without somebody prompting her. Flushed with excitement, she wondered what other memories might peel through her mind, if she was healing, truly healing, with each passing day. *First, I remember the car keys. Next, my childhood!*

Anne collected her purse, snatched the printed map to her sister's house, and beeped open the car's locks. She marveled at the camel-colored interior, black leather and chrome accents, and ran her hand along a leather steering wheel, subtle as calfskin.

She turned the ignition, pressed a button overhead, and flinched as the garage door trundled open against the bright morning light.

"All right!" Anne exclaimed, hopping up and down in her seat. "All right! All right!"

That was when the eagerness died and she sat in the driver's seat, seized with worry. It hadn't occurred to her before that she might not remember how to drive.

Don't think about it, she ordered herself. *Just do something. Maybe it's like cooking.*

Anne closed her eyes, lifted her hand, and let it drop. It adjusted its descent to land on a long rod. *A gearshift,* her mind supplied. She shifted into gear, tapped lightly on the pedal, and eased out of the driveway. With a single, deft movement, she clicked it into drive.

"Okay," Anne said with a grateful breath of relief. "Here we go."

She shut the garage door and carefully navigated through her quiet neighborhood. Most of the houses were like hers, restored Victorians, but a few new construction sites appeared as the surrounding forest thinned and other roads bisected the neighborhood.

Anne drove like an arthritic old woman, dipping well below the speed limit to reconfirm every turn and resetting the odometer to gauge every mile marker. Two vehicles honked at her sharply, and both times, Anne jumped and almost dropped the map. She recovered with a quickened pulse and avoided the glares of the other drivers. She pushed on, intent on making it to her sister's without getting lost or arrested.

When she arrived at her sister's house—exactly 43.5 miles later, after just one wrong turn—she glowed with the triumph of winning an award. The sedan hummed as she sat in the driver's seat. The small brick colonial had blue shutters and window boxes stuffed with bright yellow flowers, presumably fake since they sprouted through the snow. A machine chimed in the distance, a high-pitched alarm that rang three times, replaced with a deep-throated growl. Anne glanced at the three green garbage cans perched on the sidewalk.

She remembered the sound—a garbage truck.

Her mind was still healing!

Proud of herself, Anne checked her reflection in the pull-down mirror. The scars were definitely apparent, so her sister was in for a shock. *Oh well. No changing that.* She turned off the engine and opened the door.

Her boots clicked against the road's black asphalt. Shards of ice and rock salt peppered the sidewalk and short walkway. No windows flanked Elena's door, so there must be an unseen peephole. Anne rang the bell and took a step back.

A few pleasant notes rang through the house, and then silence. Anne crossed her arms and waited, her breath pluming like smoke. After about thirty seconds, she rang the bell again.

Nothing.

Unwilling to give up so easily, Anne lifted her fist and knocked three times. Then again, harder. "Elena?" she called. She leaned towards the door and cupped her gloved hands around her mouth. The cold leather scraped her cheeks as she yelled, "Elena! It's me! Please open the door!"

"Hey! Are you okay?"

Anne almost slipped as she turned to meet the voice. A lithe man with a flop of brown hair, ruddy cheeks, broad sunglasses, and a gray tracksuit stared at her from the sidewalk. He removed a pair of white earbuds, lifted his sunglasses, and said, "Do you need something?"

Anne stepped a few paces from the door. "I do, actually. Do you live in this neighborhood? I'm trying to find my sister. Her name's Elena Lewiston."

For a moment, the man stared at her as if Anne had said something infinitely confusing. His eyes narrowed, then grew so wide that Anne could see the hazel rims of his irises. Slack jawed, he said, "Anne? Is that you?"

She peered at his face, but didn't recognize him. "Yes, I'm Anne. Sorry, do I know you?"

"Are you serious?" The man stepped closer and wiped his nose with the back of his hand. She could hear the roar of music emanating from the earbuds dangling at his waist. The man pressed a button and the surrounding space quieted, save for their breaths, and the sound of metal scraping plastic as trash poured in the distance.

"I'm trying to find my sister," Anne said. Then, realizing that she might have the wrong house entirely, she consulted her map again. "54 Cherryhill Drive," she read aloud, and glanced at the numbers at the door. They matched. "No, this has to be the right house. Do you know a woman named Elena? Elena Lewiston?"

"Anne," the man said, his voice low and cautious, "don't you recognize me?"

Anne studied his thin face and dark, sweat-peaked hair, but remembered nothing. Not even an inkling. She shook her head.

He pointed to himself, then back at her, as if signing to a chimpanzee. "I'm Andrew. Your brother-in-law."

It took a second for his words to register. Breathless, Anne said, "Oh my god! You're Elena's husband?"

His eyes widened. "Holy shit."

The details of the investigation report were on Anne's lips, but she caught herself. If she said he looked unrecognizable from his driver's license, he'd probably think her a crazy stalker.

Anne shuffled down the steps to meet him in the middle of the brick pathway. She thrust out a hand. "It's a pleasure to meet you! I mean, I know we've met before, but I, uh..." Her words stammered into an awkward silence.

Andrew ignored her hand. His mouth dropped open. "Oh, Anne. What did you do to yourself?"

"What *I* did?" she returned, shocked at his choice of words. "I didn't do anything. I was in a car accident. I mean, a car hit *me*. In New York." When he said nothing, Anne added, "It wasn't my fault."

His face scrunched. "What is this? You seriously don't recognize me? You don't remember me at all?"

"Sorry, no." In that moment, Anne envisioned a row of trick mirrors, where her reflection echoed into infinity. She pictured having this conversation—or variations like it—for the rest of her life. Repeating her flimsy explanation and enduring her audience's concern, doubt, or disbelief. She mentally cursed herself for leaving the medical paperwork at home, since it appeared the people in her life didn't believe her. "I lost my memory," she told Andrew, hoping he believed her. "My doctors said it may be permanent, but I'm really trying to remember things."

Doubt shadowed Andrew's face. "It's all for real? This amnesia thing?"

"Yes, it's real." Anne frowned. Why didn't he believe her?

"You seem so sincere." He reached out to her, but Anne withdrew a step. His voice softened as if to a shying horse. "It's okay. I'm not going to hurt you."

"No, I know," Anne said, not understanding her reaction. "I just, um...do you know where my sister is?"

Andrew sighed. "She doesn't want to speak to you. I thought she was clear on that."

"But does she understand about my memory? Did she tell you?"

"She told me. And no, I don't think she understands. But I don't think it'll matter."

"Why not?" she said, tears pricking the back of her eyes. She rubbed her nose furiously, telling herself she would not cry in front of him.

Andrew sighed again. "Because of everything that you've done. Everything that you are."

"I'm her twin sister!"

"That may be," he said carefully, "but Elena doesn't forget." With a rueful smile, he added, "She's like an Italian that way."

"I don't know what that means," Anne snapped, her voice swelling with anger and hurt. "She won't even see me? She's my twin sister! We have to love each other. It's..." She tore her mind for the words, and lamely finished, "It's a rule. A rule of biology."

Andrew closed the distance between them to study her face. In the silence, Anne breathed in the muskiness of his sweat. Glimpsed the dark patches under his arms, across his stomach, and V-ed at his groin. "Look at me," he said, his eyes locking onto hers as if trying to catch her in a lie. "You really remember nothing? Truly?"

Something dark slid across Anne's mind. She flashed to a different moment in time. Thick hands upon her. Sour breath on her face. Her mouth filled with a familiar taste as her hands traversed a man's heaving back. And then—

She stopped herself, knowing this memory was not of the man standing before her now, but someone else. She pushed the image from her mind and said thickly, "No. I don't remember anything."

"Unbelievable." Andrew's eyes grew sad, as if recognizing the depth of her loss.

Anne's throat tightened. "Please, just tell me where my sister is. I have to see her. She doesn't have to know that you told me."

Andrew cupped one of her small shoulders in a heavy, icy hand. "I guess you'd find out eventually. She's at the mall with her class."

"Her class?"

"A Mommy & Me thing. You know. A big group of women who get together once a week with their kids."

"Oh. Okay." Anne stepped out of his grip. "And, uh...where is this mall, exactly?"

Chapter Fifteen

TWENTY MINUTES LATER, Anne still couldn't shake the feeling Andrew had left upon her, as indelible as any of her scars. What was wrong with her? Why had his presence shaken her so?

She tried to steady her breath. Her insides twisted with fear and shame.

What was their relationship before the accident? Had they been on friendly terms? Did she even like her sister's husband, or was theirs a relationship built out of forced affinity?

Anne tried to reclaim her earlier memory, but it had faded like a mist.

She followed the directions Andrew had scrawled on a sheet of paper, once again enduring the disgruntled honks of passing vehicles. Despite making several U-turns in half a dozen parking lots, Anne found the

Cincinnati Mall and snagged a parking space several rows into the back.

An enormous snowplow crawled through the lot, its giant red shovel pushing drifts of snow effortlessly aside. Anne followed a group that meandered around it, careful not to slip on the twinkling ice as they bottlenecked through a pair of double glass doors.

A blast of hot air hit her face as she skirted past the makeup, perfume, and bath stalls. Shoppers pushed past each other, clutching thick coats and enormous bags in their arms.

Anne ducked outside a Claire's jewelry store and watched the shoppers for several minutes, trying to gauge her bearings. She didn't know how to find her sister. She might have already passed Elena, or his sister could have left.

"Bitch, I *know* you didn't just say that to her!" cried a teenage girl as she walked past Anne with a tight group of friends.

"She was a skank," drawled a nearby tall blonde, opening a compact to check for lipstick stains. "She deserved what she got, flirting with my boyfriend like that."

"Girl, you made her cry!" another girl piped in, smirking with glee. "I saw it!"

"Bitch had it comin'," quipped the blonde. "I saw how she was eyein' him like he was some prize. I just put her in her place."

Anne listened to their derisive banter and blinked

against a wave of dizziness. She saw herself in a similar mall—the same one?—outside a jewelry store with friends. Their hair was big, teased from their scalps in a fray. She saw her youthful face reflected in a small purple compact with bright red lipstick smeared on her lips, and oversize gold bangles on her ears.

"She's a slut," Anne heard herself saying. "She deserved what she got."

"You sure told her!" said her friend admiringly. "God, did you see her face? I thought she was going to cry."

"She was crying," added someone else. "I saw her in the cafeteria. You really showed her, Anne!"

"I can't believe you dumped Coke on her head!" cried another. "You soaked her good. You're so lucky there wasn't a teacher around. Did you plan it like that? You're amazing!"

"Yeah," Anne said, grinning at them. "Who does she think she is? She thinks she's better than the rest of us."

"She wishes. She's just jealous."

"Who wouldn't be?" Anne returned. "Everyone wants to be us..."

And then it was gone, the memory—or whatever it was—darkening to silence.

Anne rubbed her eyes. She tried to see past this memory, to get more details, but the images remained fixed and repetitive, like a broken record. Had she really been the type who bullied others? The kind who made her classmates cry? What sort of student had her sister been?

Perfect, answered a voice in her mind. *Elena was always the perfect one.*

Anne itched to move, to put pavement between herself and a feeling she could not shake. She fell in with a group of women debating the quality of their Pashmina scarves and followed them to a crowded food court. The greasy smells of burgers, fries, and tacos weighed on the air, shifting Anne's darkness into ravenous hunger.

Anne slipped a twenty-dollar bill from her purse and purchased her first item in her new life. A slice of pepperoni pizza with mozzarella so stringy she had to catch it with her teeth.

With no available table, Anne stood at a column and consumed her slice slowly, enjoying her covert people-watching. Two nearby women confided marital woes and various divorce options. A husband and wife reprimanded a young boy for spilling his banana smoothie across the table. A man appeared to be animatedly talking to himself until Anne realized he spoke into an earpiece.

She chewed the starchy crust thoughtfully and scanned the wide expanse of the food court, then lifted her eyes to the crowded walkway between the stores. Her eyes focused on a group of women when something clicked in her mind.

She saw her, Elena, in the distance, pushing a

stroller past a Footlocker. Anne knew her instantly, as if she had spotted herself in a mirror. The long black hair pulled into a slick ponytail. Her thin, graceful body. Her lack of makeup save for a singular swipe of burgundy lipstick.

Anne rushed from the food court, ignoring the faceless strangers she collided into during her race to catch her sister. But Elena was quite a distance from her, and Anne's body was slow to pick up speed. Still, she kept sight of her sister's ponytail, following her down a wing to an exit.

"Elena!" Anne cried as her sister and another woman pushed their way through a set of double doors. "Elena, wait!"

The doors swung shut. Anne jogged the remaining few steps and opened the doors into a group of shoppers. Muttering apologies, she threaded her way into the parking garage. Her heart leapt when she spotted her sister's distant ponytail.

"Elena!" she cried again, louder than before. "Elena! *Stop!*"

Her sister turned around, confusion writ on her face. The woman next to Elena met Anne's eyes and scowled.

Anne closed the distance between them with ragged breaths. She sidled up to her sister, surprised that they stood identical in height. But any similarity ended there. Elena's hair and eyes were the color of spilled ink. Her skin pale as ivory, with cheekbones sharp as irons above a projecting clavicle. Like Andrew, Elena looked much thinner than her DMV photo, as if someone had let the air out. The bold color on her thin lips—now pressed together in an angry line—was the only thing keeping Elena from disappearing entirely.

"What are you doing here?" Elena demanded. "I thought I told you—"

"I know, I know," Anne stammered. "But you've got to hear me out. I'm telling the truth—"

"Please!" Elena's eyes rolled skyward. "Like you've ever told the truth."

"I am!" Anne protested before adding in a rush, "I was in an accident, and I don't remember anything. If we can just talk for a minute, I think that I—"

"Oh my goodness!" interrupted the woman next to Elena. "What happened to your *face*?"

Anne lifted her hand to her most prominent scar. Perhaps she should have attempted to cover them with makeup. Or combed hair over the bald spot stamped above her ear.

"What did you do to yourself?" the woman asked.

"I didn't *do* anything," Anne replied, shocked for the second time that anyone would presume she had done this to herself. "A car hit me. Who are you, anyway?"

"Who am I?" the woman echoed, her brows shooting up in surprise.

"Just leave it alone, Lauren," Elena said as she

peered into Anne's face. "It looks like she got them taken care of, anyway. Did your doctor friend help you out again?"

Anne blinked at Elena in confusion. "Doctor friend? You mean Luke?"

Elena sneered, as if she had finally caught Anne in a verbal trap. "Hah! I knew this whole thing was a charade. You *do* remember."

"But I don't!" Anne's frustration edged dangerously close to tears. How could she explain she didn't remember? That she'd pieced her history together with an investigation report launched by a movie star's lawyer and a stack of e-mails left behind by her husband?

"Then you have a selective memory," said Elena. "How convenient."

Anne opened her mouth to respond when there came a tug on her arm. She glanced at a chubby fist attempting to dislodge the pizza crust in her hand. Anne gazed at the child strapped securely in the stroller. She couldn't have been more than a year old, yet was stunningly beautiful. Her hair and eyes mirrored Elena's, with features in perfect proportion. The child's lips shaped into a lovely Cupid's bow, with skin flawless as an enameled plate. *She fits the golden ratio better than Jack,* Anne thought.

The little girl blinked up at Anne and murmured, "Mommy?"

Anne lowered herself, careful not to break the

child's grip on her pizza's remnants, and said, "Charlotte?"

Elena jerked the stroller backwards, and the little girl's hand sprang from the crust. Tears filled the child's eyes. "See what you've done!" Elena said, furiously unbuckling the shoulder straps and yanking her daughter to her chest.

"Mommy!" the girl sobbed, her voice a pathetic warble. "*Mommy!*"

Anne's heart dropped. "I'm sorry. Here, does she want my crust? Is she hungry?" She offered the bread as one would an olive branch, but her sister turned away.

"Leave her alone! She doesn't need anything from you." Elena jogged the child in her arms, and the cries faded. "And neither do I."

"Elena, please," said Anne desperately. "I know you don't believe me, and I'm sorry for whatever I've done to make you so mad at me. But I spoke to Andrew, and he said—"

"You spoke to my *husband*?" Elena's voice cut into her, barbed with pain. In seconds, her dark eyes shone bright with unshed tears.

Why was *she* crying?

"How could you do this to me?" Elena's voice was almost a whisper. "How *could* you?"

"What are you talking about?" Anne tried to make sense of it, but couldn't wrap her mind around her sister's accusations, her seemingly bottomless hurt. "I just went to your house—"

"You went to my house!" Elena pinched her eyes closed, as if warding against Anne's words. When she opened them, whatever tears had been close to spilling had disappeared. "What's *wrong* with you? Do I have to move? Take out a restraining order? Get out of my life!"

"Please," Anne begged. "Please, Elena. I don't know what this is. If you can just listen to me. If we can just talk—"

"I think you've done enough talking," Lauren cut in. "Just leave her alone." She pointedly took Elena's elbow and guided her away, presumably towards her car. Then Lauren threw their shopping bags and purses into the stroller and thrust it around.

Anne snapped out of her stupor. "Elena! *Please*."

"You know what I think?" Lauren interjected. She stalked up to Anne and stabbed a manicured finger up at her. "I think once a bully, always a bully. You think you can manipulate people to do whatever you want, but I'm on to you. Always have been."

"I don't even know you," Anne said, and made a move to pass her.

Lauren shoved the stroller in front of her. "Well, I know *you*. You used to be the only person who mattered in my life, because you were the only one would could ever make me truly miserable."

Anne stared at the woman for the first time.

Lauren barely cleared Anne's throat. She had a mousy face and chestnut hair infused with brassy highlights. Something in her glinting eyes tugged at Anne's memory. "Who are you?"

Lauren's lips curled into a humorless grin. "Who am *I*? I'm the girl you bullied for four years in high school. So *fuck* you!"

Lauren yanked the stroller around and marched after Elena.

Anne's heart sank past her ribs.

She had lost her sister all over again.

Chapter Sixteen

IT TOOK Anne almost two hours to find her way home, but she would be damned if she was going to call anyone for help. As she endured half a dozen enraged honks while U-turning or pulling across lanes, Anne realized her sister may never speak to her again. Frederick would probably stay oversees until she'd packed her bags and left their house altogether. After thirty minutes, she pulled into a gas station and sobbed into her hands. Yet by the time she rolled into her driveway, her tears were dry, and she was angry.

Why doesn't anyone believe me? she thought, stabbing at the garage door opener. She parked and turned off the car, then sat until the overhead lights turned off and she was alone in the near-darkness.

What had she done that was so wrong? Was it so

terrible, so unforgivable, that she was never to be given a second chance?

Okay, she thought. *Yes. I did cheat on my husband. That much is clear. But what drove me to that?*

Perhaps Frederick was cruel. Perhaps he beat her or drank himself into a manic stupor. Maybe he neglected her and only returned home once every six months. Maybe they'd never had passion between them, but an asexual bond. Perhaps he had cheated first or cheated too, and her actions had been out of revenge.

Yet none of these scenarios rang true. Anne sensed she once loved Frederick, and he loved her. That her actions had cut him to the quick, and now he wanted nothing to do with her.

With a sigh, Anne got out of the car and let herself into the house. She thought, *It really is over for me. I'm just going to take Jack's money and start a new life. It's clear no one wants me here. Perhaps it's better if I never remember.*

A voice called her name as a hand fell on her shoulder. Anne jumped and let out a scream. She snatched a stainless steel spatula and brandished it like a sword. "Who are you?" Anne demanded, waving the makeshift weapon.

The unfamiliar woman put her hands up and withdrew several steps. "Sorry! Sorry! I didn't mean to scare you. It's me, Anne. Nicole. Nicole Burns. I'm one of your housekeepers."

Anne marked the sincerity in the woman's face and connected her voice to the high warble she had twice spoken to on Jack's house phone. Anne dropped the spatula on the kitchen island and put her hand to her chest. "Jesus Christ. I think I almost had a heart attack."

"Me too," said Nicole, laughing awkwardly. "God. I'm really sorry. I know you lost your memory. I don't know what I was thinking, just coming out like that. I probably should have left a sign or something on the door."

"It's okay," said Anne, then—after letting Nicole's words sink in—said, "Wait. You believe me?"

"Believe what?"

"That I lost my memory?"

Nicole blinked at her. "Why wouldn't I?"

"Why wouldn't you?" Anne released the spatula with a trembling hand. "No one else believes me. My sister doesn't. I don't think my husband does either." She lifted her eyes to Nicole, who stared at her as if she was an animal that could sprint from the room any second. "You really believe me?"

"Sure. I mean, *look* at you." Nicole stopped, her face twitching with regret. "God! Sorry! Sorry. That's awful. I mean, it just looks like you've been through something terrible."

"But you believe me," Anne said again, unable to comprehend that someone from her past took her at her word.

"Sure. I mean, stranger things have happened. *Way* stranger."

"But what did I do to you?"

Nicole frowned. "What do you mean?"

Anne waved her hands, wanting to get to the end of this as soon as possible. She knew it'd be painful, and that there'd probably be a few tears—all on her end. But she didn't want to lull in pleasantries when this woman likely harbored malice. "What did I do to hurt you?" Anne clarified. "You know, to piss you off? I assume you hate me. Or at least, aren't too happy to see me."

Nicole's eyes widened. "Why would I hate you?"

"Everyone here hates me," Anne said in a rush. "Why would you be any different? So why don't I just apologize for whatever I did to piss you off? I may not remember what I did, or why, but then you might at least feel better."

Nicole laughed a full, belly-hugging, tear-inducing laugh. The sound of it filled the kitchen, vibrated through the house.

Anne stared at her in shock. "Why are you laughing?"

Nicole wiped her eyes, her guffaw fading into a chuckle. "Oh my god. I see you kept your sense of humor. You're hilarious."

"Hilarious? How am I hilarious?"

"Well, for one, you've never pissed me off. I mean, maybe you pissed off my mom? But then anyone can piss her off, even a priest. So your doing so isn't any sort of accomplishment."

Anne remembered Miranda Burns at the front door, hesitating to let her in the house. The dark look that had passed over her face. "What'd I do to her?"

"You want the truth?"

Anne tensed. Uncovering truth was like pressing her hand to a burning stove. It hurt anytime she got close. "Um...okay."

Nicole counted on her fingers. "She never liked how you left Mr. Strafford to go out at all hours. Or how you'd flake on appointments or dinners out. Or your outfits. Or what you talked about. Or your friends. Or that you came back."

"Came back from where?" Anne asked. "New York?"

"Yeah. When we found out where you went and that you hadn't come back, we figured you and Fred— Mr. Strafford—had officially split up. Mom was really disappointed when I told her I'd talked to you, that you'd be coming home. She never thought you were good enough for him."

"Great," said Anne, aching as if someone had repeatedly punched her in the stomach. "Does she like *anything* about me?"

Nicole nodded emphatically. "Oh yeah. Your sister, and her husband. Oh! And your niece. She loves them."

"Right. Of course." *They must be perfect to every-*

one, Anne thought. *I'm the one who's the failure. The one everyone despises and wants out of their lives. The one no one wants to come home.*

Nicole must have seen something in Anne's face, because she drew close and patted her arm. "I'm sorry. I didn't mean to upset you. You know how Mom can be—well, I guess you don't. Anyway, she pisses me off too. She's got the same amount of criticism about me as she does you, believe me."

"Really?" Anne said hopefully.

"Sure. Truth is that I always liked you, even if you drove Mom crazy. I think you're a riot."

"A riot?"

"Yeah." She smiled brightly. "I mean, you were always nice to me."

"I was?" Anne said, while thinking, *I was nice to someone?*

"Sure." Nicole pointed at a white leather purse with a silver buckle that was suspended on the doorknob to the basement. "You see that Valentino? You gave that to me."

Anne stared at her blankly. "What's a Valentino? A type of purse?"

"Oh my god! You can't be serious!" Nicole let out another laugh, but recovered quickly. "You're all about designer bags and shoes and stuff. Or at least you were. That purse alone probably cost a grand."

"A thousand dollars?" Anne sucked in her breath. She'd spent that much on a purse?

"I know, right?" Nicole said with an admiring shake of her head. "Anyway, when my old purse broke, and you saw me trying to re-sew the straps for like the eighth time, you gave me yours. You just said, 'Here, Nicole. Take this. And I won't take no for an answer.' I knew you didn't use it anymore, but it was still really nice that you gave it to me." She sighed as she gazed longingly at the purse. "It's the most precious thing I own. I never, *ever* let it touch the floor. I even bought one of those purse holders to keep it off the chairs at restaurants, because who knows what they've got on them, right?"

Anne gazed at the purse, flooding with memory. The white textured leather soft under her fingertips. The zippered top enclosure sliding back and forth smoothly. The faint tanning smell of the inner lining.

Anne returned her gaze to Nicole and tried to measure the sincerity of her words. She seemed genuine enough. Her bright, expectant eyes betrayed no malevolence. "So, you like me?" Anne said at last. "You really do?"

"Sure," Nicole said. "Does that make you feel better?"

"You have no idea."

As they smiled at each other, Anne's heart surged. Here was a kind, spirited person from her past. Someone who actually *liked* her.

"So, what are you doing here?" Anne asked.

"Me?" Nicole pointed to herself. "I'm here to set up the Christmas party. Didn't Mom tell you?"

"She mentioned something like that. Is it going to take a long time?"

"I only got here a minute before you. So it depends. How much did Mom set up?"

"Set up?" Anne glanced about and a shadow of a frown passed over her face. "For the party?"

"Yeah. Did she put up any lights or order the tree or anything?"

Anne shook her head. "No. I don't think so. I've not seen any ornaments or anything."

"Huh." Nicole put her hands on her hips, snapped her head back and forth as she shot her focus throughout the house. "Well, what'd she do? Didn't you two go over the plan?"

"No," Anne said as she mentally reviewed her exchange with the other housekeeper. "I mean, Mrs. Burns told me that whenever I got home, she was supposed to be dismissed for the day."

"She *what*?" Nicole shook her head and laughed.

"What? Did I do something wrong?"

"Sneaky bitch," Nicole said under her breath. "God, you gotta admire that."

"Admire what? What do you mean?"

"She was supposed to start on the Christmas decorations and I was supposed to finish up. It's the same every year, since Mom has the talent. It's part of what you pay her to do. When you get here, you're supposed to go over any plans for the house, not dismiss her."

Heat rose in Anne's cheeks. "I didn't know that."

"Well, you wouldn't, would you?" Nicole shook her head, still grinning. "No wonder she had time for that movie yesterday."

Anne wanted to move on. "So what do we do?"

"Well, are you up to helping me decorate your house?"

"I guess," Anne said. "What's this party for, anyway?"

"It's for Mr. Strafford's department at the firm. They have a rotating Christmas party, and you're the next in line. Actually," Nicole said, her voice perking with excitement, "it's my first time helping with the party. And from what Mom says, it's a really big deal. Schmoozing with some big guns, I guess."

"Oh," Anne said. "I see."

Her grin broadened. "So then, are you up for decorating?"

Anne warmed to Nicole's enthusiasm. Her energy was almost contagious. "Sure. Sounds like fun."

"Great. I'll go in the garage and grab the cans from the storage closet." Nicole paused at the door. "Oh. And Mom never goes by Mrs. Burns. It's Miranda. Always has been, at least to you guys."

"Right." Anne shook her head and thought, almost admiringly, *Sneaky bitch.*

The top of the ten-foot Douglas fir nearly brushed the ceiling and filled the family room with the crisp scent of pine. Nicole smoothed out a red and gold checkered tree skirt while Anne opened the first canister of ornaments and arranged the baubles into sections. Handblown glass. Glitter and crystals. Polished enamel. She took her time setting the pieces into the cool, scented branches of the fir.

"You're *so* not like my Mom," Nicole said.

"Why's that?" Anne tilted her head, trying to determine why the tree looked off balance.

"It's gonna take you a decade to finish this tree."

"It will not." Anne moved to replace an enormous egg ornament with one cast in gold and silver, in the shape of a jolly Santa Claus. *There,* she thought happily. *Now it's even.*

Nicole stood up and admired their work. "Wow. You're a natural!"

"I probably do this every year," said Anne as she spread a cluster of golden orbs more evenly throughout the tree.

"Actually," Nicole said, "you don't."

Anne glanced at her. "I don't?"

"Nah. Actually, I don't think I've ever seen you decorate the tree. You were always out with Cindy or getting a pedicure or something. As big a grouch as she can be, that's part of Mom's appeal with clients.

They're out for a few hours buying presents or picking up some eggnog and appetizers, and *boom!*—everything's done when they get home."

"Sounds nice," said Anne, even though she wanted to decorate it herself. She enjoyed clasping each individual ornament in her hand, wondering when she'd bought them. Did they hold any special meaning? Had they passed down generations? Was she cradling her family's history?

Anne unwrapped a Swarovski crystal star from the delicate folds of white tissue paper. She held it up, taking a moment to admire how its facets exquisitely caught the light, and gently suspended it near the top of the tree.

"Careful," Nicole warned. "You told me last year that one's expensive."

Apparently everything in this house is, Anne thought, suppressing the urge to roll her eyes. Of course, if she shattered the star on the hardwood, it was hers, wasn't it? It was sort of liberating, thinking that she could, if so inclined, punch a hole in the wall, overturn mahogany tables, or fling china into the backyard.

But her smile faded as she realized nothing actually *was* hers.

At least not after the divorce.

Anne dislodged the lid of the second canister and gasped at its fill of plastic ornaments. Garish gnomes.

Neon red elves and Santa Clauses. Bright Disney and Looney Tunes figurines.

"What's this?" Anne held up an ornament of two skunks staring lustily at each other, their tails entwined into the curved angle of a heart.

Nicole, who was busy positioning several strands of white lights throughout the middle of the tree, poked her head out. "Shoot. I forgot. You don't use those. I was supposed to leave them in storage."

"They're kind of cute." Anne picked up another figurine, this one a small, bald yellow bird with enormous, innocent eyes. She had a flash of holding this ornament before, but sensed it was years ago. The tree then had been considerably smaller, but she remembered being happy suspending this bird near the top of that tree.

"I guess they're sort of cute," Nicole allowed, "but you don't use them."

"Why not?"

Nicole shrugged and returned to the lights. "I don't know. Mom said they used to be the only thing you'd put on the tree, but then you changed it up a few years ago. I don't know why."

"But they belong to us? Or are they Frederick's?"

Nicole paused her work. "No, I think they're both yours. I think you used those your first year here. But after that, you bought the fancy ones."

"Huh." Anne stared into the depths of the metal can, then shifted her eyes to the tree with its perfect—

and altogether impersonal—arrangement. "You know something? I think I like these better."

"Seriously?" Nicole stared at the tree, at the glass and gold winking back at her. "But these are *gorgeous!*"

"Yeah. But I like these better." Anne gazed down into the can, at the dozens of painted eyes and plastic limbs, with wire hangers instead of smooth white ribbon. "They're not something you can order out of a catalog."

"No way. I bet you *could* order them out of a catalog."

Anne gripped a plastic ornament in each hand. A little boy in a red scarf on a sled, and a golden retriever with what appeared to be a femur in its mouth. "I think these are just better."

Nicole blinked at her. "Why?"

But how could Anne explain? How could Nicole possibly understand her draw to anything shedding light on her murky past? That Nicole was lucky to remember her family and their shared Christmases? The pomp and circumstance of every holiday?

Anne gave a vague shrug. "They have a history."

Nicole shook her head. "You're crazy. This tree is gorgeous. I'd order this tree for myself!"

"You can have it," said Anne briskly.

"I wish. If there was a way to shrink it down to pocket-size, you know I'd do it." Nicole snapped her fingers for emphasis. "Like *that!*"

Grinning, Anne replaced a Fabrergé egg with a

black and white Snoopy figurine. It dangled from the tree, not at all bright, but it seemed—if it was possible to be—*happy* there.

Nicole let out a groan. "Does this mean we have to redo them all?"

"We'll be quick," Anne assured. She plucked down the baubles cast in silver and gold and hundreds of appliquéd crystals, replacing them with bright yellow and green and red plastic ones that looked fifty years old, but made her smile.

Anne stepped back to admire their work. Nicole had reluctantly changed the white lights she'd roped around the tree to colorful ones. Ornaments weighed nearly every other bough, each selected for its size or color. Taken in its entirety, the tree was beautiful. It wouldn't display at a Macy's or Nordstrom's, but belonged in a cozy living room surrounded by family. Maybe it was like what she'd grown up with. Maybe Frederick too.

Anne folded her arms over her chest, breathing in the sharp scent of pine and residual smoke from the fireplace. Yes. It felt like home. And that made her happy.

"Well, I hope you're happy!" Nicole said, as if reading her mind. "Was it worth all the effort?"

"Entirely." Anne grinned at her. "Oh, don't be such a pain. You know you enjoyed it."

Nicole couldn't suppress a smile. "Okay, maybe I did. It was neat seeing all those old ornaments. I can't believe you have every character from Winnie the Pooh!"

"Me neither."

"In my family," said Nicole, "each of us is a Winnie the Pooh character."

"Really?" Anne's eyebrows perked with interest. "Which one are you?"

Nicole didn't hesitate. "I'm Piglet."

The miniature pink pig hung suspended in the middle of the tree. Anne smiled at the plucky little creature snuggled in the arms of a golden Pooh Bear. "Why are you Piglet?"

Nicole shrugged. "I guess because I worry. I stress a lot about things. But I'm sweet too. And people like me."

Anne considered this. "Who's your mother?"

Nicole barked a laugh. "Rabbit, of course! Hello, *housekeeper?* Rabbit's all about cleaning."

"That's clever," said Anne. Had she and Frederick ever considered which character mirrored their personalities?

"Maybe we should start on the stockings?" Nicole suggested.

Anne nodded. "Sounds good. What comes after that?"

Nicole squeezed her hand into her tight jean pocket and removed a scrap of notebook paper. "Okay, first the tree. Then the stockings...oh. We need to set up the dining room table and get the butler's pantry ready with the display dishes. And hang some decorations in the foyer, and of course go outside and take care of the front and back planters. And then there's the stairway. The guest and master bedrooms. And the mistletoe—"

"Sounds like a lot," said Anne, her mind swimming.

"That's why Mom usually splits the work with me." Nicole shoved the list back into her pocket. "God. I must have done something to really piss her off."

"Maybe both of us did," Anne said, then sighed. "Okay, then. What should we do first?"

Chapter Seventeen

ANNE FINGERED the two monogrammed stockings dangling from the fireplace's mantle. Her initials and Frederick's rendered in gold thread. Anne hadn't admitted to Nicole that they were just for show. *Frederick won't celebrate the holiday with me,* Anne thought. *Not after what I did.*

Nicole polished the dining table while Anne arranged crimson chargers, linen placemats, and porcelain china banded in gold. After sliding the napkins into sterling reindeer holders, they set long ivory tapers into the pewter candlestick holders and finished with a stunning centerpiece: a miniature Douglass fir smothered in holly and sparkling sprigs.

"Are we done?" Nicole asked, breathless.

"Not yet," said Anne.

They hung mistletoe in the entryway and unearthed the chrysanthemums and sunflowers from the porch planters. Into the black mulch they shoved in poinsettias as big as Anne's hand, framing them with holly and branches peppered with gold glitter. Next, they went to the butler's pantry and lined the pastry and appetizer china sets along the granite countertop for the party in two days' time.

As Nicole inspected their work, Anne realized she must entertain five couples she no longer remembered. Had any of them heard of her condition? Was she already a cautionary tale in the neighborhood, or even the city?

"Everything looks great," Nicole said with an approving nod.

They stood in the foyer. Anne admired the garland spun around the stairway. The gilded ornaments they had tied to the knobs of the banister. The chandelier suspending mistletoe and ivy. And the two Santa Clauses that flanked the front door, fake presents at their boots, ready to greet visitors.

"It looks great," Anne agreed.

Nicole started for the kitchen, and Anne trailed absently behind. She took in the smooth, gleaming surfaces of the furniture. The fresh fragrance of pine that infused the air. The glimpse of the fireplace with the dangling of his and her stockings. All that was missing was a pile of presents beneath the tree, and a roaring fire in the hearth.

For someone else, Anne thought. *Not for me.*

"You excited about the party?" Nicole asked, folding her arms over the kitchen island and openly regarding her.

Anne sighed and brushed a sweaty strand of hair from her eye. "Not at all. You think I should just cancel?"

"Cancel?" Nicole gasped. "Are you joking? After all the work we just put into decorating the place? You must be crazy!"

"Maybe I am." Anne sighed. "But really, think about it. What am I doing this for? I won't remember anyone. It'll be like greeting a group of strangers."

"But Frederick needs you," Nicole insisted. "It's a big deal!"

"So I'm told," said Anne. She closed her eyes and pressed her fingers against her eyelids, blowing hot air into her palms.

"You okay?"

"I don't know." Anne dropped her hands. "What am I going to do when you leave? I've no one else to talk to."

"There's Cindy," said Nicole, as if having this answer ready in her back pocket. "You guys are best friends."

"I don't even like her." The second the words were out, Anne realized it was true. Perhaps she had once liked her, as she had once liked Luke and Eddie, but those feelings were gone. She no longer had to be swayed by a complex history, only by her intuition.

And the fact was that these people weren't good for her. She knew this somewhere deep within herself, the closest thing to who she really was.

"So, what will you do?" Nicole asked, and looked at her—*really* looked at her. It was as if Anne was the only person in the world, and her next step could change the course of her life.

"I'm not sure," Anne said finally. "I mean...do you know about my husband? About our relationship?"

Nicole shifted uneasily. "You mean about your marriage?"

Anne nodded. "I just found out that it's over. He wants a divorce."

"Yowza." Nicole dropped her eyes to the floor, as if the slats of hardwood might offer some answers. "Are you happy about that?"

"Am I *happy?*" Anne echoed, flummoxed. What sort of question was that? How could she be happy about a divorce?

"Sorry, that came out wrong," Nicole amended quickly. "I just mean you weren't happy. In the marriage, I mean. Maybe you were in the beginning, before I started working with Mom, I don't know. But when I met you, you seemed like someone whose light had turned off. You just moped around. The only time you ever seemed to get excited was when you went out with Cindy, and sometimes you were gone for like two days at a time."

I was probably with Luke, Anne thought, unable to

imagine spending the night in Cindy's melodramatic presence.

A memory struck her like a lash. Anne saw herself in a hotel bed, a man beside her, a rake of dark hair and a smile beneath a trimmed goatee soft as fur. His body slanted across hers as they drew together in a kiss. His tongue in her mouth. His hand pressed against the small of her back. She remembered desiring his touch, desiring *him*, yet fighting an emptiness and desperate need to escape.

Maybe those nights made me happy, Anne thought. *But only briefly.*

She shook her head to clear it, then saw her husband's face. His icy blue eyes with their perpetual assuredness. His thin, angular face that cracked a smile sideways, always in the right corner of his mouth. His thick, formerly coffee-colored hair—now streaked with gray—that he had professionally cut every other Saturday or else it would run wild. She even remembered the smell of him: Corsican mint mixed with the woodsy amber of his cologne. And she knew what the underside of his chin felt like, and the prickly stubble above his smooth throat.

These moments came to Anne unexpectedly—triggered by a smell, a reflection, or touching something once familiar—and they were gone just as swiftly. Giant gaps between memories. Flashes of insight that she could never be certain were true. But she had to trust herself, for she had no one else. "No," said

Anne eventually. "I think I was happy. At least in the beginning. Sometimes, when I think of him, I have these feelings..." She paused, unsure if she could describe it. She *knew* it was real. She had the same dizzying, falling-from-a-swing feeling whenever she thought about Frederick—that inner warmth whenever she heard his name. Was that love? Or something close to it?

"But then there are other things," Anne continued. "Like how this house hardly has any pictures of us together. At least not after the wedding. I even found these portraits on the floor in the bedroom. He never even hung them up!"

Nicole glanced away from her, and Anne knew instantly that she was hiding something. "What?" said Anne. "Do you know something I don't?"

She probably knows lots more than you, said a voice within her, Anne's voice, shot through with rancor and guilt. It was the voice that said she wasn't good enough for this place, or her husband, or her sister. Or anyone.

"What is it?" Anne pressed.

Nicole wouldn't meet her eyes. "That's the thing. Those pictures *were* hung up."

"They were? Where?"

"In the master bedroom," Nicole said, almost painfully. "Mr. Strafford asked us to take them down. Mom was supposed to...uh." She hesitated, then sighed. "Well, put them away. I guess she forgot."

"Oh. I see." Anne's throat tightened. She had presumed the portraits were to be suspended from the walls, and so had finished the work herself. Should it have occurred to her that someone—her husband—had wanted them taken down? Stored forever, or perhaps even burned? "Well, that's his choice. I'm sure, with everything that's going on, it was hard for him to look at them."

"Probably," Nicole said.

Anne buried her face in her hands and thought, *This is too much. Maybe I should just leave. Take a flight somewhere and never look back.* She said through her cupped fingers, "I should just cancel this stupid party. It's too embarrassing. Plus, Frederick's not even here, and they're his friends."

"I'm sure he'll make it back for the party."

Anne dropped her hands. "You do?"

Nicole nodded. "Well, he has to, for obvious reasons. I'm actually shocked he's not back already."

A rising feeling built inside Anne—a mélange of excitement and nervousness in equal measure. She reached forward to grip the cold granite of the kitchen island. "So I may still see him," she said, mostly to herself.

"Well, of course you'll see him," Nicole said, clearly baffled. "The question is, do you *want* to?"

"Yes," Anne said. She wanted to see him and hear his voice. Perhaps standing in the same room would free the mental tourniquet closing off her past.

Keys scratched the lock, turning the deadbolt. The front doors opened and footfalls sounded on the hardwood.

Nicole blanched but forced a smile. "Hello, Mr. Strafford! Welcome home!"

Anne froze as the footsteps drew closer. She should turn around. Greet the man behind her. But her limbs wouldn't budge.

A low and familiar voice said, "Hello, Miss Burns. Happy holidays to you." The footsteps stopped just behind Anne. Then one word, spoken with icy formality: "*Anne.*"

Anne's feet stayed rooted to the floor. Nicole gave her an encouraging smile, but her eyes screamed, "What the hell are you doing? Say something! *Do* something!"

A burning pressure built behind Anne's eyes. What was she afraid of?

"Anne," repeated the voice.

Anne waited for him to touch her, hoping that would break the spell. But Frederick made no move. She'd have to free herself.

With an effort, she released the granite—now hot and clammy from her grasp—and turned around.

Anne faced her husband, home at last.

Chapter Eighteen

FOR A LONG MOMENT, they stared at each other. Frederick, in his pressed black suit and canary yellow tie, had a colossal presence in the kitchen. His salt-and-pepper hair, a streak of gray stubble, and cold blue eyes crackled with power.

He was a man whom others followed. And he was furious.

Anne had truly, deeply wronged him. His gaze challenged to vaporize her on the spot.

But Anne didn't shrink away. Instead, she surprised herself. She took a step toward him, then another. She looked him straight in the face and said, "Hello, Frederick."

He blinked first, but said nothing. Anne waited for him to betray some sort of emotion. He saw her roping scars. Her garish eyebrows. The purple scabs dotting the periphery of her face and neck. Yet he exhibited no surprise at her appearance. Even Jack Post, the illustrious actor, had openly gaped at her wounds. But her husband remained an unreadable stone.

Nicole broke the uneasy silence. "I should go. Mr. Strafford, everything is ready for your party. I've confirmed with the caterers like you asked. They should be here to set up at 9 a.m. the day after tomorrow."

"Thank you, Miss Burns," Frederick said, his eyes still on Anne's.

Nicole walked around her, lightly grazed Anne's shoulder, then padded out the front doors. That's when Anne noticed the two black leather suitcases by the stairwell. How long had her husband been out of the country?

"So," Anne said, when it was clear Frederick would say nothing further. "Did you just get home?"

Frederick blinked again, then narrowed his eyes as if he suspected something. "I'll be in the study. We'll need to discuss certain arrangements."

"Oh. Okay." Anne hated the weakness bleeding in her voice. She cleared her throat and said, more strongly, "We can discuss them now if you'd like."

"No," he said, his tone forceful. "I have calls to make." Frederick turned away and strode down the hall, disappearing behind a distantly slammed door.

Great, Anne thought. *What the hell do I do now?*

Anne trudged upstairs to the master bedroom, where the folder whose contents made her sick lay splashed across the bureau. She had not signed the divorce papers, and she sensed that was what her husband wanted to discuss. He would want her still-unfamiliar signature so his lawyers could legally sever their ties. Perhaps he even wanted to discuss her eviction. Was he calling her a cab even now, securing her a one-way ticket to nowhere?

Anne sighed, then resignedly pulled her suitcase onto the bed and began stuffing her socks and panties and fleece sweatpants inside. She cast a backward glance at her walk-in closet—hers alone, since Frederick had taken over the guest bedroom's—and took in the rows of posh satin hangers suspending Gucci jackets and pants, Prada blouses and skirts, with three rows of designer shoe boxes stacked by the season, from red-soled Christian Louboutins to Manolo Blahnik slingbacks.

A small chandelier hung just past the closet door, its twinkling lights warming the space. Anne stared up at all of her clothes, painstakingly pressed and arranged, with not a single item out of place. In a section clearly designated for winter, Anne grasped the tail of a fox fur scarf, its plush white fur streaked with shadow. She buried her face in the tufts and inhaled, catching fragrances of sandalwood and vanilla, and the faintest hint of smoke.

In that moment she saw herself supine upon a

bearskin rug, naked save for this scarf and a black satin thong. The heat of a fire crackled nearby as a muscled man slid on top of her, his starched shirt rasping her bare skin. She moaned at the touch of his practiced fingers.

While she told herself it was Frederick, inside she knew it was Luke.

Anne sighed, wishing she could destroy all reminders of that man, and the guilt stapled to every one of their shared memories. She remembered the heartbreaking e-mail from his wife. The pain that had practically emanated from the computer screen.

Did I even care? Anne wondered, furious with herself. *Did it ever matter that he was married? Did it matter that I was too?*

She ran her fingers through her wardrobe, ordering herself to summon more memories. She inhaled various fabrics—silks and cashmeres and smooth leather jackets—but the lot had been dry-cleaned and bore not a single trace of a personal scent.

Anne gazed up at the rows of shoeboxes, wondering if she had worn them all, and when, and to where. Standing on tiptoe, she brought down a box and slipped on a pair of silver stiletto pumps with a white Badgley Mischka label sewn into the heels. But they were so tall she had to balance on the two clothes bars on opposite sides of her, to prevent from toppling.

As her heels sank into the carpet, Anne realized

these were only shoes. She'd hoped for a sudden rush, something different from when putting on any other pair. She felt nothing that justified the over two-hundred dollar price tag, still affixed to the side of the box.

Teetering in the heels, Anne skimmed her gaze over the king-sized bed to the double-paned window where snow fell in furious silence. It would be a cold evening and night—a harsh one to face if Frederick kicked her to the curb. She was an iceberg in the middle of a vast ocean. One superficial tip in plain view, the rest submerged beneath freezing water. It would take something more substantive than bravery for her to dive in and uncover the rest.

Heaving a sigh, Anne turned her gaze to the black cherry jewelry case tucked just inside the closet's doorframe. One drawer held thick turquoise bangles and matching hoop earrings. Another had sapphire and diamond rings. The next, three sets of diamond tennis bracelets.

How many of these pieces had been gifts from her husband? How many others were secret tokens from other men? She imagined sending the latter pieces home to the wives of these philandering husbands, smiling as confusion etched on the men's faces.

Anne slipped a silver ring onto the fourth finger of her left hand. Its multi-faceted stone caught the entire color spectrum with a twinkling brilliance. She thought, distantly, that it was as if she had harnessed the rippling energy of the aurora borealis—a thought that instantly frustrated her. How could she recall this rare phenomenon when she couldn't remember most of her own life? How many more rings, shoes, and blouses must she touch to restore her mind? How long until she was something close to normal? Where her own family didn't look at with disgust and derision—and actually *trusted* her?

And did she even want to keep trying?

Anne sighed as the questions weighed on her mind. Her own family wasn't speaking to her, for reasons she only half-understood. What would happen if she discovered the true depth of their hurt, and what she had done? Could it possibly be all her fault, everything that had happened? Or did others play a role in the outcome as well?

The enormous ring hung on her finger. Anne wondered what had happened to her diamond wedding ring, the one she had flaunted in her wedding pictures. Had she lost it in New York? Had someone stolen it? What about everything else she had presumably brought with her on the trip? Her driver's license, cellular phone, a purse with—what?—tampons and lipsticks and a roll of Mentos? What had happened to those things? Had she left them all somewhere, or were they taken?

Anne tried to remember, worked hard at her mind, because she sensed something there, just beyond her reach.

But it was too far.

Her eyes dropped to the two suitcases yawning open on the bed, ready to accept anything she put in them. Anything at all.

But it's all from another life, Anne realized. And though it was a life she was trying to expose and, more to the point, understand, a part of her was also putting it behind her. Or trying to.

"I want nothing," she said, her voice quiet but firm. Perhaps Frederick could donate everything to charity, or give some to Nicole. Anne smiled, thinking of the girl inheriting every one of her favorite designers. Her little dance in too-big shoes as she twirled about in Anne's fur coats, silk dresses, and saltwater pearls.

Anne stepped out of the wobbly pumps and placed them back in their crinkly folds of tissue paper, then returned the box to its place on the second shelf. She pulled off the ring and pushed it into its velveteen slot in the case, closed the mirrored lid. Then she clicked off the light, the chandelier above her head fading to black, and shut the closet door.

Anne flung the rest of what Jack gave her into a suitcase. She knew these clothes. Their existence wasn't suspect. Anne couldn't say the same about the wardrobe of her previous life.

She zipped a suitcase closed. All that remained was to collect her few toiletries scattered across the bathroom vanity, but that could wait. She would have to see what Frederick wanted her to do.

But to do that, she would have to face him.

Anne's cheeks warmed. She pictured Frederick in the study, reclining in his favorite black leather club chair. A fire crackling in the hearth. The low strings of Beethoven or Bach playing through hidden speakers. Him reading for work or pleasure, with the door shut for privacy.

Anne had to tell him. And now, before she lost her nerve.

When she reached the study, Anne knocked three times on the heavy door. No answer was forthcoming. Deciding against a second attempt—she knew he was there, just ignoring her—she turned the knob and shouldered her way inside.

Frederick was exactly how she pictured him, except that the fireplace was cold, and it was, she somehow knew, Strauss playing on the stereo.

"Hello, Frederick," she said.

He grimaced, but didn't look up from the book opened across his lap.

Anne waited a few seconds and tried again, her voice low and pleading. "Listen. I know you're mad at me. And I am so, so sorry."

The right corner of Frederick's lips tightened.

Anne sighed, realizing this would be much harder than she expected. She swallowed hard. "Understand that I truly don't remember a lot of what's happened between us. Almost all of it, in fact. The accident I suffered in New York was real. I have papers to prove it, or you can call my doctors, or Jack. They'll tell you everything I'm saying is the truth. And I'm trying to remember. I really am." Anne hesitated, and then stumbled over her next words. "I found the...uh, papers. You left. On the bed." She swallowed again, wishing Frederick would look at her, or at least move. He could have been an oil painting. "I found the e-mails too. And I'm sorry, because I know it must have hurt you so much to have found them."

Frederick's blue eyes met hers. Their piercing gaze came almost as a physical slap, and Anne took a nervous step back. "Do you, now?" he said, his tone mocking. "You know how much they hurt me? That's awfully *empathetic* of you. To imagine how your actions affect other people. I didn't know you were capable of that."

"Right. I guess I deserve that." Anne swallowed again. A part of her wanted to flee the room and race into the cold outside. Another part wanted to take Frederick in her arms, bury her face in his neck, and absorb the hurt and pain that stretched from him like a noon shadow.

"I am sorry, Frederick," she said again. "I can't know exactly how you feel, or understand all of it, but I'm trying. I want you to know that I've had..." She paused. How to put this? "I've had certain...flashbacks.

About what happened before. And you're right." She stopped again, then sighed and pushed on. She had to tell him the truth, give voice to her actions, because without acknowledging them, she could never truly move on. "I cheated on you. I know that now. His name was—*is*—Luke Harris. He's a plastic surgeon."

"I know who he is." Frederick's eyes dropped to her chest with a look of infinite loathing. "I shudder to think what you traded for that kind of work."

Anne ignored the jibe. She had to hurry to the finish before doubt consumed her. "And there was someone else—Eddie something—and I think I must have been with him too. But I want you to know that it's over with these men. I've written to them—" She purposefully left out that she had spoken to one, "—and it's over. I'll never see them again." She passed her hand over her face, where the beginnings of a headache pulsed behind her eyes. "It's really, truly, over."

"It's over," he echoed. "And that's supposed to make it all right? That's supposed to erase what you did?" He laughed hollowly, and it hurt her to hear him make that sound. "I guess I should consider myself lucky you didn't give me some disease. You can't imagine what it was like, waiting for those results to come back. The humiliation of it. The *pain*."

Frederick shut his book and dropped it on the desk with a thud. Anne jumped, but said nothing. She waited.

Seconds passed. The brass nautical clock ticked

overhead. She started counting—sixty-seven...eighty-two...one-hundred-and-five—before, after nearly three minutes, Frederick finally broke the silence.

"In any case," he said, drawing out his words, "you realize that your admittance of adultery releases me from any financial obligation to you. That fidelity was a stipulation of the prenuptial agreement." He paused, letting her absorb the weight of his words, before adding, "So you can kiss your half of my assets goodbye."

Anne had actually thought of this, but she didn't care. She didn't want his money. She had no intention of tricking him out of it. Her husband didn't know about the money Jack had given her, and it was enough to get her started somewhere. She could rent an apartment, pay for the first few months, secure some savings, and find a job. She could bag groceries, or waitress, if her memory healed enough to remember orders. She could make a new life for herself, with brand-new memories—if it came to that, which she hoped it wouldn't. Because this man pulled her like an opposing magnet. She had to chase those feelings wherever they led.

"I know," Anne said finally. "But I don't care."

"You don't care." The words came out as an accusation, not a question. "You don't care about money. *You*."

"No," she said. "I don't."

Frederick met her eyes. The icy threads of white in

his blue irises struck Anne as beautiful. She wondered if she'd ever admired them, or admired him. If any of her warm feelings for Frederick had been legitimate.

Frederick grimaced. "I highly doubt that, Anne. It's who *you* are. You're a money-grubbing, manipulative little bitch."

His words cut her like a knife. She hoped her face didn't betray her.

"Even now. That look you're giving me. It's all calculated. You think about how to present yourself to me—a young, pretty ingénue at first, and now a helpless woman without a memory—and you prey on me. You're a parasite, Anne. Nothing more than an opportunistic parasite. You feed off whomever you can get a hold of until they're sucked dry and then move on. Right now, at this very moment, you're searching for your next golden ticket." He stood up then, and though he was not a tall man, his fury practically shot him up a foot. "I won't fall for it. Not again. *Never* again."

Anne didn't fight him. She simply absorbed his words like a sponge, despite how sick they made her. When he said nothing else, Anne whispered, "I must be all of those things you said, or at least I was. But I'm different now, I promise. I'm not that person anymore."

Frederick glared at her. "Then who are you?"

She opened her hands at her sides, then dropped them. "I'm finding that out. But I want you to know that I don't want your money. And that I understand if you want a divorce. I'll sign all the papers. And I'll leave. I won't take anything. You can have everything, or donate it to charity..."

"...or throw it out," he finished with a mirthless grin.

Anne swallowed. "You can do with it whatever you want to. Whatever feels right. But I think you should give it to someone who needs it."

"Who the hell needs six-hundred dollar shoes?" Frederick snapped. "You think some battered women's shelter hands out ridiculous five-inch heels? Or three thousand dollar dresses? No..." He shook his head emphatically, drawing closer to her. "I think I'd rather take it out into the backyard and have an enormous bonfire with it. Then I'd throw in every piece of jewelry you ever conned me into buying. And every one of our pictures together. Throw it on top and watch the whole thing burn." He was inches from her, his presence as menacing as a natural disaster. But Anne stood her ground and met his gaze. "What do you think about that? How would that make you feel? Watching everything you've ever cared about go up in flames? Would that hurt you, even a little? Would that finally get to you, watching all your precious things melt away? Or are you even capable of caring?"

He hates me, Anne thought, taking in his pinched face, his eyes dark and cruel. It was then that she realized his anger stemmed from something else. She had hurt him, perhaps irrevocably. And he was lashing out at her, trying to hurt her back.

But why? she wondered. *If he doesn't care about me anymore, why does he care to hurt me?*

Time seemed to slow. She stared up into her husband's face and measured his words and the meaning behind them. She wondered if he still cared for her. If a part of him still loved her. If he didn't, wouldn't he act calm, uncaring, and aloof? He'd simply show her the door, speak to her through lawyers, and rid himself of her.

Perhaps his rancor meant a chance to resurrect old feelings. But was she willing to fight for it—for him— at any cost?

What do I have to lose?

Before Frederick could summon anything further, Anne said, "You still love me."

His mouth was open—he had clearly intended to cut her with another remark—and now he closed it, surprised. He took a step back. "What the hell are you talking about?"

Anne waved a hand. "All of this. If I look past what you're saying, it's clear that you still care about me. And that I hurt you."

"Of course you hurt me," he said, his voice leveling. "You hurt everyone and everything you touch."

"I'm sorry." She closed the distance between them. Anne reached out to touch him, but he recoiled from her, almost instinctually, as if she were an open flame.

She moved to grip his hands, but he tore away. She took another step, grasping for him.

"Stop it," he warned.

Anne reached out again, touched his hands. He pulled back, but not as violently as before. She'd backed him into a corner between the fireplace and a built-in bookshelf. Without dropping her gaze, she reached for Frederick's hands, and—this time—he let her touch him. She squeezed his fingers.

"I'm sorry, Freddy," she whispered. She saw herself saying this name, lying beside him in bed. His vulnerable expression. His hand stroking her hair, caressing her face. The memory leaked into her core. "I'm so sorry," she said again. "I know I can't take back what I've done. I don't remember most of it, but I know I loved you. I know that. I remember us together, and that we were happy. And maybe I'm holding on to expired memories, but I want to think that there's something there. That there's something to fix. Because I know I loved you once, and that I can love you again—if you give me that chance."

Frederick stared at her for a long moment. Anne flashed to him surveying business accounts, deciding if past performance foreshadowed future benefits. His eyes narrowed. "Does it hurt? Your face?"

For the first time, Anne didn't move to touch her scars. Instead, she kept her grip on his hands, which were steady and warm. "Not that much," she said. "Not anymore."

"But it must have. In the beginning."

"I don't remember. I was in a coma through the worst of it."

Frederick studied her scars as if needing to recall their placement for an exam. "They did good work," he said in a measured tone. "Your doctors. It must have been horrific."

"I don't know," she said, unsure where he was going with this. "I never saw what I looked like right after the accident."

His face darkened, and she wondered if she had said something wrong.

"You're not wearing any makeup." He said this almost accusingly, as if her dearth of foundation and eyeshadow was suspect.

"I don't like makeup that much."

"You don't like makeup. *You*."

"No. I got a bunch in New York, but I don't really see the point. Maybe if you're going someplace nice, but it's just not me. Besides," she added, having given some thought to the subject, "You don't wear any makeup. Why should I have to?"

Frederick's stony expression cracked. She saw the ghost of a smile playing on his lips, though he tried to force it back. He shook his head. "Certainly I've not heard that argument before, coming from you. You once asked me to keep a makeup artist on permanent retainer. You said the process was too laborious and kept you from your other daily activities."

Anne gave him a sardonic smile. "What activities? Shopping?"

There. A smile twitched at the corner of his mouth. He let out a low chuckle, not checking himself this time. "You're so..." He searched for the word. "Different. I can't believe it. I would actually call you sincere."

Anne carefully traced his knuckles with her thumbs, running her fingers over his hands and squeezing the underside of his palms. "I am sorry, Freddy," she said. "I am."

For the next few moments, Frederick seemed at war. Conflicted emotions pulled at his face. Hatred. Suspicion. Tenderness. Fear. Loathing. Love. They were all there, and she recognized them all. Anne marked the truth, knowing without a doubt that her nights with other men had shattered something deep. He looked lost, like a child newly orphaned. But this time, he didn't pull away.

Anne held his hands and squeezed his fingers with her own, enjoying the pressure of the contact, of the warm proximity of his body. The softness of his suit jacket pressing against her arms. The clean smell of his linen and cologne. His chest rising and falling.

"I'm sorry, Freddy," Anne said again. She wanted him to hear her, truly hear her. Tears streaked down the sides of her face. She didn't bother to wipe them away. "I'm so sorry. Please, Freddy. *Please.* I'm so sorry." Her voice caught against a strangled sob. Her eyes stung from the salt of her tears.

Frederick bit his lip as he reached to touch her face.

Anne caught his hand and closed her eyes, pressing her face into his palm. She longed for his touch, for him to hold her. She wanted to stop time, or to reverse it, to erase everything bad that had happened between them and replace it only with the good.

Frederick sighed as he lowered his hand, but she still held on. She saw a new emotion register on his face: pity. "I have to go, Anne," he said, his voice thick and strange. "Please look over the papers I left you."

His fingers slipped through hers.

She let him go.

Chapter Nineteen

IN HER DREAMS, Anne was a young girl sitting at a kitchen table. Elena read a book beside her, every few seconds pushing up the glasses sliding down her nose. Their mother flitted wildly about making breakfast, hips swaying to the beat of the Gipsy Kings' "Bamboléo".

Their mother kept her long brown hair plaited, with gold hoop earrings shining on her lobes. She always sang and kept in constant motion, like a river striking its own path. Even when reading, their mother's feet tapped a syncopated beat.

Anne had not inherited her mother's gift of dance, and struggled to keep up with the quick and fluid steps. Elena had the ability but refused it, claiming that dancing embarrassed her, or distracted her from more serious endeavors.

Anne didn't mind. She loved when their mother shook her hips down the hall or in the kitchen. With a bright smile splashed across her face, her mother inevitably invited Anne to dance. She'd spin Anne under her arm, rock with her, and butterfly their arms. She never made Anne feel anything less than a natural dancer, even when Anne stumbled in a salsa. "I can teach rhythm to a platypus," her mother loved to say. Sometimes her father overheard their joy, set aside his papers, and joined in their infectious dancing.

Anne loved seeing her parents together. Loved how easily they moved, the contrast of their skin and bodies. Her father was tall and pale and freckled anytime the sun glanced his skin. Her mother's skin was olive in the winter, chestnut in the summer, and flaunted her curves.

When her parents were happy, their house filled with light and music. When they fought, shouts vibrated the walls like thunderclaps. Anne crouched at the door, trying to listen, while Elena rolled her eyes and said, "It's just noise. Ignore it."

She always acts like she's older than me, Anne thought, but said instead, "Don't you want to know what's going on?"

"Nope. Don't care."

Anne cared. Even during the worst fights, Elena read with stoic detachment while Anne listened at the door. Their mother wanted to stop spending money on bars and friends. To move to a better neighborhood. For their father to leave his English department and find a college that respected him. But these fights never lasted long. After a day or two, they inevitably forgave each other. And their mother would smile at them again and resume her dance.

That morning, as her mother beat eggs, milk, and cinnamon into a froth, Anne's heart swelled with love. She needed her mother's affection like oxygen and did everything she could to please her. She did her chores without complaint. Accepted scoldings and lectures without a fight. Even massaged her mother's feet after a grueling dance rehearsal with her troupe. Anne absorbed her mother's stories about Argentina. How her birth city, Córdoba, was unlike any place in the world. "It has wide cobble streets," her mother said. "Endless stone buildings. Movie theaters with wooden armchairs that seat a thousand!"

Elena never asked their mother questions. She rarely spoke to her at all. She told Anne their mother was too "flighty"—a word Anne still didn't understand—and that it was their *mother* who needed a better job. Anne thought her sister was crazy because their mother was beautiful and perfect.

"*Hola, Nena,*" their mother said, catching Anne's eyes. "*¿Tienes hambre?*"

"*Hola, Mami,*" Anne said with an enthusiastic nod, responding that she was starving.

Mouth-watering aromas filled the kitchen as their mother cooked steaming slices of bread in the pan.

After plating them, she ladled whipped cream in glistening mounds and sprinkled cinnamon and powdered sugar. Anne snatched the syrup—maple for her, strawberry for Elena—and some napkins and forks, and waited at the table. Their mother appeared with two plates stacked with French toast. Elena mumbled thanks and grasped for hers, while Anne reached up for a kiss, which her mother never denied.

"*Te quiero,*" their mother said, smiling at them. "*Mis hijas lindas.*"

"Thanks, Mom," Elena said dutifully.

"*¡Gracias, Mami! ¡Te quiero muchísimo!*" Anne chirped, hoping her accent wasn't too thick, because she tried to speak Spanish as perfectly as her mother.

Elena dug into her toast, her eyes still rapt upon her book. Anne took in a forkful and glanced at her mother, hoping she was looking at her too, but her mom stared at Elena with a wistful expression. "*¿Está bien, Mami?*" Anne asked hesitatingly.

Her mother blinked, as if caught in a dream. "*Por supesto, Nena,*" she said. She bent to kiss Anne again. "Of course."

Anne awoke with a start. Cooled sweat pooled around her in dark circles, and she was shivering. The room was black as pitch. She glanced at the clock: 3:12 a.m.

Still, Anne couldn't sleep. When she closed her

eyes, she saw her mother. That braid of dark hair. That ready smile. The way she danced every spare moment. How much Anne had loved her and needed her.

Mami, Anne thought, hearing the familiar intonation in her mind, how it settled at her heart. She had one memory of her mother. One. And it felt as vivid as if it had happened mere minutes ago.

She tried chasing her dream past the point of waking, but her efforts landed in a fog. The same happened when she tried to go backwards before her breakfast with her sister. She caught occasional glimpses of her past, but found them impossible to align. It'd be easier to piece a reflection in a wind-cut pool.

Anne sighed and pressed her arm over her eyes. Maybe if she went back to sleep, more memories would surface.

But sleep never came. She lay in bed—in an adjacent spot unspoiled by sweat—with the covers pulled to her chin, trying to force a dream. When she glanced at the clock again, it read 3:51 a.m.

This is ridiculous. Anne turned on the lamp, swaying with dizziness as she stood from the bed. The house groaned from the beating of snow and wind, creating a ghostly ambiance that sprinkled goose pimples along her flesh.

Anne crossed her arms but found no warmth.

She had to get out.

Creeping down the hall, she didn't quite know her

destination until she found herself outside the guest bedroom with its door slightly ajar. Anne eased open the door and padded to the bed.

She gazed down at her sleeping husband. Frederick lay on his side, one hand caught under his pillow, the other wrapped tightly around the comforter bunched at his waist. His face was to her, and by the light of the iPhone glowing nearby, she could see the softness of his features, how the earlier creases had relaxed into thin lines. She wanted to reach out to touch his face, to kiss him, but she resisted.

Anne wondered how long he had been sleeping in this bedroom, away from her. It was before the accident, based on the arrangement of the closet and the state Nicole Burns had kept this room. She wondered if her old self had minded her husband sleeping down the hall, if she had missed him, longed for the proximity of his body, and his touch. She didn't know, and couldn't sense, the answers to these questions. All she knew was that she wanted him back. And if he didn't come back, she wanted him happy.

Frederick stirred and opened his eyes. Anne froze, unsure if she should stay or go, if he even saw her. Then his eyes met hers. For a few seconds, neither one said a word.

Her husband broke the silence. "What are you doing here, Anne?"

"I'm not sure," she said truthfully.

He sat up and pulled his phone before his eyes to check the time. "How long have you been here?"

"Not long." Anne told herself to return to her room. But her feet wouldn't listen. Instead, she drifted to the bed, where she stood only inches from Frederick. They stared at each other as the street lamps cast shadows on the walls.

Frederick lifted his hand to touch her cheek, flooding Anne with warmth. Memories surged through her—opaque and jumbled, and out of time. She remembered curling in Frederick's arms. The pressure of his lips on hers. How the pillows always creased the same part of his face. Yet for all of her experience, she still felt strangely virginal as she stood there with his hand against her pitchfork scar, a stranger in her own body. She saw her feelings mirrored in her husband's eyes as he took her in. Any thought of sleep evaporated.

Anne braced to tell Frederick what he meant to her. But before she could speak, his lips stoppered her voice. He kissed her with a violence that startled her, his hands crushing her face. At first Anne squirmed, but she forced herself to fight with him, sensing that's what he needed. She kissed him back with equal savagery, sliding her body over his, holding his face in her hands.

Frederick's tension eased. He cupped her face with a quiet tenderness, releasing her sore lips to kiss her cheeks, neck, and behind her ears.

Anne melted into his embrace. It hadn't been like this with Jack, the most handsome man in the world. She remembered seeing Frederick's face—for she knew now that it *had* been him—when Jack kissed her. She wondered if she'd ever felt this way with anyone, Luke, or Eddie, or any of those faceless men she hid in that album by the bed. Something stirred within her, something both leveling and empowering. She longed to seal Frederick to her core, never letting him go.

Frederick opened the comforter, and she slipped inside, relishing the delicious heat of his body. He groaned when she kissed him, his hard arousal lodging against her stomach. Anne didn't hesitate. She brought her hand down, touching him there. He sighed and pressed her hand closer.

Anne pulsed with desire. She needed to be held and fulfilled. As Frederick worked on his pants, she opened his nightshirt and splayed her hands against his heaving chest. She let him slip between her legs and up her trembling thighs, gasping when he pushed inside. She wrapped her legs around his waist, loving his closeness, his smell, and how his fingers knew exactly where to be.

When it was over, she lay tucked inside his arm, her body flush against his, with her right leg thrown over his muscular thighs. The comforter heaped at the base of the bed. His kettledrum heartbeat thumped in her ear as she inhaled the lingering scents of his sweat and cologne. He wore only white boxer shorts, the rest of his clothes puddled on the floor. Panties hooked Anne's right ankle. Her nightshirt lay somewhere in the darkness, but Anne wouldn't break the moment by searching for it. She wanted to remain in this foggy dream state for as long as possible.

But it would not last. Frederick shifted against her. She whispered for him to stop, to linger, to stay in this exact position forever. But he pushed up from the mattress and avoided her sightline as he turned on the light. The room flooded with harsh incandescence, illuminating Frederick yanking on his pants. He jerked his arms though this wrinkled shirt and thumbed the row of buttons.

He did all this without looking at her. The residual warmth of his touch faded. Everything seemed different in the light. What was soft before now had hard edges. Her husband's brows furrowed like caterpillars. A sickly flush crept over his stubbled cheeks. Her own heartbeat faltered as sweat slicked her skin and her groin ached.

Anne began searching for the rest of her clothes when she saw Frederick make a deft movement, tossing her nightshirt over.

"Thanks." She smiled tremulously over at him. But he said nothing. It was as if the buttons of his shirt were the most interesting thing in the world, something from which he couldn't bear to tear his eyes away.

Anne sat in the middle of the bed, her panties

dampening as she searched for tissues. Finding a box on the nightstand, she whispered an awkward, "Excuse me," as she leaned over him, snatched a few, and shoved them between her legs. And then she waited for her husband to say something. *Anything.*

Frederick finished the last button on his neck and gave her a tired glance. "Were you able to look at the papers I left you?"

Anne swallowed. Did he still mean to go through with everything? Despite what had just happened? "You mean the divorce papers?"

Frederick nodded wordlessly.

"Yes," Anne said. "I read them when I got here."

"Good." He ran a hand through his tussled hair, parting it to the side. "It would be prudent for you to hire an attorney to review the papers first before signing. That way, you know what you're getting into. Eventually, the four of us'll schedule a joint meeting."

"Joint meeting?"

"Yes. To discuss the dissolution of various assets. Even if—as you stated earlier—you would like your items to go to charity."

Frederick's words pummeled Anne like rocks. He was so formal, so detached, even though they were both in the same bed, her bare legs only inches from his. She longed to be close to him again, but something kept her rooted in place. Anne forced herself to nod, unable to align her thoughts. She could still feel his fingers on her skin, his lips on hers, him inside her.

And now it was as if an ocean separated them, and they were looking at each other from opposite shores.

Anne hugged her knees as she waited for him to continue. But Frederick gazed at her expectantly, as if she should make the next move. Anne jolted with anger. "So nothing's changed?"

He blinked at her in surprise. "Changed?"

"Between us," she said. "After what we just did. You feel nothing for me?"

Frederick massaged his eyes with his hands. "Look, Anne. See that for what it was: a momentary lapse in judgment. We were just seizing upon an opportunity that presented itself, but we cannot let that color how we really feel about each other. We're just not suitable together."

"Stop talking like I'm some sort of merger!" Anne cried, swaying with *déjà vu*. She had said these words before, in this very house. How long ago? How many times?

Frederick's eyes lit with recognition. "Perhaps some things never change, despite circumstance."

After a long silence, Anne said, "Do you want me to go?"

"I think that would be best, don't you?"

Only an arms-length separated them now, and Anne was having trouble believing they had been as close as two people could be only minutes before. Her voice broke on the words, "How can you be so cruel?"

Frederick's face darkened. "I would hardly call this cruel, all things considered."

"I would."

He sighed. "We can't be together, Anne. Not anymore."

She slid from the bed, but lingered to say one more thing. "Despite what you said, I still feel something for you. What we did means something to *me*."

"At least it did to one of us," Frederick said coolly. It seemed like he had practiced these words before, had been waiting for the right moment to say them to her, so that she might understand his splintered heart.

Anne opened her mouth to respond, but found herself at a loss for words. She left him then, shutting the door behind her, and padded down the hall. He turned off the light before she made it back to her room.

Her bed was cold when she climbed into it, and she stared at the ceiling for a long time, thinking, remembering, trying to forget. She should no longer love her husband, not after what had just happened.

She rolled on her side and hugged her knees to her chest. Would they ever stop hurting each other? She waited, but the darkness offered no answer.

When Anne finally closed her eyes, she thought of her sister, their parents, lost love, and empty houses.

Chapter Twenty

ANNE ROSE EARLY the next morning. After several failed attempts on a gleaming espresso machine, she made coffee on a Keurig. Two pods, and she had a travel thermos filled for Frederick. After finding a crimson ceramic mug that fit perfectly in her hands, she made herself a vanilla biscotti blend. She took a sip and winced. She stirred in four spoonfuls of sugar and thought about last night. Was that the last time she would kiss her husband?

"Maybe you'd like some coffee-flavored sugar," Frederick said as he strode into the kitchen and tucked his briefcase behind a table chair. He adjusted the striped tie at his neck and then slid on his suit jacket.

"I made you some," said Anne, trying to sound cheery as she passed him the thermos. She had been waiting for him to come downstairs for some time.

The ceiling groaned as the shower turned on overhead, his footfalls thumping the floorboards. It had taken him so long to emerge that she thought he might have slipped out through the window, just to avoid her. Pacing the kitchen while light dawned had afforded her plenty of time to decide how she would act when they saw each other. She had decided that his harshness the previous night was likely justified, if not expected. She resolved to set aside her hurt and focus on the sliver of love she'd experienced—and possibly draw it out of him again.

Frederick frowned at the travel mug. "I don't take sugar. And I don't like flavored coffees. Sorry."

Anne's smile broadened. "I *knew* it! Don't worry. I picked you the plainest one I could find. And there's absolutely no sugar," she added.

He hesitated before taking a cautious sip. He grimaced, but nodded. "Thank you."

"You're welcome." She came to sit with him at the table, her elbows a tripod in front of her as she clasped her hot mug to her lips. When he opened a folder and began riffling through its contents, Anne asked, "So what are you doing today?"

He shook his head. "Not now, Anne. I'm busy."

"Right." She set down her mug and flattened her hands on either side. Then, unconsciously, she began drumming her fingers, much like her mother would have—always ready to fill the silence with rhythmic noise.

Frederick glanced at her, clearly irritated. "Anne. Please."

Her fingers stalled in midair. "Right. Sorry."

She sipped her coffee, liking the bitter taste and its vanilla fragrance. As the minutes passed, she covertly studied her husband. She admired his concentration. How he licked his thumb to turn the pages, scowled at a certain paragraph, and jotted notes in the margins. His reading intrigued her, but she knew better than to interrupt. She contented herself with watching him, wondering how many more mornings like this their future held. Was this their last? Or next to last?

Frederick stood from the table, took a last gulp of coffee before dropping it on the countertop, then closed the folder and shoved it into his briefcase. "I've got to run," he said, barely meeting her eyes as he lifted his briefcase and started for the door.

Anne shot up, nearly overturning her mug, and intercepted him. "Okay. That's fine. But I have a question."

He sighed. "What?"

"Are you still wanting to go through with the Christmas party?"

He glanced at the clock on the stove. "Too late to back out of it now, don't you think?"

"Okay." Anne smiled and leaned up to kiss him. But he deflected her, and her lips landed on his cheek, smooth and scented with aftershave.

Frederick gripped her upper arms and flinched as if

his next words pained him. "Listen, Anne. I certainly gave you the wrong impression last night. I shouldn't have acted on those feelings. But I'm past that now. We can't go back to the way things were, okay?"

Anne hesitated, then nodded, not trusting herself to speak. She wanted to tell him she didn't know how things were, only sensed what she wanted. And she wanted him.

Frederick dropped his hands and checked his watch. "Shit. I'm running late. Listen, everything we discussed earlier still applies. I'd advise you to consult an attorney. You can ask Louis for a recommendation. But we have to get this thing rolling. Have you signed the papers?"

"No," she said, the word thick in her mouth.

"Please do." He glanced at his watch again, then tightened his grip on the briefcase. "I'll see you after work. Try to get that done today, okay?"

Anne said nothing, didn't even nod. Frederick didn't wait. He was out the door and in his Mercedes, his forehead lit by the overhead light. Then the garage trundled open, and he reversed quickly down the drive.

Cold air and a few snowflakes blew into the garage. Anne crossed her arms as her husband disappeared into the cold, grisly morning.

A long, sonorous note sounded. Anne tingled with recognition.

The sound came again.

The kitchen phone was ringing.

Anne shut the garage and reentered the kitchen, catching the phone on the fourth ring. "Hello?" she said, before mentally kicking herself. What if it was Luke Harris again? Was there a way for her to know?

"Anne," said a voice, a man's voice, and it took her a few seconds to recognize it.

"Jack!" She couldn't believe it. Jack Post was on the line! "What are you—how...why are you calling?"

"I wanted to check in on you!" he said against a clash of discordant background noise. "I've been wondering how things are going. You haven't returned Maria's calls. She's left several messages."

"I didn't know," Anne said, searching for an answering machine. Or were messages now stored in phones?

"We've been a little worried," he continued. "You doing okay?"

Anne shot back to those few short weeks of limbo in Jack's palatial home. She wanted to tell him everything, but her throat closed on the words. Instead, she managed, "I'm okay. I've been meaning to call. I should have. I miss you all so much."

"We miss you, too." A pause. "How is everything? You sound down."

"It's been rough adjusting," she admitted. "My husband..." Anne couldn't say, *My husband wants a divorce!* That failure was still too fresh. Instead, she said, "My husband's really trying to get me to remember things, but it's frustrating."

"I can only imagine. Listen, do you need any help? Did my PI help you track down that friend of yours?"

Trust the world to keep Jack in a perpetual status update, Anne thought with a wry grin. "Yes, he did. Thank you."

"It's good for you to have friends, Anne. They're going to help you. I know it."

Doubtful, Anne thought. *Besides, I think I need all new friends.*

"Have you looked into those support groups? Maybe they can help too. It might be good for you to be with..." He hesitated before continuing. "Well, with others in the same or similar circumstances."

Anne remembered the printout her physician had given her just before discharge. That list was now a crumpled ball at the bottom of her purse. "Not yet," she said, "but I will. It's been a long process, but I am remembering more things."

"That's fantastic." He sounded relieved. "Listen, I'll be out-of-pocket for a few weeks. We start principal photography on a new film in Alberta, and the service there is spotty. But if you need me, call Maria. She'll contact me."

"I will," she said. "Thank you, Jack."

"Of course," he replied. Anne sensed he wanted to say something more, but decided against it. "Anyway, if you need me, I'm here for you. Good luck settling in. I hope everything continues to go well for you."

"Thanks, Jack." She held the phone to her ear, willing him to stay on, to spend the next hour—or day —talking to her, like they used to do.

But Jack, like her husband, had to go. He gave a quick goodbye and was gone with a click.

Anne returned the phone to its cradle. Frederick wanted her to contact an attorney, to continue with the divorce proceedings. He wanted her signature on the papers. Her agreement to become strangers. Their spousal ties severed. He'd suggested she talk to someone named Louis. His lawyer, perhaps?

Anne pressed her chest against a burning heart.

Maybe it was really over.

She cast her eyes to the Christmas tree she'd decorated, its smell of pine tingeing the air. She sensed a well of undiscovered memories. This was *her* home. And she was about to be driven out.

Anne balled her hands into fists.

No. She wasn't leaving without a fight.

Chapter Twenty-One

ANNE SAT in the front seat of her car staring at her sister's house, arming herself with the perfect words. True, her sister had said she never wanted to see her again. And Elena had also threatened to move or call the police should Anne attempt further contact. But before Anne could abandon her last remaining family member, she needed to know *why* Elena wanted out of her life. Maybe then there'd be hope of mending their relationship.

Anne turned off the car, letting the chill creep in. "Okay," she said to herself. "Here I go."

She padded down the walkway. Small white lights glimmered from the path, along the roofline, and around the two posts flanking the front door. Suspecting her sister wouldn't invite her in, Anne braced her hand against the cold brick and peered inside. Past the curtains in a small living room twinkled a Christmas tree. Ropes of colored lights and plastic ornaments weighed the branches, reminding Anne of her own tree. Beneath the boughs were stacks of presents and bags tufted with tissue paper. The scene could have been lifted from a magazine.

Anne's throat tightened. *It's a real home.*

There'd be no presents under Anne's tree. The only gift her husband wanted was her signature on the divorce papers.

Steeling her resolve, Anne rang the doorbell. A voice called in the distance, "Coming, Lauren!" and excited footfalls followed. When the door opened, Anne faced her sister, who had a candy cane jutting comically from her lips.

Elena's bright expression soured. She withdrew the candy cane like a cigarette and hastened to shut the door.

But Anne had expected this. She shoved her foot in the jam, letting her boot absorb the weight of the door as Elena ineffectively tried to slam it.

"Move your damn foot!" Elena cried. "Get out of my house! Get off of my porch!"

"I'm not moving an inch," said Anne, "until you talk to me. And you can change the locks, and you can call the police, and you can take out that restraining order. But until I die, I will track you down and bang on your door until you talk to me."

The two women glowered at each other. Elena's

dark eyes narrowed as her lips formed a thin, hard line. Anne wondered how many times in their lives they had faced off like this, if this animosity had always existed between them. She'd assumed twins were automatically best friends. But perhaps she and Elena were closer to adversaries, purposefully existing in separate hemispheres. Anne wondered, as she recognized the distrust and anger burning in her sister's eyes, if they had ever been friends, or if these feelings ran back into the womb. That even as zygotes, they'd fought for dominance, absorbed in an epic battle from birth until this chilly December afternoon.

"Everything okay?" Andrew said as he came to stand by Elena's shoulder. Shock stole into his face. "Anne! What are you doing here?"

Without averting her gaze, Anne said, "Telling your wife that I'm not leaving until she talks to me."

Andrew's gaze vacillated between them. "Elena, maybe you should hear her out. Even for just a few minutes." When neither woman replied, he added, "At least it'll get her off our porch."

Elena relaxed her grip on the door, but her eyes burned with rage. "Fine. Have it your way, Anne. You *always* do. I'll give you fifteen minutes. Not a second more."

Anne bit her lip against a clever retort. "Thank you. I appreciate you listening to me. Can we talk inside?"

Elena didn't hesitate. "No."

Andrew said, "Honey, it's freezing—"

"I told you she's never to set foot in my house."

"Why not the coffee shop down the block?" Anne suggested.

Elena shook her head. "No. We'll talk in your car. If that's not good enough for you, then forget it."

"That's fine with me."

Elena sighed and snatched a thick red parka suspended by the door.

"I'll be inside, honey," Andrew said. "Let me know—"

"It's fine!" Elena snapped, and her husband winced.

Anne stepped aside as her willowy sister blew past and stormed down the walkway. Andrew opened his hands, as if to say, *What can you do? She is who she is. Take it or leave it.*

Anne followed her sister to the car. Elena was practically tapping her foot in frustration as Anne fumbled for the keys and popped the locks. They both slid inside. Anne turned the ignition and put the heat to full blast.

"Not so high," Elena said, turning down the heat. "You'll roast us."

"Sorry." The second the apology was out of her mouth, Anne regretted it. She hated apologizing to everyone.

Her sister tapped the dash, just underneath the

digital clock. "It's 10:41. You've got until 10:56. And then I'm out of here."

"Right." Anne drew a breath, trying to inject strength and resolve into her voice. "Listen, Elena. I know that you're mad at me. And that's fine. You can feel how you want to feel."

"How very Oprah of you." Elena crossed her arms over her chest.

Anne wanted to call her callous and unfeeling, but stopped herself because Elena looked like a petulant, sulking child. Anne would have to try other tactics. "I wanted to meet with you because you're the only one who really knows what's happened in my life. At least I hope you do."

Elena said nothing.

"I've been remembering things." Anne let these words sink in. She needed her sister to understand the magnitude of the statement. But nothing flickered across her sister's face. Perhaps Elena couldn't comprehend the significance of these memories, or that Anne could recapture them at all. "Yesterday, I had my first memory of our mother. I remembered that time when she was making us French toast. She was dancing at the stove and you were reading a book. Remember that?" Anne's breath caught. She hoped against everything that the memory was real, and not something conjured by her broken mind.

Elena toed the carpet. "I don't know. That sounds

like a lot of mornings. Mom was always dancing, and she knew you loved French toast."

Anne's spirit lightened. "Great! That's great."

"Congratulations." Elena rolled her eyes. "Can I go now?"

Anne tried to keep the smile on her face. She wouldn't have this moment ruined by Elena's dour mood. "Not yet. My fifteen minutes aren't up." She pushed on. "I've been remembering other things too, how happy Mom and Dad were—"

"Not all the time," Elena cut in.

"No, I know," Anne amended. "I remember arguments too. Like how Mom wanted him to change departments, or maybe schools. For us to move. Does that sound right?"

Elena nodded. "It was always the same argument. Get a better job. Get us to a better neighborhood. Mom never let up on that."

"Right." Anne drifted through the threads of her past. "But that's where my memory of our family stops."

Elena glanced at her. "That's it?"

"So far. I'm sure I'll have more memories. At least I hope so."

Elena grimaced. "You don't even remember the accident?"

"No. I woke up at the hospital—"

"Not *your* accident. Mom and Dad's."

Anne's heart thumped hard in her chest. "No. But I read about it. How a drunk driver hit them."

"But there's so much more to that. You don't remember the hospital visits? Or the court hearings?"

"Court hearings?" said Anne. "What are you saying? They weren't killed instantly?"

Elena made a noise, something between a snort and a sob. "Hardly. Maybe if a merciful God existed, it'd have been instantaneous. No, it took Mom two weeks to die. She was in intensive care all that time, but a blood clot in her lungs finally sunk her. Dad was in a coma for six days, but he was brain-dead." Elena swallowed hard before continuing. "You and I took him off life support."

Anne sucked a breath against a pinch in her chest. She combed her mind for these memories. She fell through a haze, glimpsing only vague images. "No, I don't remember that."

"You'd think you'd have those moments burned into your brain. They are in mine." Elena sighed and shook her head. "Well, consider yourself lucky."

Anne's eyes stung. "I guess."

"Oh for God's sake. Why are you crying?"

"I'm not crying," Anne snapped, wiping her eyes.

"You actually *want* those memories?" Elena said, as if Anne itched to contract a fatal disease just to understand its symptoms.

"No." Anne gave a hard shake of her head. "Yes! I

don't know. Maybe. They sound awful, but they were my memories. They belong to me."

"Seriously, you're lucky not to remember." Elena scrubbed her face with her hands. "I wish I could forget half the things I know."

Now it was Anne's turn to frown. "You say that, but can you imagine forgetting your daughter? The day she was born, or what she was like as a baby? Or meeting Andrew? Falling in love?"

"So you're saying you remember *nothing*? You've got a few memories, and that's it?"

"Pretty much," Anne said. "That's why I need your help."

"I don't know how much I can help you. They're not my memories."

"But you were there for most of them."

Elena dropped her hands to her lap and then opened them, palms upward, as if casting an entreaty to the saints. "But it's all open to interpretation. My memory always differs from yours, Anne. That's what drove us crazy as kids."

"What do you mean?"

Elena shrugged. "You know. Kids do dumb things. They play tricks. We'd tell different stories, get into trouble. Point is we always had different perspectives. Still do, obviously."

"I don't care about that. I just want to hear it from you what it was like growing up. Tell me about Mom and Dad. Or what it was like meeting Frederick—"

"You've forgotten Frederick too?"

"A lot of him, yeah." Anne gritted her teeth. "He wants a divorce."

Elena muffled a laugh behind her hand. "Call CNN! There's a breaking news bulletin here."

"It's not funny," Anne snapped. "Besides, something happened. And maybe it's different now. I don't know."

"What?" For once Elena seemed genuinely interested.

Anne shifted in the seat. "Well, we sort of slept together."

"Sort of?" Elena scoffed. "You sort of had sex?"

Anne nodded.

"Again, with the evening news. And you think, what? That it's going to change everything? How do you know it wasn't out of revenge?"

Anne tried to sort out her sister's words. "No, it was nice. At least, I thought it was. Now he's acting like things aren't any different. He said it was a..." She tried to remember Frederick's exact words. "A momentary lapse in judgment."

Elena rolled her eyes again. "Come on. You can't be surprised. You cheated on him, Anne. Practically every chance you got. Of course, he's going to put distance between you two."

Anne's mouth fell open as if someone pulled a locking pin from her jaw. "How do you know about that?"

Elena shrugged, her demeanor nonchalant. "You told me back when we were still talking. You'd had like two or three affairs by then. After a while, when it was clear you wouldn't stop, I said I didn't want to hear any more."

Anne tried putting the pieces together, but they still weren't connecting. "So that's why you won't talk to me? Because of Frederick?"

"Frederick? What are you talking about?"

"About what I did to Frederick. Cheating on him?"

"You think I'm upset because you were sleeping around?"

"Isn't it?" Anne said, trying to grasp the situation. "Maybe I betrayed one of your moral codes?"

"More like your marital vows." Elena's wry grin disappeared. "Don't get me wrong. I think what you did was deplorable, stupid, dangerous, and completely self-serving. Not to mention the hurt that it's caused Frederick. Thank God you guys never had kids."

Anne scowled, perturbed by her sister's judgment, but still desperate to understand. "So if it's not about Frederick, why are you mad at me?"

"Wow. You really did lose your memory. Listen, I can't rehash the past for the next twelve hours. If you've got specific questions for me, then ask them. Otherwise, I'm going inside."

"That is a specific question. Why are you mad at me?"

Elena glowered at her. "Maybe it's a question I don't want to answer. Have you thought about that?"

"Why are you like this?" Anne demanded, even as her heart frayed like a garment caught in a ringer. "We're sisters. Twins. We're all that's left of our family."

Elena stretched for the door handle. "I *have* a family. I don't need you."

"Stop it!" Anne leaned over and swiped her sister's hand. Elena, clearly shocked, sat back. Anne tried to cage her fury. "I had a serious accident and was in a coma for days. You know this. You know I sustained permanent brain damage, but you'd still toss me out like garbage. Nothing I've done to you deserves this. Nothing."

"You tried to seduce my husband!" Elena spit at her like acid.

Anne lost her breath. "What?"

"You heard me." Elena's eyes glistened. "You tried to seduce my husband. You knew his history, everything gruesome he went through. You knew he thought you were pretty, and you preyed on his affections. You didn't care that he was my husband, that I loved him. All you saw was another conquest. Another notch on your bedpost."

"I'm sorry," Anne said, unable to see herself doing this, but—marking the vehemence in her sister's eyes —knowing it had to be true. "I'm sorry."

"Yeah. You're sorry."

"Did I...?" Anne hesitated, feeling sick. She forced herself to say the words. "Did I sleep with him?"

Elena's gaze was unwavering. She let time stretch for an agonizing half minute before she finally answered. "No. He's probably the only guy you didn't fuck."

Anne's heart twisted with both repulsion and relief. "Oh thank God."

Elena's lips curled. "I'm out of here. Screw your fifteen minutes."

"No!" Anne reached over to grasp her sister's hands, but Elena buffeted her efforts. Anne punched the lock closed, and Elena—with a confused glare at her—immediately tried to pry it open. Anne laid her body like a brick over her sister, gripping the door handle with resolute fingers.

"Let go!" Elena cried, trying to push her away. "Get off me, you bitch!"

"No!" Anne cried with a ferocity that startled them both. Elena stilled behind her. After a moment, when the only noises were their ragged breaths, Anne managed in a calmer voice. "I'm sorry. But I can't let you leave. Not until we finish this. Not until I remember some things."

Perhaps it was only a minute. Perhaps it was ten. Anne lost track of time. Her hands sweated against the door handle as her body sunk against Elena's jagged limbs. Her sister's clavicle, xylophone ribs, and knobby knees poked from unseen angles. Neither said a word.

Anne hoped her resolve shown as bright as an exploding star. That her sister now understood the depth of her commitment to finding the truth.

That's when Elena did something surprising. The right corner of Elena's mouth twitched, and then trembled. Her chest vibrated, and heaved, while a low, gurgling noise traveled up her throat. With eyes pinched against the tears that tracked down her temples, Elena erupted with a laugh.

"What's so funny?" Anne asked with a chuckle.

"You are!" Elena managed between gasps. "God, you look like a crazy woman. Look at yourself!"

Anne saw herself squashed against her sister's lithe body. An outsider would think Anne physically trapped Elena in the car—which, of course, she had.

Anne relaxed her grip on the handle and arranged herself so that her sister could draw a full breath. "I'm sorry," Anne said. "I just...reacted."

"I can see that." Elena wiped her eyes.

"You won't leave, will you?" Anne's hand still lingered on the door.

Elena's laughter faded. "No. I'll stay a while longer. You can stand down, soldier."

Anne finally released the handle and pushed back into her seat. They both took a moment to smooth down their hair and wipe their watery eyes. Anne noticed that Elena's dark lipstick had smeared up both cheeks, giving her a comical clown appearance, and told her.

"God, what a pain." Elena flipped open the mirrored visor and wiped her face with her thumbs. She couldn't entirely erase the streaks of lipstick, but made it look more like blush than circus makeup. She snapped the visor closed and glanced at Anne, shaking her head.

Anne frowned. "What?"

Elena stared at her intently, as if a tiny phrase printed Anne's forehead. "It's just...weird."

"What's weird?"

"I'm just—well. I'm not used to seeing you like this."

"Like what?"

"Without any makeup. I mean, *look* at you! You don't so much as have mascara on."

"And that bothers you?"

Elena shrugged. "I guess people get used to seeing others in a certain way."

Anne had given little thought to makeup, especially since returning home. She found no thrill in it and only dabbed cover-up on the worst of her scars. But today, with only one thought driving her mind, she'd forgotten her scars entirely. Her face, according to the world, was disturbingly naked. When she touched her skin, she felt her own warmth and the soft, nearly invisible, down on her cheeks. No trace of chalky powder. Nothing coming away on her fingertips. She preferred it that way. "What were you used to seeing me as?" Anne asked.

Elena smirked. "You were Miss Makeup. Ever since you learned how to unroll a lipstick. Before you left for New York, you wore so much it looked like a kabuki mask."

"What's a kabuki mask?"

Elena explained the Japanese masks with thick eyeliner and rouged lips. How Anne never emerged without at least three shades of eyeshadow layering her lids like striations in igneous rock.

Anne stared at her, wide-eyed. "And you prefer me that way?"

"Well, it's what you are—were, I guess."

"Huh." Anne considered this. She remembered how the methodical application of makeup had once warmed her with a rush of familiarity. But it was too much effort, and in the end it wasn't really her, was it? It was her hiding behind a mask of someone else, someone with perfect skin and no visible imperfections. And that wasn't her anymore.

What am I going to do with my life? Anne wondered as the question echoed in her mind. Often she felt a prisoner in her own body, trapped in someone else's life.

"So what do you want to know?" Elena asked, breaking Anne's reverie.

"Know?"

"About yourself. Maybe I can help." For once Elena seemed sincere, even a little excited.

Anne tensed. Was there a chance for them?

Anne tried not to reveal her burgeoning hope, but her heart fell when she saw the time. "Oh."

"What?" Elena asked.

No point in hiding it. Their fifteen minutes were up. "It's 10:59. I guess we're supposed to be done."

Elena checked the clock and glanced back towards her house.

Don't leave me, Anne pleaded silently. *Please don't leave me here alone.*

Elena tucked a piece of hair behind her ear, the same way Anne did. "Forget the clock. I've got some time. What's your first question?"

"Really?" Anne couldn't believe it. Her grin threatened to overtake her face.

"Really." Elena crossed her legs, got comfortable. "Shoot."

"Okay." Anne knew where to begin, but feared to ask. She wet her lips and said in a rush, "Start with Andrew. How'd you meet him? How long did you date? How many years until you had Charlotte? And was it love at first sight?"

"Wow," Elena said, her brows pursing together. "That's a lot of questions. You sure that's where you want to start?"

Anne could read the hesitation on her sister's face. "Forget it. How about—"

"No, it's fine," Elena interjected. "Fine. We'll start with my husband." She drummed her fingers lightly against her lips. "Well, technically, we met him together. When he was on TV."

Anne's mouth went slack. "He was on TV? Was he famous?"

"More infamous," Elena began.

The tension eased from Elena's face as she spoke. She told Anne the stories they shared. Together, they pieced the fragments of Anne's broken life, spilling light into her mental darkness. Anne sewed each new piece of history together, wrapping them around herself like a quilt. She told herself she would never forget, never again. As details whirled through Anne's mind, unbidden memories sprang forward. Those once trapped in darkness now surging into light.

Part Two

A LIFE IN FRAGMENTS

Chapter Twenty-Two

THAT NIGHT, when Anne closed her eyes, she saw her sister as clearly as if peering through a pane of glass. But it wasn't Elena of the present, but a much younger version. Her face perpetually flushed and pimply since the onset of puberty. Her expression as hard and unforgiving as one of those handprints punched into the sidewalk. Anne sat next to her in their parents' living room, watching the boy's tragic interview on TV. Elena blurted, "That's the man I'm going to marry."

"Oh, *please*," Anne said, rolling her eyes as she picked at the pedicure curling on her toenails. "How can you possibly know that?"

Elena crossed her arms over her chest, defiant as always. "I just sense it. I *know*."

That was her sister: haughty and headstrong. A person who could get whatever she wanted if she just worked hard enough. Elena was like that in school, too. From earning top marks in all of her classes to funding college with dozens of scholarships.

Now they were juniors, a mere two semesters from college. And while they were twins, everyone knew they were hardly the same. Their academic schedules had intersected several times, but for years, Anne requested separate classes. She flamed beet-red whenever Elena's hand sprang into the air with an answer while Anne herself struggled to follow along.

And then there was her sister's dowdy appearance. How she spent her allowance and any part-time salary on clothes from the Salvation Army and Goodwill, never noticing their worn seams and musky scent. Elena didn't care that she was hopelessly unpopular. Or that she had only one friend—Lauren, a chubby girl with buck teeth who was just as much a nerd. Or that everyone made fun of them behind their backs, and occasionally to their faces. When one of Anne's friends had poured Diet Coke all over Elena and Lauren after homecoming, their parents grounded Anne for three weeks. And all because she *laughed*.

Elena snapped at Anne all the time at home, while rarely making eye contact with her at school—yet everyone acted like Elena was so much better.

Until that afternoon, Elena had never expressed an interest in boys—calling them a "distraction from education"—while Anne had swooned over the opposite sex long before she'd started her period. When Anne snuck out to parties, enjoying a boy's hands on her skin, she could always count on her sister's nightly vigil. Elena's eyes rapt on her homework, a nun trapped in her own personal convent. Though she never outwardly appeared to prefer women, Anne had privately wondered if her sister might be gay, though she was too afraid to ask.

After watching that TV special, Elena hand-wrote a letter to Andrew Lewiston: a boy they just learned had spent most of his infancy in a dog cage in a leaky basement, the punching bag of two psychopathic parents. When the authorities finally caught on two years later, the boy looked as emaciated as a concentration camp survivor. Cigarette burns marked his little body like chicken pox and sections of cross-bars had etched permanently into his skin.

Anne had wanted to watch an episode of *The Brady Bunch* or *I Love Lucy* or anything that made the world silly. Not watch other people's depressing lives. But Elena snatched the remote and said that *she* was interested in the interview—and that Anne's juvenile programming needed to grow up.

When Anne asked their mother for help, she only shrugged and said, "It is strange, yes, but who are we to determine the fate of her heart?"

That was their mother, whom Elena often whispered was a New Age nutcase. But she was beautiful, and Anne adored her. Elena was drawn to their father, who regaled them with stories of his time in college, his research on nineteenth-century British history, his many students, and the latest book he was teaching. It was everything Anne could do to keep up with their witty repartee.

Anne tried to be smart like her sister, to snag their father's notice. But whenever she cracked open a book on his syllabus, she needed Merriam-Webster for help. Elena recalled everything she came across, as if she were the human embodiment of an encyclopedia. Whenever their father dropped words like "existential," "curmudgeon," or "paradigm," Elena nodded with cheerful confidence. Anne gave up asking her father to define the words, because interruptions slowed his tales. Sometimes Anne wished to trade her face for Elena's mind—but only for a day. Maybe then the world would make more sense to her.

After the boy's interview, Elena disappeared and quickly returned with a stack of paper, a pencil, and a ballpoint pen, and began drafting a letter. Anne knew her method. She'd brainstorm for several minutes, edit for half an hour, then carefully transcribe a letter in a perfect schoolgirl's ink. Anne said nothing as her sister tapped the pencil to her lips and scribbled notes in the margins. When she finished, Elena sealed the envelope and set out to uncover the boy's address.

Anne shouted, "You'll never find it!" But Elena was already gone, booting up the computer and clicking frantically on the keyboard. After several calls,

Elena tracked down the show's producers and somehow convinced them to speak to her.

Elena's letter was in the mail the next morning.

Their parents said to be careful, but Elena got her way, like she always did. Anne watched the whole scenario play out like one of her father's nineteenth-century novels, and—much like those books—she couldn't relate to any of it. Elena scurried to the mailbox every afternoon after school, tearing through the mail like a mouse searching for cheese. Twice a week Andrew wrote to her sister, and Elena would write him back. Their lengthy correspondence only lacked Elena writing by the light of a fire, a quill to her lips, her body corseted until her lungs fused. It was as if modern technology didn't exist. Anne had never seen them talk on the phone or e-mail. They wrote everything longhand, on stiff stationary. Every word carefully chosen. Every revelation methodically studied, as if Elena had trapped herself in a provincial love story.

But then Anne caught her usually guarded sister smiling dreamily, or—most bizarrely—singing to herself. Since they shared a room, she heard the crinkle of Elena's letters as she reread them by the glow of the nightlight. Sometimes Anne awoke to Elena's laughter, a rare, melodic sound. Elena had even stopped giving

Anne critical looks or her usual cutting remarks. Actually, she seemed not to notice Anne at all.

Elena was happy. Perhaps for the first time in her life.

But did that mean Elena had always been unhappy? Anne shied at broaching the subject with her parents, who seemed content to listen as Elena read letter after letter to them. To Anne, they seemed relieved, as if they had been holding their breaths for years, waiting for something. Elena's perpetual cloud had dampened their household, but she hadn't realized the greatness of the impact until that cloud lifted. Without Anne and Elena's constant bickering, dinner became a pleasant affair. Anne noticed their parents smiled constantly, and even occasionally sneaked in a kiss. The four of them circled each other like dancers at a cotillion—nobody wanting to misstep and ruin the fun.

Their parents didn't stop Elena from communicating with Andrew Lewiston, but when she wanted to meet him after only two months, they were cautious and skeptical. But—yet again—Elena got her way. Their father even said Andrew could sleep on the couch, enraging Anne since none of her boyfriends could stay overnight.

How cunning her sister had been, allowing them to read their letters, pretending she had nothing to hide. Elena had invited their parents into her romance, acting innocent as a courted princess.

After dinner, Anne caught her sister just outside the bathroom. "So you're really going to meet this guy?" she demanded. "Isn't that going to be weird? I mean, you've never even spoken to him!"

Elena looked at her, *really* looked at her, for the first time in weeks. It was as if a gauze fell from her eyes, and that familiar cold judgment crept back in. "Actually," she said in her holier-than-thou voice, "I've already spoken to him."

"What?" Anne's eyebrows shot up in surprise. "You have? When?"

"About a week ago."

"I never saw you..."

"Are you spying on me now?" Elena, who had been clutching her bathrobe and pajamas in one hand, angrily shoved the bunch to her opposite elbow. "I can have secrets too, you know."

Anne blinked at her, uncomprehending. "What are you talking about?"

Her sister tilted her nose up in the air, as if trying to avoid a foul smell. "I know all about your stupid parties. How you sneak out at night. You'd think you'd be more careful, seeing as we share the same room."

Of course Elena had known, because she had always been there when Anne returned drunk or stoned. But Elena had never said a word, never once confronted Anne on her late nights, or told their parents. Elena studied in bed, books and papers in her lap, listening to Beethoven or Vivaldi. She never glanced up when Anne slipped through the window, collapsing into bed, fully clothed.

Anne's throat ached with shame. "You've never said anything."

Elena shrugged. "What's there to say? You're going to do what you're going to do. You always have."

Anne crossed her arms, trying to quell the tremors that began anytime she challenged her sister. "I might say the same about you."

"Please. You've always gotten your way, ever since we were kids. You'd just have to bat your eyes and things just came to you. Whereas I—" Elena stabbed herself squarely in her chest with her thumb. "—have to *work* at it. But all this effort will be worth it in the end. You'll see."

"So, what? You're going to marry this guy? You've never even met him!"

"That'll soon change," Elena said, smiling maddeningly. "When you meet him, you'll see."

"See what?"

"What I see." Elena opened the door to the bathroom. "Now let me shower. What do you care about all this, anyway? Don't you have more important things to do? Like hanging out with your friends or one of your boyfriends?"

"You're just jealous," Anne snapped. "You've always been jealous that I'm popular, and that boys want me."

"You're wrong." Elena stepped very close to her

then. And even though Elena was only two minutes older, Anne felt like a child next to a hulking adult. "What bothers you the most is that I don't care about that, and never have. You have nothing in your life that I want. Not a single thing. And it kills you to know that."

Words built in Anne's mouth, but before she could voice them, Elena shut the door. In seconds, the shower was on, and Anne could hear her sister singing through the bathroom door.

Chapter Twenty-Three

IN ANNE'S DREAMS, someone said, "It's not fair. It's not fair!"

It was her own voice, again and again, the words haunting like a ghostly echo. It wasn't fair when her sister mounted the Greyhound bus to visit her boyfriend, and again when Andrew's Phillies blanket became a permanent fixture on their parents' couch. It wasn't fair when Elena scored a full scholarship to Ohio University, using residual funds to purchase herself a used Honda, a rental off-campus, and their parents a brand-new washer and dryer from Sears. It wasn't fair when Anne's own unremarkable grades and low SAT scores had her wait-listed at the University of Cincinnati, gaining acceptance only when her father called in favors from their English Department.

It wasn't fair how tenderly Andrew stroked Elena's

face when they thought no one was watching, while Anne's own boyfriends were callous and mean. How many more times would Anne lie beneath a man she didn't love? How many more times must she feign pleasure to make someone like her? How much longer did she have to pretend to be happy?

It wasn't fair when a semi collided into their parents' sedan, slamming them into the guardrails and pitching them straight into the side of a building. And again as her sister collapsed into Andrew's arms, while Anne had nothing to hold on to but her own elbows.

It wasn't fair when the doctors told them nothing could be done. Andrew clasped her sister's hand when their father's life support turned off. The three of them watched as he drew his final breaths. It wasn't fair when a pulmonary embolism claimed their mother only a week later. And again at the funeral, as Anne stood next to her sister while distant relatives and friends of their parents offered condolences.

A resolute Elena took care of everything, with Andrew by her side, while Anne broke apart piece by piece. She lost bits of herself in the hearse, at the church, at their parent's overturned plots, in the long nights she spent in her childhood house.

What do I have? Anne thought, clutching one of her mother's dresses to her face and tasting the salt of her tears. *Nothing. Nothing. Nothing.*

An unfamiliar voice whispered, *You can make*

something of yourself. You're a chameleon. You can adapt. You can be anything you want.

Others may have perceived Anne as weak and shallow, but she told herself she was a *survivor*. She could turn her life around. Perhaps she didn't have Elena's brains, but she had something better—something *greater*. But it needed to be used soon, before it expired, or at least until she accrued the funds for the upkeep of plastic surgery.

I'm going to find my own dream man, Anne thought as she drew together a plan in the darkness. *Someone a million times better than Andrew. Smarter. And loaded. Someone who can treat me exactly the way I deserve.*

Anne's husband flared in her memory: his face, those ice-blue eyes, the warmth of his skin. How he loved telling the story of their chance meeting at a butterfly arboretum—but that wasn't the truth. Anne had known him before and sought him out. In all their years together, she'd never told him.

She'd seen Frederick for the first time at Best Buy. He strode through the automatic doors as she scraped through the clearance DVD bin. He wasn't a large man, or tall, but he had a presence that Anne recognized meant wealth. The smooth lines of his suit denoted a designer brand. His loafers appeared custom-made. When he scanned the store, small wrinkles creviced across his rugged face.

Anne found herself instantly drawn to him. She followed him through the store as he purchased a five thousand dollar big screen television as easily as buying a package of AA batteries. She'd wanted to say something then, but she was in a sweaty pair of workout shorts and an oversize T-shirt, having just finished a marathon cardio session at the gym. Hardly the "meet cute" she had in mind.

She watched him until he disappeared in the parking lot, her heart caught in a net of longing, yet with a keen premonition they would meet again. True, she had noticed the flash of a gold band on the only finger that mattered, but she told herself this was just a detail. She only had to wait.

As if by fate, she saw his picture in the paper two weeks later. His company had just donated two million dollars to a halfway house reconstruction project downtown. The tax breaks probably outweighed the humanitarian desire, but he said all the right things in the article. His team wanted to better society by assisting in the economic depression. He wore a tailored suit and a tight smile, with a hint of gray streaking his temples. He was older—Anne had known that when she first spotted him—but their fifteen-year spread did not deter her. It only meant that he had the resources to fund the life of her dreams.

Anne Googled him and discovered, unsurprisingly,

that he was something close to brilliant, or at least as smart as her sister. His degrees impressed her less than his company's charitable donations. That meant he had money to burn. It didn't matter that he was married, or had two children. Like her sister, she felt on a deep, almost simian level that she'd found the man of her dreams. She tried confiding in Elena, but her sister dismissed her with contempt. "Andrew was single. This guy is married. Leave him alone."

"But it could be love," Anne protested.

"It's lust," Elena countered. "Find someone else."

When a month passed and fate dealt Anne no further hands, she heeded her sister's advice. Her "someone else" came as a Starbucks barista named Stephen that made love like a train and bought her the best turquoise jewelry he could afford. But when his rings turned her fingers green, Anne checked her heart. Stephen was a distraction, nothing more. He would *not* be her husband.

Her life turned on a casual Sunday morning as Stephen made cappuccinos and split the paper. He took the sports section and the hard news and handed her *Parade* and the comics section. Flipping through the leaflets as she sipped her coffee, Anne found herself in possession of the obituaries. Something guided her interest through the small squares of ink, reading them as if browsing through apartment listings. As if strings pulled her eyes, she drew to the now-familiar name: Frederick Strafford.

"Philanthropic entrepreneur Frederick Strafford laid to rest his loving wife, daughter, and son Wednesday evening at a private service..." the obituary began.

Hands shaking, Anne read how a drunk driver cut their lives short. She pictured hands at the steering wheel. Glass splintering as tires screamed on the asphalt. A confused Frederick dragged from the managed vehicle. Him awakening alone at the hospital— only to discover that his entire family was dead.

Anne read the obituary again and again. The words hurled her back to a memory she tried to suppress. Alone at the hospital, devastated by the deaths of her parents.

Destiny linked her with Frederick Strafford. She couldn't deny it any more than her own heartbeat.

"You okay?" Stephen asked, causing her to jump.

"Yeah." She wiped her clammy forehead. "I'm fine."

"You look like you've seen a ghost. What's going on?"

"Nothing, nothing." Anne forced a smile until Stephen returned to the sports forecasts. Stephen knew only that her parents were dead, none of the specifics. She was never comfortable sharing those moments with him, or anyone. In fact, the only people who knew her part in terminating her father's life support were Elena and Andrew, and they had never spoken of it. Not since they heard their father's heartbeat echo on a machine, and then the machine turned off, and the long line of death tracing across the screen. They had walked out together: Elena tucked against Andrew, Anne clasping her elbows as pain and loss ossified in her bones.

In the beginning, it took almost nothing for Anne's eyes to burn with tears. Hearing a line from *Jane Eyre* and remembering her father reading its pages. The faintest trace of sofrito that took her back to her mother's cooking. Remembering her parents dance to the distant beat of the Gipsy Kings.

Sometimes Anne could visit an Argentinean restaurant without her throat closing. Or breathe in a new book's smell without suffering a panic attack. She was healing, but it had taken years. Poor Frederick Strafford, with a triplicate wound, freshly carved. What would become of him?

A second memorial service was scheduled for the following week to accommodate out-of-state friends and family. Anne, who had dropped out of college and worked at Starbucks with Stephen, took the afternoon off. She sat at the back of the church as Frederick gave a heartbreaking eulogy. When his voice broke, his brother led him from the dais with Frederick sobbing against his shoulder like a child.

Behind Anne, a couple spoke of Frederick visiting the arboretum in a search for peace. How he walked the winding paths and fed the ducks and geese, speaking to no one.

Anne knew the arboretum. She learned he visited on Thursday and Saturday, between conferences. A plan unfurled in her mind. They'd meet casually at the butterfly house. She'd thrill him with her charm, and he'd invite her to dinner. She'd spread her seduction over many weeks, aiming for a proposal with a five-carat diamond.

The plan evaporated as soon as it formed. Sitting in the back of a melancholy church, Anne knew she couldn't do it. She saw this man with his racking shoulders, his pain emanating like the foulest stench.

Who am I? she thought. *What am I?*

Anne fled the church, vowing never to think about Frederick Strafford again.

Anne awoke in the night, her hair tangled with sweat, her mouth bone-dry. The memories were flooding through her, turning over each other, surging, bending. When she closed her eyes, she fell through time again. Voices bubbled to the surface of her dreams. Sunshine warmed her face. Mosquitos itched her bare calves.

"We tag the monarchs before they're released for their migration to Mexico in November," explained a volunteer to a cluster of listeners. She pointed out the breeds of butterflies: the painted lady, the red admiral, the black and tiger swallowtail. They fluttered about inside the netted gazebo.

Anne recognized these various breeds from her family's trips to the arboretum. It'd been a year since she stepped through the squeaky doors. She inhaled the pungent scents of wet soil, leaves, and the dusty filaments tracking through checkered beams of sunlight. She flashed to her father, squatting beside her as he explained the metamorphoses of moths and butterflies. The wonder when they emerged from their spun or glistening shelters—completely transformed, and ready to begin a new life.

Anne wasn't sure what had returned her to the arboretum. Unable to rid her mind of Frederick Strafford, she had visited on a Thursday the previous year, shortly after his family's memorial service. She had seen him wandering alone on the paths, sitting on the grass by one of the dark ponds. With grim purpose, he'd uprooted and discarded countless shards of grass. Anne watched him for close to twenty minutes, not once speaking. She needed to observe, not interact. What could she possibly say to him, anyway? His vacant expression made her doubt he'd even see her, much less form words. When he left, she bid him a silent goodbye, hoping his life turned for the better, and that—perhaps—he could find love again.

As a pair of black spicebush swallowtails fluttered past, a chill blew across Anne's neck and a familiar hum rattled her ears.

She turned to see a man push through the gray metal door and meander between visitors, his hands cupped behind his back. Now he rested at a squat next to a series of bright green host plants, their leaves heavy with dots of eggs and the batting wings of mating butterflies. Wearing the same nondescript tracksuit from the previous year, he scrutinized the autumnal wings of a pale Cecropia moth.

Frederick Strafford.

It was an experience foreign to Anne: knowing so much about a man who was unaware of her own existence. She sensed destiny clicking into place. She was there with him, as if guided by the hands of Fate. Finally, like her sister had been with Andrew, Anne was at the right place at the right time.

With forced casualness, Anne stepped over to stand at his shoulder, feigning interest in a shimmering sack that wriggled from a leaf a few feet away. "Hmmm," she said, loud enough for him to hear, "what an interesting cocoon. I think it's going to hatch!"

Frederick glanced at her tanned, lean legs, draped in a white linen skirt. Anne sent a prayer of thanks for her flattering outfit, makeup, and perfectly dyed blonde hair. She sensed his interest the second their eyes met. She *had* him.

Frederick Strafford rose and said in a friendly voice, "Actually, it's called a chrysalis."

"A chrysalis?" said Anne, as if hearing it for the

first time. She didn't say her father had drilled the correct word since reading "The Hungry Caterpillar". Most of the world believed butterflies spun cocoons, but only moths did. Anne flashed a smile and asked in an innocent voice, "How is that different from a cocoon?"

Frederick pointed to the wriggling sack. "From what I've gleaned, a chrysalis is the residual skin shed by the caterpillar—the would-be butterfly—after attaching to a leaf or twig. A cocoon is something closer to silk, spun by moths." Frederick rubbed the back of his neck, a gesture Anne would grow to recognize as his only betrayal of nervousness. "At least I think that's how it goes. Does that make any sense?"

"Absolutely." Anne's grin broadened as she leaned towards him. "I can't believe I've been saying it wrong my whole life. How embarrassing!"

Frederick chuckled. "Don't feel bad. I didn't know the difference until about a year ago, and I've got some years on you."

"Do you?" She arranged her face in what she hoped was the picture of innocence. "You're not in your thirties?"

"You flatter me." He smiled then, genuinely, as he openly regarded her. "I'm sure you're closer to twenty than thirty yourself. Or is it rude to ask a woman's age who isn't broaching menopause?"

"I'm twenty-six," she said, tucking a stand of hair

playfully behind her ear. With a shy smile, she added, "And old enough for a lot of things."

Frederick's eyes shifted. She sensed he recognized the buried meaning in her words, but wondered if he had misinterpreted—suspecting he had, while praying he had not.

"If I were to guess," she said, turning to him fully, "I would put you at thirty-five."

He chuckled again. "Try forty-one."

"Really?" She tried to look surprised as she calculated a number she already knew. "Well, that's only fifteen years."

"You're quick on the math," he said, his tone admiring. "You in school?"

"Not anymore," she returned with an airy laugh. "And I certainly wasn't in math. I studied British literature."

"Really? I—" A small boy running for his friends knocked Frederick into her. "I'm so sorry," said Frederick, his heavy hands gripping Anne's exposed arms.

"It's okay." She brushed her fingers against his and gave him a coy smile. She was near enough to catch the scent of his cologne, ounce-for-ounce more than she earned in a month.

His hands lingered many moments longer than necessary. In that instant, Anne knew she had him, as she knew she had all the men that had traipsed through her life, looking at her first with curiosity, then desire. The trick would be in keeping him. But how, when her longest relationship had only lasted four months?

"I'm Frederick," he said, taking a step back and offering his hand. "Frederick Strafford."

Anne almost gave him the name she used at clubs: Victoria Winslow. It was a name she had invented in high school, coupled with her desired personality. She'd used this name when ordering cocktails at clubs too old for her, then with casual flings, saving her real name for long-term boyfriends and family. The V was on her lips, her teeth pressed to form the word, but she corrected herself quickly, and, beaming, replied, "Anne Turner. Pleased to meet you."

"A pleasure, Anne." He smiled and closed his hand over hers. "So. Tell me about yourself."

I'm a chameleon, Anne thought as she answered him, her answers light and charming. She watched her reflection in his eyes, her own beauty mirrored back. *I can be anyone you want me to be, Frederick Strafford. Anyone at all.*

Anne began by exaggerating some of her interests and concealing others. She supported Frederick's training for half-marathons, standing—uncomplaining—in the early-morning chill with other families at the finish line. She feigned wonder whenever he presented a word he thought she didn't know, even though she often knew its definition. At dinner parties, she tried to contribute to the conversations. But more often than not, his colleagues' wives and girlfriends either possessed PhDs or were incapable of calculating a ten percent tip. Anne found herself curiously stranded somewhere in between: not that smart, but certainly not dumb. She struggled to keep up with the academics discussing string theory and Venetian mercantilism and was bored by the women who only wanted to talk about Botox and weight loss.

Though no one directly remarked on their age difference, Anne caught many conniving looks. She'd inevitably blurt, "Harrison Ford, Michael Douglas, and Warren Beatty all married women twenty years their junior! It's actually normal in Hollywood."

The women gave her a pitying glance, sipped their cocktails, and turned elsewhere.

Anne's only recourse to keep Frederick's interest was to sleep with him as many times as possible. She delayed their first time as long as she could. Two months of dinners, park visits, feature films, and Sundays watching football (which she secretly abhorred). When she could keep his hands off her no longer—and, she judged, he'd fallen for her much more deeply than her previous boyfriends—she gave in.

A fifteen year age difference was a lifetime for many, especially in their age brackets. She was relieved to discover that Frederick needed no help in the bedroom. He was vigorous, loving, tender, and longed to spend hours with her in his king-sized bed, their limbs a tangle in his 800-thread count sheets. She used every trick she had accrued in the eleven years since that bumbling afternoon on Bobby Flenderson's pool table. Anne slid her hands against Frederick every morning and every night, their sessions often so intense that it negated his workouts. Or perhaps he couldn't stand to be away from her any longer than necessary.

Anne guarded her heart. She couldn't risk putting all of herself into a relationship that might not last the summer. But then Frederick surprised her at the steakhouse she waitressed on their three-month anniversary, his arms heavy with pink roses. As the other waitresses shot her envious glares, Anne's spirits surged. She wanted to sneer, "Look at me *now*, bitches!"

Frederick listened to Anne like no one else. He massaged her feet whenever she vented about a new manager, her awful co-workers, or how her face ached from smiling so she could earn bigger tips. Yet his tenderness made the evenings with his friends that much harder. Was she good enough? The first wives looked at Anne like she was nothing more than a bimbo with manicured claws ready to sink into rich, available flesh.

Maybe there was some truth in that. Anne was reinventing herself, aligning everything she was to what she believed Frederick wanted. Her sister had noted the change and mentioned it the first time the four of them went out to dinner. "Who are you trying to impress?" Elena demanded as Anne powdered her nose in the bathroom mirror. Elena stood with her back to the sink, arms crossed in disapproval.

"What do you mean?" Anne asked, not meeting her eyes.

"I mean, *look* at you!" Elena spread her hands. "Dinner was all about Frederick. It used to be all about you."

Anne grinned despite herself. "Well, maybe it's a good thing. You always said I was too self-absorbed. Isn't this better?"

"I'm not sure." She hesitated. "You're like a robot: nodding at everything he says. Laughing at everything. Agreeing with everything. The Anne I knew wouldn't think he was so interesting. It's like you're turning yourself into a Stepford Wife."

Anne glared at her. "I might say the same thing about you and Andrew."

"Excuse me?"

"You heard me. I had to be happy while you had a boyfriend when I suffered though the worst time of my life. *Alone.* Now it's my turn to be happy."

"He's too old for you," said Elena.

"Age is just a number," Anne returned.

Elena let out an exasperated groan. "It's not just a number! It's an enormous factor! Christ, you're from two entirely different generations. What do you have in common?"

"Lots of things." Anne pursed her lips, reapplying lipstick over two unsmeared crimson lines.

"You know that sex doesn't count," Elena snapped.

Anne's cheeks flared. "God, why can't you be happy for me? Can't you see that I'm happy?"

"I *want* you to be happy. I just want this to be sincere. For this to be what you really want."

"You've never known what I've wanted." Anne flung her lipstick back into her tiny purse. "Do you even like him? He's been perfect to you. And to Andrew."

"It's not..." Elena paused, tried again. "I'm not... it's just..."

For the first time Anne could remember, her sister struggled with formulating a sentence. Anne wanted to flee the ladies' room, to return to the comfort of Frederick's arms, but her sister's bumbling efforts rooted her to the floor.

Elena sighed again. "I want you to be happy. I've always wanted that. And if you say that you're happy, that this relationship is real, then I believe you. Okay?"

"Fine." Anne squared her shoulders as she faced her sister. "I'm happy."

Elena gave a grudging nod, but Anne sensed she didn't believe her.

As the restroom door swung shut behind them, Anne wondered if she even believed herself.

As the months passed and his touch became as familiar as her own skin, Anne fell into her new role as the woman on Frederick's arm. Dutiful, compliant, subservient to his power and intellect, and—above all—sensuous and beautiful. She both feared and hungered for those evenings when he took her out and paraded her like a prized peacock to be viewed in all her splendor. He must have seen the admiring glances of his colleagues, and what she hoped were envious ones from their female counterparts. Although Anne never truly fit in, she'd won a rare prize.

She knew the exact day Frederick would propose because he kept smiling at her like a love-struck teenager, his hand in a constant swipe at the back of his neck. That morning, he announced that he had made reservations at La Florine, the most expensive restaurant within a four-hour drive. Upon their arrival, he ordered a bottle of Cristal. Anne had dressed in a low-cut, black sequined dress and matching heels, her hair and makeup professionally done that afternoon. She swayed when the four-hundred dollar bottle arrived in a dewy champagne bucket stacked with flawless ice.

Frederick took her hand after they finished their scallop risotto appetizers and said, "Anne. You know I love you more than I ever thought possible, especially—" His voice caught. Pain flashed through his eyes.

Anne squeezed his fingers, trying to regain the momentum. "I know, Frederick. I love you, too."

His gaze lingered on her a moment longer, and he sighed and clasped her hand tighter. "I never thought I could feel this way again. You make me feel wonderful. Whole. You make me want to get up in the morning. You give me..." He searched for the words. "You make me feel *alive*."

Anne smiled. "Thank you. I hope I do."

"Indeed, you do." He withdrew his hands and reached into his jacket.

Here it is, Anne thought, her mouth dry as sand. *My new life is about to begin!*

His smile wavering, Frederick revealed a small black velvet ring box. He stood from the table, discarded his linen napkin on his seat, and came to kneel beside her. "Anne Turner," he said, his voice low but firm. "Will you do me the honor of marrying me?"

He opened the box, and Anne's heart lurched. It wasn't the Hollywood rock she had envisioned: a perfect stone as big as her thumb. It was a simple white gold band, with a diamond that barely pushed the single-carat range.

Anne hid her disappointment, knowing she only had herself to blame. Frederick made no secret that he despised women who lusted after expensive jewelry. Anne had even agreed with his diatribes that the diamond industry was a racket. She'd lied to him, because that's what he wanted to hear. How could she have expected him to go against his beliefs, caving into societal pressures that expected men to mortgage their houses for a ring? Anne was probably lucky he didn't present her with a brassy trinket from a Cracker Jack box. Yet for all his derision of brainwashed women, Anne still wanted a ring that proclaimed she'd made it. That someone of worth had chosen her above all others. That she *deserved* it.

Anne's mind pealed over the past six months. Her pursuit of this relationship. The hundreds of hours she'd used her body for his pleasure. The evenings spent listening to him, agreeing with him, making him feel like the greatest man in the world. Everything she had done, this new person she'd become, had led to this—and this was exactly what she wanted, the life she had always dreamed of attaining.

It was hers. She had *won*.

Anne forced a smile and slipped the simple ring over her finger. She took Frederick's face in her hands, kissed him exactly as she had seen in the movies, and said, "Of course I'll marry you, Freddy. You're the only man for me."

Chapter Twenty-Four

HER DREAMS DARKENED. Time jumped as she skipped months and years, leaving behind blank and disjointed segments of memory. Then the blur slowed and sharpened into focus, and Anne was in a hotel bed, and not alone.

"You're the only man for me," Anne moaned against Luke Harris's shoulder, gripping him tightly as he sagged against her, spent. Their sweat lingered on the crisp hotel sheets, mingling with the vanilla and orange blossom gels from their shared Jacuzzi bath.

Luke rolled onto his back, his chest heaving. "That was awesome," he said, his breath ragged. "God. It's never been that good. Ever. Where'd you learn that stuff?"

A smug smile warmed Anne's face. "I aim to please."

"You sure do." He ran his hands over her naked skin, eliciting trembles and a squeal of delight.

"Not just yet," she said, covering his hand with hers. "I need a minute."

"I'll give you ten." He kissed the curve of her neck and stood from the bed, unabashed by his own nakedness. He strode to the bathroom and shut himself away to brush his teeth and wash his hands. It was an inexplicable ritual he performed each time they made love, and Anne had never asked why.

Anne let her hands skim across her bare skin. She touched her clavicle first—a long, tender bone looking more defined by the day—then across her breasts and nipples. Then down her slender waist, hips, and the slope of her thighs. She'd lost most of her curves over the past few months from vigorous dieting and a harsh trainer at the gym. Anytime the scale registered another pound of weight loss, she squealed with victory.

Frederick said she needed to slow down. That she didn't need to lose weight. That she was perfect. But Anne waved him off. Luke had shown her the truth, what she lacked, what she needed to improve. And he was the expert, wasn't he? He was one of the best plastic surgeons in the state. Later he'd tell her of his occasional Hollywood starlet, which augmented the tedium of women making themselves over for their new husbands.

Anne remembered their initial consultation. Watching him across a wide oak table as he showed her a diagram of a woman's face. He pointed at Anne's faint frown lines, the shallow etching on her forehead, and the barely discernible wrinkles beside her mouth. Frederick said she had been crazy, that she was thirty-one years old and didn't need facial fillers. But Anne knew her teenage habit of roasting herself in the sun had prematurely weathered her. She hated the marks that forked across her skin. Luke had seen them, too. He'd read her face like a fortuneteller reading palms and pricked her with Botox and Restylane.

She remembered the cologne Luke Harris wore to the office. How his muscular side pressed against her as he massaged the serum into her forehead. How she'd snuck glances up at him when the nurse wasn't looking. Had she known even then? Or was it later when he warned about the return of "dynamic wrinkles"? "Look in the mirror," Luke instructed. "Try to look surprised or laugh. You'll see them."

And she did. Every time.

"You're beautiful," Frederick assured her later. "You're being ridiculous."

Anne knew she wasn't. The best part of her was rotting away.

Anne dressed her best for her next visit with Dr. Harris. When his nurse left, Anne slipped him a card with her number, even though he had it in her chart. What he didn't have was the hotel's address, which she had helpfully provided.

Luke had taken the paper slowly, his dark eyes

meeting hers as he tucked a strand of his black hair behind an ear. How she had longed to do that herself, to touch his hair, his face, the heat of his skin, the pressing weight of his body. When he had read her face again and saw her brazen desire, lust filled his eyes, and Anne reveled in the effects of her power.

Luke had not been the first lover she had taken since her wedding day. He was, by Anne's count, her fifth and—she hoped—her final. Her first six months of marriage had been pleasant enough. Gradually her time with Frederick thinned as work took him out of the country, sometimes for six weeks at a time. Anne often wandered the empty house touching the cold, empty bedsheets. She missed his attention like a lost limb.

Cindy provided some comfort in their frequent trips to bars and movies. Her sister less so now that all she could talk about was work, her yearning for babies, and impending motherhood. Anne had no other friends and had lost touch with her girlfriends from high school. Most had moved away. Almost all were married with kids, often to be raised by au pairs as her former friends ossified in their country clubs.

When Cindy flirted with men she met at bars, or danced provocatively with them at clubs, Anne joined in. Shyly at first, wondering if she should. Then openly accepting their slippery drinks and suggestive banter, craving their lust like an addict. That's how she met Mark. A stranger at a bar, Mark was gorgeous, which

at first made her overlook his strange mannerisms: he
fled immediately after sex and left angry voicemails
whenever Anne couldn't see him, prompting Anne to
delete his phone number and blacklist their favorite
haunts. She vowed never to cheat on her husband
again.

Time passed, and she grew restless. Anne amended
the vow to never sleep with anyone *single*. Why
threaten her marriage with a jealous lover? Two years
passed before Derek, a married optometrist, who made
her feel beautiful and important. But Derek left her to
pursue marriage counseling, and Anne fell in with
Charlie, a manager at RadioShack, with hands that
crushed her exquisitely. Then Eddie, her most recent
conquest. He traveled domestically three times a
month, bragged about his hotel points, and burned
through money like cigarettes.

These relationships were fleeting. All men were
married or living with girlfriends. None endangered
her life with Frederick. She even kept a secret album of
her conquests to reflect upon during lonely times.
Anytime Frederick flew to New York or Miami, Anne
pulled out the album and traced the faces of her lovers,
remembering their sizzling touch. She and Derek in
Puerto Vallarta. She and Charlie in a local bar drunk-
enly snapping a picture on a disposable camera. Sipping cappuccinos with Eddie at the Dallas Ritz-
Carlton. Spending a long weekend at the Marriot with
Luke.

As she lay in the enormous hotel bed, her heart filled with pleasure and remorse. It was always this way. She adored the moments when she could release herself, to give and receive pleasure, but when these feelings faded, she saw her husband's face. She remembered his initial tenderness, and how his hands held hers less and less. Could she ever be happy again? And if not, should she even stay?

Anne turned on her side and tucked her face into a pillow. No, she could never divorce Frederick. They had been married five years, and in that time she had grown accustomed, even entrenched, in the life he provided, unable to imagine any other existence. She figured it was the same with him.

Besides, what would she return to? Waitressing at Longhorn Steakhouse? Stealing other people's Sunday papers for dollar-off coupons? Scouring supermarket shelves for sale items? Borrowing money from her sister? Waiting for Elena to scrawl out check after check, both of them knowing it wasn't a loan? Enduring those judgmental looks as her sister tore the paper from the billfold and handed it to her as if surrendering the deed to her house?

No. She couldn't go back. Not to that life. That wasn't living.

Luke emerged from the bathroom, scrunching a towel between his hands that he discarded by the bed before climbing in. "Hi there, beautiful." He nuzzled her neck. "Did I give you enough of a breather?"

"Do you ever miss your wife?" The question was out of her mouth before she could stop it.

The air seemed to chill around her, as if Anne had opened a window to a snowstorm. Luke froze, then slowly shifted to meet her eyes. "What?"

"I'm sorry," she said, berating herself. What was she thinking? Luke had been clear from the beginning. Never, ever, mention his wife or children. Anne pretended they didn't exist, as Frederick didn't exist for him. Their spouses lived on a different plane, in a different universe. Their hours in a hotel were a stolen gift, theirs only to enjoy, with nothing and no one from their real world ever to intrude.

Luke grimaced. "You know what we agreed to."

"I know, I know." Tears pricked the back of Anne's eyes. What was happening to her? "I just...I was thinking about Fred—my husband."

Luke winced, as if the mere mention of another man pained him. "Please. Let's not talk about this."

"I'm sorry." But even as she said this, she filled with questions. Did Luke love his wife? Did he miss her, what they once had together? Or was she the monster Anne envisioned? Luke had never told her anything about his wife, not even her name, though he had once said he had two young children. Certainly she had never spoken of Frederick, and Anne knew him not to be a monster. He was certainly distant, especially recently, aloof and somewhat cold. But not a monster.

"I'm sorry," Anne said again. She pulled Luke closer, wanting to put this behind them, but his arousal had dimmed. They laid in each other's arms for a long time, Anne stroking Luke's hair through her fingers as his breathing deepened. She thought of her husband in Philadelphia, far away from her, and wondered if he was lying in a hotel bed with someone else in his arms, someone better. The pain of that thought and the image it created burned like acid. Yet something told her that Frederick was not with anyone else, if for no other reason than she recognized the signs—and was an expert at hiding them herself.

He can't find out, Anne thought, sending a prayer that Frederick never learned her secret. It wasn't just the prenuptial agreement. It was his heart. Frederick would think it the ultimate betrayal, which it *wasn't.* This was something she needed. Something he couldn't give her. Maybe nobody could.

Her mind turned to Luke's wife, perhaps even now tending to their two children. Maybe she was putting them to bed or grappling with their slippery limbs in a bath, hoping her husband would soon come home.

Did she know? Did she even suspect? Anne often thought the woman had to be a fool not to know. Anne would've demanded details of any overnight trip. Would have searched Frederick's clothes for hints of perfume or smears of lipstick. Would have watched his face when they made love to ensure he wasn't thinking of somebody else, someone not *her*.

Anne wondered if Luke still cared for his wife. Did they even have sex anymore? Or was their lovemaking as rough as Anne's? Did he cradle his wife's face or whisper loving words?

Anne needed Luke to tell her something, *anything*, about his wife and their life together. But when Anne opened her mouth, she found her lover already asleep.

Chapter Twenty-Five

TIME SPED FORWARD AGAIN. Skipped several beats. "But I need to talk to someone..." Anne was saying. And she saw her sister before her, older now, with a face drawn and unhappy. Her eight-month-old niece stretched out on the beige carpet at her sister's house, playing with a plastic ball.

"Talk to Cindy," Elena said. "I think she's the best person for this mess you're in."

Anne couldn't admit that Cindy frayed her nerves. Her mood flipped from sycophantic to jealous in the space of a heartbeat. Their trips to Vegas and Atlantic City eventually wore on Anne. Cindy complained endlessly of her husband, whining he spent too much time away in countries she couldn't even pronounce.

"I'd rather talk to you," Anne said, wincing at the desperation clawing at her voice. Why hadn't she made more friends? How pathetic to keep running back to her sister.

"I don't want to talk about it," Elena snapped. "I'm tired of hearing about it. All the affairs. All the cheating—"

"They're my lovers," Anne corrected.

"And that too." Elena gave a threatening wave of her rice cake wafer. "That word. *Lover.* It's a euphemism for what's really going on. A bunch of adults cheating on their spouses. It's disgusting. *Disgusting.*"

Anne put up her hands. "I get it. I get it."

"Do you? Because I'm serious. I don't want to hear any more about these guys you're seeing."

"Guy," she corrected again. "Singular." Anne wanted to say more, but knew she shouldn't disclose further details. How she both loved and despised Luke. The crazy bet Cindy had concocted over cocktails. No, her sister would never speak to her if she caught even the slightest whiff of *that.*

"Cheating with one person at a time doesn't make it any better. It's gross." Elena dropped herself on the couch across from her, taking another crunching bite from her rice cake, which flaked shiny bits of wafer across the room.

"You're gross," Anne said, turning her lips in disgust. "Seriously. How can you eat that stuff?"

"It's good for you. It curbs the appetite."

"Curbs the appetite? Are you trying to lose weight?" Anne gestured to her sister's stomach, which had shrunk from a pumpkin to a washboard three months after Charlotte's birth. Elena *never* dieted. Anne couldn't remember her sister ever being critical of her body—a quality that secretly riled her. Did she see a flaw in herself? A pouch of fat? Hanging skin? A web of stretch marks?

"I'm not trying to lose weight," Elena said. "I'm just trying to instill healthy eating habits for Charlotte. It's the same reason I eat salads. It's good to model that kind of behavior."

Anne rolled her eyes around the house that had once been the epitome of modern sparseness, choking now with giant stuffed animals, jumpers, Pack 'N Plays, walkers, rattles, blocks, and neon plastic cups. Before, Elena was a savvy marketing executive. Now she was a stay-at-home mother who recited French to her newborn in a moronically high-pitched voice. "Of course. It's *always* about the baby."

Elena scowled. "What's that supposed to mean?"

The words came out in a rush. "Everything you do is for the baby! All you ever talk about is the baby! Charlotte, look at this! Charlotte, look at that! Do you know how to spell 'encyclopedia', Charlotte?" Anne let out a grating laugh. "As if she understands what you say. Honestly. You act like she's some sort of miracle. She's just a kid, Elena. People have them every day."

Her sister's expression shot Anne with regret. Of course she remembered, too late, about the miscarriages. Three over the past four years. Each time, Anne stroked her sister's hair. Assured her she'd have a baby one day. That maybe the time wasn't right. Elena sobbed bitterly into a pillow, into tissues, into her hands, rarely speaking.

Anne hadn't known that her sister was pregnant with Charlotte until halfway through the second trimester. She had received an update via text message when the two were barely speaking. When Anne told Frederick, clutching the phone with its blurry ultrasound photo, he said Elena was probably worried about another loss. That perhaps she wanted to feel secure before announcing the news.

"She used to feel secure with *me*," said Anne, but inside she knew the truth. Elena had never been secure with her. Not really. She kept her heart locked in a box, like Snow White's huntsman. Most of the time, Anne never knew what went on in her mind, even though she was her sister—her *twin*.

"I'm sorry," Anne said, meaning it. "I'm sorry. Forget what I said."

No tears glistened in Elena's eyes. Her sister's face was as smooth as a porcelain plate. She gave Charlotte's head a comforting pat, then disappeared into the kitchen. Anne heard the garbage can open, the rice cake presumably tossed inside.

Elena returned to the couch and let her daughter play with stacks of *Winnie the Pooh* books. Finally, she steepled her fingers under her chin. "Perhaps you're right. Maybe eating rice cakes sends Charlotte the wrong message. I don't want her thinking I'm on a diet."

Anne smiled with relief. "Good. I just—"

"But who are you to talk?" Elena interrupted. "You're practically transparent. I don't think I've ever seen you this thin in my life."

Anne sat up straighter. "Really? You can tell I've lost weight?"

Elena frowned as she arranged herself on the floor, dragging her daughter away from Anne. "It's not a compliment. You look emaciated. Sickly."

"Come on. That's not true." Anne knew she looked like she'd stepped off a *Vogue* cover. At least, that was what Luke said. She just needed a few more adjustments, and she would be perfect. "I don't look sickly."

"You do. Have you looked at yourself in the mirror?"

All the time, Anne wanted to say. "Of course I have. I think I look great. Fantastic, even."

Elena paused as she openly regarded her. "What are they shooting into your face? Are you even capable of making discernible expressions? What's next? Breast implants? Liposuction?"

Anne had had enough. Forget what she had said, the hurt she might have caused earlier. What about the hurt her sister had piled on for years? What about that?

Anne launched from the couch and balled her hands into fists. "Can you stop coming down on me? God, it's always been like this. Even when we were kids, you were always judging me. Always lecturing me. You're not my mother."

"Don't you think I know that?" Elena didn't bother standing up. Instead, she lifted her child to her chest and let Charlotte rub her small, tired face on her shoulder. Seeing them cradled together, Anne wondered at the last time Elena held her. It must have been years—probably not since their parents' funeral. "Sure," her sister continued, "maybe I criticize you too much, and maybe I point out your flaws. But have you taken a good, hard look at yourself lately? What have you become? I don't even recognize you anymore."

"I'm everything I've ever wanted to be," Anne said, though this wasn't entirely true. She needed one more thing fixed and had all the intention of having it done soon—and for free. It only required persuasion, and she had that quality in spades. Anne would have her breasts enlarged, from an ample size C to an enviable DD. Then she'd be perfect. Then she would show her sister and everyone else. *Then.*

Elena let Charlotte crawl away and then crossed her arms over her enormous chest, the very chest Anne secretly sought. "So why are you here? Tell me that."

"I came here for marriage advice, but I can see that I don't need any from you." Anne rushed to pick up her purse, scrambled for her heels.

"You want marriage advice?" Elena called after her. "Divorce your husband or stop screwing around on him! You can't have both!"

I can too, Anne thought, her mind dark as she slammed out of her sister's house. *I can have both. I can have anything I want. You just watch me.*

Anne stomped out to her car, but when she saw her hand shaking on the door handle, she knew she should probably take a walk before driving. And so she stalked down her sister's sidewalk, angry tears pushing at the back of her eyes. All her life she had wanted her sister to...what? Envy her? Be jealous of her? Love her unconditionally? But now Anne had the distinct feeling that all Elena felt for her was disdain. That the mere sight of Anne filled her sister with thoughts and memories she would rather have locked away, buried, or burned.

Anne was so absorbed in her own thoughts that she didn't notice Andrew jogging down the path.

"Anne!" he said, coming to a stop. When he saw her face, he pulled out his earphones. "What's wrong?"

"Nothing." Anne pushed a bright smile into her face. "Just thinking. I didn't know you ran."

"Lately, yeah." With a sardonic grin, he gestured to his double chin and stomach roll. "I thought since Elena's busy, I'd catch a run. Try to burn off this weight."

"And how's that going for you?"

He shrugged carelessly. "Okay, I guess. It's going to

take some time. Maybe when Charlotte graduates high school, I'll be back to my old self."

Anne walked the neighborhood with Andrew as he cooled down, keeping the topic light and avoiding the subject of her sister. Doubtless he would return to his house and hear soon enough. Better, Anne decided, to make it look like their argument hadn't affected her.

As she walked beside him, Anne remembered the first time she had seen Andrew on television. That lost teenage boy who kept his eyes downcast through an endless series of devastating questions. His voice filling that long-ago living room as she, her sister, and parents listened with rapt attention. Then his letters filling their mailbox, and finally meeting him at the bus station that frosty December morning. Elena had loved him even then, perhaps before, and maybe even when she had first seen him pixilated on their television screen.

With a sinking feeling, Anne realized she'd never experienced the sweeping love that had overtaken her sister and brother-in-law. With Frederick, she performed the motions without her heart.

Why did Elena get everything? Why couldn't Anne have what she had? Why was life so unfair?

Anne focused on the positive. She'd never have to work again. Meanwhile, Elena spent years scrounging enough money for infertility treatments and, eventually, maternal leave. Anne had no mortgage or car payments or student loans. Elena had all three.

Anne had the life she wanted. But even as she told herself this, doubt shadowed her thoughts.

Anne half-listened as Andrew talked about juggling work and his home-life. He claimed to barely have a minute to himself now that Elena demanded he take Charlotte from the second he came home until their daughter's bedtime. "It's exhausting," he admitted. "She has every half-hour regimented. The alarm is constantly going off."

Anne hid her smile. Elena had once been a workaholic. Now she applied that same focus to her child.

"Of course, Elena's amazing," Andrew added with a touch of guilt. "Motherhood is a huge undertaking. But she's exhausted too. I wish she'd give herself a break."

"Doesn't she run?" Anne asked, while thinking, *A lot, by the size of her waist!*

"Yeah, but even then, she takes Charlotte with her. It's like she can't stand to be away from her, even for an instant."

"You guys ever go out?"

"Go out?" He stared at her as if she'd just switched languages.

"Sure. Go out. You know, like a date. Dinner? A movie? Who do you have to baby-sit?"

"No one. We haven't been out since Charlotte was born."

"That was eight months ago!"

"I know."

Anne stared at Andrew in shock. Eight months without a single night in town? Without going to a play or a film? She couldn't fathom it. Of course Anne had offered to baby-sit, but Elena had insisted that Charlotte was too young, that it was too soon. Anne figured it was because Elena was a new mother, but that eventually she'd crack and research babysitters on Craigslist to escape for a spa day.

But nothing? In eight entire months?

"That's crazy," Anne said, unable to buffer her words. "That's absolutely crazy. How do you feel about that?"

"Well, it's fine. I didn't mean..." Andrew's voice trailed away, as if he'd overshared.

He probably did, Anne thought, smiling inwardly. *Elena would probably kill him for telling me.*

Andrew was like that. He perpetually kept himself on guard until he wasn't, and that always seemed to happen around Anne. He'd relax and open himself, revealing pieces of his history like chapters in a book. He once described the cage his parents locked him in. The endless court hearings to find suitable guardians. The press interviews and articles in the paper. Trying to make new friends and hoping they wouldn't find out about his past. Praying that parents wouldn't tell their children to stay away because they worried his pain was contagious. How nervous he'd been to meet

Anne's parents, especially their well-read father. How their mother's beauty made him anxious until she put him at ease with her natural warmth, effortless charm, and home-cooked meals.

All of this Andrew told her over the years, and Anne was a sympathetic audience. She and her sister were the only women in his life he felt comfortable enough to truly talk to. That trust was a quality he rarely gave to people. Perhaps he trusted Anne because she was her sister's twin. Despite their constant bickering and bouts of silent treatments, their connection defied everything. Their biological tie made them almost the same.

"Sometimes it's hard," Andrew said at last, cracking a wan smile. "There are days I just want to grab a hamburger and fries with Elena and not have to fire up the grill at home. The cleanup never ends."

"Doesn't Elena help with that?" Anne never considered their division of chores. Anne herself rarely cooked. Their housekeeper, Miranda Burns, was vigilant in cleanliness. But one look at Elena's house said there hadn't been a dust rag or a bottle of Windex used in weeks. Maybe in months.

"Not really," Andrew said. "She keeps saying that she's not a housewife. That's she's a mother, and that's it."

"You should hire someone," Anne suggested, envisioning her sister laying out the rules. "I am a mother *only*," Elena would say, clutching her hips. "Not a cook. Not a maid. I gave up my career to raise our child, not become a housewife."

"Can't really afford it," Andrew said, then halted their walk. He tensed as to say something else, then waved a dismissive hand. "It's fine. It's just tiring. It'll get better."

I doubt it, Anne thought. Without thinking, she dropped her hand on his arm and gave a sympathetic squeeze. "Well, I sure hope it does. You know I'm here if you need to talk."

"Thanks, Anne," he said, meaning it. He smiled at her then, and the wall between them momentarily vanished. Anne sensed something there. Had she mistaken his closeness, that look in his eyes, for something more than brotherly affection?

She grinned and said, "Sure, Andy. No problem."

Andrew gave a sigh of relief and resumed their walk. Anne waited until they stepped beyond the sightline of her sister's house before stopping him a second time. "What you said makes me wonder. Are you and Elena still able to get together?"

Andrew blinked in confusion. "Get together?"

"You know," she said, letting a few beats of silence pass. "Be intimate?"

"What?" His voice cracked on the word.

Anne kept her tone playful. "I know how hard it is on couples, especially when a new baby enters the picture. The sex goes right out the window. Am I right?"

There. She saw it. He couldn't keep the truth from his face.

Andrew gave an awkward laugh and glanced toward his house. "Sorry, Anne. I don't think we should talk about this."

"Come on." She put a careless hand on his chest. "We're *family*. Family should be able to talk about anything. It's only natural."

He cleared his throat. "We're fine. It's been rough these last few months. We're just adjusting."

"Hopefully you still find time for yourself," Anne said. "It's an important thing, especially for a man. I should know."

There it was again. That look of recognition. Anne knew without a doubt that Andrew desired her, even if he'd denied it all those years ago. How could he not, when compared to her sister? Sure, Elena had the brains and the clever repartee, but she lacked Anne's sensuality, her sexy confidence, her natural draw of men. Anne had all those qualities. Now she'd prove their power.

"I'd like to give you something," Anne said, as if the thought had just occurred to her. Holding up a finger, she opened the door to her Mercedes, released the glove compartment, and pulled out a crisp white envelope. She closed the door with her hip and passed the envelope to Andrew with a radiant smile.

He hesitated. "What is this?"

"Just a little gift from me to you." She tossed her

hair over her shoulder, a practiced movement. "It should help you get through the slow times. I know there's going to be a lot, especially when the baby demands more of your time. It may be weeks before you're able to find some relief."

Andrew opened the envelope, removed the picture halfway, then immediately shoved it back inside. His cheeks flared. "Anne! I can't—"

"Shhh." She folded her hands over his. She was so close she could reach up and kiss him. But as much as she enjoyed the game, as much as she wanted him to want her, Anne didn't desire him. She yearned only for what he could give. "It'll be our secret," she whispered. "No one has to know."

She leaned up to kiss his cheek, letting her breasts linger on his heaving chest. "Hope it helps, Andy. I'll catch you later."

Anne walked back to her car and slipped into the driver's side. She saw Andrew through the windshield, frozen in place, holding the envelope like an amputated limb. She waved at him playfully, then started up the engine and pulled away. When she glanced at him in the rearview mirror, she saw him slip the envelope into the side pocket of his shorts, and start up the walkway to his house.

Anne imagined him alone in the bedroom, removing the picture carefully, so as not to mar the image. He'd see Anne rearing up against a bear-skin rug. Her platinum-blonde hair a tousled cascade behind her head. Her arms braced against plush animal fur. Her breasts exposed for the camera's lens while the clean sweep of her taut stomach and buttocks provided a delicious contrast against a roaring fire. Her legs bent at two perfect angles, cleverly hiding the V of her groin, while a pair of sparkling crystal heels caught her manicured feet.

The photographer had told her to radiate sensuality, that her husband would appreciate her efforts. And Anne had, imagining herself as a pornographic Cinderella, her electric candor surprising even herself. They took a blur of shots before settling on this singular portrait. Frederick would take it with him on his extended trips. He'd gaze at his wife and not believe his luck.

Anne printed several copies and recently gave one to Luke. Unlike her husband, who admired the shot from every angle, Luke gave it a fleeting glance and handed it back. "It's a pretty picture, sure. But you're even more striking now."

Embarrassed, Anne kept that photo in her dash. Every so often, she'd pull it out. Most would say she was beautiful. But Anne couldn't see past the imperfections. Her smaller left breast. Those matching grates of cellulite on her otherwise smooth thighs. That snaggletooth incisor. The unfilled lines beside her eyes and mouth. That small roll of fat just below her bellybutton that no amount of sit-ups flattened. Taken together, she was practically a monster. She'd put the picture away, deciding that all the injections, dieting, rounds of liposuction, and the pain of recovery—it had all been worth it.

But with Andrew, she knew none of that mattered. Andrew would see her old picture and still find her perfect. Because some men were like that. They couldn't see what was actually there.

As Anne drove home, she imagined Andrew pleasuring himself to her image. Triumph burned through her veins like liquid fire. Her sister's smarts and accomplishments didn't matter, because Anne had won. Now, anytime Andrew was with Elena, he'd be thinking of Anne instead.

Chapter Twenty-Six

In the predawn hours, Anne's last memory returned in glimpses. She saw herself checking her makeup in an airplane lavatory. Hailing a taxi to The Plaza. Huddling in a white pea coat as her black suede boots sank into the cold ground of Central Park.

She'd found the film's location easily enough. She followed a throng of people behind a taped-off area where men with earphones and clipboards stood guard. Occasionally, some held up signs that read "QUIET." Anne tried to see past the wall of shoulders. She thought she saw Jack Post standing near a glimmering pond trading lines with another actor. But then sunlight poured through the clouds, and she realized it was someone else.

"Step back fifteen feet!" ordered a crew member.

The audience moved aside. Anne couldn't see past

the shifting throng, enormous filming equipment, and scattered crew. "Can you see anything?" she asked a woman in front of her.

The woman gave her a cursory glance, then pulled her hood down over her reddening ears. "Nothin'. And we've been here for two hours. I'm hoping they'll sign autographs after this."

"Unlikely," said the man next to them. "They won't even let us use our cell phones!"

"Bastards," said another.

Anne blew hot air into her hands and reviewed the Jack Post Loves List. Parasailing. Sashimi. Matinees. *Braveheart*. Catholicism. Impressionist paintings. Graham Greene martinis. Rock climbing. Crate & Barrel. Warren, Michigan. Private planes. Horseback riding. Skydiving. Frette linens. Organic produce. Purple. Tantric yoga. Magnum condoms.

On the printout, she'd highlighted several items. Jack's favorite paintings: Monet's Haystack series. The best places to rock climb: Yosemite and Joshua Tree. His favorite color (purple, which Anne thought odd) and least favorite (orange). Also his strict preference for salmon sashimi with ginger and sesame seed oil over the mundane spicy tuna.

She and Cindy had accrued Jack Post's likes and dislikes over many weekends. They poured over copies of *People*, *US Weekly*, *In Touch*, *Vanity Fair*, and *Time* and took notes on anything relevant. They watched five documentaries and scoured the Internet. They memorized Jack Post's website and his press statements upon the release of his biggest films. Together they giggled and slurped chocolate martinis and wondered at his bedroom skills. Was he as good a kisser in life as he was in the movies? Cindy theorized he had a tiny penis, so he compensated with illustrious mansions and decadent sports cars. Anne thought him brilliant. Wasn't he always perfectly poised on television?

"He's an actor," Cindy chided.

"A *smart* actor," Anne returned. "He spends his spare time reading all the Tom Clancy novels. And those are huge!"

"That's just so he can star in them," Cindy said with a roll of her eyes.

Anne knew his birthday. His hometown. That he was left-handed. That his high school voted him "Most Likely to Succeed". His discovery by a casting director during Jack's second year of law school. Anne knew about his three sisters. His single mother. His humble origins. That Jack eschewed the paparazzi and only did the marketing required for his films. That he enjoyed skydiving and deep-sea diving.

"How are you going to handle that?" Cindy demanded. "You're terrified of heights!"

"That's a future problem," Anne quipped. She figured while the former terrified her and the latter bored her, she could successfully fake an interest. She'd gotten good at that from all of Frederick's cocktail parties.

Cindy learned Jack was due to film scenes for his new movie, *The Night Watch*, in Central Park. Anne researched his favorite nearby restaurants. The full implication of the bet didn't hit Anne until Cindy insisted she buy a plane ticket. Cindy had hunched over the computer and entered all the required information, needing Anne's help only when the payment was due.

"Right," said Anne, swallowing hard. Was she really going to do this? It was just a joke, right? A silly dare. Anne didn't take it seriously until Cindy handed her the confirmation receipt and squealed that it was *really* happening.

Three days. That was all the time Anne had allowed herself. Frederick was due back from Miami in less than a week, and she didn't want her time in New York to overlap with his arrival and add to his mounting suspicions. It was enough—should Frederick ever pry into the exact details of her trip—that Cindy was going to vouch for her, make up some story that they had taken a girls-only weekend. Not that Frederick liked Cindy. He had told Anne countless times that she should make better friends, that Cindy was a "bad influence." But Anne had scoffed at this. What did Frederick know? Cindy loved her, she loved Cindy, and—okay, yes. They didn't get along as swimmingly as they had in high school, but wasn't that all part of getting older? Cindy always had Anne's best interests at heart, though Frederick never believed Anne when she told him this.

Operation Seduce a Movie Star was originally Cindy's idea. She'd encouraged Anne to pursue Jack Post since they agreed he was the most handsome bachelor in Hollywood. Cindy bought the ticket with Anne's credit card and drove her to the airport. Cindy believed in Anne when no one else would. She was Anne's one loyal friend and sincerely thought that she could do this, if only Anne put her mind to it.

I wonder if I'll even see him, Anne thought, imagining the presence she had seen on screen for years suddenly becoming a reality. It was like chasing Santa Claus. People talked about him the world over, but she suspected only a handful had any sort of meaningful interaction with him. What if she never saw him? What if someone kept her from seeing him? She imagined a security team, their arms crossed with faces like stone, as daunting as a line of FBI agents. What if she met Jack Post but couldn't win him over with her beauty and charm? He was used to beautiful women and had probably entertained hundreds—if not thousands—of knockouts. What made her think she could stand out from such a striking crowd?

But I'm not looking for a relationship, Anne reminded herself. *Just a score.*

This thought eased her coiling mind. She could secure a one-night stand, given the proper meeting. She knew she could. She had done it before. Jack Post was a just man. She could conquer him. Now that she was here, there remained two choices. Go big or go home.

And she wasn't about to admit defeat, at least not yet. She needed to get in the right mindset. She had to play the part.

After a white-gloved bellhop whisked her suitcases from the cab into her hotel suite, Anne skimmed her hands over the silky bed linens and scrunched the plush Mascioni towels in the mosaic-tiled bathroom. Anne adored luxury. She had once stayed with Frederick at The Plaza just after their wedding, when he asked her to accompany him to a meeting with his partners. She spent her time watching pay-per-view movies while nursing a Snickers ice cream bar and a bowl of popcorn, then luxuriated at the spa. Upon Frederick's return, Anne launched into his arms and covered his face with kisses. Frederick laughed as they tumbled into bed. Later, Anne would marvel at the twinkling lights as they drove to Broadway plays and five-star restaurants.

That was six years ago, but it felt more like twenty. Anne couldn't remember the last time Frederick had asked her to come with him on a business trip. When had that stopped? Probably within the year they married.

"It's just getting too hard," Frederick had said, not meeting Anne's eyes as he knotted his navy tie in the mirror. "You demand so much when I take you out.

I'm tired, Anne. All the dinners. The plays. The entertainment. Sometimes I just want to stay in, you know?"

"I can stay in," Anne had replied, although even to herself she didn't sound convincing.

"But that's not you, honey." He had kissed her complacently on the cheek. "Maybe next time, okay? When I'm not so tied up at work?"

But work took all of Frederick's time. There was always another project, another deadline. Anne no longer asked for details, and he stopped explaining. She tired of using her body to entice him. When he turned to her in the night seeking his pleasure, she'd grimace and comply, but he could tell she was forcing herself. Eventually, he stopped trying altogether.

As Anne paced the hotel room alone, she stretched out her arms, feeling the energy of the place. She parted the curtains and gazed out at the New York skyline, at the hundreds of jagged silver buildings that reared into a sky gauzy with a darkening sunset. Then below, at the streets glowing like rows of Christmas lights. But she could hear no sound. She pressed her hand against the cold glass, sensing the promise of a hard winter.

Anne's first sight the next morning was her room-service tray with its remnants of dinner still on the table. She glimpsed the earthy tips of strawberries, rinds of Gruyere cheese, cracker dust, and a wineglass with a single splash of Chardonnay.

Anne rolled over in bed and pressed her hand to her eyes, hoping to stop the mad beating of her heart. What had awoken her?

On the nightstand, her phone—her *secret* phone— vibrated and chimed a voicemail message. It could only be three people: Cindy, Luke, or Eddie.

Anne hesitated, unsure if she wanted to speak to any of them. That was strange. Usually, she couldn't wait to hear their voices. She grimaced as she paged her voicemail and brought the phone to her ear.

"Anne!" came Cindy's unmistakable warble. "Sweetie pie! You didn't call me last night. How's it going? What's the plan? Call me as soon as you get this!"

Anne did. She endured Cindy's hollow encourage- ments for several minutes before making an excuse to hang up.

"Fine, but call me as soon as you hear something," Cindy said, almost breathless.

"Sure thing. Bye." Anne tossed the phone on the comforter and folded her arms over her eyes.

That's when a thought that had been scratching her mind finally bubbled to the surface: *What the hell am I doing?*

Hours later, she felt enormously foolish, and—for the first time in a long time—pathetic as she stood in the freezing cold waiting for a movie star. What did she honestly think would happen? That Jack Post would take one look at her and instantly fall in love? That

only worked on unseasoned ingénues, drunken no-
bodies, or those searching for someone, anyone, else.
And Jack Post was none of these. Even without
meeting him, Anne knew this much.

A distant horn blared, and the crowd dispersed.
Anne checked her watch: 1:15 p.m. They were probably breaking for lunch.

The crowd lightened as workers altered the set.
Lights and cameras rolled down the slope of a hill.
People in matching black hats and coats moved chairs
and directed people outside of the park. She saw no
sign of Jack Post.

Anne sighed and started back for the hotel. Insane
joggers—Anne suspected her sister would have been
one of these—blew past with arms pumping to the
beat of their iPods. Fast-paced dog walkers trailed the
sidewalks, plastic bags swinging on their hips. No children bounded about making snowballs from the three
inches of snow. No homeless huddled in the corners
she could see. A few of the elm and oak trees clung
stubbornly to their autumnal reds and oranges, but
most had shed their leaves in darkening drifts. Anne
crunched through the papery mounds, her heels
sinking into the chilling earth before returning to the
sidewalk.

The wind picked up. Shivering, Anne pulled her
coat tighter. Her gloved fingers turned to ice. Her eyes
watered. Her ears pounded, then burned.

When she arrived back at the hotel, she considered

calling Cindy, but she didn't want to hear that syrupy voice. Anne held the small black phone in her hand, thinking about her husband, his voice, the touch of his hands. Was he thinking about her now? Did he ever?

She spent the rest of the afternoon in bed watching television and munching on a chicken panini she ordered from the kitchen. On one of the entertainment channels she glimpsed Jack Post, and the reporter said that he was filming in Manhattan, after a near two-year hiatus. She wondered what he did with his time, where he went, who he spoke to. If he had people who loved him, truly, for who he was.

Anne skipped dinner and went to bed early. She awoke a few hours later when her other phone—the *real* one—trumpeted loud as a marching band.

She fanned through her purse's contents, fished it out, and blearily read the caller ID. It was her husband.

"Hi Freddy," she said, wondering why he was calling. He used to call her twice a day when he was on business, but lately they had settled on catching up every third night.

"Hello yourself. Did I wake you?" A pause. "It's only 9:30."

"Yeah. I'm not feeling well." She yawned, hoping he heard it.

"I'm sorry. Have you seen a doctor?"

"It's just a head cold." Her heart gave a sickening lurch. What other questions would he ask? What if he was coming home early? She tried to keep her voice level. "Where are you?"

"Still in Miami. That trip to Saudi got moved up."

"Will you be home for Thanksgiving?" She'd already made the arrangements. The wife of one of Frederick's senior partners was lending them her chef—a welcome relief, since the only dish Anne knew was her mother's almond risotto. Frederick had missed Thanksgiving last year and promised to be home this time.

"I'm trying," Frederick said, sounding distracted. "I have a lot more work to do, but I'm making every effort to be there. Of course, it would be easier for me to stay here."

"But it's Thanksgiving," Anne said, wondering why his presence seemed so important.

"I know. I'm trying." He sighed. "Sorry to wake you. Get some sleep, okay? I'll call you tomorrow and we'll talk specifics."

Anne blinked hard. "Okay."

"I love you," he said.

Her heart pinched. "I love you, too."

"Sorry I'm always gone. It's going to get better."

You always say that, Anne thought, *and it never does.* But she was tired of fighting him, and so she said, "I know it will."

"Get some rest. I'll see you at the end of the week."

He clicked off and Anne's phone screen faded to black. She pressed her hands against her eyes, anticipating tears. None came. She was as hollow as if someone had painlessly removed her insides.

What the hell am I doing here? she wondered, then thought of Cindy. Why had her oldest friend been so adamant that she come, and why had Anne listened? She longed to call her sister, to confide everything, but feared Elena's reproach. No. She couldn't call her sister. She couldn't tell her husband. And she didn't want to talk to Cindy.

She thought of her mother, the image of her paling in her mind. Anne's memory only recalled the warmth of her love. A fleeting glimpse of her sashaying hips. Her deft way of cooking. The easy naturalness of her dance. *She'd hoped I'd be different, more like her,* Anne thought. *What if she could see me now?*

Anne awoke the next morning thinking of the people in her life and the empty room around her. She threw on her clothes and chugged down a cup of orange juice, deciding to abandon her fool's errand. She'd never find Jack Post. Even if she did, she couldn't go through her plan of seduction, Love List or not.

Cindy called repeatedly that morning, leaving at first perky voicemails that grew thin with annoyance. But Anne didn't want to divulge her revised plan, didn't want to hear the smugness in Cindy's voice that Anne had given up. Anne wanted what little time she had left in this city to be special, so she'd visit the Museum of Modern Art. She'd liked art from the moment she saw a painting of men in top hats and women with parasols strolling beside a stream. Her father explained it wasn't just a painting, but a clever arrangement of colored dots.

"See how they don't connect?" he had asked, bringing the enormous hardback close to Anne's face. Indeed, thousands—possibly millions—of unconnected pinpricks formed a distinctive picture.

"It's called pointillism," her father explained, "using dots in a pattern to form an image."

"I can draw dots," Anne announced with pride.

"Give it a try, then."

Anne snatched a black Sharpie and a piece of white construction paper. After considering the proper model, she went outside to study the front of their house. Knowing she couldn't erase, Anne carefully dotted a picture of their small colonial, the white metal mailbox that never wiped clean, and the gangly tree with the rotting remnants of a starling nest. It took almost an hour, meticulously pressing her pen to paper so that the points didn't bleed together. Her father lauded her work and even tacked it onto the refrigerator. There it remained until he pushed it aside for Elena's newest report card: a cascade of perfect A's.

The New York sidewalks were thick with bustling crowds. Anne glimpsed Carnegie Hall on her left before being almost knocked into traffic by a throng of people.

"Watch it, lady!" barked the man that had plummeted into her.

Anne shot him an angry glare, clutching her coat and purse. She followed the crowd across 57th Street onto Sixth Avenue, feeling the rip of wind funneling through the buildings overhead. Her hair spiraled into corkscrews and her face blistered from the wind.

Unable to stand the cold any longer, Anne ducked inside a small bar. She pushed through the glass door, surprised to see the space nearly deserted, save for a few patrons at the mahogany bar-top and a few distracted waiters.

Anne wiped down her hair and made her way to the barstool closest to the television. Maybe a show would distract her from the cold weight on her bones.

"What'll it be?" asked a balding man behind the counter.

Anne glanced about. "Do you have a menu?"

"You want to order lunch?"

She was actually famished, but a bar probably wasn't the best place to sate her appetite. One round of nachos or a greasy quesadilla would sabotage her months of scrupulous dieting. Not to mention she may not squeeze into the only coat she thought to bring on her trip. "Just a drink menu," she said.

She was relieved to see that a non-alcoholic hot chocolate was available, and ordered it. "Skim milk," she clarified before he turned away. "And no added syrups or whipped cream, please."

"So tasteless?" said the man, cracking a grin as he slid over a sweaty glass of ice water. "Your call."

As she waited, Anne took a cautious sip, ice clinking against her teeth. She counted eleven people in the bar. On her left, two men in business suits engaged in conversation. On her right hunched an older gentleman in a Burberry coat, matching scarf, and a down-turned trilby hat. Anne wondered why men didn't wear more hats, like a cute newsboy or classy fedora.

Anne tried to remember the type of hat her father wore when her neighbor drained his martini.

She lost her breath. *Oh my god.*

The bartender leaned over the counter and said to the man in a quiet, formal voice, "Another Greene, sir?"

"Please." He slid over his empty glass.

Anne couldn't believe it. That face. Those eyes. How had she not recognized him instantly? Had fate once again led her to exactly the right place at exactly the right time? Because there he was, not three feet away.

Jack Post.

Strangely, her first instinct was to bolt. But that couldn't be right. She should try to get his attention, to say something, *anything*, because wasn't that the reason she had traveled so far?

Wasn't that why she was there, in this city, to see him?

But what about earlier? She'd wanted to forget the purpose of this trip. Embrace the role of a goggle-eyed tourist and see the sights.

But now he was here.

Jack Post was shorter than she'd envisioned, though she knew him to be exactly six-foot-one. She covertly studied him, comparing reality to her previously aligned image. His muscled shoulders slumped. His blue eyes were bleary, red, and evasive. His normally smooth face had collapsed like an old jacket.

What was wrong with him?

The bartender slid him another martini—in a fresh glass, Anne noticed. Jack Post gulped down half in an instant and wiped his lips with two trembling fingers.

"Are you okay?" Anne asked. These were not the words she and Cindy had rehearsed, the beginning of a seduction that they had jointly conspired.

Jack glanced at her again, briefly holding her gaze before returning to his drink. "Leave me alone."

Anne's face flamed. What was she doing, talking to Jack Post? Of course, he wouldn't be interested in conversing with her. She was a nobody—she was nothing, if she really thought about it. Her whole life had led to this moment, and she saw the dismissal in his eyes like the world had turned against her. She wanted to leave, and was actually standing to do so, when the bartender passed her a mug of hot chocolate. No curl of whipped cream. No chocolate shavings. Just a pebbly brown surface that looked like mud.

"Enjoy," said the bartender, his gaze flitting between her and Jack Post. Then he stepped aside to serve another patron.

Anne opened her wallet and extracted a ten-dollar bill. Without looking at anyone, she dropped it on the counter and shouldered her purse.

"You're not gonna finish your drink?" blurted Jack Post.

Anne stalled, her body paused in a hunch. Did he just speak to her?

"I didn't mean—see, you don't have to leave." Jack wiped his eyes, took another drink. "Sorry I snapped at you. It's been...a hard day."

Anne sat back on the barstool. She reached for her mug, welcoming the enamel's stinging warmth. *He's just a man,* Anne reminded herself. *Just a man.*

"I'm Jack," he said, nodding to her.

Anne didn't smile. She could scarcely nod. "I know who you are."

"Do you, now?" Jack grinned without humor, without kindness. His lips pursed as if tasting something sour. "Can't believe I just blew twelve years of sobriety. But goddamn if Charley doesn't make the best Graham Greenes." Jack held up his glass, turned it in the dim light of the bar. "The trick is finding a good cassis, one that blends with the gin and vermouth.

Most places don't even know what the hell this is. Haven't had one in years. But if not today, if not now, then when? When the hell else can I lose myself. To forget..."

Jack glanced at her as if she had interrupted him. "So. You want an autograph? Maybe snap a picture for your webpage?"

She frowned. "No. No, thank you."

Jack's expression strained. "Not what you expected? Thought I'd be more...debonair?"

"I don't know what I thought." Anne paused. "Maybe happier?"

Jack shook his head bitterly, finished his glass, and put his hand up for another. "Not after today. My sister died. Just this morning."

Anne's heart caught like it did on the morning she had first read the obituary of Frederick's family. Her knees were only a foot away from Jack's. She longed to touch his hand, but stopped herself. He was like a figure trapped in stained glass. He might shatter if she moved too quickly. "I'm so sorry," she said instead.

Jack gave a morose shake of his head. "You didn't know her. Anyway, I hadn't seen her in years."

Anne wondered which of his sisters it had been. She knew them all, but wasn't about to tell him that. "Were you close?"

"Aren't all siblings?"

"No," she said, surprising herself with her quick

response. "I have a twin sister and we barely speak half the time."

Jack's face lit with interest. "Twin, huh? Identical?"

"Fraternal."

"Ah. Well, then you know how it is. No, we weren't close. Obviously."

"How did she die?" Anne asked, then instantly regretted the question. What was she thinking, asking something so personal?

He blinked at her. Perhaps it was because she was a stranger. Perhaps it was because he was clearly drunk. But Jack told her, as casually as if informing her of the time. "Endometrial cancer. Diagnosed too late. Terminal after three weeks."

"I'm sorry. That's awful." Even to her own ears, her words sounded weak. What else could she say? "I wish you'd been able to see her."

"I do too." He shook his head again, stared into the depths of his refreshed drink. "You ever hurt someone you love every day you're alive?"

Anne's pulse quickened. "What?"

But Jack didn't hear her. "Hurt that person every day with something other than words? I think neglect is the worst thing you can do to a person. Just ignore them. Pretend they don't exist, like they're not even worth shit. That's what I did to her, and the rest, once I became famous. I forgot where I came from. Or maybe I didn't forget. Maybe I chose not to remember, because they reminded me of who I used to be. The nothing that I was. Know what I mean?"

Anne gazed into his blue eyes. "I do. I know what you mean." She glimpsed the face of her husband, the faces of all those men. Something dark coiled within her. It bit at her stomach, her chest, and snapped up her throat.

Anne dropped her mug on the counter. A splash of hot chocolate burned the top of her hand. She stood shakily as she put her hand to her mouth. "I've got to go."

Jack stared at her, slack-jawed. Anne knew from the bleary redness of his eyes that he wouldn't remember her, which was probably for the best. "You don't have to go," he said as she slipped her arms through her coat and shouldered her purse. "Wait a sec! What's your name again?"

She'd never told him. She wanted to run, to disappear, to put as much distance between them as possible. "Goodbye," she said. "Sorry for your loss."

Without a backward glance, she shuffled out to the street, a blast of frozen air punching her face.

The art museum was only a block away, but she couldn't go in. She realized she wanted to lose herself in the mass of people, the anonymity of the city. She tracked the pavement as if she had a destination, when she had no other purpose but to move because a vise of guilt closed her heart.

Luke, Eddie, and all the men flared through her

memory like apparitions. She saw Frederick—her Freddy—and his face when she told him the truth, because she *must*. She saw herself before the Botox, before the surgeries. She saw Elena, and the distance driving them apart. And Andrew, who didn't know any better.

Remorse hit Anne with a physical force. For a few eternal seconds, she couldn't breathe.

What have I done? she thought. *What's wrong with me?*

She wished she could tear away the memories. Burn them all down. But she had no way of erasing her shame. She'd carry the indelible mark for the rest of her life.

When she stopped, a surge of people pummeled into her. Anne pressed a hand to her chest and staggered sideways to sag against a building. *Breathe. Just breathe.*

Her chest lifted with a sharp intake of air. She kept her eyes closed, her hand cupping her thumping heart. *You're okay,* said a voice in her mind, but it wasn't her own. It was her mother's, in that smooth, once-familiar cadence. *Está bien, nena. Está bien.*

Anne opened her eyes. Where was she? She couldn't see a street sign. She swayed, disorientated. When the crowd thinned, she tried reentering the sidewalk, but a fresh throng pushed her into an alleyway. Pulling her coat close, Anne opened her purse and extracted her phone, holding it above her head for a signal. She'd call her husband. Tell him everything. Beg his forgiveness. Ask him to press rewind on their marriage, to start over, that she loved him. That despite everything, she loved him. And she was so, *so* sorry.

A slim man shoved her backwards. "Move, please."

Anne clasped her phone. "Sorry," she said, letting him guide her down the alley. She probably wasn't supposed to be there and so she said with a ready smile, "I just need a minute. I've got to make a phone call—"

An explosion of stars. A jagged pain behind her eyes. Something clattered on the pavement—her phone? her purse?—and someone yanked at her hand. Anne slumped onto cold brick. Wet snow burned holes into her jeans. Through a mist of tears, she saw a man snatch her purse and dissolve into the crowd.

No one came to help.

It took a few minutes to orient herself, to realize what had just happened. Someone had mugged her. What was she supposed to do? Call the police? She searched the wet pavement for her purse. Her phones. Her wallet. Her driver's license. The plane tickets. All gone.

When Anne's chest closed again, she told herself to breathe. To get up. To get out. She placed her left hand on the cold brick of a building. An angry red line tracked along her fourth finger.

Her wedding ring was gone. There remained only

the paler band of skin, marking its position for the past six years.

Tears sprung to her eyes, but she quickly blinked them back. She had to think. To *think*.

But her *head*...

Anne staggered back onto the sidewalk and blearily retraced her steps. She spotted the bar where she had seen Jack Post, then the park, and finally her hotel: a huddling mass of steel and glass and artificial light.

I'm so dizzy, Anne thought. She touched her forehead, where a welt pounded against her icy fingertips. *What did he hit me with? Am I okay? Should I go to a hospital?*

Across the street, she spotted a policeman surveying the crowd. She should go to him, tell him everything. He would help her. He had to. Anne tried to form a picture of the attacker in her mind, but all she could remember was a slash of dark hair and his thin, wiry frame.

She saw a break in the street and crossed. She caught a patch of ice and briefly lost her balance. *Halfway there,* she thought, eyes set on the sidewalk and its mass of people. This was taking forever. She should've worn different shoes.

A taxi whipped past, blaring its horn. Anne lurched backwards, her heart thudding. That was *way* too close. She balled her fists and started forward again. *Almost there...*

Tires screeched. Rubber burned. Anne glimpsed a face she swore she knew: a set of surprised blue eyes. Then the fender slammed against her hips, toppling her over a glossy black hood.

Her face splintered on the windshield. She slid down the side of the car and toppled across the frozen pavement.

Silence. And then a voice from high above.

The policeman, his dark eyes on hers. Gray stubble moving with his jaw.

She couldn't understand the words. She tried to stay awake even as the smoky sky descended.

Sour liquor flooded her senses. She blinked into a handsome, stricken face. Cold hands pressed her wet fingers. "I'm so, so sorry," he said. "Don't worry. We'll get you to a hospital!"

Anne wanted to touch his agonized face, to tell him she was okay. But her hand froze midair, because she saw the blood. The shards of glass and rocks embedded in her skin.

Her hand dropped, and her world heaved into darkness.

Part Three

FINDING HOME

Chapter Twenty-Seven

ANNE OPENED her bedroom door to find her sister on her bed, back propped against a stack of decorative pillows. "Did you find the marshmallows?" Elena asked with an eager smile.

"Yes. It took long enough." Anne passed over a mug and tucked in beside her. They sat in reflective silence for a time, sipping their hot chocolates as snow drifted across the windowpane. "You sure Andrew's okay with watching Charlotte while you're here?"

Elena waved a dismissive hand. "It's fine. I'd tell you otherwise, right?"

"You sure would," Anne said. She took a slow swallow and the gooey peppermint marshmallows stuck to her upper lip. It took her several attempts to lick away the glossy residue.

Her sister smiled at her. "How much did you put in there?"

"Only a handful," Anne said in mock defense. She brought her mug up for another sip.

"God." Elena shook her head.

"What?"

Elena gave her a look that Anne recognized meant, "You are not who you used to be, the person who I've always known."

"Well," said Elena, "you've been off sugar for over a year. And yet here you are, chugging high fructose corn syrup. Come to think of it..." She glanced critically at her own mug. "When did you last use marshmallows? Don't they expire?"

Anne rolled her eyes. "No idea. They probably preserve for a century. Just enjoy your stupid drink."

Elena grinned and squeezed Anne's thigh, warm beneath a thick down comforter and faux bearskin coverlet. Anne leaned into the touch, enjoying her sister's body slanted alongside. How long had it been since they had been like this? Years? Decades? Possibly never?

"I'm glad you're here," Anne said.

Elena didn't look at her. But she nodded and sipped her drink.

Cold air drifted through the bedroom door. Where was Frederick? He hadn't returned home in two days. Even though Anne had recovered his personal cell phone number, he hadn't answered her calls.

Would he avoid her until people arrived for the Christmas party, less than two hours away?

Nicole and Miranda Burns were downstairs sweeping hardwood, vacuuming carpets, and polishing every surface. Anne had volunteered to help, but Nicole pushed her away and said, "We've got this. Your husband is paying us overtime to work this party. Go enjoy being with your sister."

"When was the last time she came here?" Anne whispered.

Nicole gave Elena a covert glance. "Once that I know of, for the first Christmas party. About four years ago. Other than that, I don't know. Not often."

Or ever, Anne thought.

She and Elena had talked on the phone often since their conversation in Anne's steaming car. Anne called Elena nearly six times a day, and their conversations had since swelled from a few hesitating minutes to a few hours uninterrupted. Even Andrew had grown used to surrendering the phone to his wife, though his tenor had cooled with her. Anne never pressured him. She only wished to speak with Elena, and did not want to do anything to embarrass Andrew further. Together, she and her sister shared countless stories, with Elena filling in the gaps. Although Anne tried, her history remained a collection of events affecting someone else. Would they ever register as her memories? And did she even them to?

"Why was I like that?" Anne asked eventually, her question a stark echo in the bedroom.

Elena tensed. "Like what?"

Anne hesitated, wondering if she really wanted to hear the answer, and if Elena even knew. "You know," she said. "Like I was."

"You're going to have to be a lot more specific."

"Okay." Anne drew a breath. "Why do you think I cheated on Frederick? Have I ever been monogamous?"

"Sure you have," Elena said. "When you were young, at least. You were a serial monogamist. Honestly, I thought you were going to get married to every guy you dated."

"Really?"

Elena nodded.

"Why did that change with Frederick? I feel like I really loved him."

Elena held her gaze, then sighed and shook her head. "My best guess is you were afraid."

Anne frowned, not understanding. What could she have been afraid of? She had the perfect life, or so it had seemed. Or maybe it was only perfect in the beginning, before reality set in. "Afraid of what?"

Now it was Elena's turn to shrug. "Of losing someone again. Mom and Dad's deaths devastated you. You even started..." Elena stopped.

"What?" Anne demanded.

Elena grimaced. "You were cutting yourself."

Anne gasped. "*What*? I cut myself?"

"On your legs." Elena dropped her eyes to Anne's lap.

Anne remembered the four symmetrical scars lining her inner thighs. Had she really done that to herself? She tried to picture pressing a blade to her skin —scissors, a razor, a steak knife—but cringed at the image. She pushed it from her mind even as a darker thought followed, *Is that why Elena and Lauren both thought my scars were self-inflicted?*

"When you told me," Elena continued, "I knew you needed to see someone. You didn't fight it, but you didn't stay in therapy either. That would've really helped you. When they put you on medication, you quit that too."

Anne shuddered. "What did they give me?"

"SSRIs. A kind of antidepressant. But that doesn't matter. Point is, I think you loved Frederick, at least in your way. But you were afraid to really open up to him."

Anne's voice was barely a whisper. "Why?"

Elena gave a faint shrug. "Only you know why."

Anne stared into her hot chocolate, swirling like creamy mud. She bit her lip and thought, *Maybe I divided my heart so that the one person who mattered couldn't break it.*

That bitter truth settled into Anne's bones. She chuffed her face and said, "It was a stupid thing to do."

Elena finished her drink and slid the empty mug

onto a glass coaster on the nightstand. "I don't know. I mean, I can sort of understand it. But that doesn't mean I approve of what you did. I never once thought of cheating on Andrew, even though I went through the same thing with our parents."

"Never?"

"No. I love him. With my whole heart. That's why..." Elena's voice trailed and she looked away.

"Why what?" Anne pressed.

Elena moved her hand to her face. Her voice strained with unshed tears. "That's why it hurt so much when I found that picture. Of *you*."

Anne's stomach dropped. Elena had found the picture she'd given to Andrew. Why had she done that? To make Andrew desire her over her sister? To prove something? But prove what?

Elena drew a shaky breath. "He was masturbating to it. I caught him in the bathroom. Holding it like some..." She waved her hand. "I don't know what. I had a meltdown. He slept on the couch for two weeks. I couldn't stand the touch of him."

"I'm so sorry..." Anne reached for her hand, but Elena pulled away and pressed her fingers to her eyes. Anne waited, the mug cooling in her trembling grip.

"He told me everything," Elena said eventually. "This was when you were gone, in New York. I called you for a week, but you never answered. Now I know why..." She shook her head. "Doesn't matter. Andrew is...he's always been..." She paused again, considering her words. Anne waited in the silence. "I guess lost is the best way to describe it. It was his stupid parents, ruining him from such a young age. A part of him has always been afraid. And he doesn't really understand women. I mean, he's married to me, of course, and I think we've always had a good sex life. We were virgins when we met. We discovered everything with each other. And it was wonderful, like writing your own chapters in a book." She smiled wistfully. "I love him. I always have. And I forgave him. But you..." Elena turned on Anne. "I destroyed the picture. Told myself I was through with you. And I thought I was."

A raw, burning ache clawed at Anne's throat. "I'm sorry, Elena. I don't know what's wrong with me, what made me do that." She thought of their life together, a life she had only just sewn from fragments, the shadows and light that played in her mind. Yet even though she couldn't remember everything, she sensed the whole, could find the music's cadence even if she didn't know the words. "I can only guess why I did what I did. And I promise I'll never do anything like that again. But you have to change, too."

Elena's eyes flashed a warning. "What are you talking about?"

"I don't want you to write me off. Despite everything, we're *sisters*. There's nothing—and I mean *nothing*—that'll make me let you go. Okay?" Anne let out a breath, winded, and waited for her sister's response. She'd spread her cards on the table and gone all in with her heart.

Elena gave an almost imperceptive nod. "I know. And you're right."

Anne blinked, surprise and disbelief adding to the weight of her constricting guilt. "I am?"

The ghost of a smile played on Elena's lips. "Yeah. And I can't really say why that is. Maybe it's because Mom said we bonded the day we were born. That twins are supposed to spend eternity together. Maybe it's because we have a second chance. Or maybe it's because I just want to believe you. I haven't been the best sister to you, and God knows you've been awful to me, but maybe we can start over."

Anne let out a relieved sigh. "And to think all it took was a bit of brain damage. Nothing an expert chronicler like you can't clear up."

Elena patted her hand. "Exactly. Too bad it took that to get us here, huh?"

Anne nodded. It was too bad. "But why do you think we're so different? You'd think we'd have more in common, considering everything we've been through together."

"I've wondered that myself, actually. Ever since we were kids. The same parents raised us. Once we even shared the same body. Yet we're as different as two people born on separate continents."

"But we're similar in some respects," Anne said. "We both like to read. Or at least I used to."

Elena smiled at the memory. "Indeed. You didn't understand most of it when we were kids, but that didn't stop you from trying. I never said it, but I really admired that about you. This stuff may come easily to me, but it means more when you have to really work hard for something. And you did, and for a long time."

Anne's heart lifted at the rare compliment. "Thanks, Elena."

"Sure."

Anne thought for a moment. "Do you still like to read?"

"Only occasionally. Charlotte keeps me pretty busy."

"You should try to make time for yourself, if it's important to you."

Elena rolled her eyes. "Just wait until you have a kid. Then we'll talk."

Anne shrugged, deciding to abandon this subject for now. She worried her sister never spent time on herself. That her devotion to her daughter might eventually breed resentment. Instead, Anne said, "I'm remembering more things. Mostly bits and pieces, but still. It's something."

"What else do you remember?"

"Reading with Dad."

Elena smirked. "Sure. We did that a lot as kids."

Anne sipped her cocoa and said, "I remember he had an enormous library. Or, at least, big in my mind. Where did he get the money for all the books?"

"That one's easy," said Elena. "He got most of them for free. He'd haunt university book fairs, exaggerate how many courses he was teaching the next semester, and come home with a car full of books."

Anne saw their father's old Honda puttering up the driveway. They'd help him carry paper bags filled to the brim with books. British and American anthologies. Essay collections. Books on Shakespeare, Chaucer, and Milton. Thick academic writing texts with corresponding workbooks and teacher guides. Their father took everything and anything the university gave him, even if he had no intention of teaching the materials.

"Every one of us is a student," he'd say in his lofty voice. "We have but one lifetime to learn."

"Thinking back on it," Elena said, breaking Anne's reverie, "what drove me the most crazy about you was your histrionics."

Anne blinked at her, not understanding the word, and thrown by the abrupt dip in her sister's tone. "Histrionics?"

"You know," said Elena. "The drama. The 'it's all about me' mentality. The exaggerations, the promiscuity, the lies. It drives—*drove* me crazy. For years."

Anne's pulse quickened. "But I'm not like that anymore."

Doubt weighed Elena's smile. "I hope not, Anne. For all our sakes."

Three taps rapped the door. Nicole poked her

head inside. "Anne?" she called, scanning the room before dropping her eyes to the bed. "Oh, there you are. Listen, I think you better get ready."

"Right now?" Anne pouted. She didn't want to leave. Perhaps she could skip the party and stay locked in her room, listening to her sister and renewing their history. What was she going to do with a house full of strangers?

"I think you better," Nicole piped in. "Frederick just got home."

The color drained from Anne's face. "Oh. I see."

"I should go." Elena slid off the bed and gathered up her mug and fallen purse. "Call me later if you can. Tell me how it went."

Anne grasped for her sister's hand, even as hot chocolate sloshed from her mug. "Please stay. Don't leave me alone."

Elena smiled encouragingly. "Oh, Anne. You're *not* alone."

But I am, Anne thought, knowing she was being irrational, but needing the security of her sister's face. She'd lost so much of her relationship with Frederick. Perhaps she didn't want to remember all of it. The hurt in his eyes. That deep pit of sorrow. She couldn't bear to see that again. "Please stay," Anne entreated. "I need you here."

"But..." Elena threw a desperate glance at Nicole. "Isn't there a guest list?"

"No problem adding one more!" Nicole quipped.

Elena snorted. "But I've nothing to wear."

"Borrow one of my dresses!" Anne motioned to her closet, a stifling array of clothes with unpronounceable designer tags sewn into their hems. "There has to be something you like."

Elena still looked uneasy. "I don't know. Shouldn't you be alone? With Frederick?"

"I'm heading out," Nicole said, but before she closed the door, she hissed, "He's downstairs. In the study."

The door closed, and Anne turned to Elena once more. "Please. Just for this evening. Then I can face him." *I'll have to,* she thought, not wanting to understand her sudden fear. Perhaps it was of knowing too much, and yet not enough.

Elena gave a grudging nod. She pulled the phone from her purse and pressed a number. "Okay, you little wimp. I'll tell Andrew I'll be late, and then I'm all yours."

Chapter Twenty-Eight

THEY EMERGED from the bathroom forty minutes later. Elena looked stunning in Anne's new look: a scooped-neck green sheath, four-inch heels, black wavy hair, and flawless makeup.

Despite Elena's protests, Anne selected for herself a simple long-sleeved black dress, matching hose, and heels. When she finished, she looked ready for a funeral. And maybe she was. Her *own*.

Anne hoped her understated attire made her disappear. But as they passed the garland and holy and stepped into the blinking Christmas tree lights, Anne realized her black stood out most of all.

But it was too late. Frederick stood at the bottom landing, sipping a cocktail.

Anne froze, imagining fleeing the scene or

sprouting wings to fly. Elena's hand clasped her elbow, guiding her forward.

"Freddy," Elena said in a pleasant voice. "Hey there!"

Frederick turned and smiled warmly up at his sister-in-law, then slid his gaze to Anne. His expression darkened.

Frederick kissed Elena on her cheek. "You look marvelous, Elena," he said. "Can I get you something to drink?"

"A Shirley Temple would be fantastic." But before he could leave with the order, Elena turned slightly to Anne and pushed her forward. "And what about Anne here? I think she looks great!"

Anne flushed at Elena's forced enthusiasm. She knew she'd done a shoddy job with her own makeup, despite having concealed her bald spot and brows with strategic hair placement. Once, in Jack Post's bathroom, Anne had been religious in her application, covering her scars and blemishes like an artist. But tonight she'd used almost all the time tending to her sister, purposefully making Elena look the prettiest. Anne didn't know what drove her until she saw Elena's face open with surprise and gratitude when she finally turned to her reflection. "I look beautiful," her sister said, her voice thick with disbelief. Elena reached out to squeeze Anne's hand. "Thank you."

Anne spent little time on herself in the remaining minutes. A few careless swipes of concealer on the worst of her scars. A rough blend of foundation on her forehead, cheeks, and neck. A dab of mascara and a hint of lipstick, which would surely rub off once she'd had a single drink. Her own reflection appeared pale, anxious, and tired: the ghost of her old self. And she saw all of this mirrored in her husband's eyes as he gave her another fleeting glance.

"Anne," he said, allowing her the barest of nods. "You look—that is..."

He was taking too long, and Elena rushed to fill the awkward silence. "Natural, don't you think? Without that old kabuki mask! Wouldn't you say she looks better?" Elena waved a hand at her own face. "Really, Frederick. She forced this makeup on me. You know I wouldn't have it on otherwise! Ha ha!"

A rush of tenderness swept through Anne. Elena was nervous. Her sister actually cared what happened to her.

Anne squared her shoulders and faced her husband fully. "Hello, Freddy. I'm so glad you're home." She planted a light kiss on his cheek, rasping against his unshaven stubble. Her heart fluttered at the familiar musk that once perfumed her sheets. She longed for his mouth, but even her slight, cordial touch turned Frederick into ice.

Anne didn't linger. She fell back on her heels and managed a thin smile. "Welcome home."

Frederick cleared his throat. "Of course. Would you like a drink?"

Anne nodded at her sister. "Same as Elena, if you can. Thanks."

He hesitated another moment before striding away, his heavy leather loafers stomping down the hall.

Elena let out a breath and squeezed Anne's hand. "Okay. I think that went better than expected. Don't you?"

Anne wriggled out three maraschino cherries from the crushed ice, not caring who saw her. She planned to down every ounce of this delicious sugary drink.

Her sister was nearby chatting up a tall, elegant blonde. The woman was a stranger to Anne, although allegedly they'd known each other in the past. Frederick huddled with three men at the bar. The remaining six guests milled in the foyer, their banter blending with the faint Christmas music emanating from hidden speakers.

Anne stood with her hip pressed against the sideboard, trying to relieve her cramped feet. What had possessed her to squeeze her toes into a pair of patent leather monstrosities? She freed her foot to massage her calf while studiously avoiding the eyes of passerby.

She knew she couldn't ignore the guests forever. She was technically half of the hosting couple. It had been interesting at first, greeting people at the door. Most didn't recognize her. Some claimed it was her hair—formally platinum blonde, now forked with auburn roots. "It's so—so dark!" blurted one woman, clearly at a loss for words. Others said it was Anne's understated attire. But Anne knew better. It was her face. Still, she considered herself lucky, with only two red lines and a pitchfork scar. She could've been much worse, and told them so after tiring of their clandestine looks.

"I was in a car accident," Anne said. "I could've woken up paralyzed. Or not woken up at all."

After that, most made excuses to leave, but a few wanted details. Where had she been? Did she know who hit her? How was her recovery? Was she in any pain?

Anne kept her answers vague.

Word spread that she'd lost most of her memory, and even though some faces stirred in her mind, she didn't connect them to her past.

Anne rubbed her temples. She wanted to crawl into bed, throw the comforter over her face, and fall into a dreamless sleep.

"How are you doing, sis?" Elena said, a little giddy after graduating from Shirley Temples to cosmopolitans.

Anne shrugged. "Fine. Just ready for the party to be over."

"But we haven't even had dinner yet! Why don't you try talking to more people?" Elena laughed, as if she'd told a joke. "Look at what I'm saying! You were the one who always had to get *me* out of my shell. And here I am, telling you to be social. Geez Louise. What are we going to do with you?"

Anne smiled despite herself. Elena's mood was infectious. "Yes. It's hilarious."

"Oh, you know what I mean." Elena rolled her eyes and slurped her drink. "God. It feels great being among adults again! Having stimulating conversations. Guess what I just talked about over there? With that woman?" Elena pointed at the blonde woman, radiant in a gold silk dress.

Celebrities? Anne thought. *Plastic surgery? Designer dresses?* "Not a clue," Anne said instead.

Elena grinned broadly. "Politics! The next Republican presidential candidate!"

Anne blinked at her. "But aren't you a Democrat?"

Elena giggled into her martini, clearly more than a little tipsy. "Who cares? I was talking about something that *mattered*. Something legitimate. *Sesame Street* and *Baby Mozart* didn't once come up! Do you know how liberating that is?"

"Not really." A keyboard tapped nearby, and Anne dropped her eyes to Elena's purse. "I think your phone's ringing."

"Is it?" Elena blinked down in confusion, then passed Anne her glass as she fished through her clutch. "Oh, dang! It's Andrew." She held up a finger and stepped from the room, and Anne was alone again, holding her sister's drink. She stared into its ruby depths, a curled piece of lemon spread almost flat against the side of the glass, and took a generous sip. Her face scrunched. That was a big no.

"If you don't want it, I'll take it," said Nicole, moving a tray of assorted crackers and cheese into Anne's sightline. "Care for some brie?"

Anne's eyes widened. "They've got you catering?"

"Don't ask. Mom's having a fight with some of the waiters. Apparently, one of them broke a wine glass and didn't own up to it. So here I am, keeping the peace."

"Great. Should I do anything?"

Nicole shook her head adamantly. "Dude, I wouldn't."

"Right." Anne took a proffered cracker, though it tasted like stale toast. "Thanks."

"Don't mention it. So..." Nicole glanced about. "You having fun?"

"I'm having a blast." Anne stared off into the distance, her eyes tracking her sister on the phone. She wondered what she was saying.

"Yeah," Nicole said. "I can totally tell. Why don't you try talking to some people? You were quite the social butterfly before. I bet it's just like riding a bike."

How would you know? Anne wanted to snap. But she suppressed the urge, knowing Nicole was only trying to be kind, wanting Anne to have fun. But a wall of strangers surrounded her, and Frederick was practically a continent away. She sighed and fingered the shimmering drink.

"You like that cocktail?" Nicole asked.

"It's not mine. I'm just holding it for Elena."

"Do you want another drink?" Nicole asked hopefully. "I can scramble one up for you. Might be the kick-start you need."

"Thanks," Anne said, "but no." She hadn't had a drink since the accident, at first because of her medication and surgery, and now because...actually, she wasn't sure why she wasn't drinking now. Perhaps she didn't want to lose herself—or *more* of herself.

"Suit yourself. But with this crowd, I'd kick back every chance I got!" Nicole sashayed away, her tray a supplication as she flitted from guest to guest.

"Hi, Anne!" said the blonde in the gold dress, balancing effortlessly on towering heels.

So, Anne thought. *This is the one of the Stimulating Conversation.* She had a hard time believing it.

"You okay?" asked the blonde.

"I'm fine," said Anne, raking a hand through her hair. Remembering she had to be careful lest she reveal her bald spot, she folded both hands around Elena's sweating martini glass.

"Sarah," supplied the blonde.

"Sorry?"

"My name is Sarah." The woman smiled in sympathy. "In case you don't remember? We've had dinner a few times. My husband's a partner. Richard Jones."

"Right." Anne nodded as if finally recognizing her, which she didn't in the slightest. She just wanted to be alone. "Sarah."

"I'm sorry about your accident," Sarah said, meeting Anne's eyes without repulsion or surprise. "It must suck not being able to remember."

"Yeah. It does." Anne took another sip, grimacing as the fire burned down her throat.

Sarah's lips crinkled with amusement. "Not a fan?"

"I guess not." Anne set the glass on the gleaming sideboard, then realized she hadn't placed down a coaster. Oh well. It was her sideboard, wasn't it? For now, at least.

"So how are you?" Sarah asked.

Anne blinked. "Excuse me?"

"How arc you? Arc you doing okay?"

"I'm fine."

"I don't mean to be rude. It's just, after the accident and everything, I wasn't sure—"

A shout startled them both. A man slammed his hand against the dining room table, his face reddening in a heated conversation with an older gentleman.

"I suppose I'd better go rescue my husband," Sarah said with a beleaguered sigh.

"Which one is he?" Anne asked, presuming he was the tall, angry one in the fitted black suit and the confident swagger.

"The shorter one," Sarah said, still smiling.

Anne hadn't expected that. The woman's husband was certainly shorter—almost a head shorter than the other man—with a paunch that flapped like an empty bladder over his khaki pants. He was older too, perhaps twenty years Sarah's senior, with thick glasses and a mop of brown hair. Anne saw him give a quick scratch to his groin.

"Don't judge him by his appearance," Sarah said, as if reading Anne's thoughts. "He's so kind and has the most wonderful spirit." She paused, giving Anne a serious look. "Sometimes that all you need, right? Someone good to go home to?"

Anne gave an indulgent nod, wondering if this woman was implying something. Perhaps that other people saw her with Frederick and presumed the worst. Anne looked away, hoping the woman would leave. Hoping they'd all leave.

"Okay." Sarah patted her hair. "Good talking to you, Anne."

Sarah Jones strode to her husband, whispered in his ear, and guided him into the dining room. He folded his arm around her waist, and she tucked her hand against the small of his back.

Anne smiled, not knowing why. Then she noticed her own husband standing a few feet away, staring at her.

He wasn't smiling.

Dinner was a slow, but delectable affair. A rack of lamb crusted in fennel and rosemary with scalloped potatoes slathered in a Gruyère cheese sauce. Anne sat directly across the dining room table from Frederick, the two extra leaves spanning what seemed like a mile between them. With the colossal glass centerpieces and poinsettia flower arrangements, Anne could hardly see him at all.

Elena sat at her right for the first half of dinner, but then had to leave when Andrew unexpectedly arrived. Charlotte had tripped into the coffee table and sustained a small cut, which had bled for several minutes. But she wouldn't settle without her mother.

Anne waved goodbye to them, wondering what Andrew thought as he offered a curt wave in return.

It's all going to change, Anne promised. *And for the better.*

For the rest of the meal, Anne listened to a lawyer's boring opinions on city laws and predictions for the country's court system. When Nicole appeared to assist with clearing the plates, Anne excused herself and made a dash for the kitchen.

"Save me!" Anne hissed. "Is there anything I can do?"

Nicole covered her laugh with a hand. "You're playing hooky at your own dinner? But we haven't even served dessert! And it's crème brûlé! With *raspberries!*"

"Forget dessert," Anne said, guiding Nicole away

from prying eyes. "Just get me out of here. I'll help with whatever you need."

Luckily, Miranda Burns was still mired with the caterers. While Nicole fetched another serving tray, Anne poured coffee into porcelain cups, set aside the chilled cream and granulated sugar, and unloaded the dishwasher.

"Never thought we'd be doing this together," Nicole said, turning on the faucet and taking up a stack of soiled salad plates. "What a crazy world!"

"Crazy," Anne agreed, her arms loaded with saucers. She glanced at the cabinets and frowned.

"Over by the fridge," Nicole instructed. "Middle one. There. You got it."

Anne chuckled and shook her head. It was the little things. Like needing a housekeeper to tell her where she stored her own dishes. "Thanks."

"Don't mention it."

"There you are!" said a tinkling voice. Anne turned to meet the eyes of Sarah Jones. A black coat shrouded her glittery dress, and white gloves swathed her hands. "I've been looking for you. I saw you disappear and wanted to say goodbye. My husband and I have to skip dessert. He's not feeling well."

"I'm sorry," said Anne. "Is there anything I can do?"

Sarah waved a dismissive hand. "It's nothing. Just flares up now and again. Here. I wanted to give you this."

Anne stared at the piece of folded paper. "What is it?"

"Just my phone number. You should call me sometime. I'd love to get together."

Anne narrowed her eyes, immediately wondering who had put Sarah up to this. Probably Elena. Now everyone thought Anne was some sort of charity case. "Thanks," said Anne. "I'll do that."

"Please do," Sarah said, then stepped closer to Anne and lowered her voice. "I know what it's like to need a friend. I think you need one."

"Uh huh." Anne set the paper on the counter. "Will do. Hope your husband feels better."

Sarah bit her lip. "I'm not saying this right."

"You're fine," Anne said. "That's really nice. But I've got a lot of work to do."

"Of course." Sarah glanced around again. "Okay. Talk to you soon."

"Bye."

Sarah nodded, waved, and swept through the set of double glass doors, back into the foyer.

Nicole lifted her brows as she dried her hands with a dishtowel. "New friend?"

Anne laughed mirthlessly. "I don't think so."

"But she seems nice."

"Yeah. I'm sure she is."

Nicole put her hands up in mock defense. "Fine, I'll drop it. You want to wash or load?"

"Load, please." Relieved for the distraction, Anne

guided the plates and stemware into their allotted compartments, careful not to crack the glass. When they filled the dishwasher to the brim, Anne closed it into the cabinet and scrutinized its stainless steel face.

"Gentle cycle, low heat," said Nicole, showing her the corresponding buttons. When the machine whirred, they stepped back and high-fived each other, as if they had just aced a midterm.

"We also have trash that needs to go out," said Miranda Burns, her voice making them jump. She held an enormous black trash bag, heavy with its contents.

Nicole frowned and was about to say something, but Anne put on a smile and accepted the bag. "Of course."

Miranda crossed her arms and smiled sweetly. "Left side of the house. Through the front door."

Anne wondered at the woman's smile, but didn't need to ruminate for long. She sensed curious glances as she staggered down the hall. She must look strange carrying out garbage in the middle of dinner. Perhaps that was the Miranda's plan all along: to embarrass her.

Anne purposefully avoided her Frederick's eyes as she crossed into the dining room. Stepping out the front door, she maneuvered down the steps and crunched through the fresh snow. She shuffled past a thicker drift by the side of the house in her search for the garbage can. It perched between a pair of snowed hedges. With a grunt, she hauled open the lid and threw the bag inside.

The wind was low, but the air was cold, so her breath hovered in a billowing gray cloud. She started back for the house and lingered on the porch, staring out into the frozen expanse of the front yard. She couldn't see her neighbors who lived over an acre away. She enjoyed the surrounding space, especially after finding New York stifling. There people scrambled for views of steel buildings and an artificial, jagged skyline, with smog impeding the starlight.

Anne let herself breathe and be still, relishing this beat of freedom before her return to the forced-pleasantries of dinner.

Distant moment caught Anne's eye. A man in a black trench coat stood at the end of the driveway, a silver sports car steaming alongside.

Must be a dinner guest, Anne thought, wondering why he wasn't shuffling down the driveway with a rush of apologies for being late.

Anne raised her hand to call out to him, but stopped.

The slope of his shoulders. The way he leaned on his toes, as if perched at the edge of a cliff.

Anne's skin prickled with recognition.

"You must be freezing!" came Nicole's voice as she plunked loudly down the porch steps.

A coat flung about Anne's shoulders. Frederick's, by the size of it. "Thanks," Anne said with a grateful smile. She was about to point out the strange man when his car roared away in a plume of white smoke.

"Who was that?" Nicole asked.

Anne shook her head. "I'm not sure."

"Probably lost." Nicole blew hot air into her cupped hands. "Whew! Let's get inside. I don't know how you stand it."

Anne hesitated a moment longer, sensing a missing piece of the puzzle. It stoked the yawning cavity of her mind, but she couldn't grasp it.

She watched the street with its line of expensive cars for a few moments longer, then followed Nicole inside.

Chapter Twenty-Nine

ANNE STOOD with Frederick by the front door as their guests shuffled down the driveway to their cars. She wished everyone good night, thanking them for their gifts ranging from bottles of red wine and port to engraved silver pens and clocks for Frederick's office. Luckily, Anne had had the foresight—in her previous life—to pre-purchase party favors: Belgian truffles, pine-scented candles, and candy cane ornaments wrapped in red and green cellophane and tied with white ribbon. Nicole had set the gifts in a giant wicker basket by the door, and the guests *oohed* and *aahed* over the parting gifts, shook their hands, or offered stiff hugs and even the occasional kiss on their cheeks as they slipped into the night.

A westerly wind cut across Anne's skin as she gazed at the stars twinkling beyond the bare branches.

She thought again about the man she had seen earlier. Her mind itched to place him, but she drew a blank.

Frederick said, "We should go in. You look cold."

Anne stepped back inside, saying nothing, as Frederick shut and locked the doors. When he finished, they stood apart and regarded each other. Anne clenched her jaw. She missed Elena and her stories, Nicole's humor, even Miranda Burns' glares.

When he said nothing, Anne broke the silence. "Did you like the party, Freddy?"

"You've not signed the divorce papers," he said, his voice an accusation.

Ah, Anne thought. *So this is how it's going to be.*

Frederick was right. She hadn't signed the divorce papers. She hadn't even bothered to read them, finding its wedges of bright stickers an open challenge. "No," Anne said. "I haven't."

Frederick narrowed his blue eyes. "And why haven't you? I was clear before I left. And I think I've been more than fair, considering the circumstances. We need to get this matter taken care of."

"I think we should talk first."

"We've talked. There's nothing more to say."

Anne fisted her hands. She wasn't about to give up. She couldn't. "I think we should talk more."

"We've talked enough." Frederick started down the hallway, calling over his shoulder, "I'll be working late. I need your signatures. Don't fight me on this, Anne."

Anne closed her eyes. The voice of her mother

blew through her mind. *He doesn't want you to fight him. So why are you?*

Anne envisioned her mother with her effortless grace and confidence. How Anne longed for that phantom presence to become realized. To fall into that comforting embrace as she had as a child. To feel the print of her mother's lipstick on her forehead. The warmth of her embrace. What advice would she give? Try to make her marriage work? Or grant Frederick the divorce he so obviously desired? What was the right thing to do?

Anne slipped her feet out of her heels and tossed them by the door. She padded across the house bare-footed, considering her options and examining her motivations. She glimpsed her past with Frederick, wondering at their division. She felt she loved him, truly loved him, but feared that love denied—and that perhaps she deserved the loss.

Questions plagued her. Had Frederick ever known her, truly? Had she ever allowed him to see who she really was? Or had the fear that he'd cast her aside paralyzed her to the point of restricting herself completely? Had that fear ultimately been her undoing, where she spiraled into a state where she didn't even recognize herself?

Did I even know who I was? Anne wondered, touching the walls that had once been home. *Did I even try?*

She floated from room to room, turning off the

lights. There was a strange finality in her movements, like she was saying goodbye. Fighting her husband was a vain enterprise, one that she'd probably lose at great emotional expense. Perhaps she should just give into his wishes. Then at least he might have the chance for happiness. For himself, or with somebody else.

Anne trailed down the hall to the study, where a ribbon of light beneath the door cast hulking shadows against the wall. Without preamble, Anne turned the glass doorknob and stepped inside.

The fireplace was cold and empty. Frederick sat at his executive desk typing at his keyboard, bar graphs and data entry sidebars lighting the computer screen.

"I don't think we've talked enough," Anne announced, standing with her hands on her hips. When Frederick didn't acknowledge her, she sat down in one of his club chairs. "Freddy. I'm not leaving until you talk to me." She counted the beat of her heart: forty-five eternal seconds. "Freddy," she said, trying to purge the emotion from her voice. "Freddy. You made love to me, remember?"

Frederick's shoulders gripped. With a deep sigh, he turned around. "We had sex," he said with a dismissive wave of his hand, "and I'm sorry about that. I meant to apologize. I shouldn't have given you mixed signals. It was a mistake."

A mistake. Both words tattooed across Anne's heart. "I don't think it was a mistake. I think you meant it."

"I was angry."

"You deserved to be."

He said nothing.

"I'll sign the papers," Anne said. "On one condition."

"The alimony is non-negotiable, Anne. You know that. You broke the prenuptial agreement when you..." He stopped again, his expression hardening. "When you did what you did."

Anne gritted her teeth. Was that all he thought she cared about? His money? "You can have every penny. I don't care."

"You say that, but—"

"I don't want it!" She needed him to believe her, though he clearly didn't. "I won't fight you. You don't have to bother with lawyers and all that. I'll sign whatever you want. Just let me explain what I know to you."

"I assure you, that won't change anything."

"Even so. I want you to know." She dropped her eyes. "You deserve to know."

Frederick massaged his temples as if to ward off an impending headache. "Fine, Anne. Fine. I'll get your signatures?"

"Yes," she said. "I promise."

He grumbled something about the legitimacy of her promises, but Anne held her tongue. He waved his hand again. "Fine. But please be quick."

Anne crossed her legs. The same nerves that

twisted at her sister's confrontation knotted again. What was this fear? Frederick was already leaving her. She had nothing left to lose.

Anne began with what she could remember of her childhood. She described the room she shared with her sister from infancy through high school. Elena's affinity for academics and Anne's own struggle to keep up. Her father's obsession with reading, vocabulary, and degrees. Their mother's love of dancing. She wanted him to know about the fights between her parents, how they loved each other despite the yelling and the swearing. How once her father stormed off to a bar and hadn't returned until dawn. How she and Elena had stayed awake all night, wondering if he'd come back or if their parents would divorce. How her parents argued about money constantly. The fear and shame that poisoned their words. How they'd gone on food stamps when her father couldn't find work—not in universities, not even in high schools. How her mother placed ads offering discounted lessons to *gringos*.

"But I thought your father was head of his department," Frederick interrupted, confusion etching his face. "Wasn't he tenured?"

Anne grimaced, wondering how much of her history she'd embellished to impress him—perhaps even convincing herself. How many lies had she fed him over the years?

The next part was the hardest. Gripping her trembling hands, she admitted to finding Frederick's name in the paper and attending his family's funeral. "It was wrong," Anne said, nausea clawing her throat. "I'm sorry."

"You were there?" Frederick's voice was barely a whisper. A tremor went through him. "You were there?"

Anne's face burned with shame. "I know you don't understand, and you may never. But I fell in love with you a little that afternoon."

Frederick shook his head, his eyes wide. "I don't want to hear it."

"But it's true—"

"Enough!" Frederick scrubbed his face with his hands. "Has everything been a lie? *Everything*, Anne?"

"Just let me finish..." Anne wanted to get it out, to pull out every drop of poison. To be free. She confessed to haunting the arboretum in the hopes they would meet. How she'd met him by pure chance exactly one year later. How she'd pretended not to know him. How she prepared a version of herself she thought he would desire and—hopefully—fall in love with.

"You mean fall *for*," Frederick cut in. His eyes locked on the carpet as if its patterns contained all the universe's secrets.

Anne swallowed hard and continued on, pressing to the finish. How she pretended to be smarter or dumber, depending on the circumstance. How she feigned ignorance over the words he defined. That she actually knew nothing of politics or current affairs and gleaned only enough facts to please him. How she used to read but didn't anymore because Frederick said fiction was a waste of time.

Anne admitted that she despised most of his coworkers and envied the rest. How she'd never fit in and never made friends. That she realized Cindy wasn't a friend at all, but something closer to a parasite. How Anne always wished she and Elena had been closer. How the wall Elena put up grew continental once their parents died, when Andrew became a permanent fixture and Charlotte was born.

Then came the affairs. The lies and the cheating. Anne related how she met these men. The luminosity in the beginning, and the emptiness that followed. Then there was Luke, whom Frederick had correctly guessed was the source of her injectables and breast implants. How she'd ended their relationship and apologized to Luke's wife.

Anne drew a deep, rattling breath. She had one last truth. "And there's the reason I was in New York in the first place."

Frederick finally met her eyes. His voice came out in a hollow croak. "Go on. You might as well finish."

In a rush, she told him everything. Cindy's bet. Their collective scheme. The Jack Post Loves List. The plane tickets, hotel, and Anne's search for a movie star. Her random sighting of Jack in a bar, and her subsequent coma caused by a mugger and Jack's drunk driving. The weeks Anne spent at his mansion. Meeting Maria, Francis, and Justin. Anne's trip to an organic market that resulted in her face splashing the glossy pages of celebrity magazines. How she had sought the truth of herself, her reaction to Sam's investigation report. Her trip home. Her slow redemption with her sister. How she still needed to make amends with Andrew, and to become the aunt her niece deserved—someone who was present, and could love.

When Anne finished, her palms were slicked with sweat and her muscles ached. Yet she felt a release. She'd found freedom by standing naked in her truth—not only before Frederick, but before herself. Because this was who she really was. Frederick should know her before he left. She owed both of them that much.

Frederick's eyes reddened. He dropped his gaze to the carpet again. "That's a lot to digest."

She wondered what flayed his mind. Was it her affairs? Her plot to marry him? Or the lies that culminated in her memory loss? Or did he just want to be rid of her completely and start his life over?

Frederick's voice came heavy and thick. "I wish you had told me this from the beginning."

"I was afraid you wouldn't like me," Anne said, wiping her eyes.

Frederick sighed. "I guess we'll never know, will we?"

Anne spread her hands and thought, *I guess not.*

They were still a long time, the room crowding with their words. Anne glanced at the door, longing for the sanctuary of her bed—at least for one more night. Tomorrow, she'd plan her next steps. She still had the money from Jack Post, but where would she go? A hotel? Live with Elena until she found a job? And what would she take with her from here, if anything?

Anne pushed these thoughts aside. She was bone-tired.

She rose from the club chair and nearly fell. How long had she been sitting in a fighter's crouch, ready to spring? She stumbled over to Frederick and stared down the nape of his neck. "I'm sorry for what I did to you," she said, her voice low and steady, "and to us. I just wanted you to know."

"And now I do," he said to the carpet.

"Now you do," Anne agreed. She reached out, hesitated, and then gingerly touched his neck. He flinched, but he didn't move away. She palmed his clammy skin. "I want you to know I love you despite everything. You deserve someone without all this baggage. I hope you find happiness, Freddy. I'm so sorry I couldn't give it to you." She didn't want to say the next words, but knew that she had to—that she'd promised. "I'll sign the divorce papers in the morning. And then it can all be over."

She kissed the top of his head and left the study. Nausea wound in her stomach as she slunk up the stairs to her bedroom. She mechanically brushed her teeth, washed her face, and shimmied into an oversized T-shirt. She turned out the light and slipped beneath the icy covers, wishing they were the fuzzy flannel of her youth.

Finally, mercifully, she slept. She dreamt of her mother and father, and Elena.

In the dream, she was happy.

In the dream, she was free.

Warm sunlight dappled Anne's right cheek. She blinked awake, stretched. She felt good. Rested beyond memory. Yet in the space of that moment, the previous night came flooding back. Telling Frederick everything. Her pledge to sign the divorce papers.

Anne wondered what time it was, if she could have a few more hours with Frederick in her life, or if that part was dead and buried. She covered her face with her hands and breathed into her palms.

"You even sleep differently," murmured a voice by the door.

Anne jolted to see Frederick leaning against the frame. He wore red and black-checkered slacks and a nightshirt, the flannel softening his appearance. He looked as if he hadn't slept. And how could he? Not with everything she'd confessed. Not knowing that almost every moment of their seven years together had been a lie.

"What'd you say?" Anne asked, though she had heard him. She just couldn't believe he was standing there. She sat up in bed, pulling the down comforter to her chin.

"You sleep differently," Frederick repeated. "Softer."

Anne combed her fingers through her hair, but the auburn/blonde nest made it a hopeless cause. What did it matter how she looked? Frederick no longer cared. She gave a faint shrug. "I slept the night. Can't remember the last time that's happened."

"Wish I could say the same," he said with a grimace.

Anne's smile strained. She glanced at Frederick's hands, expecting to see a pen, but they were empty. "Do you want me to sign the papers now? Or can it —"

"Before we get to that," he said, then abruptly came to sit at the edge of the bed. His shoulders tensed as he swiped the back of his neck. "I thought you should know some things, too. About me. I haven't been fully honest with you either."

"What do you mean?"

"I mean, you were honest with me last night. Perhaps for the first time that we've been together. And you deserve the same. From me."

"Okay," Anne said, her stomach hollowing at his tone.

"I never..." Pain stopped his voice. He recovered with a trembling breath. "My wife—my first wife, Susan. I never told you much about her."

Anne frowned, searching her mind. She couldn't recover a single memory of his late wife, or his children. Was it she couldn't remember? Or had Frederick simply never told her?

"I want you to know," he began, "that she wasn't anything like you."

"I see." Anne didn't trust herself to say more, and couldn't control the scowl that deepened in her face.

Frederick touched her hand. "I don't mean that as an insult. I just mean you two were very different. And not just in age, but in so many respects. All except one."

"Which one is that?" Anne asked, bracing herself.

"I mean, you were different, but I loved you both. But I could never share what Susan's death did to me, or my children's. Whenever I tried to tell you, I felt—" He stopped again, struggling for words. "It was like my insides were coming out. Like I was being cut open."

"That sounds awful," Anne said, for lack of anything better. Because what else could she say? It was a cruel twist of fate that his children had passed before him, and she knew he struggled to make sense of it. Her parents' deaths—although sudden and violent—could never compare to his triple loss.

"I think you understand more than I ever gave you credit for," Frederick said. "I never allowed myself to acknowledge that before, when I should have."

Anne squeezed his hand. "It's okay. I never wanted to talk about my parents, either."

"Maybe we should have. Maybe sharing that could have brought us together. It affects us every day, and holding that back only breeds resentment. And more pain."

Anne nodded. He was right.

She listened as Frederick shared glimpses into his twelve-year marriage to Susan and their two children, Rebecca and Levi. The day of their deaths, and how he endlessly replayed their last moments. His only attempt at suicide with a bottle of Vicodin, only to be saved by Miranda Burns. The numbness that ate his insides unless he disappeared into work. How for ten months he'd kept his children's rooms as shrines until the emptiness threatened to swallow him whole and he sold the house. How he felt he could never, should never, love again.

"But then I met you," he said, his eyes wet. "And you were pure light. You netted me like one of those damn butterflies. You made me feel *alive*. I loved you beyond anything I thought possible. I thought I could take care of you, but I fell into a role you didn't deserve. I shouldn't have neglected you or treated you as anything less than an equal. For that, I'm sorry, Anne."

Anne couldn't believe his words. "Frederick—Freddy. I don't deserve your apology."

"You do. You deserve more than you think. What you did. The cheating. I don't know if I can ever forgive that. But I want you to know that I acknowledge my role in it. You deserved better."

We both did, Anne thought. "Maybe the problem is that we weren't right for each other. Maybe we fell in together because something was broke inside of us."

"Maybe," he allowed, dropping his eyes. "Maybe."

Anne shivered against a creeping chill. She pulled the comforter tighter.

Frederick rose from the bed. "Are you cold?"

"Freezing."

"I'll turn up the thermostat—"

"No!" she cried, surprising them both. "I mean, I don't want you to leave."

"Why not?"

"I just...I—" She scrambled for the right words, but she didn't even know what she wanted to say. It was all so much to take in: their marriage, their pasts, their collective baggage that clung like lead vests.

Anne looked at Frederick—at her husband. He was a kind man. A good man. He was someone to come home to.

She wondered if this was her first time acknowledging that truth. He didn't deserve what she had done to him. He never had.

You're a good person too, whispered her mother's

voice. *You are, nena. Know that you are, because it's true.*

Anne's throat closed, and she swallowed with great effort. To distract herself, she reached down and rubbed her toes through the coverlet.

Frederick stepped to a corner of the room and returned brandishing a pair of red, fluffy slippers. "Here."

She reached for them with a smile. "Thanks."

"I can put them on, if you'd like."

Was it just her, or did he sound almost sheepish? "Okay," she said, opening the comforter.

Frederick guided the slippers over her feet. "There you go," he said, grinning in triumph.

Anne inhaled his residual cologne. Glimpsed the uneven stubble along his neck, the small scar under his ear, and the barely discernible cleft in his chin.

Her pulse quickened.

"What do you think?" Frederick asked.

"It's perfect," she said. "I just—"

"What?"

She didn't answer. Instead, she met his lips with a gentle kiss. There was a moment she feared he'd pull away. Then he returned the kiss with a moan. Anne pulled him into bed, breaking contact only long enough to pull the covers over their legs. Frederick caressed her face, nuzzled her neck. She relished his scent, his taste, and the tenderness of his touch.

They didn't make love, but lay holding hands,

their fingers locking and releasing. They shared their dreams, their fears, and the most painful parts of their histories. She let herself cry when she spoke of her parents. That long evening at the hospital when she and Elena took their father off life support. She laughed with Frederick when he spoke of his children's first steps, teaching them to speak and to write. Driving them to school. Watching them at soccer practice, and brushing their teeth, and opening presents at Christmas. Anne held him through every memory, and he never left her side.

"I can't remember doing this," he said, pulling her closer.

"What?" she asked, kissing him lightly under his chin. "Laying together?"

"Exactly."

His heart thumped through his flannel shirt. The smell of him. The warm familiarity of his body. All of it washed over Anne like a warm tide.

Frederick shifted in her arms and said, "I can't remember the last time we were just still. We always seemed too distracted. Something always got in the way."

"I'm glad we're here now," Anne said, meaning it. She felt at home in his arms, beneath the heat of the comforter, his legs intertwined with hers. She wanted to hold on to this moment as long as possible, as long as the world would let her.

"Indeed," Frederick said, and kissed her.

When they had exhausted themselves, they lay in silence. Anne's head propped against Frederick's shoulder as she gazed at the window glimmering in the early morning light.

"I speak Spanish," she blurted. "Well, not fluently. But pretty well." Then, before Frederick could respond, she added. "I just thought you should know."

He chuckled as he nuzzled her neck. "That I already knew."

Anne smiled. She said nothing for a long, long time.

Chapter Thirty

ANNE SPENT the next three days with Frederick in a state of uninterrupted bliss, of lovemaking and rediscovery. They spent their mornings lounging in pajamas, drinking coffee and nibbling English muffins slick with butter and raspberry preserves. That first day, she asked Frederick if he wanted her to wear makeup, to spend the requisite fifteen minutes covering her scars.

"You don't have to do that for me," Frederick said. "I think you're perfect."

So she didn't. Anne put away her makeup bag and subsisted on the barest essentials: washing her face, brushing her hair, and massaging moisturizer into her dry skin. Frederick came to stand behind her—his day-old scruff flourishing into a salt-and-pepper beard that scratched the nape of her neck in an exciting way—and whispered, "You're so beautiful, Anne. You are." He kissed her hair, and she closed her eyes.

She didn't need him to say those words, but it was nice to hear them. Sometimes in the harsh fluorescent her scars were startling. But it was her face, and Anne felt an almost choking relief to be alive, and to be here, with him. It all could have turned out differently. A part of her feared it still would.

On Christmas morning, she awoke in Frederick's arms, his bare chest rising and falling beneath her cheek. She felt rested and loved.

She wanted to tell him again how much she loved him, but her adorations felt closer to an invitation. *Tell me you forgive me,* she willed him to say. *Tell me you love me too.* He seemed to love her, at least in his actions, his attentions, and his slow, tender lovemaking. And he hadn't mentioned the divorce papers again.

"I thought I'd have my sister and her family over for lunch today," Anne announced, hoping she sounded casual. Inviting them over was as rare as a solar eclipse.

"Sounds nice," said Frederick. He stirred sugar and a curled slice of lemon peel into his espresso, took a slow, savoring sip, and turned the page of the Wall Street Journal.

"Great!" Anne glanced around the kitchen. "I'll cook."

Frederick's face lit with surprise. "Really? What would you cook?"

"Oh. I don't know." She regarded the machines stacked across the granite countertops. A standing mixer, blender, food processor, coffeemaker, and a flat machine with a long silver handle hard enough to squash a turkey. She pointed to the last. "What's that?"

"A panini maker." When Anne said nothing, he added, "It makes hot sandwiches. But they're flat. With grill marks."

"Sounds easy enough. I can make sandwiches. What do you think?"

"I think throw in a bag of salt and vinegar chips and you've got a party."

Anne agreed and tucked into her toast, topped with peanut butter and generous slices of banana. It felt good to eat again. She sensed she hadn't eaten many breakfasts in the past, perpetually fearful of overindulgence. That morning, along with her makeup, she'd slipped the accusatory scale into the cabinet beneath the double vanity. She didn't need that pressure staring up at her every morning when she brushed her teeth. Not any more.

She'd also discarded something else: the photo album of her affairs. While Frederick slept, she'd eased open the lingerie drawer, snatched the album, and crept from the room. She hoped the squeak of her footfalls wouldn't wake him, and she was in luck. In the kitchen, she pawed through the garbage and buried the album near the bottom, watching as pizza crusts, sludgy cans, and other refuse covered it completely.

She washed her hands at the sink, gazing out the window into the moonlit backyard. A tightness released in her chest. She could breathe again.

"I've got something for you," Frederick said. He opened the overhead kitchen cabinet and returned with a present wrapped in green and white foil.

Anne held the gift in her hand, realizing she had nothing to give him in return. What to do?

"What's wrong?" he asked.

She gritted her teeth. No point in denying it. "I have nothing to give you."

He stepped close and stroked her leg through the slit of her terry-cloth robe. "You've already given me a tremendous gift. And you never could have wrapped it."

"Hopefully more than that," she said with a playful wink.

He chuckled. "Much more than that."

Anne's heart lifted. She smiled up at him hopefully. *Tell me,* she thought. *Tell me...*

"You came home to me," Frederick said, as if this was the most natural thing in the world. "Just you being here is a gift."

"Really?"

"Really," he said. "No more games."

She knew exactly what he meant. She was glad to be rid of them, too. "No more games," she agreed. Light danced on the foil as she jostled the gift. "May I?"

He grinned. "Please."

She tore it open, cast the paper aside. It was a book bound in clear plastic, like the novels she'd once read in the library. Anne turned it over in her hands. *Playing the Jack*, it read. By Mary Brown.

"I've not heard of it," she said, taking in the glossy cover. A young woman with short, spiraled hair wore a ginger and white petticoat. She held a mask of a mustached man in one hand and fanned four faceless cards with the other. On her left was a swarthy man, frozen in a gesture of greeting. On her right, a turbaned juggler.

Frederick's smile grew as he regarded the cover. "I went to this independent bookstore in town. Asked the owner if she could recommend a book with adventure, romance, and new identities. She said to try this one. Said it was a favorite among her family, especially her grown daughters, who discovered it as teenagers. She said it's about a young girl who happens upon a traveling circus during the French Revolution, and how she has to journey great distances to find herself." He stopped, and Anne sensed his eyes upon her. "I thought you might enjoy it," he continued. "You know I'm not fond of reading, so I couldn't think of anything myself. But the shopkeeper seemed happy with this choice."

Anne opened the book, glimpsing a small black stamp from a British library, and thumbed to the middle. She brought it to her face, inhaling deeply.

"What are you doing?" Frederick asked.

Anne lifted the book to his nose. "Here. Smell it."

He looked doubtful, but indulged her. "Mmm."

"What do you think?"

"It's musty as hell. What do you get out of it?"

"My dad taught us this. Elena and I did this every time we started a book." Anne drew the pages to her face again, luxuriating in the scent of the decades-old paper and ink. "This used to be a library book. I love thinking about how many people have read this. What they thought. Who they were."

Frederick's eyes shone with pleasure. "So you like it, then?"

"I love it." Anne gave his cheek a quick kiss before turning to the first chapter. "I can't wait to start."

"That's good." Frederick shifted on his heels.

Sensing something amiss, Anne tore her eyes away. "What is it?"

He rubbed the back of his neck. "I'm really sorry, Anne. But I got an e-mail from the office. They need me to come in to clear up some paperwork."

Anne's smile fell. "On Christmas morning? Seriously?"

"It doesn't have to be until this afternoon. And it'll only take an hour. I promise."

"All right." Anne nestled the novel against her chest. "At least you got me a good book."

They showered and dressed together, giggling as the dressing took longer than necessary. They were a wet tangle in bedsheets by the time the doorbell rang.

"Shit!" Frederick pushed himself from the bed and rushed for some boxers. "That's probably them. Can you be ready in ten minutes?"

"I'll try," Anne said with a grin. She felt like a teenager, sneaking around school halls, making out with her boyfriend when the teachers' backs turned. As Frederick dressed, she took a moment to admire his body, thinking he outmatched men half his age. Or perhaps it was her love for him that made his tufts of gray hair and few wrinkles distinguished. She loved every inch of him and loved him even more naked. She smiled as he shuffled into a black cashmere sweater and khakis. Laughed when he jumped up and down to slip on his black socks and favorite loafers.

Frederick gave her a fleeting kiss before rushing down the stairs. The front doors opened, and her sister and husband traipsed inside. Charlotte cried out, "Mommy! Mommy!" as Frederick loudly proclaimed Anne was still dressing.

Anne slid from the bed and picked up her discarded panties and bra. She found a red wool sweater in the closet and a pair of soft black slacks. She dismissed the rows of high heels and settled on fuzzy red slippers. "What the hell?" she proclaimed. "It's just family." Even saying the words made her smile.

Anne arranged her hair over her bald spot and retrieved her makeup case. First she covered her pitchfork scar, then the thin red lines flanking her face. She etched black liner over her lashes, blended in chestnut and ivory eyeshadow, and rouged her cheeks. With a final swipe of ruby lipstick, Anne was done. But she wasn't wearing the kabuki mask her sister was so fond of recalling. No, this was something more natural. More *her*.

Beaming, Anne blew herself a kiss in the mirror before turning off the bathroom light.

***

"No, really. I think they turned out fine," said Elena, but even she didn't look convinced. The bread on her panini was clearly burnt, the Gruyère cheese charred to black, and the deli slices of turkey Anne had slapped inside might have had a questionable expiration date.

"I like it," said Andrew, already finishing his second half.

"Try the chips," encouraged Fredrick, although his sandwich had only two bites.

"Well, I tried!" said Anne, attempting to sound hurt, but couldn't stop from bursting out laughing. "I'm sorry. I didn't know you had to watch the machine so carefully. Who's up for pizza?"

"Sounds good to me!" Elena set her plate down on the kitchen table. "Do you have any Italian sausage? I've always wanted to try your Gaggenau."

Anne shook her head. "No, I mean, we have pizza in the back freezer. It's good. We've had it the last couple of days."

"Frozen pizza?" Elena uttered the words as if they were a betrayal of the culinary community. "My God. Mom would never forgive you!"

Anne grinned. Elena was right. The only things frozen in their mother's house were homemade meals she'd doubled to save herself from cooking on her busiest days. Homemade meals, and ice.

They settled on Chinese takeout, which was really their only choice as the fridge was practically empty and everywhere else was closed for the holiday. They talked gamely as they feasted on crab rangoons, shrimp fried rice, orange and sesame chicken. Frederick heated kimoto sake on the stovetop and chuckled as he passed around miniature cups fit for a child's tea party. "Who says we can't mix cultures?" he said, then toasted everyone at the table.

As the room filled with their boisterous banter, Anne took a moment to gaze at the four of them: her family. For the first time, she felt no tension. Not even with Andrew, who found a buddy in Frederick with his passion for sports. Frederick was a natural in conversation, finding shared interests with Elena and Andrew and avoiding anything controversial.

Later, while Charlotte busied herself with a plastic ball and stack of blocks, Elena told poignant and hilarious stories. With a sharp pang, Anne realized this was probably the first time Elena and Andrew had been out with them in a long time. She glanced at Frederick, hoping it wouldn't be the last.

"You two are getting along well," Elena whispered as she helped Anne clear the table. The men were out in the family room watching an old football game on DVD while Charlotte lolled on the carpet, attempting to crawl. Elena grinned and said, "Andrew was pure *gringo*, arriving twenty minutes early. I told him we were probably interrupting some mad love session."

Anne couldn't hide her blush. Elena squealed and jabbed her in the ribs.

"Oh my god! I was kidding!" Elena exclaimed, grinning from ear-to-ear. "Wow. I knew something was up when you didn't call. I didn't want to jinx it by prying. I was worried when I left the party, but it appears you two made up well. Bravo."

Anne gave a small shrug. "Yeah. I don't know."

Elena's smile wavered. "What?"

Anne spread her hands. "I mean, it's going fine. It really is. But he hasn't said he loves me yet."

"Do you love him?"

Anne nodded, more sure of this than anything. "I do. I really do."

"Then give him time."

"You think he can forgive and forget?"

"Anybody can forgive. Trust me. It's the forgetting that's the hardest part."

"Depends on who's doing the forgetting," Anne said pointedly.

Elena passed over a stack of plates. "*Touché*, sis."

As everyone said their goodbyes, Anne knelt and helped her niece into her jacket while Elena and Andrew shouldered into their coats. "Goodbye, Charlotte," Anne said, kissing her little face. The girl stared up at her with eyes wide and curious. "Merry Christmas," Anne added. "I hope you like your new book." Anne had scrounged up her old copy of *Little Women*, realizing too late that it'd be years before Charlotte could digest its contents instead of its cover.

Anne passed Elena a heavy white shopping bag, to which Elena shook her head in wonder.

"I still don't know if I can take this," Elena said, but Anne could tell by her tone that she would. For Elena's Christmas present, Anne offered a choice of three outfits from her designer closet. After much sorting and trying on, Elena emerged with a black sequins cocktail dress, a strapless sundress with a matching belt, and a bohemian tunic. Elena held the items as guiltily as if she had just stolen them from Nordstrom's. "I don't know, Anne. This is too much!"

"They're yours," Anne assured. She figured the fewer clothes, the better. And she couldn't remember her favorites, anyway.

Frederick had pulled a good bottle of wine from the cellar and a few cigars for Andrew.

Elena glanced guiltily at their simple tin of homemade sugar cookies. "Our gift doesn't compare to yours. Seriously, Anne. If you want these back—"

"Forget it!" Anne said, guiding her out the door. "Just promise to enjoy them."

"Want me to walk them out?" Frederick asked, reaching for his coat.

Anne waved him off. "Let me walk them. I won't be long."

Frederick stepped back to pump Andrew's hand and give Elena and Charlotte a quick kiss. "Pleasure to see you all. We should do this again soon."

"Absolutely," said Elena. "Merry Christmas, Freddy."

"Merry Christmas," he replied. "Enjoy the rest of your day."

Frederick waited behind as they crossed the porch. They waved back as they started up the unplowed driveway. Anne drew in a shaky breath, hoping her nerves didn't get the better of her. "Andrew?" she called, her voice a croak. "Mind if I have a word with you?"

He gave her an anxious glance. "I don't know, Anne. We're on our way out."

"It'll just take a moment," Anne assured. "I promise."

Andrew glanced at Elena, as if gauging her response. Elena gave Anne a hard look, nodded, and reached for Charlotte. "Give her to me. It might be good for you guys to talk."

Anne waited for her sister and niece to reach the car. "Andrew," she began. "I want to apologize. About the picture. That was an awful, stupid thing to do."

There. The words were out. Anne waited for his response as they crunched through the ice into the deeper layer of snow.

Andrew said nothing. His eyes remained fixed on his car.

"Andrew?" Anne touched his arm, thought better of it, and quickly dropped her hand.

"It's fine," Andrew said.

He doesn't sound fine, Anne thought.

They clomped through the snow in silence. Finally, Andrew blurted, "I should have been stronger with you."

"What?" Anne said, stepping closer.

He shook his head bitterly. "I should've told you it was wrong from the beginning. But I've never been the best with women—or really people. Most times, I don't know how to handle them or even myself. You know that. You've always known that." He chuffed his face with his calloused hands. "Thanks for apologizing.

What you did—yes. It was stupid. And it hurt people. It hurt us."

Anne winced. His words stung, but she knew they were true. "I'm sorry for a lot of things," she went on, needing to explain, for him to understand. "I think most of this has to do with me being jealous of Elena. And I know we're not perfect. Nobody is. Especially me." Anne chuckled, hoping Andrew would too, but he didn't. She pushed on. "Anyway, I'm hoping that we can be friends. And that we can put this behind us."

Andrew stopped and turned to her. In the distance, Elena strapped Charlotte into the infant car seat. "I know you're going through a lot," Andrew said. "And I know it's been a struggle, remembering everything. I'm glad that you and Elena are making amends. That you're finally acting like real sisters should."

Anne folded her hands together to stop the shaking. "I know. It's not been easy."

"Truth is," Andrew continued, "neither of you made it easy. You're so lucky and don't even know it. You had parents who loved you. Really loved you. You've never gone hungry. You went to school. Had a shot at college. And all of this—" He gestured about. "You married a guy who can give you anything you want. And you pissed it all away."

Anne's heart faltered. She glanced back at the house. The front door was closed. Frederick must have gone inside. "I know," Anne said in a halting voice. "It was wrong. And stupid."

Andrew lurched forward to grip her shoulders. "Don't piss this new opportunity away too. This is your second chance. I hope you really, really try to make the most of it."

"I will," she whispered, leveled by Andrew's hard grip and the intensity of his gaze. He stared straight through her, as if recognizing something unseen by everyone else. Anne swallowed hard and tried to look confident. "I promise."

"Good." Andrew released her. "I hope things go well with Frederick. He's a good guy. Maybe now we can be a real family."

"I'd like that," Anne said. She tried to smile, but tears stung her eyes.

"You okay?" said Elena, her gaze switching between them as they approached the car.

Anne nodded as she forced back tears. "I apologized. I hope we can all get past the stupid things I did."

Elena pulled Anne into a fierce hug. "We're trying. At least we're trying."

Anne breathed in her sister's White Shoulders perfume, which so reminded her of their mother. She closed her eyes and held Elena tight, hoping she'd remember this moment forever: standing with her sister in the snow on Christmas Day, holding her, and loving her.

Tears glinted in Elena's eyes. Anne smiled and said, "Merry Christmas."

"Merry Christmas," Elena and Andrew said together.

Anne waved as their car puttered down the driveway. She waited until they were gone before starting back home.

"I'll be gone an hour, maybe less," Frederick said as he buttoned his coat and snatched up his briefcase. "You okay?"

"I'm fine," Anne called from the leather divan. She'd tucked her legs beneath a plush Ohio State blanket, set a mug of hot chocolate on the adjacent table, and had her new book open across her lap. "I'm perfect, actually. Call if you're going to take longer. I don't want to start on those cookies without you."

"You got it." Frederick leaned down to kiss her forehead, but Anne caught his face for a deeper kiss.

After he left, Anne read and sipped her drink. She was halfway through the second chapter when the doorbell rang.

"Great," Anne muttered, setting down the book and flinging back the blanket. It was probably a poor mail clerk working on Christmas. She paced down the hall and squinted through the peephole. It was a man in a black trench coat. A hat obscured his face.

For a fleeting moment, Anne thought it was Jack Post. But that was impossible. She hadn't heard from Jack since he'd left to film in Canada, and he certainly wouldn't have appeared on her doorstep unannounced. "Who is it?" Anne called through the door.

"It's me."

Her memory instantly connected with the low, sulky voice.

Luke Harris.

"Open the door, Anne," he said, shuffling along the porch. "It's fucking cold out here. Come on."

Anne didn't want to talk to him or let him inside. She wanted him to vaporize on the spot, but she sensed he wouldn't give up that easily. She realized he'd been the stranger to haunt her driveway the night of the Christmas party. How many other times had he driven by her house?

No. He wouldn't give up without speaking to her.

Thank goodness Freddy's not here, Anne thought as she reluctantly unlocked the door. Before it open fully, Luke pushed through, slamming the door open so hard it bounced against the wall.

"Watch it!" Anne cried, putting up her hands.

"Sorry for that," Luke said, towering over her small frame. "But what the fuck have you been doing, avoiding me all this time? Are you trying to drive me crazy? Because it's working. It's really working."

Anne stepped back, mentally cursing herself. Why had she opened the door? What had she been thinking? What if he turned violent? "Listen, Luke," Anne said, hoping to calm him down, "I'm sorry that you think—"

"You're sorry?" Luke exploded. "That's all I get? How about an epic blowjob for ignoring my seventeen calls? Or my twenty-three e-mails? All you give me is a lousy, 'I'm sorry?'!"

Anne took another step back, crowding against the foyer wall. "Listen to me. When I lost my phone—"

"Yeah. Sure," Luke snapped. "You lost your phone. You also lose your computer?"

"I've not been checking e-mail."

His laugh was a harsh, grating sound. "Like you've ever gone an hour without checking your e-mail." He closed the distance between them, flattening one hand against the wall by Anne's ear and breathing into her face. "Listen, I'll forget everything if you admit this is just a phase. I can try to understand that. Just tell me what's going on. You owe me that much."

Anne stepped sideways. "Listen. It's over between us. I'm back with my husband. Go home to your wife."

"I've left my wife!" Luke flung at her. "Just like you wanted me to! Just like we talked about!"

Anne couldn't believe it. She knew Luke had told his wife about their affair. She remembered the woman's heartbreaking e-mail. But to actually leave his wife and their children? That was another level entirely. "No. Please, don't say that."

Luke laughed without humor. "It's what you always wanted, right? To be together and finally be happy? Well, where's my happiness, Anne? I'm waiting for you to give it to me."

She shook her head. "Please. Just go. "

He gripped her upper arms. "You love me, Anne. You always have. This isn't just some fling you can end like it's nothing. What we have is real." He shook her once, then twice. "Tell me you love me. You know you love me."

His fingers ground into her flesh. Anne knew she couldn't show her fear, not after coming so far. She looked him straight in the face and said, "I don't love you, Luke. I don't think I ever did. I'm sorry for what happened to your family, and my role in it. But it's over between us."

His face twisted into a combination of fury and hurt. "But...but—"

"I was in an accident in New York," Anne blurted, hoping the truth would bring him to his senses. "I was in a coma. I lost most of my memories. It's called retrograde amnesia. I really don't remember you."

His expression broke. "What? What are you saying?"

"A car hit me." Anne pulled apart her hairline to reveal the bald spot. She touched her scars, wishing she hadn't covered them so well. "I was in the hospital. I don't remember you."

Luke's face darkened with suspicion. "What sort of game is this?"

"It's not a game. I remember you a bit. But for the most part, it's a blur. These feelings you have—I don't have them because I can't remember. Okay?"

"You don't remember this?" He fumbled at her shirt, groping for her breast.

Anne shoved his hand away. "Stop that!"

"Come on, baby. That's how you like it." He clutched at her harder and slid his opposite hand between her legs. "You don't remember this? Don't remember how I touched you better than any man, like you said?" He pressed her against the wall, his lips on her throat as he whispered, "You don't remember these awesome tits I gave you? This ass? Don't remember me going down on you? How I made you come harder than ever? How do you not remember that, baby?"

"No," Anne said, while thinking, *God help me, I do.* It was returning to her, quick as a train. The roughness of his touch. The smell of his sweat and cologne. She remembered him in bed. Her unsated hunger. And how she hated herself on the long drive home. Her lies that mounted by the day. The cold bitterness that crept into her heart.

"No," Anne said again. She pushed Luke back, wanting him gone. "I'm not that person. I've changed."

"Please," he said with a sneer. "You can't change. A chair will always be a chair."

"I'm not a chair," she said firmly. "And I can change. I did. I want you gone. It's over, Luke. *Over.*"

"Baby," he said, more gently this time. "This is all because you can't remember me? Well, I can make you remember..."

His lips were on hers, his tongue in her mouth. Anne choked and pushed him back, but he held her in a vise-grip. She struggled, but he swallowed her cries. She searched for a weapon. Her fingertips grazed a silver candelabrum when a voice called from the front door, "I think you better explain what the hell you're doing."

Luke jumped back as if stung. Anne rubbed his salvia from her face and yanked her sweater down.

Frederick stood in the doorway, clutching his briefcase in a white-knuckled fist.

Luke stammered for words. "I—I thought you were gone."

"Came home early," Frederick returned in a flat monotone. "Didn't think it'd be to this. I asked what the hell you're doing."

Luke straightened his jacket. "I'm Doctor Luke Harris. Anne's plastic surgeon. You must be the husband?

"I guess I am," said Frederick.

Luke clutched Anne's shoulder. "We're in love. Anne wants to leave you—for me."

Anne stepped out of Luke's grip, her voice coming in a rush. "Freddy, that's not—"

But Frederick held up a hand as he stepped aside, his eyes narrowed almost to slits. "Be that as it may, I want you out. Now. Before I call the police."

"Listen," said Luke, "you don't need to—"

"Out." Frederick glowered with the intimidation of a man twice his size. "*Now*."

The two men stared at each other for a long time. Luke snapped his eyes to Anne, then back to Frederick. "Fine. I'll leave. But not without her. She's coming with me."

"What?" Anne cried in shock. "I am not—"

"She loves me," Luke continued, as if not hearing her. "She's always loved me. She told me she doesn't love you anymore. Accept it."

Frederick leveled his eyes on Anne. "Is that true? Is that how you really feel?"

"No!" She shook her head wildly.

"Yes, you do!" Luke tried to catch her hand, but she wriggled from his grasp. "Anne, don't be like this! You love me, goddamnit!"

"I don't!" she cried. "I don't love you. And I don't think I ever did. You're not a good person!"

"I'm not a good person?" he shouted, his face the picture of shock. "What the fuck does that mean? Not a good person? You said I was your goddamn knight in shining armor for taking you away from this life! From him!"

Anne stepped to Frederick's side. "Like my husband said. We'll call the police if you come back again. Now get the hell out!"

Luke's glare burned. "Fine, Anne. That's just fine. Have it your way. That's the thanks I get for giving you those tits. I should sue your ass."

"Just try it," Anne said. She wanted to spit at him, wanted to vomit, thinking about how she'd been intimate with him, told him things—secret things. She wanted to scrub her mind with steel wool.

Luke glanced between her and Frederick. "I don't need this. You're completely replaceable. You always were." He threw his hands up in disgust and stormed out.

Anne slammed and locked the door behind him. "Oh, thank God you came home, Freddy!" she said, turning to him. But Frederick had stomped down the hall, still clutching his briefcase. "Where are you going?"

He stopped, but didn't turn around. "I thought I could do this, Anne. But I can't."

Anne's heart fell past her ribs. "What are you talking about?"

His shoulders slumped. "I want to go through with it."

"With—what? What are you saying?" But she knew the answer even as she asked the question.

Frederick turned to face her. He passed his hand over the back of his neck, looking infinitely tired. "I know you've apologized. I know you probably meant it in your way. But the past isn't just in the past. It's here, in my own house, coming through the door. I thought maybe if I could forgive..." He gave a solemn shake of his head. "But I can't forget. I'm sorry, Anne. I'm done with all of it. I want you out. And by tonight. Go stay with your sister."

And with that, he was gone, the click of the study door heavy behind him.

Chapter Thirty-One

THREE WEEKS LATER, and Anne still couldn't sleep on her sister's couch. She stared up at the ceiling as the clock over the small fireplace mantle ticked away. Charlotte's wails always came around midnight and 6:30 a.m. A groggy Elena would plod from her bedroom, across the living room where Anne slept, and down the hall to nurse her eager child.

Anne lifted her head and punched the pillow beneath, wishing it had the give like the one in her old home, or in Jack Post's guest suite. She also wished for the hundredth time that she'd thought to pack one goose down pillow. But her flight from the life she once shared with Frederick had been swift, without time to consider the implications of anything left behind. She still had the money from Jack Post, his gift of a wardrobe, some underwear, and her makeup bag.

Anne had figured she needed nothing else. She'd told Frederick that she wanted the rest of her items donated to charity and she wanted that request granted. Let some other woman benefit from the life she had pissed away.

In the note Anne left for Cindy, she claimed the Gucci "trophy" coat returned and told Cindy never to contact her again. Afterwards, Anne set her keys on the foyer table and closed the front doors, managing not to cry until she slipped into the passenger seat of her sister's car.

Anne rolled over on the couch and re-tucked the three layers of quilts. She was grateful Elena had opened up her home. Elena had not only braved the cold picking Anne up, she sat in sympathetic silence as Anne sobbed and told her everything, sparing no detail.

"I can't believe this is how it turned out," Elena said with a sad shake of her head.

"Me neither," Anne blubbered. "That bastard Luke. Why did I ever sleep with him? What did I ever see in him? I remember how insecure he made me feel. How he said I needed to change myself when I was fine the way I was. Look at me!" Anne flung down the mirrored visor. "That's the face of someone who needed medical attention. Someone who survived a car accident, not someone with boobs that aren't as big as some movie star, or a face that's getting slightly older. He made me a monster! A stupid little Frankenstein!"

"You're not Frankenstein," Elena assured. "Come on, Anne. Pull yourself together. At least you purged him from your life. *Finally*."

"But at what cost?" Anne stared down at her hands, her vision swimming with tears. "He left his wife for me. I broke apart someone's family."

"Sounds like it was already broken," Elena said reasonably. "And it was his choice."

"Even so. I was the one who started it."

"You don't know that you were the only one he cheated with. There could be others!"

Anne covered her face, enduring a fresh wave of humiliation. "I guess Freddy was lucky not to get some disease."

Elena scowled. "What are you talking about?"

Anne shuddered. She didn't want to tell her, but knew she had no choice. "Freddy said after he found out about everything, he got himself tested to make sure I hadn't given him anything. Thank God I didn't."

"Thank God you're fine yourself," Elena said. "Just think about *that*. Forget about Frederick. Forget about Luke. Forget all those men. Just focus on what you're going to do for yourself, with your own life. Let go of the rest."

Elena's words rang true, as they did every night when Anne stared up at the whitewashed ceiling. In the darkness, the series of events played through Anne's mind like a stuck movie reel.

Charlotte's hiccuping sobs crescendoed into a full-blown wail. Elena appeared from her bedroom, slinging on a robe. She rubbed her tired face and groped her way towards the living room.

"Let me help," Anne said, flicking the lamp on behind her head.

"I didn't know you were up." Elena's dark hair nested about her head and she blinked tired, red eyes. Anne figured she didn't look much better.

"I couldn't sleep," Anne said. "I just feel so—"

Elena held up a finger as Charlotte mewed in the distance. "Hold that thought," she said, sweeping from the room.

Anne lay back against the single pillow and hiked the quilts to her chin, seeking their warmth and comfort. Her life was at an impasse, and she didn't know how to cross. She had determined the "where" of her next step, but there remained the "what". Hopefully, she hadn't squandered every opportunity.

Anne considered returning to college to finish her lapsed English degree. She'd been only fifteen credits shy of graduating. She'd passed the requisite core curriculum, but still had several upper-level courses to complete.

Anne told herself she could do it. Nothing held her back except money. That meant she needed a job.

Her mind was a whirling dervish by the time Elena returned to sit at the end of the couch. With a yawn,

Elena drew Anne's feet onto her lap. "Why are you up? It's 3 a.m."

"Really?" Anne threw a glance at the digital clock.

"Something's on your mind. Want to unload?"

Anne fisted the quilts. "I've been thinking about doing something, but I don't know how you'll feel about it."

Elena's eyebrows lifted, but she said nothing.

"I've been thinking about going back to college." When her sister said nothing, Anne went on, "Finishing my degree. And I know what you're going to say—"

"How do you know what I'm going to say?" Elena interjected.

Anne began ticking off her fingers. "That I'm ten years too late. That I don't have a job to pay for it. And even if I find a job, it'll take forever. That there are other things I should take care of. Like finalizing my divorce. Or buying a car. Or finding my own place."

"That may be what you're thinking," Elena said, "but I'm thinking that it's actually a fantastic idea."

"You do?"

"Yup."

"But don't you think—"

"Pursuing an education is rarely a bad idea," said Elena, her voice thick with authority. "You don't have children or any outstanding debts. I think it could benefit you in the long run. Question is, what will you do once you finish?"

Anne pulled her feet from Elena's lap and notched her chin against her knees. "I was thinking I could teach."

Elena gave a curt nod. "That's good."

"But I don't know. Maybe I should just take some time to see what I really want to do. I like to read. I remember mostly enjoying my classes." Anne gave a dejected sigh. "I shouldn't have dropped out of college. I should have stuck with it!"

"That's in the past. You're living too much in it, especially for someone who can't remember it all." Elena gave Anne's calf an encouraging squeeze. "Focus on the future."

Anne heard the echo of Frederick's parting words. "But it's not just in the past. It's here. It's putting me in your house. Dropping me out of school. Making me rope my self-worth to how many drinks a guy buys me."

"All that stuff you can change. Listen. You've got a home here however long you need it. You're my twin sister. You're my family." Elena's smile was soft and genuine.

Anne pulled her into a tight embrace. "Thanks, Elena."

"You got it."

Anne wiped her eyes with trembling fingers. "God, I'm a mess."

"It's okay. You're going through a lot."

Anne shot a glance at the landline on the side table. "I've called him every night. Sometimes twice."

"I know you have."

"He hasn't called me back," Anne said. "Not once." In fact, the only person to call Anne was Sarah Jones, the blonde woman she'd met at the Christmas party. Sarah left messages inviting Anne to coffee or lunch—offering friendship.

"I think she's nice," Elena said. "She might be good for you. You should call her back."

But Anne didn't want to speak with anyone tied to Frederick's work, especially the wife of a partner. They'd all side with Frederick eventually, once the divorce was finalized. Yet unlike most divorces, theirs would have no splitting of assets, of friends and acquaintances. Frederick would have it all.

Anne winced at the memory of calling Frederick's office the previous week. Before she could deliver her message, the secretary told Anne to contact Frederick's attorney. After reciting the number, the line went dead.

The next afternoon, a courier arrived with a fresh set of divorce papers and a ballpoint pen. Anne signed everything on the kitchen table while her sister looked on. "Are you sure?" Elena asked. "Maybe if you—"

"No," Anne interrupted. "I'm not forcing him to do anything." She scrawled her final signature and numbly returned the stack to the uniformed man.

So now I'm divorced, Anne thought once the door closed. *Just like that.*

"Frederick doesn't mean to be cruel," Elena said to her now. "He just doesn't know how to deal with this. Truthfully, I wouldn't either."

"What would you have done?"

"You really want to know?" Elena waited for Anne's nod. "I would have thrown Andrew's ass to the curb. Hired some lawyer."

Anne's spirit drained. "So it's what I deserve. I guess I was never good enough for him."

"No," said Elena. "That's where you're wrong. You were always good enough for him. Always. You just—well, sometimes you weren't the best for him."

Anne blinked at her. "What?"

Elena sighed, clearly frustrated. "Do you get what I'm trying to say?"

"Not really," Anne said, feeling helpless all over again. "I just know that I love him. I do."

"It'll pass. Broken hearts always heal. It just takes time."

"I don't think mine will."

Elena rubbed her leg. "It will, honey. Trust me."

By the following week, Anne felt markedly better. She'd investigated classes at the University of Dayton and even called the registrar to see if her credits could transfer from Cincinnati. The classes ranged from contemporary drama to postcolonial literature. Unfortunately, open enrollment had ended in November, and the spring semester had already begun. The earliest Anne could begin courses was in the summer, but that was fine. It gave her time to secure a job and lease an apartment.

Anne scoured newspapers and the Internet for job postings, even created a résumé with the help of her sister- and brother-in-law. She kept everything organized in a manila folder, which she carried with her for every interview. Anne dressed casually but professionally, smiling brightly through every question. Since restaurant turnover was so high, Anne landed a waitressing position in three days. That night, Elena opened a bottle of champagne and toasted Anne's success.

"Thanks for letting me stay here," Anne said, clinking her flute to theirs. "You don't know what it's meant to me. And don't worry," she added with a guilty smile at Andrew. "I won't be here much longer."

"Take all the time you need," Elena said, glancing pointedly at her husband. "Right, honey?"

"Right," Andrew said, slurping down his champagne and tucking into his macaroni and cheese. "Mind if I turn on the game?"

"Sure," Elena said.

When Andrew left to search for the remote, Anne touched Elena's hand. "Thanks, sis."

Elena winked at her. "You got it."

That night, as the house slept, Anne broke out the worn copy of *Jane Eyre* she'd found in Elena's bookcase. Anne had already finished the Mary Brown novel Frederick gifted her, followed by several Harlequin romances. Now she craved the comfort of something from her childhood. Their mother had read *Jane Eyre* twice that Anne could remember.

At least I didn't lie to Jack about everything, Anne thought. She wondered if Jack was still filming in Canada, if he was still sober, if he was lonely. He'd been good to her when he could have left her at the hospital, where she likely would have degraded in her solitary quest for answers. What would she have done without his help? Certainly, she wouldn't have had the insight or the funds to hire a private investigator to uncover her origins. For all Anne knew, she'd still be a ward of New York Presbyterian.

Anne picked up the phone and dialed a number she hadn't recalled in quite some time. As she waited through the few clicks and a distant ring, Anne worried she might have called the wrong number, when a familiar voice crackled down the line, "*¿Alo?*"

"Maria!" Anne's grin threatened to overtake her face. "It's Anne—or Vickie. Remember me?"

"Vickie!" Maria cried. "*¡Ay, Dios mío!* How are you? But I suppose you are Anne now!"

Anne laughed at this. "I suppose I am. How are you? How was Christmas?"

Maria enthusiastically filled her in. Jack had returned home from principal photography in time for Christmas. He'd invited his two remaining sisters to spend the holiday with him—something that hadn't occurred in over a decade. "He had so much fun!" Maria declared. "I've not seen him so happy since—well, since you were here!"

"That's great," Anne said, her heart pinching. *Good for him.*

They shared stories. Anne revealed that much of her memory had returned, that she was fostering a closer relationship with her sister, and—when pressed —admitted Frederick had filed for divorce. Maria countered with all the exciting details of the house. Most riveting was Jack Post's newest love interest: a makeup artist who was warm, unpretentious, and made everyone laugh—especially Jack.

Before they said goodbye, Anne related a message to Jack. "Please tell him I'm reading *Jane Eyre* and that I thought about him. It's not a first edition, of course, but it's wonderful. I thought it'd make him smile."

"*Sí, señora.* I will tell him. It is so good to hear from you. And please, don't forget us. *Recuerdalos.*"

"I'll remember you," Anne assured. She could never forget the man who had pushed her over the brink and helped bring her back, nor the people that warmed his home. "Tell Jack thank you. For everything."

"*Por supuesto, querida. Adios.*"

Anne tensed, not wanting to close the receiver. Her chest hurt when she said goodbye.

Anne lay alone in the silence, staring at her favorite spot on the ceiling. After twenty minutes, she sat up, snapped on the lamp, picked up the overturned book, and began to read.

By midnight, Jane Eyre had left her teaching post at Lowood and applied for a governess position. That led straight into the arms of Edward Rochester and down the wings of his mysterious mansion. Jane had just startled Rochester's horse in a darkened wood when Charlotte awoke, crying for her mother.

Elena shuffled into the living room and blinked groggily into the light. "Good grief. You're reading at this hour? Must be a good book."

"It sure is," said Anne, revealing the spine.

"Ah! A classic. But if you like the book, you've got to see the movie." Elena gave a mischievous wink. "In fact, I know a version with a certain gorgeous actor. It actually earned him an Oscar."

"Thanks," Anne said with a wry grin, "but I'd rather have the book for now."

"Interesting."

"What?"

Elena clasped her hips. "Nothing. I'm just shocked you're picking a book over a Jack Post movie. You sure you weren't replaced with an alien?"

"There's no telling," Anne said with a laugh.

After Charlotte quieted, Elena settled down on the couch.

"What are you doing?" Anne asked. "Aren't you heading to bed?"

"Nah. I'll wait up a bit. Nothing's worse than going to sleep, only to get jarred awake three minutes later."

Anne fingered the book's faded spine. "Want to talk?"

"Sure. What's up?"

"I did more research on the school. I can enroll this spring and start classes in June. What do you think?"

Elena beamed. "I think it's great. June's not too far away."

"I know!" Excitement sparked all the way to Anne's toes. Who knew she'd be so excited to go to school? *I'm a different person now*, Anne thought.

"Have you considered what you'll do with your degree?" Elena asked for the dozenth time.

Anne gave a noncommittal shrug. "Still not sure. Maybe it'll come to me in a flash of inspiration, like in these books. I want to finish something that'd make our parents proud—and make myself proud, too."

To her surprise, Elena leaned over to kiss her forehead. "You'd make Mom and Dad proud right now. I know that's what you make me."

Anne's eyes flooded with tears. "I love you."

"I love you too," Elena said, her eyes shining.

They smiled at each other. Anne flashed to their rocky childhood. Their wasted years bickering. Their distance since their parents' deaths. Yet here they were, putting the past behind them. Loving each other.

If only our parents were here to see this, Anne thought. *If only they could have heard us say it.*

Chapter Thirty-Two

ANNE GRITTED her teeth as she bussed her tables. She refilled the sugars and condiments at the sideboard, lined up the silverware, and wiped down the booths. Anne hadn't predicted just how much she'd have to memorize, or how quickly she'd have to recall the shorthand for so many orders. Some of her coworkers thought her a little strange. They spoke of her scars, the hot cocoa she sipped when everyone else smoked or chugged coffee, and her total lack of flirtation with the male customers. Despite this, Anne remained friendly, kept her orders straight, and completed her shifts efficiently. She had only one goal: save enough money to go back to school.

With three months until her summer courses, she took as many double shifts as possible, often not returning to her studio apartment until 11 p.m. on weekdays and 2 a.m. on weekends. The wages were terrible, but the tips were decent, especially on Friday and Saturday nights, when patrons ordered booze and were in a more generous mood. While Anne enjoyed greeting the customers, she hated rushing to satisfy up to thirty people at a time.

In the beginning, she worried one of Frederick's partners would be seated in her section, or—possibly worse—one of their wives. After a few weeks, Anne realized those sorts of people shied away from establishments with sawdust on the floor and peanut shells littering the booths. That was just fine with her.

When Anne returned home after a grueling shift, she sunk into her only couch to read or watch TV. Her home was small and sparsely decorated, the biggest pieces coming from Elena and Goodwill. Even Lauren, whom Anne thought would hate her forever, had donated a coffee table and matching stool refurbished from an old telephone pole. Anne had a double bed, a dresser, and a small kitchen table with two chairs. With a television mounted on a cheap plywood entertainment stand, Anne lived in modest comfort.

When nights got too quiet, Anne called her sister and, more recently, Sarah Jones, who rang during Anne's first week at the apartment. "Elena gave me your number," Sarah said in a rush. "I hope that's okay."

"I guess," said Anne, squinting with suspicion. "So...um. What's up?"

"Not much. I know it must seem strange, me calling you like this. I just thought we could meet for lunch? My treat? I know what you're going through can't be easy."

Sarah wouldn't give up, so Anne reluctantly agreed to brunch that Sunday at a downtown café. Before Anne had settled at the table, Sarah passed her a filled champagne flute. "I ordered us mimosas," she said cheerily. "I hope you don't mind."

"Thanks." Anne took a cautious sip. *Mmm,* she thought. *Not bad.*

"Better than the cosmopolitan, right?" Sarah gave her a conspiratorial wink.

Anne stared back blankly. "Sorry?"

"From the Christmas party. Remember how you didn't like it?"

"Oh! Right." Anne shook her head, wondering how the woman remembered that particular detail.

After they ordered, Sarah said, "Let me get right to it. I know you must think me—well, odd. I know you don't like me—"

"It's not that," Anne said.

Sarah waved her hands. "Or maybe it's that you don't trust me. It's okay. We didn't know each other that well before the accident. But when Richard told me your story, I knew I had to help."

"Richard?"

"My husband. He's a close friend of Frederick's."

"Oh. I thought he was a partner?"

Sarah nodded. "He is, but he's also a friend. Has been for over twenty years."

Anne wondered why Frederick hadn't mentioned him. Or perhaps he had, before the accident. She couldn't remember.

"I've wanted to talk to you for weeks now," Sarah continued. "About Frederick."

Anne set down her flute. "What about him?"

Sarah folded her hands on the table. "Frederick's dragging his feet at work. He's acting depressed. People think it's this merger coming up, where they stand to lose a lot of money, but Richard says it's because of the divorce. Because of *you*."

Anne tried to picture Frederick morose at his office. How could he be depressed over her? It didn't make sense. He'd wanted her gone. "So everyone knows about the divorce," Anne said flatly.

Sarah shook her head. "You don't understand. Frederick's a very private man. To my knowledge, the only people who know about the split are his secretary, my husband, and myself. But I sense it's weighing on him." Sarah paused, then added, "I thought you should know. I think he really misses you."

Anne drained her mimosa. "What makes you think I care?"

"Because Elena thinks you miss him. That you still love him."

"You talked to my *sister*?" Anne exclaimed, while thinking, *What else did you two talk about?*

"She didn't betray your confidence," Sarah added, as though she'd given offense. "I just told Elena he misses you, and she implied you feel the same. All of it just supports my case."

"What case?"

"That you and Frederick are meant for each other."

Anne snorted. "You think we're meant for each other?"

"Yes. I do."

Anne suspected the woman was a silly romantic idealist, but still. Anne had to know. So she spoke the question Sarah clearly wanted to hear. "What makes you think we're meant for each other?"

Sarah splayed her hands on the table. "I went to your wedding. I heard women taking bets on how long you'd last. The whispers that you were nothing but a gold digger." Anne winced, but Sarah continued as if she hadn't noticed. "But I saw genuine love. Richard saw it too. He said you switched a light on in Frederick. That you made him happy. But then, things took a turn."

Anne tensed, sensing where this was going.

"Frederick became distracted at work. He told Richard he thought you were cheating on him, but couldn't prove it. It was my husband's idea to hire an investigator, but we thought he wouldn't find anything. That it was all baseless." Sarah picked at her fingernails. "We didn't know it was true."

Anne lost her breath. So Sarah's husband was the reason behind the divorce papers that greeted her that first afternoon home? The copies of her e-mails? Everything else that had followed? Anne didn't know whether to cry or scream. She surprised herself by doing neither. She simply held Sarah's gaze and said, "So what? Why are you here?"

Just then the waiter returned to slide a three-cheese omelette in front of Anne, and eggs Benedict before Sarah. Anne ignored her plate. She had long since lost her appetite. Apparently, Sarah had too.

After fiddling with her napkin for half a minute, Sarah drew a fortifying breath and said, "I just thought you should know. That you *deserve* to know. Were the situation reversed, I'd want someone to tell me if my husband missed me. That he still loved me. Especially if pride was the only thing keeping him from telling the truth."

Love. The word rang through Anne's mind like a clarion call. Did Frederick love her, still? Despite everything? How would she ever know? "Thanks, I guess," Anne said with a sigh. "I'm sorry I snapped at you."

Sarah flashed a relieved smile. "It's fine. I hope I didn't ruin your day."

"You didn't," Anne said, taking up her fork. "You've just given me a lot to think about."

Anne had been out with Sarah twice since their initial brunch, surprising each other with their overlapping life experiences. Sarah had a father she was still close to, but lost her mother to lung cancer as a teenager. Like Anne, she'd married her husband after he'd lost his wife. Unlike her, Sarah had tried to get pregnant for the past three years, with each round of in vitro sapping both their savings and emotional strength.

"We've given up for now," Sarah said as she sipped coffee from her Styrofoam cup, her legs tucked under her on Anne's couch.

Anne smiled at her new friend, once more chiding herself for writing the woman off so quickly. It was nice having someone to talk to other than her sister, someone else that knew her name, who even seemed to care about her.

Readying her tables, Anne thought of Sarah and their planned dinner with Elena and Andrew the next night. Elena had finally hired a babysitter, and was enjoying more intimate time with her husband. *I did that!* Anne thought in triumph. *I helped her!*

Her thoughts broke when someone touched her arm and said, "Anne?"

"Yeah?" Anne said, glancing anxiously at the hostess. Hopefully, she wasn't adding another table to Anne's queue. "What's up, Bethany?"

"Someone's here to see you."

"Who?"

"Wouldn't give his name. Some guy who says he's

your friend." Bethany dropped her voice. "And he's cute!"

Anne asked the waitress Stacy to cover her shift as she followed Bethany across the restaurant. "Where is he?" Anne asked, hoping it wasn't Luke Harris, come to find her after all this time.

Bethany pointed at the bar, but it was so crowded it took Anne a moment to pick him out. But there he was. His unmistakable profile. His salt-and-pepper hair. His pressed jacket and tie. All he missed was a leather briefcase.

Freddy, Anne thought, her heart catching in her throat.

"Who is he?" Bethany hissed in her ear.

"My hus—" Anne paused to correct herself. "My *ex*-husband."

"Oh." Bethany pouted. "I can tell him you're on a shift. You can't break for long, anyway."

Anne shook her head, already pushing ahead. "It's fine. I've got this."

Anne threaded between the tables and stopped at the bar. Frederick idly thumbed through his Blackberry, his face unusually scruffy for a Thursday night. A glass of water sat untouched by his elbow.

Anne swallowed hard. "Hello, Freddy. You wanted to see me?"

The phone jostled in his hand. He lurched to stand. "Anne! I didn't see you."

His face was less than six inches away. Anne suppressed the urge to touch his cheeks, telling herself, *You're over him. You had to let him go.*

"How'd you find out where I work?" Anne asked. She crossed her arms, trying to put some physical distance between them. Hoping he wouldn't hear her thudding heart.

"Elena told me," Frederick said in a sheepish voice. "Is that okay?"

Elena. Her twin could always be counted on to surrender personal details. Good thing she didn't work for the CIA. "What do you want? Did I forget to sign something?"

Frederick winced. "Can we talk outside?"

Anne could barely hear him anyway, so she nodded and told him to be quick. Frederick guided her from the bar, opened the front door, and led her outside. They stood a short distance away from a family clustered on a wooden bench, waiting for their buzzers to vibrate.

"So..." Anne said, staring up at him. "What is it?"

"How've you been?" he asked, attempting a smile. "You've been okay? Do you need anything?"

"I'm fine," she said, purposefully keeping her tone measured as she thought, *Why does he care? What does he want?* She hoped whatever he told her would be fast as ripping off a Band-Aid. Then she could return to work and try to lose herself in the blur of faces, writing orders until her hands cramped.

"Good, good," he said, toeing the pavement. "Your sister said you got a place. Is it nice?"

"Nice enough," Anne said.

He swiped the back of his neck. "I'm glad you're settled. And that you've found work. And friends."

"I've met some people," Anne said, glancing back at the restaurant. "Listen, Freddy, I need to—"

"Richard told me you've been meeting with his wife."

Ah. Now it makes sense. Frederick was about to tell her not to associate with his co-workers or their families. Well, that wouldn't happen. "I can make friends with whomever I want," Anne said, irritation edging her voice.

Frederick put up his hands, palms outward. "No, that's not what I meant. I think it's good. Sarah's universally better than Cindy."

Cindy. Anne hadn't thought of her in close to a month, not since sending directions to retrieve her prized Gucci. "Did you give her the coat I left?" Anne asked.

"Yes. She didn't seem too happy with the note."

"Well, it *was* the friend equivalent of a divorce."

His eyebrows rose. "You're no longer friends with her?"

Anne shook her head.

"That's good," he said, swiping his neck again. "That's very good."

Footsteps sounded nearby. Bethany sidled next to

Anne and said, loud enough for Frederick to hear, "We need you back inside."

"On my way," Anne assured her. When the hostess left, Anne leveled her eyes on Frederick. "Just get to the point, okay? I have to go."

Frederick opened his mouth to speak, reconsidered, and tried again. "I'm sorry. I'm doing this all wrong. I came here to tell you something."

"What?" Anne snapped, hoping she appeared tough and uncaring, even as her insides turned to water. She still sheltered a flame of hope, but dared not acknowledge it. Not here, not with him. Freddy could never know. "Just tell me," Anne said. "Just get it over with."

"I came to tell you I miss you."

Anne blinked, fearing she'd misheard. "What did you say?"

Frederick's expression crumpled. "I miss you, Anne. I've missed you since the night you left. Every day is worse than the last. I miss you. I miss my *wife*."

"But you told me to go," Anne said, her throat closing on the words. "You sent me the divorce papers. I signed them. We're not together anymore."

Frederick hesitated. "They're not finalized."

Anne stared up at him in shock. "What's not finalized? The divorce papers?"

"Yes."

"You still have them?"

"Yes. I never filed them."

"So then..." Anne paused as the facts clicked into place. "We're still married?"

He nodded.

"But why?" Anne blurted. "Don't you want to be with somebody else? Someone who didn't hurt you? You deserve that, Freddy. You do."

"I want you," Frederick said, reaching to clasp her arms. "I want you. I *love* you."

Anne trembled. These were the three words she'd longed to hear, but they'd come too late. She wriggled free of his grip. "No. You can't do this. I won't make you happy."

"But you do." His voice was thick and insistent. "Do I—*did* I make you happy?"

"You did." A hot pressure built behind her eyes. She shook her head to clear it. "Yes. You did. Once."

"Then we can be that way again." He reached for her once more, and this time, she let him. "Please, Anne. All I'm asking for is a second chance."

Frederick's eyes were a radiant blue in the lamplight, his face pale around the scruff of his beard. It was the face of her husband. The love of her life. He was there, asking for her to come back to him—to build a new life from the ashes of old.

Anne lifted her chin. "If I give you another chance, some things have to change."

His lips twitched into a smile. "A negotiation, is it? Fine. What's your first item?"

"I'm going back to college."

His eyebrows shot up, but he said nothing.

"I start classes in June. I'm making that a priority. So you will too."

"Agreed."

"Second..."

"Yes?"

"I want to stay in my own place for a while. See how things go."

He hesitated. "Agreed."

"Third, you have to make time for me. Not to where your work suffers, but enough that I feel like I matter. That I come first."

"That's a definite yes," he said, then stopped. A shadow crossed his face.

"What is it?" Anne asked, troubled.

"It's just..." Frederick's voice trailed into a sigh. "Do you think you'll ever regain all your memories?"

Anne bit her lip and gave a sad shake of her head. "I don't know. There are parts I wish I had, like my parents and my sister. Growing up. But then there are other parts. The ones I messed up so badly. Those I'd rather not have back. What do you think?"

"About what?"

"About starting over. With me."

Frederick lightly stroked her shoulders with his thumbs. "Starting over is exactly what I mean to do."

Anne's flame of hope glowed brighter. They would start over. *Together.* "What made you come find me?"

He cracked a wry grin. "You won't believe it."

"Try me."

"Jack Post called me at work. *The* Jack Post."

"Oh, I believe it. What'd he say?"

"He said he'd been the one to care for you in New York. That he found out I'd filed for divorce. And that —short of you being a serial killer—I was a fool not to crawl back to you on my hands and knees and make total amends."

Anne's eyes misted. *Jack Post. A hero on the silver screen. A guardian angel in real life.* "So you're here because of him?"

"No," said Frederick. "Not because of him. He just got me here faster than expected. I planned to wait until Sunday, when Elena said you got off work. But I decided I couldn't even wait that long."

Anne's heart expanded. *Don't hope too soon,* she warned herself.

A buzzer sounded nearby and the family waiting for their table lumbered past. Anne glanced into the restaurant, knowing her stations were piling up and that Stacy was likely nearing a stroke. "I'm sorry," Anne said, "but I have to get back."

Frederick caught her hand. "One more thing."

She met his eyes, and didn't pull away.

He gave her a sheepish grin. "I thought I could take you out on a proper date. Somewhere you didn't work."

Anne returned the smile. "I think that sounds wonderful."

For a long moment, they simply stared at each other. Anne's pulse quickened as her hands slicked with sweat. She'd be less nervous on a first date. "I guess I'll go in," Anne said at last.

"Right," he said, his gaze uncertain. "So then I'll call you?"

"That'd be great." Anne smiled and was about to turn when Frederick opened his arms. That was all the invitation she needed. She fell into his embrace, breathed in his familiar cologne, and nuzzled against the rapid rise and fall of his chest.

When Anne looked up, her husband's face was coming down, and then all that existed was the kiss.

Epilogue

ON A WARM DAY in July exactly a year and eight months since her fateful accident, Anne Strafford stood with Frederick in Punderson State Park, minutes away from renewing their wedding vows. Behind them stood a Tudor-style manor swathed in a cascade of white trillium, and ahead lay the gray expanse of a lake, dappled in sunlight.

Anne had dressed in a mermaid silhouette gown adorned with seed pearls and sequins. Adjusting her grip on a bouquet of stargazer lilies, she smiled at her small throng of friends. Elena and Sarah looked radiant in their cerulean bridesmaid dresses, while Charlotte giggled in her white taffeta flower girl dress and clutched a petal caddy.

Anne cast a glance at Andrew, who stood at the end of the makeshift aisle next to the Justice of the

Peace and Richard Jones, Sarah's husband. Both men wore matching tuxedos with blue pocket swatches. Nicole and Miranda Burns sat in the front row talking with the few other couples from Frederick's office that Anne had grown to know over the past few months. But the most impressive attendee of all was Jack Post, sitting with his third wife as well as—to Anne's happy surprise—Maria and Justin. Everyone from Anne's New Jersey convalescence had flown out for the occasion, save for the mercenary lawyer, Sam, whom Anne had expressly forbidden.

"Are you ready?" Elena asked, eyebrows dancing.

Anne rolled her eyes. "Please. It's not like I haven't been here before."

"But it's your wedding," Elena insisted.

"Technically, it's a vow renewal," said Sarah, flashing Anne a sidelong grin.

"Whatever it is," Elena continued, "I'm glad we're all here."

Anne nodded, her smile genuine. Once, she doubted she'd ever be back with Frederick. While she wished it had happened differently, they'd arrived at a better place. Frederick had finally opened his heart to her, and Anne did the same. They rebuilt their trust one brick at a time. No more secrets. No more games.

Frederick supported Anne through her grueling coursework, thesis, and defense. She took a job as a bilingual advocate for battered women. Associates at

Frederick's firm had even commissioned her to translate during trials.

I'm finally living my life, Anne thought, closing her eyes as she warmly embraced her sister and friend.

The Justice of the Peace made a motion for everyone to sit. Jack Post, who'd insisted on choosing the musical score, pushed PLAY on the iPod speaker system and nodded to Anne from across the lawn. Frederick had asked if Anne wanted a harpist or even a quartet, but she'd kept it simple. She wanted this vow renewal to be completely theirs.

Anne picked up her dress and strode to Frederick. After tucking her arm through his, Frederick escorted her to the strumming notes of Pachelbel's Canon in D. Three photographers snapped pictures like crazed paparazzi as they advanced. As their audience smiled and waved, Frederick motioned to the photographers and whispered, "There they are, taking the million photos you requested."

"Wonderful," Anne said, returning the waves of their beaming friends.

"Out of curiosity, why so many pictures?"

Anne gazed up at her husband, smiling as if the answer was obvious. "So that I'll never forget."

Thank you for reading!

Like this book?
Please leave a review on Amazon/Goodreads.

Join Katherine's newsletter to stay up-to-date with new releases, sneak peeks, giveaways, and more.

www.katherinetiradoryen.com

Forgetting Me
READING GROUP GUIDE

1. What was your initial impression of Vickie/Anne? What about the movie star, Jack Post? Were you surprised that Jack took Anne home from the hospital? How much guilt do you assign Jack over the car accident?

2. Jack has a team of assistants: Maria the housekeeper, Sam the layer, Justin the personal assistant, and Francis the chef. Which one is your favorite? How do they compare to Frederick's housekeepers, Miranda and Nicole Burns?

3. Who is "Vickie" to Anne and Jack Post? Why did Anne assume that identity? What is the "Jack Post Love List"?

4. After landing back in Ohio, Anne meets Miranda Burns, Cindy Harper, Andrew Lewiston, Elena Lewiston, and finally Frederick Strafford. What do their reactions suggest about their shared histories with Anne?

5. On a scale from healthy to toxic, how do you rate Anne and Frederick's relationship? Apply the same rating scale to Elena, Andrew, Cindy, Lauren, and Luke. Do you have similar relationships in your life?

6. Do the flashback scenes influence your opinion of Anne? How did her upbringing impact her life? What did you think of Anne's bullying history with Lauren? Was Lauren justified in confronting Anne at the mall?

7. Is Frederick justified in his response to Anne's affairs? Why do you think Anne sought the attention of other men? Are Anne and Frederick right for each other? Why or why not?

8. This book asks the question: are we more than the sum of our experiences? What do you believe? Do you sympathize with Anne's quest to find herself?

9. The novel opens in a hospital and ends with a vow renewal. How does Anne grow and change between both of these key moments?

10. Discussing books is sometimes almost as exciting as reading them. How would you describe *Forgetting Me* to someone who has not read it? Would you recommend it to a friend or loved one? What do you imagine Anne will do next?

For more by Katherine Tirado-Ryen, visit
www.katherinetiradoryen.com

Made in the USA
Middletown, DE
11 January 2024